"Readers looking for atmospheric mystery set in the period following the Great War will savor the intricate plotting and captivating details of the era." —*Library Journal* (Starred Review)

"Action-filled . . . Huber offers a well-researched historical and a fascinating look at the lingering aftermath of war." —*Publishers Weekly*

"A historical mystery to delight fans of Agatha Christie or Daphne du Maurier." —*Bookpage*

"Huber's historical mysteries are always multilayered, complex stories, and *Penny* is an especially satisfying one as she interweaves social commentary and righteous feminist rage into the post-War period. With a perfect blend of murder, mystery, history, romance, and powerful heroines, Huber has yet to disappoint." —*Criminal Element*

"A thrilling mystery that supplies its gutsy heroine with plenty of angst-ridden romance." —*Kirkus Reviews*

"Masterful . . . Just when you think the plot will zig, it zags. Regardless of how well-versed you may be in the genre, you'll be hard-pressed to predict this climax. . . . Deeply enjoyable . . . just the thing if you're looking for relatable heroines, meatier drama, and smart characters with rich inner lives." —*Criminal Element*

MURDER
MOST
FAIR

Novels by Anna Lee Huber

This Side of Murder
Treacherous Is the Night
Penny for Your Secrets
A Pretty Deceit
Murder Most Fair

MURDER MOST FAIR

A Verity Kent Mystery

ANNA LEE HUBER

KENSINGTON
PUBLISHING CORP.

www.kensingtonbooks.com

KENSINGTON BOOKS are published by

Kensington Publishing Corp.
119 West 40th Street
New York, NY 10018

ISBN-13: 978-1-4967-2850-0 (ebook)
ISBN-10: 1-4967-2850-5 (ebook)

ISBN-13: 978-1-4967-2849-4
ISBN-10: 1-4967-2849-1
First Kensington Trade Paperback Printing: September 2021

10 9 8 7 6 5 4 3 2 1

Printed in the United States of America

For my youngest brother Matt,
who has always viewed the world through unique eyes, and
in doing so has made the rest of us do the same, to our better-
ment. Your peaceful, easy-going nature is a balm to those
around you, and your dedication and zeal for the things
you love is inspiring.
You are gracious, kind, and intelligent, and an
amazing uncle. I'm so proud of you.
Thank you for always being there!

Acknowledgments

2020 was not the year any of us anticipated it would be. In many ways it was extremely difficult for everyone, including us creative types. As such, I struggled more than usual with my writing—with finding the inspiration, the will, and the impetus to create. But a number of individuals helped me to keep going, and to believe that the stories flowing from my fingertips weren't completely rubbish. Chief among them was my darling husband, who not only encourages and uplifts me, but serves as an excellent sounding board, and wrangles our children to give me extra hours to write when needed. I also must thank my two daughters, who spent more time at home than usual, and were mostly patient and understanding of the fact that Mommy and Daddy had to get their work done.

Another huge thank you goes out to my readers, particularly those of you who wrote to tell me how much my books meant to you, especially during a time of tumult and uncertainty. At times your messages arrived at just the moment when I needed something to spur me on, to remind me why I write stories in the first place. So thank you for sharing your lives and your precious time with me and my tales.

I also wish to thank all my author friends. We commiserated and empathized with each other about how difficult it all was, and then encouraged each other to keep going. I've never been more grateful to be part of such a broad community of amazing individuals. You all make me aspire to do better.

Heaps of thanks also go to my friends and family, whose support uplifts me and means so much. In particular Jackie Musser and Stacie Roth Miller, my indispensable beta readers.

I'm incredibly grateful to my agent, Kevan Lyon, whose guidance is always stellar; my eagle-eyed editor, Wendy McCurdy; and the entire team at Kensington, including, but not limited to, Elizabeth Trout, Ann Pryor, Carly Sommerstein, Lauren Jernigan, Alexandra Nicolajsen, and Kristine Mills; as well as the creator of my gorgeous cover illustrations, Andrew Davidson. You all make my books better and help them find their wings.

Slowly, slowly, the wound to the soul begins to make itself felt, like a bruise, which only slowly deepens its terrible ache, till it fills all the psyche. And when we think we
have recovered and forgotten, it is then that the terrible
after-effects have to be encountered at their worst.
—D. H. Lawrence, *Lady Chatterley's Lover*

CHAPTER 1

※❦※

Fair is foul, and foul is fair: Hover through the
fog and filthy air.
—William Shakespeare

November 1919
Seaford, Sussex

"Did you thrash the fellow?" my cousin Reg asked my husband eagerly.

"Nothing so brutal," I protested, casting Reg a chiding look
he couldn't see, having lost his sight during the war, but could
no doubt hear in my voice.

One corner of Sidney's lips quirked upward as he slid a hand
into the pocket of his gray worsted trousers. "No, I simply
helped the chap back over the fence where he belonged."

I turned to hand him a gin rickey, arching a single eyebrow
wryly. "And by 'helped' you mean, 'shoved him off a six-foot-
high wall.' "

Reg tipped his head back and laughed while Sidney shrugged,
his amused gaze lingering on me as he took a sip of his drink.
The ice clinked against the glass.

"Well, the photographer *was* trespassing, wasn't he?" my
friend Daphne countered from her perch beside Reg, whose side
she hadn't strayed far from in the past fortnight. She fluffed her

blond bob with one hand. "He was certainly up to no good. Probably after some *scurrilous* pictures he could sell to the papers."

I appreciated her outrage on our behalf, something that brought color into her cheeks and a sparkle into her blue eyes.

Not that Reg could see it. Though he didn't seem averse to her company. At least, not after I explained to her that he was merely blind, not a doddering old fool. Kindhearted Daphne had meant well, even if at times she was a bit thick. In this case she'd made the same mistake as much of society, including my aunt, in thinking that *blind* meant *incapable* and *inept*. Reg might have lost the use of his eyes, but his mind and wit were still as sharp as ever, and Daphne had swiftly remedied her error.

For my part, I was pleased to see my cousin looking so merry. Escaping from his overbearing mother and the ever-present troubles at his estate, Littlemote House, had done wonders for his spirits. I suspected the fact that—Daphne's momentary blunder aside—everyone here treating him like he had a brain and a working set of limbs also helped.

My brilliant friend George Bentnick, who'd worked as a codebreaker during the war, reclined in a chair across the terrace of our cottage. The curls of his black hair ruffled in the evening breeze as he took a drag from his cigarette before turning to blow a long plume of smoke out into the garden. But I hadn't failed to note the smirk stretching his lips.

"And just what do *you* find so amusing?" I asked as I draped myself over one of our lounge chairs, making certain the ends of the georgette silk scarf wrapped around my neck weren't caught behind me. I arranged the skirts of my aubergine gown so that only my ankles peeked out.

"That photographer's folly. What did he expect would happen when he scaled the fence of dashing war hero Sidney Kent and his beautiful and intrepid wife, Verity?" George questioned, quoting almost verbatim the description so often ascribed to us in the press. He scoffed, lifting his glass. "Kent certainly wasn't going to invite him in to tea."

"You underestimate me, Bentnick," Sidney replied. "Perhaps next time I'll do that very thing."

"Oh, but surely there won't be a next time." Daphne leaned forward to protest.

This comment was met by four silent looks of disbelief. In my experience, photographers and newspapermen were not so easily deterred. Not when their quarry was guaranteed to sell papers and gossip rags. I supposed it was our own fault for remaining in the limelight for solving murders. Otherwise, our celebrity would have already dimmed five months after Sidney's celebrated return after the fifteen months he had been believed to be dead, and the revelation of the traitors I'd helped him unmask.

In any case, I was tired of discussing the incident with the photographer. I tipped my head back to admire the streaks of red, mauve, and golden orange painting the sky, and providing a stiff competition to the leaves still clinging to our maple and black poplar trees for the most brilliant prospect. At least, temporarily. I wrapped my juniper-green woolen jumper tighter around me and breathed deeply of the air tinted with the smoke from the hearths burning inside, the earthy aroma of autumn decay, and a faint tinge of saltiness from the sea a short distance away. The breeze sawed gently through the trees overhead, rustling the leaves like castanets, and I allowed my eyes to drift shut. The evening was a lovely one, especially for mid-November.

Certainly lovelier than the evenings I'd spent at our cottage during the four long years of the war. Just a little over a year earlier, nature's chorus before sunset—no matter how sweet the sound—would merely have been a prelude to the nightly growls and grumbles of the guns echoing across the Channel from the Western Front some seventy miles away. This was why the few times I'd retreated here I hadn't remained more than a handful of days. Knowing Sidney was over there, his section of the trenches even at that moment perhaps being shelled and fired upon... It was too wrenching to not only be intellectually aware of the danger he was in, but also audibly reminded of it.

Even the relative peace of daylight had been periodically

shattered by the sounds of gunfire and explosions from one of the military camps nearby, the gentle scents of honeysuckle and sweetbriar soured by the drifting stench of gunpowder or some other noxious fume from their training exercises.

A distinctive metallic *kak-kak* cry filled the air, and I opened my eyes to scowl at the black-winged menace landing on the gable of the cottage roof. "I thought Harley was going to take care of that jackdaw," I grumbled to Sidney, doubting I was the only one who found the bird's calls unsettlingly reminiscent of a Vickers machine gun.

"I'm afraid that's my fault," a deep voice admitted from over my shoulder.

I turned to find Max Westfield, the Earl of Ryde, grinning sheepishly down at me. His dark blond hair proved to be in need of a haircut, curling upward against the back of his collar.

"One of the tires on my Rolls went flat, and I asked him to change it," he explained. "And then he uncovered an issue with the axle."

I couldn't help but soften at this news. Harley was a wonder with motorcars. Along with his duties as a man-of-all-work here at the cottage, he also repaired motorcars for the local village and its sharp influx of visitors in the summer months. Given the option between catching a jackdaw and tinkering with a motorcar as fine as Max's pale yellow Rolls-Royce, there was no question what would take precedence. And given the fact that Max was our guest, I couldn't begrudge Harley the choice he'd made.

"Is that where you've been?" I teased him, having wondered where he'd disappeared to for half the afternoon, but having been too lazy to bestir myself to find out.

"Did it happen when we were over at Pevensey?" Sidney queried with a frown. "I noticed there were a number of ruts in that road that needed to be repaired."

"More than likely." Max turned toward the drinks trolley, which had been wheeled out onto the terrace. "But then the maintenance of little-used rural roads has hardly been a priority these past five years."

Our visit to Pevensey Castle, the site of one of the Romans'

Saxon shore forts built to defend Britain from invaders, had been less of a holiday—though we had taken a picnic with us—and more of a matter of unfinished business. A month prior, a letter written by Max's late father had sent us off on a sort of Romano-British treasure hunt in search of what we'd thought was proof he'd held of the infamous Lord Ardmore's guilt. One of the clues had been hidden at Pevensey, but we'd been able to sidestep it and skip to the last site. But we hadn't figured out the purpose of the key he had also left his son, so we'd decided it would be best to search Pevensey for it. However, our visit had been disappointing in that regard. We'd found the clue that would have led us to Littlemote House and the deadly concealed treasure we'd uncovered there, but we still had no idea what the key was meant for.

Part of me was worried whatever the key unlocked had already fallen into the hands of Lord Ardmore. Ardmore had all but openly admitted he was responsible for the deaths of more than half a dozen people, and had implicated himself in a number of treasonous proceedings. He had proven himself wily, cunning, ruthless, and remorseless. But his somewhat shadowy position with Naval Intelligence and his highly placed friends made him untouchable until we possessed the definitive proof required to bring him down.

Proof that was supposed to lie at the end of the late Lord Ryde's infuriating treasure hunt. Instead, we'd merely found ourselves with more disquieting questions. For Max even more than the rest of us. Though he presented an unruffled exterior, I could tell he was more unsettled than he wished to appear. When he lifted his drink to his lips, downing the contents in one long swallow before pouring himself another glass, I was even more convinced of it.

I wanted to say something to reassure him, to promise him we would figure out what his father's key unlocked, to vow that we would find the proof we needed to stop Ardmore and avenge his father's death. But not everyone on the terrace was privy to the knowledge of our investigation. Besides, I knew that wasn't what truly disturbed him. It was his father's culpability in Ardmore's *Zebrina* plot, which had enabled the devious lord to smuggle an unknown quantity of the poisonous gas phosgene out of Britain to an unspecified destination—possibly somewhere in Ireland. The late Lord Ryde's missives from beyond the grave had tried to downplay his role, to deny any knowledge of the *Zebrina*'s true cargo and Ardmore's intentions for it, but I knew Max must hold the same doubts I did about the level of his father's ignorance.

So in the end I remained silent, though I couldn't help monitoring him from the corner of my eye with growing concern. He took a deep drink from his second glass of scotch, but rather than refill it, he crossed the terrace to sink into the vacant chair across the table from Reg.

"What have I missed?" he asked with forced cheer. "Are there any grand plans for this evening? It is our last night here, after all."

"Aye, Ver," Reg chimed in. "What have you got planned for us? Another cribbage tournament? Some nocturnal sea bathing? A spot of snipe hunting?" This last was uttered with a particularly impish grin, poking fun at me for the time Reg and our older brothers had convinced me and my younger brother, Tim, to sneak out of the nursery after dark to join them on a snipe hunt. Of course, had we realized the snipe we were hunting was mythical, and that the pillowcases they'd told us to bring to capture the bird were actually going to be used on us, Tim and I wouldn't have been so eager to tag along.

"Are you sure hunting is the best idea?" Daphne voiced in concern, artlessly unaware he was teasing me.

"He jests," I assured her.

"Do I?" he challenged, the natural lines and tiny scars near the corners of his eyes crinkling.

Max chuckled into his drink, and a glance at Sidney and George told me they were also familiar with the general joke.

"Yes, unless you intend to be the hunter strung up in a tree with a pillowcase over your head this time," I replied pointedly before taking a sip of my gin rickey.

"That wasn't my idea," Reg replied as he echoed the others'

laughter. All save Daphne, that is, who merely frowned, either in confusion or disapproval.

"No, it was undoubtedly Thomas." His older brother had always been the most domineering. "Or Freddy," I conceded, for my oldest brother had possessed a reckless and impulsive streak. "But you were also content to leave us there all night at their urging," I muttered wryly, unwilling to let him off the hook as I recalled the fear I'd felt and the chill of that autumn evening, which had made me shiver in my thin coat. Though even as I'd listened to Tim's whimpers, I'd refused to cry, determined not to give the older boys the satisfaction.

"Only because I knew Rob would return to release you." A smile still curled his lips, showing he was far from chastened.

"Yes, Rob always looked out for those who were younger and weaker." A sharp pain lanced my heart as thoughts of my second-oldest brother tinted the memory with sadness. He had always been the best of us, and when his aeroplane was shot down over France in July 1915, he'd taken a piece of me with him. That I still hadn't reconciled myself to his loss even four years later simply made matters worse.

I drained my glass of its cool libation, resolutely pushing back the other memories battering at the door to my consciousness. When I opened my eyes, I found my husband watching me from his position leaning against the stone balustrade. It was obvious he knew where my thoughts had strayed, but I knew he wouldn't say anything. Not now anyway. Not until we were alone. And there was time enough to distract him from doing that.

"No snipe hunting," I declared as I set my glass on the table nearby. "And I suspect another cribbage tournament would only result in Reg routing us all again."

Reg's teeth flashed in a cocksure grin.

I had happened to stumble across a deck of Braille playing cards in a specialty shop I'd visited in London and brought them to the cottage. Reg had initially struggled to adapt to them, but with Daphne's assistance he had quickly acquired proficiency with them and sightless game play. This did not surprise me in the least. Reg had always possessed a quick mind and a dogged determination. Now, a fortnight after his arrival in Seaford, he was trouncing us all, with the possible exception of George, whose mathematical genius always made games of chance more interesting.

"Nocturnal sea bathing, then?" Reg persisted merrily.

Sidney straightened, crossing closer to the rest of us. "Not this evening. Not with those storms that hovered over the Channel earlier today. The water will be too choppy."

"Perhaps Verity means to surprise us," Max chimed in to say, possibly hoping to save me from Reg's further harassment. But he looked to me with the same enthusiasm.

Given the reason behind my and Sidney's retreat from London, and our decision to host this extended house party, we'd gone to great lengths to entertain and distract ourselves and our friends. After all, the one-year anniversary of the armistice ending the war had passed less than a fortnight earlier, and each of us had struggled with the tides of our own grief and loss. We had each lost loved ones, each sacrificed for the war effort— some more than others. While Sidney, Max, and Reg had served as officers in the trenches of the Western Front, George, Daphne, and I had worked for the British Intelligence Services. George had been a brilliant codebreaker for Naval Intelligence, while Daphne worked in the Registry for MI5 counterintelligence, and I had operated in a number of capacities for the Secret Service, even spending time behind enemy lines in German-occupied Belgium and France, liaising with our intelligence-gathering networks there.

Given our collective memories, our collective desire to escape the pomp and circumstance being orchestrated in London to mark the occasion, I'd had my work cut out for me. Though I'd known it was foolish to hope to pass that day and those around it without confronting some dark emotions and painful recollections, I'd done my best to strategically sprinkle our itinerary with welcome distractions. Some mundane and some outrageous. Some peaceful and some dynamic. Each of us had also done our fair share of strolling alone through our gardens or along the rocky beach. Each of us coming to terms with what had passed, our own part in it, and the fortune of our survival to see this day when so many others had not.

So I met the looks on their eager faces with some sense of chagrin as I was forced to admit the truth. "Actually, I didn't make any specific plans for this evening. I thought we might all be preoccupied with preparations for our return to London." I glanced anxiously at each of them in turn, searching for signs of disappointment. "But we could make up a table of whist or brag, if you like. Or play some music on the gramophone and roll back the rug in the parlor so we can dance. We're short on ladies, of course, but I'm sure Daphne and I can rise to the challenge if you gentlemen are willing to take turns."

George lowered his leg from where he'd crossed it over the other knee and leaned forward so that a curl of his dark hair fell over his forehead. "Don't fret, Ver. I fear we've become quite spoiled in your charge over the past few weeks. We seem to have forgotten we can entertain ourselves."

"Bentnick's right," Max chimed in, tipping his glass to me. "A relaxing evening is just what we need."

I offered them a tight smile, appreciating their desire to reassure me, but I still felt that I'd let them down. Fortunately, I would have all of dinner to come up with something clever and diverting. Mr. Parson should be appearing at any moment to inform us the meal prepared by his wife was ready. We rarely stood on ceremony at Sweetbriar Cottage, and so had taken to not dressing formally for dinner as we would elsewhere. Someone of an older generation like my mother or my aunt might have balked at such informal behavior, but none of the men minded eschewing their evening attire, and Daphne was accustomed to my ways.

So when the door behind me opened, I sat upright, swinging my legs over the side of the chaise in anticipation of Mr. Parson's announcement. But rather than declare dinner to be served, he spoke in a strained voice. "Mrs. Kent? It appears you have a visitor."

My brow furrowed at his choice of words. "It *appears* I do?"

He cleared his throat, his brow puckering in disapproval.

"Yes, well, she claims to be a relation of some kind, but I'm not quite certain."

I glanced at Sidney in confusion as I pushed to my feet. "What is her name?"

But I could now see beyond his shoulder to the woman standing behind him, having refused to wait in the entry as he must have requested. So when he pronounced her name it was all but drowned out by my exclamation of astonishment.

"Mrs. Ilse Vischering."

"Großtante Ilse!" I rushed forward, forcing Mr. Parson to step aside as I threw my arms around my great-aunt.

A fur stole was draped around her shoulders, and she smelled of the eau de cologne she had worn for as long as I could remember—a blend of peony, spices, and jasmine. Her husky voice when she whispered in my ear was the same, albeit frayed at the edges with the same rush of emotion I felt. *"Mein Liebchen."* However, her shoulders were frail beneath my arms, her body thin, and when I pulled back to look into her eyes, I could see that she had aged greatly in the past five years.

"How did you make it out of Germany?" I gasped.

CHAPTER 2

Perhaps the more pertinent question was, How had she been allowed into England? For I knew that very few visas were being granted to German citizens seeking to come to Britain. Of course, this was more to keep out those who might pursue employment here rather than elderly women with their own means of support, but the authorities were still being rather strict about which applicants they would even consider.

I stepped back, studying her more closely. Whereas before she had been Rubenesque and pleasantly round, her skin now sagged on the fine bone structure of her face, its color pale and sallow, while dark circles ringed her sunken eyes. But those green eyes, so like my own, were still sharp and brilliant, albeit watery with emotion at the moment.

"And why didn't you inform us you were coming?" I pressed. "I would have met your ship at the dock."

"There was no time, dear. When our visas were finally issued, I was just anxious to be gone." Her hand shook slightly as she raised it to tuck a tendril of my bobbed auburn tresses behind my ear. "As to the rest, I think your father vouched for me with your Home Office. Or at least convinced them that I could not be a threat."

That was very like Father. To quietly arrange matters and set things into motion, and then tell no one about it. But in this instance I rather wished he'd said something. At least then I might have been better prepared for his Tante Ilse to appear on my doorstep. But perhaps he had worried I might be disheartened if the Home Office had denied her application. He knew how much Tante Ilse meant to me. How close we had been before the war tore everything apart.

"You must have traveled to London first," I surmised. My parents lived hundreds of miles farther north in the Yorkshire Dales, while Sidney and I spent most of our time at our Berkeley Square flat.

She nodded as a guardedness entered her eyes. "Your housekeeper was reluctant to tell us where you were at first."

Just as Mr. Parson had been reluctant to admit her here. Because she was German.

Her English might be excellent, but her accent and inflection, even refined as it was, gave her away. Because of the war, Germans were shunned, if not outright reviled, by most British. It didn't matter that the Germans had lost even more soldiers than the British Isles, or that their economy was in shambles, its population starving. The Germans were the enemy. They had killed our boys. They had caused our suffering. And the vicious propaganda put out by the government had done its job too well, splashing images of Huns brandishing babies on spikes and trampling over the bloody ravished bodies of innocent Belgian women.

Even knowing the greater facts of the matter as I did, even mourning the deaths of my second cousins who had fought for the other side, I still had to check my reaction to the German people at large. After all, I had witnessed firsthand what they had done to the populace of the territories they occupied in Belgium and northeastern France. I had listened to the stories the people there had to tell of their atrocities, and beheld the people's stripped homes and empty larders. I'd also endured the groping hands of the German soldiers at checkpoints and among the streets of the cities and villages, ever fearful they would realize I was not a local civilian but a British spy.

But when confronted individually, it was harder to ignore their humanity and their equal suffering. And I could never disdain my *Großtante*. Especially not knowing what she'd done for me during the war at terrible risk to herself.

I squeezed her upper arms gently, conscious of how fragile they felt beneath my hands. "Well, I'm glad you found me." My gaze slid over her shoulder, expecting to find her longtime maid, Schmidt, hovering there, but instead there stood a new girl. She couldn't have been much older than twenty, and although she lingered in the shadows across the room, I could tell she was quite pretty.

Tante Ilse turned to look behind her, anticipating my question before I could ask it. "Schmidt died. The Spanish influenza," she explained.

"And you?" I asked in alarm, wondering if the virus that had ravaged the rest of the world in subsequent waves of infection since the summer of 1918 was at least partly the cause of her decline.

"It spared me." She sighed. "Though not your cousin Gretchen."

My heart clenched at this news.

She shook her head wearily. "Why is it the young that the world seems so insistent on taking from us?"

First the war, and then the influenza, which had disproportionately killed more young adults in the prime of their life than children or the elderly. I had no answer for her, for I had found myself wondering the same thing.

Her eyes widened as they drifted toward the terrace beyond me. "Oh, but I am sorry. I seem to have interrupted a party."

I had all but forgotten about the others who were gathered there, so intently was I studying Tante Ilse's face and trying to come to grips with the fact she was here actually standing before me.

"Allow me to introduce you while Mr. Parson shows your maid to the Primrose chamber, where she can settle your things." I turned to the man who still stood stonily to the side, offering him a stern look of my own. He might despise Germans, but he would treat my great-aunt and her servant with respect or else he would hear it from me.

He nodded his head once before turning to usher the young maid toward the entry hall and then the stairs.

"Tante Ilse, allow me to introduce you to my husband," I declared, guiding her toward Sidney, who had already crossed to meet us halfway.

"So you're the fellow who captured Verity's heart," she murmured with a soft smile as he clasped her hand. Her eyes twinkled as she scrutinized his handsome visage, clearly liking what she saw. "I can see why she chose you."

Sidney laughed before his gaze briefly brushed over mine. "And I can see where she gets her charm."

Tante Ilse giggled. "It's certainly not from Frederick or Sarah," she jested, naming my parents by their given names. "As much as I love them," she added, perhaps worrying she had been too severe. But she wasn't wrong. My father and mother had never been noted for their charm or joviality. Not even before the war.

"I wish I could have attended your wedding, but . . ." She shrugged, as eloquent a gesture as could be made to explain the impossibility of a German traveling to England for such an occasion in the midst of a bitter war between the two countries.

He patted her hand. "Well, I'm pleased to meet you now. Verity has told me so much about you."

A bold-faced lie if ever I'd heard one, for I'd told him almost nothing about her. Not during the summer before the war or during his all-too-brief leaves from the front—days that we'd mostly spent wrapped up in each other—and not since his return from the dead five months prior, when we'd teamed up to catch the traitors he'd feigned his death to apprehend. But we had been rather preoccupied since then—readjusting to each other and investigating unsolved crimes from the war and after.

In any case, Tante Ilse didn't try to tell the same lie, for she couldn't. It had become all but impossible for mail to slip through to Germany during the conflict, and only recently had we been able to resume exchanging letters. She had no telephone and, as I understood it, little chance of being able to make a call from her home deep in the countryside of Westphalia even if she had, as Germany's broken infrastructure was still in pieces.

I turned to find that the other gentlemen and even Daphne had stood to greet her, and I introduced them each by name. She lingered longest with my cousin Reg, who was also her grand-nephew, though they had never been close. My Aunt Ernestine had always disapproved of her mother's German lineage. Or perhaps that wasn't true. Perhaps she had become critical after her marriage to an English baronet. Either way, the war had hardened her desire to distance herself from that branch of the family, and Reg's reaction to Tante Ilse, while polite, was far from effusive. Tante Ilse responded in kind, seeming to take her cue from him.

Or maybe she was merely too tired to display more warmth, for I could see the effort it cost her to perform even this most basic of social rituals. Her shoulders slumped, and lines of fatigue and possibly pain scored her brow, even as she smiled graciously and said all the right things.

"We were just enjoying some drinks before dinner," I explained. "But perhaps you would like me to show you to your room. I'm sure today and many of the days before it have been long ones."

"Yes, please. You are all so kind." She reached for my hand, and I was alarmed to discover hers trembled. "But I think I would like to lie down."

Everyone murmured their consent and best wishes as I guided her toward the door, before speaking over my shoulder. "Don't hold dinner for me. I'll join you once I've settled Frau Vischering."

I slowed my steps, noticing how much more she leaned on me with each passing moment. Fearing her legs might give out completely, I leaned my head closer to whisper. "Shall I ask Sidney to assist you up the stairs?"

She offered me a flicker of a smile even though her face was pale with strain. "As much as I would enjoy being swept up into the arms of your handsome young man, I'm sure I can do it on my own. If you help me," she added, and I took a firmer grip of her arm, bracing her elbow.

We climbed with plodding steps, but eventually we made it to the Primrose bedchamber, where my great-aunt's maid had already turned down the bed and was now in the process of unpacking her valise. She hastened over as we entered and assisted me in settling Tante Ilse onto the bed. In the soft glow of the bedside lamp, I was surprised to discover the maid was even lovelier than I expected. A tendril of brown hair, the soft shade of a fawn's pelt, had escaped from its pins to trail along her jawline. Although she was overly thin, her sunken skin forming hollows in her cheekbones, her complexion was the smooth and creamy shade and consistency that society women paid hundreds of pounds trying to achieve. Long curling lashes shaded her wide amber-brown eyes. She spoke to my great-aunt in German, her voice an airy soprano, asking if she wanted her medicine.

"*Nein. Nicht jetzt,*" Tante Ilse responded, patting the girl's hand where it clutched hers. Then she dismissed her, asking her to fetch her a glass of water.

"Did Mr. Parson show you the stairs that lead to the kitchen?" I piped up to ask the maid in German as she rounded the bed.

She turned to me in surprise, perhaps not having expected me to know the language, or dare to speak it. She nodded.

"Mrs. Parson will be making arrangements for a room for you, as well. Though I suspect she has her hands full preparing dinner at the moment."

She nodded again and then hastened out of the room, almost as if she could not wait to escape. I stared after her for a moment, puzzling over what I had said to unnerve her.

"Never mind Bauer," Tante Ilse told me, returning to English. "She has gotten a little shy since we arrived. I don't think she anticipated all of the unkindness."

I couldn't help but wonder if her English had failed her or if she was deliberately understating the matter. *Animosity* was the word I would have chosen.

"And you did?"

She blinked open her eyes to gaze up at me. "Oh, yes. I knew how it would be."

"I'm sorry . . ."

"*Nein, Liebchen,*" she interrupted, gripping my hand. "*Es ist nicht deine Schuld.*"

It might not be my fault, but I still felt somehow that it was. She stared up at me, the firm will she had always possessed shimmering in her eyes, and waited until I nodded in agreement—though it was more acceptance on my part—before relaxing her gaze.

She breathed deeply as she settled deeper into the bedding, her fingers trailing over the floral counterpane for which the chamber had been named. The pale yellow flowers speckled across the white background matched the primrose shade of the room's walls. In the spring, they bloomed in the meadow to the west of the cottage, which could be seen through the window, but by mid-November there was little to see but grass and gorse.

While her eyes were closed, I sank down in the chair next to the bed, taking the opportunity to scrutinize her more closely: The lines etched into her face, even in repose. The sunken appearance of her eyes and the paleness of her lips. "Your maid mentioned medicine?" I ventured in German, half afraid of her answer.

"It is nothing," Tante Ilse responded in English. "I am almost eighty years old. If you were my age, you would sometimes need medicine, too."

My mouth curled reflexively. I supposed that was true. But my great-aunt had always seemed so indomitable. "Would it be easier to speak in German?"

"No, I need the practice." She crossed her hands one over the other at her waist. "And I have learned that it is always better to speak the language of the country you are in, so that they do not believe that you are conspiring against them."

I flushed. Not at the truth, for I had operated with the same understanding during the war, whether in neutral Holland or German-occupied Belgium. Nothing made one stand out more or aroused more suspicion than speaking a foreign tongue. However, I had never thought to have the same implication made within my own country, especially when speaking with my own family member.

She opened her jade-green eyes. "Your husband," she began uncertainly, but then her thoughts seemed to change course. "You understated how good-looking he is," she murmured almost in scolding, before adding anxiously, "He will not mind that I am here, will he?"

"No, of course not." I reached for her hand, hastening to reassure her, though there was no "of course" about it. For all I knew, he minded very much, but I wasn't going to let my great-aunt suspect such a possibility. Not for a moment. "He knows how much I've missed you."

But the look in her eyes told me perhaps she already knew more than I was saying. "I would not have come, not like this." Her gaze drifted to the side, and her voice turned pensive. "But sometimes you must seize the opportunity when it is presented, lest it slip away."

I wasn't certain where her thoughts had gone, but it wasn't to a happy place. "How bad was it?" I finally dared to ask, not knowing how to voice it any other way. In any case, she knew what I meant.

"Very bad," she stated succinctly. A moment later she inhaled a ragged breath as if to rally herself to give a more complete answer. "Between the crops failures and the blockade, and after our army commandeered almost all of our supplies, nobody had anything. It improved a little when the *treaty*"—she nearly spat the word—"was signed, and the blockade ended, but not enough. Nowhere near enough."

In such conditions, money mattered little. Not when there was nothing to be had.

"And with cousin Gretchen gone . . ." I couldn't finish the sentence, but the implication was clear. There was no more family in Westphalia for her to rely on. Not when her two grand-nephews had already lost their lives fighting for the German Army.

She nodded.

My heart ached at the realization there was no one left in my grandmother Lina's family. No one but her own offspring living in England. Großtante Ilse had never had children, and Großonkel Carl's daughter and her sons were now dead.

"Why didn't you tell me any of this in your last letter?" I asked, having known she was being deliberately vague about her living conditions, but not to this extent.

"Because you could not do anything." Her expression turned stern. "And because I know you too well, Verity. You would have stormed into Germany after me, which would have led to catastrophe."

I frowned. "Why would it have led to catastrophe?"

"Because my neighbors already distrusted my English connections." She paused, and I could tell there was more. Her brow furrowed, perhaps irritated she'd spoken so rashly and unsure whether to continue. "And . . . because of the threats."

CHAPTER 3

"Threats?" I repeated, struggling to control how aghast I was. "You've received threats?"

She lifted her head, tugging at the fur stole that was still draped around her shoulders. I helped her remove it and then crossed the room to lay it on the oak bureau while she resettled, smoothing the coat of her red-brown woolen travel ensemble. A strand of pearls rested against her neck, peeking out of the gap in the collar above her silk blouse. When finally she clasped her hands over her abdomen again, I knew she was ready to speak. And that she was more rattled than she wished me to know.

"At first, I thought it was just a few boys, upset by the unguarded gossip from their elders, and the fact that the war ended before they were old enough to fight. The threats were childish enough. Words painted on a shed wall or scribbled on rocks thrown through a window."

These didn't sound childish to me. A rock hurled through a window? What if it had struck her or Bauer?

"What words?" I asked.

She shook her head, brushing them aside as if they were of no consequence. "But then the letters showed up on my doorstep. Letters threatening that they knew what I'd done. That if I didn't leave Germany they would tell everyone."

There was no accusation in her gaze as it met mine, but I felt the blood draining from my face anyway.

"What you'd done?" I choked on the words. "Do you mean . . . when you helped me?"

"Maybe," she hedged.

My anger with myself and irritation at her reluctance to incriminate me made my words terse. "Could it be anything else?"

She withheld her response, as if she already knew the self-recriminations spinning in my head, but I hardened my glare, compelling her to speak the truth. "No."

I turned away, fighting to restrain my emotions. "Then this is my fault," I bit out, my jaw taut with repressed fury. "I never should have told Captain Landau about you. I never should have agreed to his plan."

"Verity, *mein Liebchen*, you could not have known."

"But I should have."

The words dropped into the room like two rocks tossed into a still pond, their truth rippling outward like waves on the water. But what was done, was done. They couldn't be taken back, no matter how much I wished it.

I pushed to my feet, no longer able to sit still, regardless of how rude it was to pace about the room while Tante Ilse reclined. "Someone must have seen us."

"I think it more likely that they saw the second man."

I whirled around to face her. "What second man?"

Her brow pleated. "The second deserter."

I stared back at her in astonishment.

"Your captain may not have told you."

"No, he didn't tell me!" I pressed a hand to my forehead, my face flush with fury. "He sent a second deserter to you?"

"Yes, a few months after the first man."

I couldn't believe Captain Henry Landau had done such a thing. I couldn't believe he'd placed my great-aunt in such danger. I'd been reluctant to impose on her the first time, to expose her to such a risk, but at least *I* had been there.

"The man *told* you Captain Landau sent him?" I asked, struggling between dismay and disbelief.

"Yes. Although . . ."

I arched my eyebrows at her hesitation.

"That morning when he showed up just before sunrise and told me who he was, I admit I was alarmed. The first time was such a risk, you know. I didn't want to repeat the experience."

I could well understand that.

"So I told him he could stay in the curing shed for the day, but that night he had to go."

"And did he?"

"Yes, he was polite and respectful, and followed my orders. But still . . ."

I nodded, letting her know she needn't say more. "I am sorry, Tante Ilse," I said, sinking down on the chair beside the bed again and reaching for her hand. "I should never have come to you. And I *certainly* never intended for anyone else to."

"It is all right."

"But it's my fault you've been run out of your home."

"I wanted to leave anyway. There is nothing left for me there. Nothing but sad memories." Her voice trailed away as her gaze shifted toward the ceiling, seeing something I couldn't see. Something from her past she didn't share with me.

I drew breath to ask her further questions about the threats, but she lifted her hand to halt me. "I'm tired, Verity," she murmured, reverting to German. "I would like to rest now."

I straightened, releasing her hand. "Of course," I replied, for what else could I say? She did look exhausted. I'd contemplated this multiple times since her abrupt arrival. And yet, I couldn't help but wonder if there was more she simply didn't wish to discuss. Though her eyes were closed and her features smooth, there was a watchfulness to her, as if she held herself immobile rather than simply relaxing.

Deciding that restraint was the better part of valor, at least in this instance, I pushed to my feet. "I'll have a dinner tray brought up to you. Let my staff know if you or Bauer need anything."

And I would say something to the Parsons to be certain they obliged, if not with a smile, then at least with goodwill.

I joined Sidney and our other guests in the dining room, though I struggled to focus on the conversation. My thoughts kept returning to my great-aunt, and the threats and the second deserter she'd told me about. I wanted nothing more than to pick up the telephone and track down Captain Landau to demand answers. But such conversations were not conducted over the telephone. Not when someone could be listening. Especially when one had a name to put to that potential listener.

After all, we already feared that Lord Ardmore had somehow tapped the telephone at our flat in London, or bribed one of the switchboard operators to listen in for him. What was to stop him from doing the same at our cottage?

An hour later, I excused myself while Reg, Daphne, Max, and George played another hand of whist. When the door opened to our bedchamber a short time after that to admit Sidney, I was still standing before the vanity, my fingers fiddling with my teardrop moonstone necklace.

He paused to look at me, his dark hair gleaming in the light of the gas lamps, before quietly shutting the door and crossing the room to stand behind me. "You've been distracted tonight."

His fingers brushed lightly over the skin at the base of my neck, undoing the clasp of my pendant. I'd already removed the silk scarf I'd draped around my neck earlier, revealing the faint bruising still barely visible from a man's attempt to choke the life out of me five weeks prior. As the chain came undone, his lips swiftly followed, trailing soft kisses across the marks, and making my skin pebble and warmth pool in my abdomen. He released the ends of the necklace, allowing them to cascade over my shoulders into my open hand still clutching the moonstone.

I pivoted in his arms and lifted my finger to trail it along his square jaw. The bristles of his facial hair were just beginning to show. "Yes, well, I had good reason to be."

His hands came to rest on my hips. "What did your great-aunt have to say?"

"A number of things," I mused, my thoughts returning to her haggard face. I sighed. "None of them happy."

"Judging by this little line between your brows"—he pressed his thumb to my skin there—"I would wager some of it was troubling."

I lifted my gaze from his full mouth to his deep midnight-blue eyes. "And you would be correct." There was no use denying it, particularly when I wished to discuss it. My mind had been circling around and around it without any greater clarity. Perhaps Sidney would see something I couldn't. Though it meant admitting to another assignment I had undertaken for the Secret Service that I'd hoped never to have to relive, let alone admit to my husband. Not already knowing what his reaction would be.

I reached out to set my necklace on the vanity, gathering myself before diving in. "She told me she'd been receiving threats."

This didn't seem to surprise him, but then again Sidney was very good at suppressing his reactions when he wished to. A by-product of his time spent on the battlefields and in the trenches, I suspected, when one false twitch could see you killed.

"What type of threats?" he queried.

"Childish ones." I scowled, still not agreeing with her assessment of the earlier threats as harmless. "And then not-so-childish ones."

The corner of his mouth quirked wryly. "That's not a very helpful description."

"I know." I stepped out of his arms, pressing a hand to my forehead as I crossed the room to sink down on the edge of our bed. "But I need to tell you something—something that happened during the war—before it will make sense."

If my words had unsettled him, he still didn't show it. Instead he reached out his arm to lean against the oaken bedpost, gazing down at me expectantly. "Go on."

I dropped my gaze to the Savonnerie rug, gathering my thoughts and trying to decide precisely where to begin my tale. "You've met Captain Landau, and you know when I was sent to Rotterdam I often took my orders from him." I looked up at his face to be certain he was following. Landau had been in charge of the military section there, tasked with organizing intelligence-gathering networks within the German-occupied areas and collecting what information from them that he could on German troop and supply movements, among other things. Periodically, I had been dispatched over the border into Belgium, past the heavily guarded, electrified fence, to liaison with these networks, as well as some of the Secret Service's own agents, or to gather other targeted intelligence.

He nodded.

"Well, from time to time, he would be approached by or stumble across German deserters wandering the streets." Holland being a neutral country, the German soldiers merely needed to escape across the frontier between it and Belgium. This hadn't been an uncommon occurrence, especially as the war dragged on and Germany's situation deteriorated. "Sometimes they had useful information to sell him. Sometimes German Intelligence tried to fool him by sending him fake deserters with false data." I shrugged. "Landau said it was all part of the job, and reason enough to keep his sword and intellect sharp."

Sidney loosened his tie and pulled it from his collar. "I suppose it was no more distasteful than some of the things we field officers were forced to do."

I gazed up at him as he tossed the tie over a chair and removed his coat, wondering if he would elaborate on what he meant. Censoring his soldiers' letters? Disciplining them for infractions he himself disagreed with? Following orders he knew would result in the deaths of hundreds of his men?

When he didn't speak, I forced myself to continue.

"One deserter in particular made a strong impression on him. A fellow named Heinrich Becker. Landau felt that he wasn't selling him information simply for a few gulden, but because he had a grievance against the German authorities. He confessed that he had a wife and three children in Berlin, and that they were barely surviving on turnips and watery potatoes. On his last leave, when he'd discovered how pale and gaunt his family was, he told Landau he'd vowed to desert to Holland and find work in order to send money back to his family. He asserted that he had a greater obligation to his family than the kaiser, and Landau thought his words were sincere."

"An ideal candidate for gathering intelligence within Germany," Sidney remarked as he unfastened his cuff links.

I was glad he understood the implication. "Indeed. And when Landau approached him about that very thing, and offered him a fair amount of money, he agreed. Even though there was no minimizing how dangerous the mission would be." I rose to my feet, moving toward one of the tall windows to peer out into the night. The gardens were thick with shadows save a thin stream of light spilling through a gap in the parlor curtains.

"Landau supplied Becker with the documents he would need to prove himself unfit for military service, as well as a pass which would permit him to travel on the German railways. All courtesy of the Service's excellent engraver." I paused for barely a second, but I was certain Sidney heard the hesitation in my voice nonetheless. "However, there was still the trouble of getting him past the frontier into Germany. After all, the man he was meant to portray would have no legitimate reason to be outside of the country."

"Verity," Sidney said in a low voice just behind me. I tensed, not having heard him move, and turned to face him. "Why do I have a sinking suspicion that I know where this is going?"

I arched a single eyebrow before answering pertly. "Because you're too smart for your own good?"

The displeasure did not ease from his face, but he did reach out to tuck the auburn strands of hair that had fallen forward to shield part of my face behind my ear. The better to see me, I supposed. "Go on."

My gaze shifted back toward the window. "Landau knew I had relatives from the North Eifel Hills in Germany." I frowned, recalling our conversations. "That information must have been in my file, for he'd asked me before about Tante Ilse. He knew her home lay just outside Montjoie. Or Monschau, as they now call it, since the kaiser officially changed its name last year," I remarked dryly, for Montjoie had been much too French.

Though we British hardly had a right to our cynicism. After all, the royal family had changed their name from Saxe-Coburg and Gotha to Windsor because the former was too German.

I crossed my arms over my chest, preparing for my husband's reaction. "Because his first objective lay just southeast of there, Landau decided that was the ideal place for him to cross over. And that I should be the one to lead him."

"Into Germany?" Sidney clarified, the muscle in his jaw ticking. "Our enemy. In the midst of the bloodiest conflict the world has ever known." He cursed, turning away from me as he struggled to rein in his temper. "And here I thought Landau was the sensible one, and Xavier the reckless SOB," he groused, naming another of my former colleagues with whom I had a complicated history. He scraped a hand back through his hair before rounding on me. "You could have been killed! Or captured!"

"I could have been killed or captured on any of my missions," I pointed out calmly. "Just as *you* could have been."

"Yes," he bit out between clenched teeth. "But I . . ."

"*You* were in the trenches," I interrupted. "While I was supposed to be safe at home. Yes, we've already established this. Months ago. And in any case, all of this is over and done with." I swept my hands from my shoulders to the ground. "I'm standing here before you now, all of one piece. So shall I continue? Or would you like to rehash the same argument yet again?"

He stepped closer, forcing me to lift my chin to continue looking him in the eye. When his hands lifted to grasp my upper arms, I could feel the heat of them through the silk of my dress. "You can't be surprised I'm upset by this news," he uttered coolly. "You've been bracing for it practically since I entered the room." He loomed. "It's also why you haven't told me this tale before."

My insides squirmed in acknowledgment of this truth even if I wasn't about to admit it. "There are a lot of missions I haven't told you about. And if you hadn't found out the truth about my war service, and wormed your way into C's good graces, you wouldn't know about *any* of them."

When I had joined the Secret Service, I'd been forced to sign the Official Secrets Act, which had prevented me from disclosing the true nature of my work to anyone without authorization. But Sidney had managed to inveigle the information from one of my indiscreet colleagues—a man whom he would not name, even to this day. After we'd unmasked a nest of traitors some months past, my former—and covertly ongoing—boss at the Secret Service, C, the chief, had unofficially sanctioned our working together and my disclosing those secrets my husband needed to know.

"And imagine where we would be then," he challenged.

My heart clutched in recognition of the fact that when he had returned from war and his feigned death, it had been even odds whether we would remain together or eventually join the thousands of other couples lining up to get a divorce after four and a half years of war had torn their lives apart. Had we been forced to continue to keep all of our secrets from each other, I was fairly certain we wouldn't have made it. Even now there were times when the divide between us still seemed unbridgeable. I couldn't imagine how wide that chasm would be if I were forced to continue the pretense that I'd merely worked as a clerk at an import-export company.

Sidney's anger faded as abruptly as mine. He pulled me toward him, tucking my head against his chest below his chin and wrapping his arms around me. I inhaled the scent of bay rum from his aftershave, which clung to his shirt, and pressed my ear over the reassuring beat of his heart. A heart that had almost been stopped forever by a traitor's bullet just twenty months earlier.

Some moments later when I lifted my head, we were both calmer.

"Go on." His lips curled remorsefully. "I promise to keep my tongue in check."

I nodded, trying to gather back together the strands of the story.

"You were ordered to lead Becker to Monschau," he prompted.

"Yes, well, it wasn't an order," I admitted. "But it might as well have been one. So I agreed. We set out for Sittard, where one of our agents belonged to a group of smugglers, and he helped us to cross over into Belgium, and then I guided us the short distance into the Hohes Venn. Or Hautes Fagnes, depending on what language you're speaking in. The High Fens. They're notoriously difficult to cross. Especially in the dark. So we knew that stretch of the border would be the least guarded and easiest to penetrate."

My words faltered as I recalled that harrowing night. Then, the frontier between Belgium and Germany stretched across the most remote part of the moors. Though that wasn't the case now, as Germany had been required to cede land in the Wallonia region to Belgium as part of the peace treaty, shifting the frontier some miles east, almost to the doorstep of Monschau. But on the night of our trek, part of the border rested in a nearly undefended patch of desolate bog. Not only would the traditional fences and wires have sunk in the morass, but few people dared venture that way, making their installment unnecessary. The fen itself served as the border's own best defense. Though we had learned it was not the sole obstacle.

"But such things often aren't as simple as they appear to be," Sidney commiserated, correctly interpreting my silence.

I lifted my hands to his shirt, feeling the heat of his skin through the fine lawn, and fiddled with the placket of shiny white buttons marching down the front, the top one of which he'd already unfastened. "I'd been instructed how to find a little-known path that would lead us safely across the fens, through an area between the Helle and Hoëgne Rivers, so that we wouldn't have to attempt to wade across. However, we did have to contend with navigating a rather precarious bog. Particularly when the weather closed in, covering the landscape with fog."

I risked a glance up at his face to find him watching me steadily. "With the area being so remote, and our sources having told us it was rarely patrolled, we decided to risk the use of an electric torch. We didn't have much of a choice if we were to have any hope of finding our way across in the gloom." The hairs on the back of my neck prickled in remembrance of that journey, ever terrified that one wrong turn, one false step could spell disaster.

I took a steadying breath, almost able to smell the peat and silt. "Unfortunately, our sources hadn't been altogether correct. Or we'd simply had rotten luck. For not five minutes later we heard a German sentry call out to us."

CHAPTER 4

❧

Sidney inhaled sharply, the only sign of his alarm on our behalf.

"We doused the light and stood still, hoping he would believe we'd moved on," I hastened to explain as my words came faster. "But we soon heard the sound of him moving toward us. So we ran, as swiftly as we dared, praying we could outdistance him or lose him in the marshy terrain." I elected not to mention the gunshots. How every time the sentry fired his gun, we flinched, fearful his bullets would strike us. "Then we heard a sort of dim splash and the sound of cursing. We realized the soldier had stumbled into the bog when moments later he began calling to us, begging for our help."

"Tell me you didn't go back to help him," Sidney demanded, recalling me to the present. I realized I'd been staring unseeing at his chest as it rose and fell rapidly, echoing my own distress.

I blinked up at him, at the lines of strain marring his face. "No, I . . . I thought about it," I admitted, my voice but a thin thread of sound. "But there was no way to know if it was a trick, or if he would shoot us anyway." By the time we were able to see him, he would be able to see us. Or at least note the direction in which to point his gun. "So, we left him there."

I recoiled from the starkness of those words. For weeks afterward, the German sentry's desperate pleas echoing across the fens had haunted my dreams, and accusatory fingers had pointed at me through the fog. My conscience had not been easy with what I'd been forced to do. It still wasn't.

As if sensing this, Sidney grasped my chin gently, forcing me to meet his gaze. "Ver, you had no other choice."

"I know."

But that didn't make it any easier to accept.

The corners of his mouth lifted in a sympathetic smile, almost as if I'd spoken the thought aloud. I would likely never know what had happened to the German soldier, whether he died there from drowning or exposure, or eventually escaped. I often wondered if knowing would make it easier or harder to accept what I'd done. Or rather, hadn't done. I supposed it depended on the outcome.

"Then you and Becker made it through the High Fens," Sidney prompted.

"Yes, and on to Monschau, where Tante Ilse received us with good grace." I frowned. "Though I'd placed her in an untenable situation." I was still asking myself why I'd allowed Landau to convince me to take Becker there, especially now that I knew it had opened the door to his sending her another deserter. It was true, I'd also been tasked with another matter dealing with some of our agents in Vielsalm, near the northern border of Luxembourg. But I could have seen Becker to the frontier with Germany and turned south. I could have refused to enter Germany and lead him to Monschau.

Except I had been anxious for him to succeed. Not only for the Allies' cause, but also for the sake of his family, whom he'd talked about almost nonstop during our journey. I knew he had two headstrong daughters and a sturdy son. That his wife loved the rain, and that she made the tenderest sauerbraten, but her spätzle was always too doughy, though she insisted it was supposed to be prepared that way. The manner in which he'd smiled when he said it had made me suspect it was a personal joke between them—the kind of cozy jest often shared between husbands and wives.

He had been about to betray his country and undertake a mission fraught with danger to gather intelligence for us. And all because he loved his family and couldn't bear to see them suffer further deprivation. I had felt the least I could do was arrange the best possible start, and that meant sending him off from my great-aunt's home with pressed, clean clothes and a well-groomed appearance, so that he could stride confidently into the train station to travel deeper into Germany.

"And someone saw you? Or Becker," Sidney guessed, reminding me that the entire reason I had been telling him this story was so that I could explain the threats that had been made to my great-aunt.

"Actually, Tante Ilse believes they may have seen the second deserter."

His head reared back. "Second deserter?"

"Yes, I was just coming to that." My voice hardened. "Unbeknownst to me, apparently Landau sent another deserter to her a few months later."

Sidney's brow lowered. "That's a steep risk to take. Your great-aunt wasn't one of his agents, after all. What if she'd turned him away, or worse, turned him in."

"I assume he thought her loyalty to me would buy her silence. And his gamble appears to have paid off, but at what cost?" To Tante Ilse, that is. Landau's mission didn't appear to have suffered.

Gathering intelligence during wartime was all a matter of calculated risk. I didn't begrudge Landau for having to utilize the tools before him—be they people or resources—to achieve results. But Tante Ilse had not been his tool to use.

"I take it you're going to confront him."

"Of course I am," I replied, returning to the bed, where I perched on the edge to remove my T-strap pumps. "I know he's in London, at least briefly. And he owes me some answers." I tossed my shoes toward the bench near the bottom of the bed so I wouldn't trip on them.

"Whatever happened to Becker?" Sidney yanked the plum-colored drapes across the window before turning to face me. "Did he succeed?"

"I don't know," I admitted. "Once he strolled away from

Tante Ilse's home, he was no longer my concern. And Landau never saw fit to confide in me about the matter further. Not that there was ever much time for such chitchat."

Most of the time my meetings with the captain had been at random safe houses spaced throughout Rotterdam and the surrounding area, which I was either going to, after an assignment behind enemy lines, or leaving from, on my way to Belgium. In the latter case, Landau normally briefed me in as few words as possible on what needed to be done, and then I was absorbed in planning my route and strategy before setting off for the frontier where I would rendezvous with one of our *passeurs*, who would help me slip across the border. In the former, I was usually exhausted and anxious to write in my reports as many of the details I had committed to memory as I could before I collapsed with fatigue. Either way, there was little call for idle chatter.

"I hope for his family's sake he made it," I mused, consigning the query to the list of questions about the war I might never have satisfactory answers to.

Sidney sank down on the bed beside me. He was quiet for a moment, perhaps contemplating his own list of unanswered concerns. "Then we're still returning to London tomorrow?"

Lifting the hem of my gown, I unfastened the clasps securing one of my stockings before rolling it down my leg. "As long as Tante Ilse feels well enough to make the journey. In any case, she'll undoubtedly be more comfortable in the rear seat of your Pierce-Arrow than transferring from train to train." I glanced sideways at him before adding wryly, "Though, for her sake, you might ease off the speed this one time."

Far from chastened, he nudged me with his shoulder. "If she's anything like you, she might enjoy it."

I wrinkled my nose at his razzing before unfastening the garter on my other leg. "Under normal circumstances, I might agree with you. But Tante Ilse did not look like herself tonight." I paused, my worried gaze searching the swirled fabric of the rug for answers. "She looked old, and tired, and drained."

Sidney did not try to make light of the fact that she was, in fact, old, and that that usually led to a person tiring more easily.

And I was grateful for that. He merely pressed his hand reassuringly to the small of my back as I sorted through my apprehensions for my great-aunt.

I turned to look into his eyes. "The fact is, I don't know if all of that is due to the five long years of war and hardship, or something else. And I think I'm a little afraid to find out."

"She means a great deal to you."

I shrugged. "She always has."

Though I wasn't certain I could put into words how to explain it. For all that I loved my mother, she had never understood me. And I supposed I had never understood her either. It was just easier with Tante Ilse. She never expected me to be anything other than I was, and that was something I had always taken comfort in. With my mother, there had been nearly constant battles and bickering. Much of it well-intentioned. I was mature enough to understand that now. But I had felt harried and henpecked all the same. With my great-aunt, there had been amity.

"Her maid mentioned her medication, but of course, that doesn't necessarily mean anything."

"But you think it does." His deep voice didn't question, but stated this as if it was a valid fact, which encouraged me to admit the truth.

"I do."

"Did you ask her about it?"

"Yes, but she claimed she was simply getting old."

His mouth flattened into a humorless smile. "As you would if you wished to deflect from the truth."

"And I couldn't shake the feeling that there was something, several somethings," I amended, "she wasn't telling me."

"Maybe she was wary of telling you everything tonight. Maybe she'll be more forthcoming tomorrow."

"Maybe," I conceded, though I wasn't convinced. My aunt had never been secretive in the past, but perhaps that was my naïveté showing. After all, I was barely twenty-three years old, and besides the single night I had stayed with her during the war after leading Becker into Germany, I hadn't seen or spoken to her in over five years. As a child and adolescent, what had I truly known about her life? What had I even understood?

My recognition of this only served to make me more uneasy, and so I sought to push it away. At least, for the moment.

I let my head tip to the side, resting it on Sidney's shoulder and nestled it into the crook of his neck. His skin was warm against my own, and as I inhaled the scent of his skin, I felt something inside me begin to loosen. That is, until he spoke.

"Loath as I am to bring him up, have you given any consideration as to what Ardmore might do with the information that you have a German relative staying with you?"

I lifted my head as alarm tightened my muscles. "Are you upset she's here?"

"No. No, of course not. I'm just . . . considering the ramifications."

I searched his face, wondering if that sounded as if he *doth protest too much*, and felt my defenses rise. "She's my seventy-nine-year-old great-aunt. I can hardly turn her away. Where else would she go?"

He gripped my upper arms, speaking in his I'm-trying-to-be-reasonable-but-you-are-making-it-difficult voice that I loathed. "Verity, I never said anything about turning her away."

"But are you thinking it?"

"What? No. Verity, stop this. I have no problem with your great-aunt being here." His hands lifted to cup my face. "I'm not so hard-hearted as to hate all Germans. I never did." He sighed. "Truth be told, if anything, I pitied the poor blighters."

"What do you mean?"

He lowered his hands, turning his head to the side as a pained expression flickered over his features. "Well, the Jerries weren't happy to sit in their mudholes and cesspits any more than we were. We were both just cogs caught up in the higher-ups' wheels of madness. In another time, given half a choice, we might have shared a joke and a pint, and gone back to our lives. I had no more reason to wish him dead than he did me." His jaw tightened. "Except the fact that the only way out, the only way to end it, was to outlast him."

At the Secret Service, I'd seen the satires printed in the various so-called trench publications produced by soldiers during the war. One had featured a poem describing an aged Tommy with a hoary, snow-white beard, still fighting in the trenches; while another had written up the details of a divisional entertainment sketch titled *The Trenches, 1950*. I had winced upon seeing them the first time, but my colleagues who had been invalided home from the front and then reassigned to the Secret Service had laughed uproariously, though the sound had also held a hollow note. One that I could imagine had been amplified in the laughter of the men who were still stuck in the trenches. Men like Sidney.

"Sidney," I whispered brokenly. I pressed my hand to his arm, hoping to draw him back from his dark thoughts.

He seemed to internally shake himself, for when he turned to look at me, the despair that had clung to him had all but vanished from his features. "But regardless of Ardmore's feelings on the matter, which are unclear, he must recognize that a large portion of the population here in Britain despise Germans. And he could seek to use your great-aunt's presence here against you."

I struggled to dismiss the anguish he'd exhibited just moments before as swiftly as he had, wanting to press him on the matter. But I knew from experience that my husband could not be forced to discuss that which he didn't want to. So I squeezed my eyes shut as I reshuffled my thoughts. "Yes, you're undoubtedly right. Ardmore is nothing if not astute, and surely keen to use whatever weapon he has in his arsenal against me. But what is there to be done? I can hardly hide her. And I'm certainly not going to send her away."

"No, but we should be on guard against it."

"Yes, of course."

"And I wouldn't recommend letting your great-aunt leave the flat unaccompanied. At least, not at first," he amended, seeing the fury flash in my eyes.

I was not going to make Tante Ilse a prisoner. But I also had to admit he had a point.

I nibbled on my bottom lip, considering another option, even loath as I was to do it. "Perhaps we should move up our plans to visit my family."

Sidney's eyebrows arched high in surprise.

"Well, we promised to spend the holidays with them anyway. Will it really make much of a difference if we arrive a fortnight earlier?"

The answer was yes. Yes, it would make a difference. For I would have two weeks less to prepare. And two more weeks of listening to my mother harangue me for the fact that I hadn't visited in over four years. Not since my brother Rob died. The fact that there had been a war going on for much of that time made no difference. My mother wasn't allowed to know what I'd really been doing with my time, how I'd truly done my part for the war effort, and so I was a cruel, inconsiderate hoyden of a daughter.

But what was a fortnight in the grand scheme of things? If the last four years hadn't prepared me to face my childhood home without Rob, then what did I expect to happen in the space of two more weeks?

Sidney's hand trailed over my shoulder to the back of my neck. "Are you certain?"

"No," I replied with brutal honesty. "But it will get Tante Ilse out of London faster. And out of Ardmore's sight."

"You do know that you don't have to face this alone." His fingers played in the hairs at the nape of my neck. "I'll be with you."

I knew he was speaking of Rob. Of facing his absence and accepting his death. But I didn't want to talk about that. Not now. Not ever, really. The very thought of it lodged a lump in my throat so tight I couldn't breathe.

So I offered him a tight, placating smile before leaning forward to push to my feet. But Sidney wouldn't let me retreat. Not entirely. With his hand still gripping my neck, he turned my head so that his mouth could capture mine. After a moment of initial surprise, I readily capitulated, melting into his arms.

Some moments later, having tumbled me back onto the bed, Sidney lifted his lips a hair's breadth from mine so that he could speak. "Don't hide from me, Ver," he pleaded in his voice grown husky with desire.

"I could say the same to you," I replied, a reminder of the on-going push and pull of our relationship. The difficulty of peeling back someone else's secrets was that too often you also risked your own.

And so we retreated to the one thing we knew we could always rely on—our desire for each other. His mouth sealed over mine even as his hands moved to sweep away every last remaining barrier between our bodies. For then, at least in this one way, we could find our limbs and our breaths intertwined even if our hearts and minds still grappled for cohesion.

CHAPTER 5

It required a degree of finagling, but I managed to contrive a meeting with Captain Henry Landau three days later. At any rate, I'd needed the time between to see my great-aunt settled in our London flat and to make arrangements for our journey to Yorkshire. Nimble, my husband's valet, had proven to be a great help with both, and Tante Ilse had taken an instant liking to the large, lumbering fellow. He had served as Sidney's batman during the war, and proved to be more broad-minded than I'd feared.

More broad-minded than Sadie Yarrow, at any rate. Normally quiet and timid, our housekeeper had made her displeasure known with her sullen expressions and the series of loud bangs and thumps that accompanied her movements throughout the flat. She was a war widow, and I knew she'd grieved for her soldier husband greatly, though she'd shared with me almost nothing about him. Not even his regiment. But apparently she placed the blame for his death squarely on the Germans.

When I rang up Landau, he had declared himself delighted to hear from me, and as I'd hoped, reminded me of my promise to dine with him when he was next in London. Never mind that I had been the one who'd had to call in a favor from a friend still with the Secret Service to track him down. We met just before noon at a café near Piccadilly. Should any of Ardmore's men or any of the chaps from the Service learn of our meeting, it would appear just like two old colleagues enjoying a meal together, for ostensibly that's all it was. Landau wouldn't be remaining in London long anyway, for he'd accepted an appointment from C to open the office in Berlin, so it was unlikely anyone would care about our conferring.

I breezed through the door, inhaling the scent of roasting meat and sautéed vegetables, along with the sharp pine scent of some cleaner. Landau was waiting for me at a small table near the window, and I greeted him with congratulations as he rose from his chair to buss my cheek.

"Yes, well, C tells me it's one of the best appointments in the postwar restructuring, but I must assume he means in terms of opportunity for advancement rather than good food and good company, for Germany is a right bloody mess at the moment."

"Still. It speaks well of you," I replied. And indeed it did. I knew C well enough to know that he wanted someone he could trust implicitly to handle matters in the German capital. Particularly given all of the backdoor wrangling going on at the moment among all of the military intelligence divisions. The relative degree of cooperation that had existed during the war years had all but evaporated as each branch jockeyed for prominence with the newly created Director of Intelligence at the Home Office, Sir Basil Thomson. C's insistence throughout the war on a uniquely high level of autonomy for the foreign division to be able to operate effectively seemed now an act of remarkable forethought, for it made it more difficult for Thomson to strip it of some of its privileges.

"Tell me, how are you and Kent?" he asked, pouring me a glass of wine from the bottle on the table. "As I understand it, neither of you has exactly enjoyed a peaceful retirement."

I wondered if he was surmising such from the stories in the newspapers, or if C or another agent had filled him in more thoroughly. "Yes, well, you know well enough that I've never been the type to rest on my laurels when there's something to be done."

"True enough. Even when perhaps you should." His arched eyebrows might have hinted at disapproval, but the grin lurking at the corners of his mouth indicated he was jesting.

The waitress approached then, and Landau ordered for us, charming the girl with his easy smile and natural manner. Though his looks weren't classically handsome—his eyes being too small and his round face being dominated by a rather misshapen nose and a pair of ears that stood out from his head like the handles of a Grecian urn—there was nonetheless something about him that seemed to readily appeal to women. I suspected it was both his confidence and the warm regard in which he held them, no matter their station. Having grown up in the Transvaal of South Africa with a strong, resourceful mother, he seemed not to have developed the condescension that tainted many men's interactions with the fairer sex. I'd certainly benefitted from his willingness to not only listen to, but at times heed my advice during the years we'd worked together during the war.

And so it was with that mutual respect we'd always held for each other in mind that I decided I needn't beat around the bush. "My great-aunt arrived here from Germany four days ago," I told him after the waitress had departed.

"From Monschau?"

I'd known he would remember.

He lifted his glass to take a drink. "How is she?"

"I'm not sure," I admitted, clasping my hands in my lap lest I begin fiddling with the silverware. "The war has certainly worn her down."

He nodded, his eyes softening with understanding, offering me the opening I needed.

"Why did you send a second deserter to her?" I asked in a carefully even voice, determined not to let my temper get the best of me until I'd heard him out.

His brow furrowed in confusion. "A second deserter?"

"Yes." I stifled my impatience. "One like Becker."

He blinked at me for several seconds, and then leaned forward, shaking his head. "Verity, I never sent her a second deserter."

Alarm trickled through me, at first holding me immobile. "You didn't?"

"No. I would never . . ." His eyes flashed as he broke off,

seeming to rein in his outrage at the very suggestion he would have done such a thing. But it had been a war. All of us had done things we'd never believed ourselves capable of. "No one but you knew where in Monschau your great-aunt lived," he continued tightly. "And I certainly wouldn't have sent someone stumbling about the village, asking for her in order to find her home."

"Becker knew," I pointed out.

"Yes, but he didn't report that to us."

"So he *did* report to you?"

He sighed and turned to gaze out the window at the traffic passing by outside, all but admitting I'd made him reveal something that in all likelihood he was not permitted to. Out of the corner of my eyes I saw a woman pushing a pram hurry by on the pavement as a lumbering red bus pulled away from the curb, a cloud of fumes marking its passing. But all the while I kept my gaze trained on Landau, who eventually nodded.

"He returned a little over three weeks later with the information we'd requested on the training camps and the new regiments they were forming, as well as details about the *Sturmtruppen*." The special storm troops, who had been so effective during the Germans' big push in March 1918—the offensive that had pushed Sidney and his battalion back from the front, creating chaos with the speed of their assault. A chaos that one of Sidney's fellow officers and oldest friends had used to shoot him and leave him for dead in order to silence Sidney before he could reveal his treasonous activities.

"Had he visited his family?" I asked, having known how anxious he was to protect them, and uncertain whether approaching them in person while he was gathering intelligence for us—the enemy—would only place them in danger.

"That, I don't know." His gaze traveled discreetly over the occupants of the café beyond my shoulder, much as mine did from time to time, searching for anything out of place. It was a practice that had become so ingrained in me—in all intelligence agents—during the war, that it was now an almost unconscious act I wasn't sure I would ever be able to stop. "But he did provide us further information about the economic conditions within Germany, bringing us back samples of the coupon cards each citizen used to obtain food, much like our ration cards. But their allotment was much less than those in Britain, and in many cases the government had resorted to producing unappetizing ersatz products to substitute for the real thing. It simply confirmed for us what we already knew." His gaze was solemn. "That starvation conditions were rapidly developing. However, the German people had not yet lost heart and still hoped for victory."

I took a drink of my wine, trying to shut out the dark emotions that always crowded close when I thought about the last year and a half of the war. My gaze lifted to find Landau's own face shuttered, his eyes trained on the tablecloth between us. "You must have sent Becker on another assignment."

He cleared his throat. "Yes. And it was a difficult one. Establishing train-watching posts along the line out of Trier."

My eyebrows arched almost imperceptibly, my only reaction to this statement, but more than enough to convey to Landau that I understood the gravity of it. Although British Intelligence had been receiving the German troop movements along the Aachen-Herbesthal-Liège line for some time, the other main artery out of Germany was all but unwatched. Landau had already tried and failed multiple times to achieve this. For one, it meant establishing a post within Germany itself. For another, the line traveled through Luxembourg, which had historically allied with Germany. Luxembourg was occupied by the Germans, but to a lesser degree, and its inhabitants were far more complacent with their circumstances. The monitoring of this line would require couriers to travel into and out of Germany as well as across Luxembourg, and at this task all candidates had balked.

Though apparently not Becker.

"He had serious reservations about the possibility of such an endeavor's success, but he agreed to try and we sent him back to Germany via a different route." He sat back in his chair. "That was the last I saw of him."

"Do you think he was captured?"

"I don't know. I do know he was afraid. I had given him an enormous, and perhaps impossible, feat to accomplish, as well as a rather substantial sum of money for him to establish the organization he would need. Maybe the temptation of that money proved too great, particularly given the unlikeliness of his success, and knowing the forgeries we'd given him had already passed muster, he decided to return to his family. Or maybe he was caught and executed. I suspect we may never know."

A clear image of Becker sprang to my mind. One of him seated beneath a pine tree somewhere in the wilderness between the High Fens and Monschau. A light snow had begun to fall while we paused for a few minutes to rest. When I'd looked up from the task of scraping mud from the cracks of my worn boots with a stick, I'd been arrested by the brilliance of the smile that flashed across his beard-shadowed face. He'd begun to tell me then how he'd proposed to his wife under just such circumstances. How they'd been walking in the Grünewald while he worked up his courage, when snow had begun to fall, and seeing how beautiful she'd looked with the flakes dusting her hair—just like a snow fairy—his nerves had suddenly melted away.

Though perhaps it was disloyal and unpatriotic, I found myself hoping he had taken the money and returned to Berlin—to his snow-fairy wife and his children. After all, he had made very clear that his chief responsibility and consideration was for them. If he'd been willing to desert the German Army in order to find work to send money to them, abandoning his allegiance to the kaiser, how could Britain expect any different?

"But Verity, this second deserter . . ." He shook his head as I shifted my attention back to him. "I didn't send him."

I searched his earnest expression, finding no trace of strain or artifice. Regardless, I trusted he would have told me the truth if he had. Even if it had angered me.

I dipped my head once, indicating I believed him. "I must admit, I'm relieved to hear that. But I'm also at a loss. For if not you, then who? Who else knew about my great-aunt?" I searched my own memory for any possible solutions. "The *passeur* from

Sittard?" The smuggler who had led us over the border into Belgium.

Landau considered it and then shook his head. "No, I don't think so. He worked with us for many years. I don't think he would have taken such a risk without direction from me."

"Could the direction have come from someone else?"

After all, Landau hadn't been the only one working out of Rotterdam, and he'd had to submit his reports to someone.

"No," he replied firmly. "I told no one about your German relation. Not even my assistant." An abashed expression flashed briefly across his features. "Truthfully, I'd wondered if the connection might prove useful at a later date, and I feared that if too many people knew, it might spoil it."

I couldn't fault him this. It was one of the things that had made him such a successful agent and superior officer—knowing when to hold information close to his vest and when to reveal it, and ever conscious of potential connections.

"In terms of my reports," Landau continued. "T was the only person in Holland to see them, and he would never have interfered in such a manner with one of my agents and operations."

I suspected he was right about that. "T" stood for Robert Bolton Tinsley, a shipping magnate who had been living in Rotterdam when war broke out. He had already been handling some Secret Service work for C, so it was natural that his company's offices should become the headquarters for all the sections of British Intelligence stationed there during the war, and that Tinsley should be put in charge.

Having worked with C in London before being sent out into the field, I was perhaps better acquainted with Tinsley than Landau had ever realized, for I'd handled his reports and correspondence. Tinsley had certainly recognized I was uniquely well-informed, though we had never discussed it. As such, I knew that he was right. Tinsley was not responsible for the second deserter appearing at my great-aunt's door.

"Maybe her German neighbors were responsible," he posited. "Maybe they saw something of you and Becker and became suspicious."

"Yes, I suppose that's possible." I frowned. "But then why didn't they report her to the German authorities?"

He shook his head, seemingly as confused as I was. "Is it *possible* your great-aunt might have misunderstood?"

Though the very suggestion irked me, I forced myself to consider it. Tante Ilse's mind had always been razor sharp, and merely the fact that she was approaching eighty was no reason to believe otherwise. But the war had been long and difficult, aging her beyond the turns of the pages of the calendar, and she was certainly malnourished. I wondered what she'd been subsisting on for the past few years, but I knew she would never tell me.

Still, I doubted she would mistake a deserter for anything but that. In truth, it was rather reckless that the man had admitted to such a thing in the first place without me being there to vouch for them both. Why not simply request shelter for the night as an invalided German soldier? That would have been the easier and safer route.

"No, I know my great-aunt didn't misunderstand," I told Landau. "But there still may be something in what you're suggesting. Something off in this second deserter's approaching her."

"It sounds to me more like a test devised by her neighbors."

One she had failed. But again, why hadn't they reported her? Or had they, but the German authorities had decided it wasn't worth the effort to investigate. Much as I'd feared and despised the German Secret Police at work in Belgium, I had to admit the authorities had to have been more lenient with their citizens within Germany itself. Especially in the rural villages where everyone knew everyone. And Tante Ilse was just an old woman living with nothing but a maid. How was she to defend herself against a soldier? What choice did she have but to comply with his request? The matter was easy to dismiss.

If so, that might explain the threats still being made against her. Some of her neighbors might be angry she was never punished, and so determined to mete it out themselves in some sort of fashion.

I nodded, deciding there was no need press the matter further. At least, not with Landau. I trusted he was telling me the truth about his not being involved. So instead I brushed the problem to the side and offered him a smile as I asked about his next appointment. "So, Berlin?"

The remainder of our meal passed contentedly, and I found my thoughts crowded with memories of our meetings during the war, as well as the ghosts of old colleagues and friends who had been lost to the conflict in one shape or form. Altogether it was more sweet than bitter, but sobering all the same. As we rose from the table to part ways, Landau had at least one more piece of welcome news.

"You'll be happy to know that each of the members of La Dame Blanche is going to receive the Order of the British Empire. Military division."

La Dame Blanche had been the brilliantly conceived intelligence-gathering network I had liaised with most in the German-occupied areas. Their contributions to the war effort during the latter years of the war—made at no small risk to themselves—had been significant, and I was pleased to hear that Landau and C had won out against the objectors, and the members of La Dame Blanche would all receive their much-deserved medals from the military division, for they had taken on as many risks as any soldier. The dispute had arisen not only because the members of La Dame Blanche were largely Belgian citizens, but because half of their rosters were made up of women, and women did not receive military OBEs, but rather civil ones. However, when La Dame Blanche had agreed to ally themselves with British Intelligence, they had insisted that they would do so only if they were considered to be soldiers. I was glad Landau was able to keep his promise that they would be.

"That's wonderful news." I thought of the brave women and men I had known among La Dame Blanche's ranks. "They will be very pleased and proud." They might have been trapped behind enemy lines for the duration of the war, but they'd still been able to serve their country and their allies.

He smiled. "I'm stopping in Liège on my way to Berlin so I can tell Messieurs Dewé and Chauvin." The two clever men who had been La Dame Blanche's leaders.

"Give them my best," I urged before we said our own good-byes. When I would see Landau again, if ever, I couldn't say, and the parting was more fraught than I'd anticipated. I swallowed a lump in my throat and hurried away, lest I make a cake of my-self by actually crying.

Fortunately, I had errands to distract me, and Hatchards Bookshop and then Fortnum & Mason stood but a block away, where I slipped inside to make arrangements for the hampers of food we would take with us on our journey to Yorkshire.

CHAPTER 6

꧁❦꧂

"I do believe Tante Ilse was angling for an invitation," Sidney leaned down to say loudly into my ear to be heard over the trumpet wailing from the stage. We had paused just inside the inner doorway to Grafton Galleries nightclub, and I turned from my scrutiny of the glittering, writhing bodies jazzing across the dance floor to look up at him. "Do you think she would have been shocked?"

My lips curled thinking of my great-aunt's unsubtle hints that she would have liked to see the inside of one of these nightclubs that were currently all the rage in London. Even though we had taken her to the theater the evening before and to Westminster that afternoon, and she had clearly been tired. So Sidney and I had waited to venture out until she retired to our guest bed-chamber, despite having made no secret of our intentions—though I hadn't admitted that our visit that evening had more to do with work than play. One of my dearest friends, whom I also relied on to supply me with information, was the best jazz singer in London, and performed at this club. I didn't want to leave London without seeing her.

"Undoubtedly," I replied. At least to some extent. "But that doesn't necessarily mean she would disapprove." If I envisioned her as she had been ten years ago, I could just imagine her twirling into the fray of dancers and laughing.

The club was packed, and a haze of cigarette smoke and per-fume hovered in the air above, slowly staining the white cornices and moldings that had been installed during the days when the building had served as an art gallery. From our position, I couldn't see the tables on the other side of the mass of dancers, but the band began a new song, one I recognized. Etta Lorraine would be taking the stage soon after, so I tugged Sidney forward, turning into his arms as we reached the dance floor.

He inferred my intentions, expertly fox-trotting me through the bodies. Our progress was slow, but I didn't mind in the least. My husband had always been an excellent dancer, and after our marriage I'd discovered his mastery of rhythm and finesse extended to other pursuits. It was certainly no hardship to gaze up at his handsome features. He always looked strikingly attractive in his evening clothes, though his glittering blue eyes and the manner in which his dark hair rebelled against its ruthless taming seemed to hint at a wildness barely contained.

When Etta took to the stage swathed in a gorgeous gown of gold lamé and green sequins, which glittered in the lights, we remained in each other's arms while her bewitching voice weaved around us. Her set tonight was new, and whoever had written the songs must have had her in mind, for her voice seemed born to sing them. The rich tones ached and throbbed in the air, raising goose bumps across my arms that Sidney brushed his hands over to soothe. In such a setting, I could burrow as close to him as I wished while we swayed to the music, and given the thin emerald silk and tassels of my gown, that was close indeed.

I was all but entranced by the magic of Etta's voice and Sidney's proximity, when the sight of a familiar figure caught my eye. Etta's beau, Goldy, stood to the side of the stage in the wings rather than circulating as he normally did, and the look on his face could only be termed smitten. I warmed at the sight, hoping the pair had come to some sort of agreement, though I knew it could never be as simple as I wished.

Goldy's parents had been pressuring him to marry a woman of good family. A white woman. But his heart belonged to Etta. I didn't know what their future held. Whether Goldy would defy convention and ask her to marry him. Whether Etta would allow herself to accept. Whether society would ever accept their racial differences. There were a growing number of people, like myself, who believed such prejudice based on the color of one's skin was rubbish. But there was also an emerging movement promoting racial purity, and I found their rhetoric alarming. I could only hope those purists were a symptom of the strife and uncertainty in these postwar years, and not a lasting cultural shift.

Sidney noted my interest, and began to maneuver us through the dancers toward the stage door to Goldy's left. Once Etta finished a set, she usually emerged from there to mingle amidst the crowd for a time. If not, we could always rap on the door. The bouncers were well-acquainted with me by now, and I knew I would have no trouble gaining access.

Fortunately, we didn't even have to ask, for Goldy caught sight of us from the edge of the stage and hurried around to admit us in the door.

"Etta hoped you'd drop by," he told me, flashing me a wide smile. "Though she wouldn't tell me why." His gaze shifted to Sidney, as if drawing him into his jest. "The mysteries of women."

"Oh, come now. If you knew all of our secrets, you'd simply grow bored," I teased back, rising up on tiptoe to buss his cheek. "Love her new set."

"It's her best yet, isn't it?" he replied with pride before offering Sidney his gloved right hand. He always wore a glove on that hand to hide the scarring from the burns he'd suffered on the right side of his torso during the aeroplane crash that had ended his war service. His family owned an aviation company that was now pursuing the burgeoning market of passenger air service, an effort Sidney had invested in.

Sidney asked after that business now, and I listened quietly as I waited for Etta to join us. I heard the applause, and then the music shifted, communicating that her performance was finished for the moment. Even so, I smelled her Tabac Blond perfume before I saw her. A long pearl necklace was draped twice around her neck, and a pair of gold earrings fringed with feathers swung from her earlobes as she strode toward us with her sashaying walk.

"*Ma petite,*" she exclaimed, peppering her sentences as al-

ways with the endearments she'd learned from her Martinique-
born mother. She clasped my arms. "I heard you were back in
town. We must talk."

Though her words were light, the seriousness reflected in her
cinnamon-brown eyes made my heartbeat accelerate. She had
learned something significant. I could tell. But was it about Ardmore or another matter?

She flicked her hand toward the men, shooing them toward
the door. "We'll find you when we need you."

I bit back a laugh at this dismissive treatment, but both men
seemed to take it in stride. Even Sidney, whose eyes twinkled
with a mixture of repressed amusement and interest as his gaze
met mine when he pivoted to leave. Evidently he'd sensed the
gravity in Etta's manner as well.

She ushered us several steps farther down the corridor and
then came to a stop below the glow of the passage's sole wall
sconce and next to a stack of old equipment that had been
shoved into a corner. The once-white walls appeared coated in a
film of dust, and grit and dirt crunched under our feet, making
me wonder how long it had been since someone had swept this
area. Somewhere there must have been a water leak, for the air
smelled dank and musty.

Etta crossed her arms over her chest. Her voice was husky
with wry displeasure. "I've had an interesting visitor."

I grasped her elbow in alarm. "Not . . ."

She shook her head before I could form the word. "Not Ardmore." Her stance softened slightly. "He said he was a friend of
yours."

I frowned.

"Attractive bloke. Popular with the ladies, I imagine." She
tilted her head in consideration. "And the chaps. He had that
way about him. A little bit roguish, a little bit irreverent, but not
too much. Never too far." She scoffed at herself in amusement.
"Even I was taken in by his whisky-brown eyes and blinding
smile." Her gaze scrutinized my features. "Know who I'm talking about?"

"I'm afraid so," I muttered, for Captain Alec Xavier fit that description to perfection. He was also the most likely candidate for such an impertinent act. "But I didn't send him to you. I didn't even know he realized we were friends."

"I gathered as much, and so I played dumb. But he still insisted on giving me this." She retrieved a folded piece of paper from the bodice of her gown. "I suppose in the end I gave myself away, for he somehow convinced me to take it." Her mouth quirked drolly. "The bounder."

I could only be glad she was able to find the humor in the situation, for if I had been her, I would have been furious. As it was, I was stifling the desire to find Alec and box his ears. His reckless move might have exposed Etta to even greater scrutiny from Ardmore and others, and she could hardly afford that.

"I apologize," I told her. "He should never have come here."

"*Bébé*, you look ready to spit nails, but I'm afraid he's long gone."

I reached for the message she held out to me, but then she pulled it back, her eyes narrowing.

"Knew him during the war, did you?"

Etta and I had never discussed precisely what my war work had been, or my unofficial role now, for that matter. I couldn't tell her. Not without breaking my oath and risking prosecution for violating the Official Secrets Act. But she was an astute woman. I was certain she had guessed at least part of it.

However, there was the appearance of plausible deniability to maintain, so I equivocated. "You could say that."

She scrutinized me a moment longer, but there was no way I was going to tell her that Alec and I had worked together in German-occupied Brussels, where he had served as a German Army officer—having infiltrated their ranks several years before the war. Nor was I going to share the more personal complications of our relationship.

Perhaps recognizing she'd pushed me as far as I was willing to go, she passed me the missive. "I've been carrying it on me for almost a week," she admitted. "So it might not be as crisp as it once was."

The foolscap was still warm from her skin, and the paper's

integrity had been compromised slightly by the moisture, but during the war I had worked with documents in far worse shape, and smuggled things out of Belgium in far stranger and more unsavory places than merely a dress bodice. I recognized Alec's bold, slanting script, and though the intelligence he relayed made my heart clutch and then sink with dread, I knew my expression betrayed none of that. Refolding and tucking the message inside my own bodice, I thanked her.

She arched her brows in mild query, perhaps expecting me to explain, but when I didn't, she merely sighed. "I trust you know what you're doing, *ma chérie.*" She gestured for me to follow her around the corner, stopping before the first door on the right, on which she rested her hand. "In any case, that isn't the only matter I need to speak to you about." She pushed open the door, allowing me to see inside.

It was a dressing room. Hers, I guessed, based on the dozens of vases spaced throughout, filled to bursting with flowers, and the powders and tubes of lip salve strewn across the vanity surface, as well as the scent of Tabac Blond, which wafted out. It certainly didn't belong to the man slumped in the far corner. One leg was thrown over the left arm of his chair so that he was half-reclined, his neck cricked at an odd angle downward that made his dark blond hair fall over his face and obscure some of his features. Regardless, I knew him immediately.

I took one step forward and then stumbled to a stop, turning to Etta for an explanation as to why Max, the Earl of Ryde, was passed out in her dressing room.

"He was already three sheets to the wind when I saw him being coaxed into one of the corridors behind the bar by Lilah Turnbull."

My eyes flared wide and she nodded. Lilah was vain, cruel, and manipulative. I could guess what lengths she would go to in order to secure an earl, including coaxing him into compromising her in a rather dramatic fashion. Societal rules might be more lax than they used to be, but upstanding gentlemen still did not seduce young ladies in the back corridors of nightclubs, or appear to have, and walk away.

"I knew he was a great friend of yours, and I couldn't bear to see such an honorable chap trapped by the likes of that *viper* of a woman." The venom in her voice indicated there was more to her animosity toward Lilah than simply anger at her attempt to trap Max into marriage, but now was not the time to pursue it. "I hoped you and Sidney could escort him home."

"Of course," I replied.

"There's a rear door that leads into the mews. I'll tell Sidney to meet you there with a cab in, say, ten minutes?"

I calculated how long I thought it would take me to sober Max up enough to guide him to the door. "Ten minutes should do it." Though I might have to be a bit ruthless.

She turned to go, but I stopped her with a touch to her hand. "Thank you."

Her lips curled into a resigned smile, and then she swept from the room, closing the door.

I moved closer to stare down at Max. Though not the most elegant of sprawls, at least he wasn't drooling or snuffling, though his mouth did gape rather like a fish. His evening attire was decidedly rumpled, and his hands rested in his lap, turned upward and open, as if in supplication.

I'd been right, then, to be worried about Max's behavior at the cottage. All told, he'd been delivered several shocking blows about his late father in the past few months. The first being that he'd colluded with Ardmore and Lord Rockham to smuggle opium to Ireland in a foolish but dastardly plot. But while he'd taken that revelation more or less in stride, the discovery that the smuggled item was *not* opium, as we thought, but rather phosgene—a deadly poisonous gas—seemed to have been too much. I could only imagine the anger and disillusionment he felt toward his father, and the pain caused by such a betrayal to his and Britain's trust. After all, Max had served at the front. He'd seen the effects of phosgene gas firsthand. Right now his emotions must be in extreme turmoil.

I'd tried to monitor him, to help as best I could at the cottage. But Tante Ilse's arrival had distracted me, and I'd given him little thought since then, too absorbed with my own concerns.

"Max," I said, pushing against his shoulder. "Max." I shoved him harder, sending his torso rocking back in the chair before it returned, nearly tipping him out of the seat completely. "Max!" I shouted in his ear several times to no avail. Glancing about me, I spied a glass of water on the vanity table. Ruthless it would have to be, then.

Picking up the cup, I dumped it over his head.

He gasped and spluttered, flopping around in the chair like a fish out of water. But at least he was awake.

Swiping the water from his eyes, he blinked up at me. "Whadja do tha' for?" he demanded to know, his sentence slurring into one long word. The sight of me clearly confused him, for his brow crinkled. He turned to look around him, evidently trying to recall where he was and how he'd gotten there.

"You're in Etta's dressing room at Grafton Galleries," I explained. "You passed out in her chair."

He slicked his wet hair back from his head and looked down at the seat below him, as if shocked to discover it there. When he lifted his face again, his cheeks had flushed, and I didn't think it was from the drink.

Something twisted inside me at the evidence of his embarrassment, and I worried I'd spoken too harshly. And that if I had, it hadn't simply been residual frustration from my struggle to rouse him. I'd become used to thinking of Max as the steady, dependable one—always there when I . . . *we* needed him. But Max had his own struggles, his own troubles. It wasn't fair to think of him as faultless. After all, he was human, too.

Sinking down on the edge of the low table next to his chair, I reached for his hand, which was still damp from the water, and offered him an empathetic smile. "Is it your father?"

He struggled to meet my eyes. "Partly."

I nodded, deciding not to press. My fingers smoothed over his larger digits, trying to comfort him, to comfort myself. "Will you let me take you home?"

I felt him stiffen, and his reaction sent a fiery blush up into my own face as I realized what could be implied from what I'd said. I dropped his hand. "Will you let *us* take you home? Sidney's waiting."

He cleared his throat, his discomposure exacerbating mine. After all, I had allowed attraction to blossom between us in the days before Sidney reappeared from the dead, and though we'd never acted on them, then or since, those feelings didn't simply vanish overnight. Even so, I'd thought we'd moved past them. But apparently not entirely.

"Yes," he croaked.

"Can you walk?"

"Yes."

But that was soon proven to be false when after three steps he stumbled into the vanity table, knocking over a vase filled with flowers. I caught the floral arrangement and righted it, before grasping Max's arm and urging him to drape it over my shoulder.

"I can do it," he protested.

"Maybe. But it will go faster if you let me help."

He could hardly argue this point, so we continued on, lurching down the corridor toward the back entrance Etta had indicated. When I managed to maneuver him through the door, it was to find Sidney already waiting for us with the cab. His eyebrows arched subtly at Max's condition, but he didn't say anything. I suspected this wasn't the first time he'd assisted a drunken friend.

Max said very little on the drive to Ryde House in Mayfair. By the pale, greenish cast to his skin, I suspected there was a reason for that. The cab driver kept glancing at him in the rearview mirror, probably worried he was about to make a mess all over his upholstery. However, we made it to his town house without incident, and saw Max into the care of his butler and valet. From the manner in which he averted his eyes, I suspected he was either very sick indeed, or too ashamed to look at us. Either way, I intended to call on him the following day to check on him. Nothing good came of stewing in mortification. Especially not when there was no call for it. Not with us.

"Is that why Etta shooed us away?" Sidney asked me as we returned to the London traffic. Even at midnight the streets were

filled with cabs and motorcars darting to and fro, carrying passengers to various theaters, nightclubs, restaurants, and parties
throughout the West End. Not until two or three in the morning
would the headlamps and noises in Berkeley Square below our
flat begin to dim and quiet.

"Later," I murmured, unwilling to discuss the matter while
the driver might be listening.

All was still when we reached the flat—Sadie having departed
for home, as she lived out, and Tante Ilse, Bauer, and Nimble
presumably having fallen asleep in their various chambers hours
before. I had yet to hire a lady's maid for myself after I dismissed
the previous one, so Bauer currently occupied what would have
been her room.

Sidney locked up before joining me in our bedchamber, neither of us in the mood for a nightcap, despite the fact we hadn't
even had time for one drink at Grafton Galleries. When he entered the room, he found me seated on the edge of the bed
rather than before my vanity, with the letter Etta had given me
unfolded in my hands.

"So that was the reason for her secrecy," Sidney deduced,
sinking down beside me. "Who's it from?"

"Alec." Certain of the fact despite the absence of a signature.

He didn't react, but I knew the wheels in his head must be
turning.

"He's been sent to Ireland." Just as I'd suspected he would
be. Now that the war was over, the places where critical intelligence was most urgently needed were in Russia, which was in
the midst of a bloody revolution, and in Ireland, where rebels
were fighting for varying aims from home rule to complete independence. Alec being one of the best field agents the Secret Service possessed, it was a forgone conclusion he would end up in
one of those countries, and from the hints he had revealed to me
over the past few months, I had known it would be Ireland.

The Irish Republican Army, and in particular Michael Collins's group of men dubbed "The Squad," had been targeting
policemen, soldiers, and political figures not sympathetic to the
republican cause and assassinating them. All told, they'd already

killed more than 150 men, though the loss was magnified when one considered the people that had been targeted. After Alec and I had seen Collins and two of his men near St. James's Park in late October, and Alec had dropped some more of those hints, I'd decided I'd better bone up on the matter.

"Is that all he says?" Sidney asked, able to tell from my expression it was not.

"He doesn't spell it out specifically, but from past comments I can read much between the lines," I explained. "At this juncture, Basil Thomson as Director of Intelligence is in charge of British Intelligence efforts in Ireland, but Alec, as well as C clearly, believe he's flubbing it. Thomson thinks the Irish are stupid and rudimentary, but Alec told me he and C have long suspected their organization and intelligence gathering to be far more sophisticated. That they have their own spies within the Dublin Metropolitan Police and other government offices."

I gestured with the letter. "Alec says Thomson has assigned one of his favorite agents to infiltrate the IRA and Collins's organization. That he's already been posing as a Marxist sympathizer." I scowled. "Except neither Alec nor I have much respect for this particular agent's methods." In short, John Charles Byrnes was a brute who would stoop to just about anything to obtain results, even falsifying evidence. "And he's strongly expressed his opinion that the Irish are stupid." I shook my head. "He's never going to fool them. Not for long. And it's going to get him killed."

Sidney loosened the knot of his tie. "Is Xavier supposed to work with this fellow?"

"No, he's being sent there separately by C, in all likelihood without Thomson's knowledge. At least, that's what I've inferred." I inhaled past the tightness in my chest. "I suspect Alec's been given the same task. And while I trust he'll do it in a more . . . subtle way, I still can't help but be concerned. Alec is undoubtedly brave." I laughed humorlessly. "He has to be to have danced amidst the ranks of the German Army for six years without detection." My fingers folded and then refolded the missive. "But he's also reckless. And I worry this time he might be in over his head."

Despite the complicated history between all of us, due to the fact I'd slept with Alec one fraught night after I'd helped him escape from Belgium when his covert identity was exposed and I'd still believed Sidney to be dead, I knew my husband understood. I'd seen the worry and care he still showed for the men he'd commanded during the war, as well as his fellow officers. He grasped the fact that the comradery that sprang up between cohorts during such a conflict didn't simply evaporate once it had ended.

He draped his arm around me. "It makes sense that you're worried. Xavier has, indeed, demonstrated he can be rash and a little too careless." He squeezed my shoulders. "But let's also give him his due. He's no green soldier. Far from it. Let's not count him out yet."

I nodded, for he was right. Alec was an excellent agent. One of the ablest I'd ever worked with. If anyone could pull off what he'd been asked to do, it was him.

Nonetheless, the dread didn't leave me completely. For there had been something in his eyes when I'd last seen him, something unmoored. It was that look that had made me concerned he wouldn't take the care he had in the past.

"Besides, we've been saying we need to send someone to Ireland to look into Ardmore and the possible location of those missing canisters of phosgene," Sidney prodded, as if I needed to be reminded, when Ardmore and whatever nefarious intentions he held for that poisonous gas were forever at the back of my thoughts.

"True, and he promises to 'look into that other matter,'" I quoted from the letter. Though how much time he would have to do so was unclear. Just as it was unclear how he was going to keep this side mission from jeopardizing his main objective. Every experienced intelligence agent knew that the more operations you pursued, the more vulnerable you became to detection. How many intelligence-gathering networks within the

German-occupied areas had been compromised by their members' intersections with other resistance efforts, such as the printing and distribution of banned newspapers like *La Libre Belgique*? They were often the gateway to discovery, exposing other intersecting networks.

Despite the risk, we needed that intelligence from inside Ireland. C was doing everything he could through his connections and commissioned agents to find out what he could here in England, including uncovering where and when and precisely how many canisters had gone missing. But that information wouldn't tell us where they were now or where they were headed. Nor, sadly, could we trust the number of missing canisters reported to be accurate. Not with Ardmore working behind the scenes, possibly interfering.

Just as he would likely interfere in Ireland. The difference was that there Alec would be on his own, without our assistance to help him evade whatever Ardmore might throw at him.

"Is that all he wrote to tell you?" Disbelief clung to the edges of his voice as Sidney removed his arm from around me to shrug out of his coat. He knew well that Alec would never have taken the effort to inform me of the rest if there hadn't been something more important to communicate.

"He says he managed to locate the man who pulled me from the rubble after that bomb went off outside Bailleul."

Sidney's head snapped up from the cuff link he'd been working free. "The bomb that killed Brigadier General Bishop and his staff?"

I nodded.

During the general chaos of retreat during the Germans' big push in the spring of 1918, I'd been given the risky task of delivering a message straight to Bishop amidst the disorder of the withdrawing front lines. There was a traitor among his staff, one we feared had a connection to Military Intelligence, or else they would have been tasked with the assignment. However, moments after I'd left the shed that constituted his makeshift headquarters, it had exploded, killing everyone inside.

Until a month prior I had believed the explosion was caused by a German shell, for I had been dazed and injured, and a shell attack had commenced soon after. However, we'd recently discovered the blast had been caused by a bomb, not a shell. A bomb that we now believed the traitor had detonated after I delivered the letter from C to Bishop. What had happened to the traitor, we didn't know, but I strongly suspected he had escaped. Hence the reason I was searching for answers. And speaking to the soldier who had pulled me from the debris and then hunkered in a ditch with me during the subsequent shelling was a start.

"He says the man lives near Kendal, and he's given me his address."

"Kendal," Sidney repeated. "That's not far from you parents' home, isn't it?"

"It isn't," I confirmed. Though how Alec had known we would be headed to Yorkshire when I hadn't told him, I didn't know, but I was certain he'd somehow become aware of it. It was just like him.

"Then I suppose we should pay him a visit."

"Yes," I replied softly, wondering just what I would say to the man. There was no way I could question him without arousing his suspicion about why I had really been there. At the time I had posed as a French refugee fleeing the Germans' renewed advance. But a refugee wouldn't be asking questions about a bomb.

"He may already realize who you are," Sidney murmured.

I smiled in recognition of his having read my mind. "Are my thoughts so transparent?"

"Only to me." His eyes crinkled affectionately at the corners as he lifted his hands to begin unbuttoning his shirt. "He's likely seen your picture in one of the newspapers."

"Maybe," I conceded. "But I was hardly dressed like a society darling when he met me, and I'm afraid I looked rather worse for wear." That was the politest way I could describe my appearance given the fact I'd been coated in dirt and blood.

But Sidney could read between the lines, and the warmth that filled his eyes slowly faded at this reminder of the near catastrophe I'd faced. "Yes, well, all the same, I wouldn't worry. Either he's realized it or he hasn't. We'll confront that when we need to. As we always do."

I took comfort in that "we," and in his willingness not to dwell on the danger I'd been in, no matter how much he might have disliked it.

CHAPTER 7

The following day was filled with a flurry of activity in anticipation of our departure from London. Since we would be gone
until after the New Year, there were a number of matters to attend to, including the purchasing of Christmas gifts, as well as a
few unique errands pertaining to my great-aunt, and a handful
of requests issued by my mother over the telephone just the day
before. As such, I spent the entire morning dashing to and fro,
ordering the purchases be delivered to our flat by midafternoon.

Sidney had his own matters to take care of, so when I arrived
at Ryde House shortly after midday, I was surprised to find him
already seated with Max in his parlor. Both men rose to their
feet as I entered and bussed them each on the cheek in turn. It
seemed in bad form to remark on the fact that my husband and
I might have made this call together, but I did arch my eyebrows
in mild query when my back was turned to Max.

"Kent tells me you're off to Yorkshire tomorrow," Max said
as we all sat before the fireplace tiled with Italian marble. The
fire burned low despite the chill in the air, I suspected because of
our host's hungover state. The dark circles around his eyes and
his pale countenance communicated he was not fully recovered.

"Yes, we decided it might be best to remove my great-aunt
from London for the time being."

His lips stretched in a sympathetic smile before his gaze
dipped to the cup of tea he clutched in his hands. "I've been
thinking of retiring from London myself."

"To Nettlestone?" I asked, mentioning his manor at the seat of his earldom on the Isle of Wight.

He nodded.

I hated to think of him alone and so far away, but then I remembered he had family who lived nearby. "Will you spend the upcoming holidays with your sister and her children?"

His eyes flooded with fondness. "Yes, I've missed them."

I thought of the bright orange streamers he, as a fond uncle, had attached to his Rolls-Royce's hood ornament. How in a way they had brought us together. Someday I hoped to actually meet that niece who had such a decorative flare, as well as her brother.

"I should apologize for last night," he declared, the warmth suffusing his features fading to contrition.

"No, you shouldn't," I replied before he could say more. "You're not the first chap to ever become inebriated." I glanced at my husband. "And I imagine Sidney and I have both passed our fair share of nights zozzled. At least you had good reason to be." I leaned forward to touch his sleeve gently. "But I do wish you'd shared how you were feeling. I know you men hate that rot—emotions and sentiments and whatnot. And I know we should have suspected you might be more unsettled than you let on. But I still wish you'd said something."

Max reached out to set his cup on the table beside him. "Yes, well, I thought I was managing it. Until clearly I wasn't." His lips twisted self-deprecatingly. "That's why I decided it would be best if I left London for a time. I doubt Ardmore is coming after me at the moment."

My elusive nemesis had been quiet these past few weeks. Which only served to make me nervous. Perhaps that was his goal.

"Well, be careful anyway," I cautioned him. "He has a habit of causing trouble where we least expect it."

"I will. And thank you for collecting me last night."

I brushed this aside. "If there's anyone you need to thank, it would be Miss Lorraine. As I understand it, she saved you from being saddled with Lilah Turnbull as a wife."

He winced. "I thought perhaps I'd imagined that."

"You didn't."

"Then I shall send her a large bouquet."

"Send her something more unique. She receives dozens of bouquets from her admirers every week. She already doesn't know what to do with them."

"Any suggestions?"

I considered the matter. "A book. I know she's an avid reader of poetry. And she recently read and enjoyed *The Scarlet Pimpernel*. So perhaps the sequel. She mentioned wanting to read it before she saw the film."

"If only her swains realized the key to Miss Lorraine's heart is through verse and not roses," Sidney jested.

"Oh, she receives plenty of poetry." I scoffed. "Pages and pages of doggerel from young men who think themselves clever." It was all I could do not to roll my eyes. More soberly, I turned back to Max. "You'll contact us if you need anything, or if Ardmore gives you any trouble? I'll leave you my parents' information."

"Yes, and I expect you to do the same."

As we departed, I embraced him more tightly than when I'd arrived. I couldn't halt the worrying sensation that I shouldn't let him out of my sight. But he was a grown man, perfectly capable of taking care of himself. Most of the time. He wouldn't thank me for it if he found out, but perhaps I should send his sister a letter and ask her to keep an eye on him.

Sidney followed me from the house, and we both turned our steps east on Curzon Street. "Back there, you sounded as if you had experience with such doggerel." A teasing light had entered his eyes. "Did the young swains of Upper Wensleydale write you verse?"

"Only once. But I laughed at them and told them to send their poetry to Nellie May Sutton instead." I grinned ruefully. "I'm afraid I wasn't a very compassionate fourteen-year-old. None of the local boys tried it after that. But the lads in Malvern were a little more determined. There was a bit of a longstanding competition at Everleigh Court as to which girl could collect the most poems from her eager admirers."

Everleigh Court was the distinguished finishing school located in the Malvern Hills where my parents had sent me to complete my education and attain a bit of a social polish. Tante Ilse had wanted me to go to the finishing school in Switzerland where the Rickenberg branch of my father's family had attended for generations, but my mother had insisted upon Everleigh. It was where she had gone, and her mother before her. So she had decided that if it was good enough for them, then it was good enough for me and now my younger sister. At least then she could rely on a proper English curriculum.

Sidney jostled me playfully in the shoulder. "And you participated?"

I flushed. "I admit that at first I got a bit carried away." The competitive streak in me had reared its ugly head, making me determined to trounce all the others. "But by my third year, it had all grown rather tedious and annoying." I shook my head in bewilderment. "Except my sudden indifference only seemed to make the young men more eager. And no amount of rebuffing or small insults would put them off."

He pulled my arm through his and leaned close to banter. "You won, didn't you?" His eyes twinkled as if we were sharing a secret.

My nose wrinkled in aggravation. He was right. I had won. But I wasn't about to admit it. "Men are *strange*."

He merely grinned wider. "That we are. That we are."

"Are you returning to the flat?" I asked as we approached the intersection with Queen Street.

"No, I've still a few matters to take care of. But I'll be back in time to escort you and Frau Vischering to the cinema, as promised."

"You know she's asked you to call her Tante Ilse," I needled good-naturedly.

"Tante Ilse, then," he conceded with grace.

"Then I shall part with you here."

We paused at the corner, and I arched up on my toes to buss his cheek.

"I'll compose you some verse as I stroll," he whispered into my ear.

I shoved him lightly and he laughed, backing away several steps as I shook my head. Then we strolled off in our separate directions, smiles stretching both of our faces, I imagined.

The day being a fine one, if a bit blustery, I elected to dawdle a short while in the garden at the center of Berkeley Square. But after ten minutes sitting on a bench in the weak sunshine, the chill drove me back to my feet.

I crossed to the north side of the square toward our building of luxury flats with Portland stone elevations, Neo-Grec detailing, and Parisian-style ironwork, only to be brought up short at the sight of my great-aunt's maid speaking to a man on the pavement outside. She looked flustered and angry, her shoulders scrunched high around her ears and her arms crossed over her chest. At my appearance, the man ducked his head, preventing me from getting a good look at his features beyond his light hair and hat, and hurried away.

"Miss Bauer," I murmured, careful not to draw undo attention to her being German by calling her *Fräulein*.

She spun about to face me with wide eyes that glistened with what seemed to be fright.

"Are you all right? Did that man hurt you?" I coaxed carefully. *"Verletzen?"* I translated in a soft voice.

She shook her head before speaking in halting English. "No, I goes good. I am not hurt."

I glanced in the direction the man had retreated. "Did that man approach you? Was he pestering you? *Belästigen?"*

She didn't seem to know how to answer this and so shrugged with one shoulder uncertainly.

I nodded, offering her an empathetic smile, and then gestured for her to follow me inside. She was a lovely girl, and I couldn't imagine this was the first time she'd been importuned by a man, but it was likely the first time it had happened in a foreign country where the man spoke a different language than she did. And a foreign country that was decidedly hostile to people of her nationality.

I greeted Sal, our doorman, and the new man working as the lift operator—a former soldier from the looks of him. But of course, most men under a certain age were now former soldiers, so that was almost a given. I waited until we reached the corridor outside our flat before turning to the maid. "If that ever happens again, don't try to talk to the man, just turn and walk away as quickly as you can. And if he won't leave you alone, walk toward other people and yell, 'Police!' Do you understand?"

"Police," she repeated, nodding.

"Yes, usually the word alone will scare them off."

She nodded again, her amber eyes solemn behind her fringe of long eyelashes.

I wasn't certain she understood entirely, but it seemed she comprehended enough. In any case, if she was going to remain here with my great-aunt, she was going to have to become more fluent in English.

Mrs. Yarrow opened the door to our flat then, probably having heard my voice in the corridor. Her gaze shifted from me to Bauer, hardening. I crossed to the bureau to set down my clutch and remove my gloves while I observed the two women. Bauer dipped her head and hurried past Mrs. Yarrow, whose spine was as stiff as the pikes on Tower Hill.

After shutting the door with a decisive click while her eyes remained trained on Bauer's retreating back, Mrs. Yarrow turned to face me. "You need to keep an eye on that one."

I set one wine leather glove down and began to work my fingers out of the other. "Because she's German?" I replied coolly.

"That, and she has shifty eyes."

"Shifty eyes?" Skepticism tinted my voice.

"Yes, I can tell she's not telling the truth."

"About what?" I asked, my patience growing thin.

"I don't know." Her eyes narrowed. "Not yet."

"Mrs. Yarrow," I stated, moving a step closer to her and lowering my voice. "I realize you find it difficult to . . . associate with Germans, especially since you're still grieving for your husband. But in time you will come to understand that they have suffered just as much as we have from this war."

A militant light flashed in her eyes, and I held up my hand to stop her before she could speak.

"I cannot rid you of your grief and anger any more than I can convince you of something you do not wish to be convinced of. And I certainly cannot make you like Miss Bauer. But I can demand that you be civil to her." I knew she would never dare slight Tante Ilse, no matter her feelings about her. She was too good of a retainer for that. But Bauer was a different matter, being a fellow servant and a member of her own class.

Mrs. Yarrow's face was flushed, her lips pressed so tightly together that they were turning white.

"We leave for Yorkshire tomorrow. You have but one more day to tolerate her."

Her shoulders lowered, and some of the color drained from her cheeks at this reminder. But her outrage had not been assuaged entirely. "And after the holidays? What then? Will they be returning here?"

I frowned, my remaining tolerance of her feelings on the matter running thin. "I do not know, Mrs. Yarrow. We shall confront that later. In the meantime, the care and maintenance of the flat shall be your sole provision. Take a few days leave whenever you wish during the holidays. Just please, let me know when you decide to do so. That way we won't be expecting you here. I've left my parents' information in the top drawer of the bureau so that you can telephone if any messages or other matters arise that we must attend to. I've also left your holiday gifts there. You needn't wait until Boxing Day if you wish to open them sooner."

The last of her fury abated at this pronouncement. Perhaps it had been rather underhanded to mention the gifts now, but if she had checked the bureau drawer, she would have seen them anyway.

"Yes, ma'am. Thank you," she replied in her typically meek voice.

Which contrarily only served to irritate me more. Swallowing my aggravation, I sought some sort of smooth escape. "Have any of this morning's purchases arrived?"

"Yes, I put them in your bedchamber."

I nodded shortly and left her standing in the entry as I escaped to the refuge of my bedchamber. One glance into the drawing room as I strode by told me it was empty, so I assumed Tante Ilse must be resting. However, when I paused in the doorway to my bedroom, I found her lifting the packages from the counterpane, some of them wrapped in beautiful paper with colorful ribbons, and holding them up to her ear to shake them. Though by rights I should have been equally as exasperated with her, I found myself charmed and humored instead. How could anyone feel otherwise at the sight of a seventy-nine-year-old woman snooping in the Christmas presents?

When she looked up to find me watching her, she didn't even have the grace to blush guiltily, but instead laughed. "I could never resist a pretty package with a bow."

"Neither can Mother," I replied, crossing toward my vanity, where I set my cloche hat. "Though she will strenuously deny it should anyone ever dare suggest such a thing."

Tante Ilse smiled brighter. "I have always suspected that Sarah has a more playful side she is determined to crush." She tilted her head to the side. "It is sad, really."

I contemplated this as I shook my head and fluffed my hair to remove the crease from my bobbed curls caused by my hat. A dull ache began below my breastbone to think of my mother thusly.

"I like your hair so," my great-aunt declared before reaching up to touch her own tightly restrained long white tresses. "Maybe I should cut mine."

I smiled, crossing to the bed and pushing away some of the packages to sit beside her. "It is rather freeing not to have to contend with so much hair. And this new style of hat fits so much better."

She reached up to touch my auburn curls, examining them in the sunlight streaming through the window. "Yes, I imagine it does."

"If you're serious, it would be better to have it done here in London rather than in the wilds of Yorkshire. I doubt the hairdressers in Hawes, or even Ripon or Kendal, are very skilled at bobs."

When she didn't reply, but instead seemed lost in her scrutiny of my hair, I thought perhaps she wished to ignore the suggestion. But then she grinned. "Yes, let's do it. Is there still time?"

"I can telephone my hairdresser and find out if he can see you after the cinema."

"Oh, yes! The motion picture." Tante Ilse clasped her hands together. "I very much look forward to it."

I felt a twinge of surprise at the tone of her voice. It was almost as if she'd forgotten our plans for the afternoon. But then I brushed it aside. It wasn't as if in my own excitement I hadn't ever momentarily forgotten something.

However, when we departed the cinema and I mentioned the hair appointment I'd managed to inveigle from Monsieur Brodeur, convincing him to squeeze my great-aunt into his busy schedule, she balked.

"Haircut? Oh, no, no. Of course, I cannot do that."

"But Tante Ilse, earlier this afternoon you told me you wanted to bob your hair. You asked me to schedule the appointment."

"Oh, no. I am sure I did not ask you to do that." She seemed affronted by the suggestion. "Your hair is naturally charming, *mein Liebchen*. But I cannot cut mine. No."

I glanced at Sidney in bewilderment. "Of course, if you've changed your mind . . ." I began more gently, but she cut me off, reverting to German.

"There is no mind-changing about it. I never said I wished to cut my hair, and that is that."

I blinked in astonishment at the harsh tone of her voice while Sidney ushered us into a cab. It was then that I began to wonder whether my great-aunt's mind was as reliable as it had always been, whether her memory was slipping. I wanted to push away the ugly thought, the dread it churned up inside me that she might be forgetting. Like my great-grandfather had—my mother's grandfather. I had been twelve when he died, old enough to recall his anger and confusion, and the pain it had caused everyone else.

Sidney's hand stole into mine, squeezing, and I welcomed the comfort, the clarity it gave me. There was no use jumping to conclusions. Perhaps Tante Ilse had merely felt embarrassed by her change of heart, and worried she would appear cowardly. Or maybe the weeks of travel in her already weakened state, and the chaos of London, had overset her.

Whatever the case, I was glad we were leaving for Yorkshire. If any place could soothe and steady my great-aunt, it was the quiet and bucolic beauty of the Dales. After all, she had no ghosts waiting there for her. Not like me.

CHAPTER 8

I had been battling a rising sense of dread since we departed the railway station at Garsdale in Sidney's prized carmine-red Pierce-Arrow roadster, which he'd insisted be transported with us to Yorkshire. Sidney and Tante Ilse kept up a steady stream of chatter, but the nearer we drew to Brock House, the harder it became for me to focus on the conversation, let alone contribute. My mind was too preoccupied with surveying our surroundings, and beating back the memories that seemed to infuse every square inch of ground.

Late afternoon sunlight bathed the hills in soft light, both the bright greens of the lower slopes cultivated by the farmers, and the dark green heather at the summits of the fells. Dry stone walls bordered the road, just as they did everywhere in the Dales, crisscrossing their way over the landscape and up and down the uplands, sometimes in indecipherable patterns. Behind them, sheep lazily grazed on the hillsides. Here and there stood a gray farmhouse, or merely one of the distinctive field barns that dotted the landscape, stolid and grim. But for the most part there was nothing but hill and vale.

At the fork in the road, Sidney remembered to turn north without my prodding, taking the shortcut around the village of Hawes on the narrow lane that skirted Bellow Hill. The road climbed steadily higher, clinging to the slope above the River Ure, before the land evened out and we entered the hamlet of Hardraw. Here, Sidney had to check his speed and patiently wait for a hay wagon rattling toward us over the single-lane stone bridge that spanned Hardraw Beck. A pretty little stone church stood next to the beck amidst trees still adorned with a few late golden autumn leaves. Next to the church's weathered lychgate, abutting the road, sat the unremarkable façade of the Green Dragon Inn.

I turned away as we passed the distinctive sign hanging over its door, even though I had few memories of the dark interior of the inn with its high-backed settles and scarred oak tables, and the perpetual game of dominoes being played by some of the older locals in the back corner. Rather, all my remembrances were of the limestone gorge beyond it into which the waterfall, Hardraw Force, tumbled. I could clearly recall my brothers splashing in it one early autumn day. I'd decided then that I was too old to join in, but I'd perched on a rock a safe distance from the water, laughing and calling out encouragement of their antics. The September air had been chilly that day, nipping at my nose, and the cold water made them shriek like little girls, which had only made it all the more comical.

It had been the last time we were all together—my brothers and I. The following morning Freddy had left to return to medical school to finish his courses in order to be able to join the Royal Army Medical Corps, and the day after that Rob had departed for training with the Royal Flying Corps. A week later I was on my way to London to prepare for my wedding to Sidney. Tim had returned to school, leaving Grace, our younger sister, the only one still at home.

Wetness burned the back of my eyes as I wondered if any of us had realized then how significant that moment would be. Had any of us known it would be our last adventure together?

I forced myself to take deep even breaths, blinking against the glare of the sun reflected in the side mirror as Sidney gunned the engine and accelerated away from the village. The stone buildings lining the road grew sparser, and I could spy the hulk of Great Shunner Fell towering in the distance away to the north. My muscles tensed, for I knew it wouldn't be long now. We passed the turning that would have taken us back south toward

Hawes, and I could see the bend of the River Ure and then the village laid out before us in the valley below. Beyond rose Wether Fell and Dodd Fell like the two shoulder muscles of a giant lying on his stomach, with the spine meandering between and the head naught but a blue swell in the distance.

Brock House itself was hidden from the road by a copse of oak and downy birch trees where we had often played as children. Sidney turned the Pierce-Arrow onto the dirt drive that wound between the trees for about thirty yards before it approached a narrow stone bridge that straddled a small brook. On the other side, the lane wound up the hill to the sprawling three-story gray stone house perched on a flat expanse at the base of a higher ridge.

I scrutinized everything with eager, but wary eyes, finding it somewhat disconcerting that nothing had changed. So much had altered in the last five years, and yet here it appeared as if time had stood still. The trees were still gnarled and twisted in the same way, their thick, deep roots anchoring them against the wind. The puddles along the drive, which never seemed to dry completely, were still filled with stagnant muddy water. The same dark weathered patch of slate adorned the roof. Even the same bluebell-printed curtains hung in the sitting room window of the structure we called "the cottage."

Sidney looked at me in concern as the motorcar rolled to a stop and he set the brake, but I knew if I looked at him, the emotion lodged in the back of my throat would break free. So instead I forced myself to focus on the familiar cracks and crevices of the low stone wall that enclosed the front courtyard and the house beyond as I opened my door and gingerly stepped out into the dirt.

The smell that struck me was almost enough to send me scrambling back inside. The scents of grass and earth and wind—the crispness and clarity of it filling my lungs as if I'd merely been taking shallow sips of it before. And that indefinable odor that could only be described as home. It was the smell I'd woken to every morning and lain down with every night until five years ago when I had moved to London and wed Sidney, but it was still lodged in my brain somewhere, and it flooded my body with sensations and memories I would rather have ignored.

I stood stock-still, my knees shaking as I warred with myself. I wasn't used to this feeling of uncertainty, of incapacity. I had confronted so many horrifying things as an intelligence agent that I'd believed nothing could ever unnerve me to that degree again. And yet here I stood, petrified and overwhelmed merely by the prospect of facing my family again, of braving this place where I had grown up.

The only thing that saved me from retreat was the sound of excited barking, which rang out from within the courtyard. Seconds later a black-and-white body came hurtling through the open gate toward me. I leaned over to greet the jubilant border collie, fussing over her and scratching her ears, grateful she'd given me something else to focus on as the sound of my father's firm, measured footsteps approached.

"My goodness, what a sweet girl you are," I praised the dog. "You've grown so strong and pretty. Tabitha must be, what, seven years old now?" I asked, lifting my eyes to my father for the first time.

He stood tall and straight in his perpetual tweed coat and flat cap, his feet planted wide in their boots. "About," he answered in his quiet, gravelly voice.

I glanced beyond him toward the gate. "Where's Samson?" I gave Tabitha's ears another scratch. "Is he being lax in his duties, old girl?"

"Samson died."

I slowly straightened before inanely murmuring, "Oh." I felt a bit foolish that I hadn't suspected as much. He had already been ancient when I left. "How long?"

"About a year." His steady gray eyes scrutinized me. "He made it to a ripe old age."

I nodded, swallowing hard. "Yes, he did."

He turned his head to gaze off toward the east. "Metcalfe has a new litter of collies, and I've already spoken for one of the males." He looked down at Tabitha fondly. "Won't be long until the old girl has a puppy to whip into shape for us."

My lips curled into an attempt at a smile. Releasing my hold on the dog, I moved the final few steps closer to him to greet him properly. "Father," I said simply, arching up on my toes to kiss his rough cheek.

"It's good to see you, Verity," he murmured, resting the back of his hand against my cheek.

This close I could see he sported a few new wrinkles and a few new gray hairs. I'd wished to see signs of change, of the passage of time, and here it was wrought on my father's face and in Samson's death. Father still stood straight backed and undaunted, like the same solid, indestructible figure I'd thought him to be when I was a child. But I now knew that was only an illusion. In time, that would change, too.

He turned to greet Tante Ilse, whom Sidney had been helping from the motorcar, and I wrapped my arms around myself against the chill breeze and wandered closer to the low wall, peering over it into the front courtyard. The rowan trees that had broken through the cobbles in the corner and now provided welcome shade in the summer months were all but stripped of their leaves, allowing me to see the stone house beyond. Tabitha kept pace with me, as if sensing I needed her undemanding company, and I rested a hand briefly against her head in acknowledgment.

There was a movement out of the corner of my eye, and I turned to see my older brother Freddy emerge from the inner courtyard and turn toward the gate. He checked his stride, sensing me watching him, and then veered in my direction. Dressed in comfortable gentleman's attire, his brown hair ruffling in the wind, he was the picture of a country doctor. "And the prodigal sister returns," he jested, coming to a stop on the other side and resting his arms on top of the wall.

"Ha ha," I retorted dryly.

His eyes crinkled in a grin before they swept down over my chic Parisian blue traveling ensemble and landed on my two-tone Oxford pumps. "You look good, Ver. Though I hope you remembered your boots."

"Of course. I've only been away for five years, not lost my

senses." I nodded in the direction he'd come. "Are you and Rachel staying in the cottage?"

"Temporarily. Our house needed some improvements." His right eyebrow quirked. "Mother believes it was heavenly intervention, as now we can all enjoy a bit of family togetherness."

"While you and Rachel merely wished to have running water and flushing commodes?" I guessed.

"Something like that."

Brock House essentially comprised a large rectangle enclosed by a stone barrier with four gates, one facing in each direction. The southwest corner boasted what we called the outer courtyard, with a gate at either end of the long L-shaped low wall that bounded it. Brock House proper took up the largest part of the rectangle, starting in the northwest corner and extending into the other quadrants. The kitchen and servant quarters were located in a long single-story offshoot of the house in the northeast corner. Though technically not part of the same building, being separated by a small kitchen garden and connected by a recently enclosed walkway, at one time they had been, so everyone continued to describe them as such.

Across the inner courtyard from the servants' quarters in the far southeast corner stood "the cottage," a small building that boasted a sitting room and bath on the first floor and two bedrooms above. It was the ideal guest accommodation for Freddy and Rachel and their baby, Ruth, being inside the barrier and close to the house, but separated by stone walls so that Mother didn't have to be wakened by Ruth's crying at night. A covered walkway connected the cottage to the billiards room at the corner of the house, but still allowed ease of movement between the outer and inner courtyards.

To the east of the servants' quarters, outside the wall, stood the barn and old carriage house, as well as a number of outbuildings. The buildings that composed the working farm portion of my father's estate stood down the road a short distance, downwind of the house. But the barn and outbuildings near the house still boasted a handful of animals, which mainly supplied

Brock House's needs. A cow or two for milking, chickens, maybe a pig or goat, and horses.

"Hullo, Freddy," Sidney said, offering him his hand over the wall as he joined us. "How's the life of a country surgeon treating you?"

His lips creased into a tight smile. "It suits me. And what of you? Society man turned war hero and investigator."

"Yes, well, let's not dredge up all the war-hero nonsense, shall we," he replied, as ever uncomfortable with the honor that had been bestowed upon him when he'd recently received his Victoria Cross.

Freddy nodded, his hazel eyes reflecting understanding. He glanced over his shoulder toward the front door, which was opening. "But be forewarned. Mother is likely to bring it up every chance she can get. You're to be her showpiece for the neighbors." His gaze flitted to mine and then back, and I could already guess what Mother's addendum had been to such a sentiment. Sidney was her compensation for having such a brazen, unfeeling daughter.

We all turned at the sounds of a second motorcar lumbering up the drive behind us. It was no surprise Sidney's Pierce-Arrow had left the older vehicle my father had sent to the station to help collect our luggage in the dust, but father's chauffeur, Sidney's valet Nimble, and Tante Ilse's maid Bauer had still made good time. I turned to see the motorcar continue on down the lane toward the outbuildings and the servants' entrance, catching a glimpse of the German maid's wide eyes staring out at us. I didn't think it was the house that awed and alarmed her—or not entirely, for Tante Ilse's home in Germany had been as large— but perhaps its remoteness and the realization that there must be a great many other servants. English servants.

But I had little space in my thoughts to spare for her or my great-aunt. Not when I was struggling with my own trepidation, especially as the voice I was most apprehensive to hear rang out over the wall.

"Why are you all hovering about the courtyard and talking

over walls," Mother hollered from the open door to Brock House. "Come inside." Then she disappeared through the double doorway, expecting us all to follow.

I knew then that my mother did not intend to make this homecoming easy. She was angry at me for staying away so long, and now that she finally had me here, she was not going to make peace easily.

Sidney cast me an empathetic look as I heaved a sigh, taking my arm to escort me inside while Father assisted Tante Ilse. Tabitha trotted along behind us.

The entry boasted the same worn but gleaming wooden floors and carved staircase. From the scents of linseed oil and beeswax still lingering in the air, I could tell they'd recently been given a polish. Only the plants on the entry table ever seemed to change, rotating with the seasons. Today the silver vase was filled with some herbs from the garden and colorful autumn foliage.

I allowed Tante Ilse to greet Mother first, which gave me some time to compose myself. I stripped off my gloves and hat, passing them to Abbott, my parents' butler, with a smile of greeting.

"You look well," I told him softly.

"Thank you, Mrs. Kent. And might I say the same of you."

If he felt any hostility toward me for staying away so long, he didn't let it show, but Abbott had always possessed a remarkable poker face. As he was one of my mother's chief allies among the household, I knew better than to presume he might feel any sympathy toward me, but I still viewed the fact that his disdain wasn't evident as a good sign.

I turned toward the mirror to fluff my curls and then waited for Tante Ilse to finish thanking Mother for welcoming her into their home. This was not simple gratitude and politeness, but also a calculated gesture on my great-aunt's part. She knew that while her nephew—my father—had the final say, things would all go more peaceably if Mother accepted the situation.

I studied Mother's face as she spoke, the new lines that time had wrought on her skin, and the sagging that had begun around her neck and jawline. Her brown hair was swept into its usual style, but it sported more streaks of gray than before. Dressed in a burgundy-and-black plaid silk blouse with black cuffs, and a black woolen skirt, she appeared as distinguished as ever, her posture and comportment impeccable. She presented a decorous, but not altogether welcoming picture.

When her gaze finally lifted to mine, I felt again like I was eight years old, standing before her for inspection before church service on Sunday morning. No matter how hard I'd tried, there had always been at least one correction to be made, if not to my attire, then to my hair or my expression, or some infraction in my behavior that week. I wasn't sure at what age I'd realized I was never going to be perfect enough for my mother's exacting measures, and that I didn't care to be, but I'd soon given up on trying to meet them. Though, by the quiver of longing I felt in my breast even now, I recognized I'd never completely squashed my desire for her approval.

"Verity," she stated measuredly.

"Mother."

"So you came."

"Yes."

Her hazel eyes flickered as she scrutinized my features. She lifted her hand to my face, but didn't quite touch it. "Well, it's good to see that London's depravities don't seem to have damaged your beauty. Yet."

And there it was. I felt my heart plummet in my chest, even as I forced a flat smile.

She sighed. "But I do wish you hadn't cut your beautiful hair."

I'd been expecting this comment, knowing my mother well enough to realize she would hate the new fad for bobbing one's hair. But the last part about her proclaiming my hair beautiful was new. In all my life, I couldn't recall her ever saying so. It was always too thick or too unruly and unmanageable, the auburn shade too garish. Never beautiful.

"I like it, Mother."

"Yes, but it was so long and lovely. This is much too . . . boyish."

"Oh, tosh!" Tante Ilse exclaimed, making me wonder where she had picked up such an expression. "The young will always have fads that those of us who are older will not understand. And as far as Verity ever looking boyish, well, she has too much Rickenberg in her blood for that." She was referring to my curvaceous figure, which obviously came from my father's side of the family, given my mother's slim angularity. She looked over her shoulder to twinkle at my husband. "And I'm sure Sidney would agree."

Sidney's eyes crinkled with gentle laughter at her having pulled him into the matter. "No, I would never mistake Verity for a boy."

"That's not exactly what I said," Mother replied in a brittle voice, but, grasping the audience was against her, moved on. "Sidney, dear, how good to see you," she declared in a warmer voice. "We were all so proud to hear of your medal." She threaded her arm through his, trapping him against her side and forcing him to escort her into the drawing room to the left of the entry. "Though why you didn't wish to take part in the ceremony on Armistice Day, I do not understand."

Her voice faded away as Tante Ilse took hold of my elbow. "Do not let her bother you," she murmured confidingly. "She struggles with what to say as much as you do."

I turned to her in question, but my father stood at the drawing room doors, waiting for us to precede him, so I kept the query to myself.

The drawing room was ever as it had always been. Mounted in their gilded frames, landscape paintings of the surrounding dales painted by various artists down through the years graced the walls, which were covered in a soft jonquil shade of painted silk wallpaper. The furniture, with its ornamental cabriole legs, was largely clustered around the rubble stone hearth, where tea was served before a cheery fire. However, here and there sat other groupings of chairs, as well as a table in the corner used for cards. A pair of double doors in the far wall could be thrown open to the family parlor beyond to form one large room for entertaining.

I did spare a moment to wonder at our gathering in the more formal drawing room rather than the cozier family parlor. Was this done on my account or Tante Ilse's? And precisely what message was Mother trying to convey?

I knew Sidney would tell me I was reading too much into it, but he didn't know my mother as well as I did. She never did anything without a reason. Or two or three.

"Will Rachel be joining us?" I turned to ask Freddy, attempting to ease the stilted silence that had fallen over us upon accepting our cups of tea.

He nodded. "She was feeding Ruthie, but I imagine they'll join us soon."

I smiled, perhaps my first genuine smile since our arrival, and asked after my six-month-old niece, and was rewarded with a beaming grin from my brother. "She's a darling."

"And smart, too," Mother chimed in, though this trait had never seemed important for a girl to possess when I was little.

Freddy's gaze dipped to Tabitha, who had returned from wherever she'd gone and now flopped on the rug in front of the fire. "She's also terribly fond of old Tabitha." He glanced at Father, who sat nodding off in one of the padded bergère chairs, having finished his tea in seemingly two gulps. "So we might want to put her in the other room before she arrives."

"Oh, Tabitha is just as fond of her as the rest of us." He chuckled. "And Ruthie can't move fast enough yet to catch her if she doesn't want to be caught anyway."

"Tabitha," my great-aunt ruminated aloud. "Strange name for a dog. Is that not a cat name?"

"Tabitha Twitchit," I proclaimed, supplying the name of the beloved Beatrix Potter character she had been trying to recall. I shared a look of amusement with Freddy. "Grace was rather enamored with Miss Potter's books when she named our Tabitha." Being nine years old at the time, it was understandable.

"She was the only one of us home when Tabitha arrived," Freddy expounded, for he and Rob had been up at Oxford, while I was at Everleigh Court, and Tim down at Rugby.

"It was her turn to name the next animal anyway."

"Tabitha is a good name. It suits her," Father declared in defense of his youngest child's choice without opening an eye.

"Though that didn't stop Tim from throwing a fit about it," Freddy muttered dryly.

The three older of us might have thought the name an odd choice, but we knew better than to object. But fourteen-year-old Tim had declared the name to be stupid and refused to use it.

Freddy leaned forward. "Remember he tried to convince all of us to call her Twitchy instead?"

"Oh, yes. Though, it wasn't as if he had done much better when he named Samson." I turned to Tante Ilse to explain. "He wanted to call that collie Damson. As in a damson plum. Or so he claimed."

Freddy gave a bark of laughter. "When he told Father, he said that if he could convince Mother of it, then he'd allow it. And boy, did he ever try to convince her. But Mother wasn't having any of it."

She lowered her cup to her saucer, shaking her head. "What nonsense to think he could sneak such a thing past me. Damson plum, indeed. I told him Samson it would be."

"None of us were very good at naming our animals," I concluded, and then giggled. "I named our mouser Roxanne, despite the fact the cat was a tom."

Freddy acknowledged this with a nod of his head. "And I named a dog Balshazzar, even though I couldn't even spell it correctly at the time." Then he turned his head as if to gaze out the window at the courtyard. "Though Rob did choose Rozier. That wasn't a bad name."

I stilled, a fist seeming to grip my heart and squeeze at the mention of our brother and the dog he'd named after the hot-air balloonist, de Rozier.

"Yes, well, he was always more reflective than the rest of you," Mother declared.

"Speaking of damson plums," I muttered, eager to change the subject. "Where is Tim?"

"Oh, he's somewhere about. And never where you need him to be," Freddy groused.

"He'll turn up," Father murmured sleepily.

My oldest brother turned back toward the window, his elbow resting on the arm of his chair and his fist before his mouth as if to stop himself from speaking. This was evidently a sore subject, and something I didn't yet understand. I wondered if Freddy could be convinced to enlighten me later.

I cleared my throat. "And Grace? When is her term over at Everleigh?"

"She'll arrive late next week," Mother replied, rising to return her teacup to the tray.

"But surely that's not the end of the term? I don't recall it ending so early."

She shrugged. "There's no harm in her missing a week or two of classes. I explained everything to her headmistress and she quite agrees."

I frowned. No harm to her studies maybe, but as to the rest . . . "There's really no reason for her to leave early. Grace *must* wish to remain. And anyway, I'll still be here when she does arrive."

"Grace does what she's told," Mother stated, her voice brooking no argument.

Perhaps so, but that didn't mean she did so happily. And I was certain to be the person she blamed for it. I remembered being sixteen. Had I been ordered home from school early because an older sister I barely knew had suddenly returned—one who'd taken little interest in me for the past five years—I would have been furious.

"Grace truly won't mind," Freddy said, breaking into these musings. His lip curled shrewdly. "Not when her beau is here waiting for her."

"Mr. Bolingbroke is not your sister's beau," Mother replied crisply. "She's too young for that."

"Well, you could have fooled me."

I opened my mouth to ask a question about this Bolingbroke fellow, when Mother resolutely changed the subject to a recitation of all our neighbors and their current health and statuses, including a reminder of those who had lost loved ones either to the war or the Spanish influenza, which had ravaged the area late the previous year. As if I needed the reminder. She had kept me apprised of these facts by telephone and letter—sometimes both—while I was away. At first we each took turns interjecting, trying to turn the conversation, but the longer she droned on, the less harder we tried. Until finally the only sound but my mother's honor roll was the ticking of the clock on the wall and the crackle of the fire.

CHAPTER 9

❧❧❧

When Sidney and I were finally able to make our escape, Father *and* Tante Ilse had fallen asleep in their chairs, and it was time to dress for dinner. Rachel and little Ruth had also failed to arrive, but I couldn't help but wonder if that was because Rachel had heard Mother droning on through the open door and slipped away again before anyone noticed her. I wouldn't have blamed her.

As I'd anticipated, we'd been assigned to my old bedchamber above the billiards room. Growing up, I'd fallen asleep many a night to the clack of the balls.

As we reached the top of the wraparound carved staircase, my mother's maid, Matilda, came bustling out of our chamber. She paused at our approach, her sharp gaze, as always, just shy of insolent.

"Good evening, Matilda," I said politely, wondering why she'd been in our chamber.

"Mrs. Kent. Mr. Kent," she replied, bobbing the barest of curtseys. "I just put fresh towels in your room, should you need them."

I nodded, but she was already hurrying away, her tread surprisingly quiet for such a large woman.

We entered the room to find our luggage had already been brought up, and our things unpacked. However, I was more arrested by the changes to the room. The furniture was the same, as was the glass painted lamp on the bedside table, but the rest of the room looked completely different than I remembered. It had been painted a soft robin's egg blue and pale yellow eyelet curtains hung over the windows. A counterpane blocked in blue and yellow squares with white daisies at each center covered the bed, and was echoed in the embroidered pillows.

I stood uncertainly at the center of the rug. While, of course, my mother had every right to change the room—it was a guest chamber now, after all, and I had chosen not to visit since late 1914—I still couldn't help but feel saddened by the complete absence of my ever having been there. Not even a figurine or paper flower remained. It was as if my past presence had been utterly wiped from it.

Detecting my distress, Sidney closed the wardrobe he had been looking into and returned to where I stood by the door. "Ver, are you all right?" He took hold of my hands, waiting for me to look at him. "I know this hasn't been easy for you."

I swallowed the sticky taste of angry confusion. "I . . . yes. It's just . . ." I shook my head, not knowing what I wished to say.

He pulled me into his embrace, and I allowed myself to rest my head on his shoulder for a few seconds, absorbing the comfort he offered. But when the first tingle of tears began to threaten, I pushed away.

"We should dress."

He released me slowly, but didn't object, watching me closely as I turned toward the vanity where the items in my portmanteau had been laid out. I reached for my hair brush, pulling it through the waved tresses of my hair until they crackled and the shaky feeling in my limbs had subsided. Then I removed my jewelry and sat down on the bench to remove my shoes.

It was then that I saw that the clasp of my handbag was opened. I parted it, and one look inside told me it was not as I'd left it.

"Fresh towels, indeed," I snapped indignantly. "She's been through my handbag." I whirled about to show Sidney.

He paused in unbuttoning his shirt, his eyes dipping to the bag and then back to me. "Are you certain?"

"What do you mean, am I certain? Of course I am."

He held up his hands in placation. "I simply mean, the bag could have been rifled another way. Perhaps it was dropped."

I arched a single eyebrow, extracting the case that contained my lip salve and mirror. "And I suppose when it fell, it jostled this open, too."

"Very well, but you can't know for certain it was Matilda."

I glared at him witheringly.

"I don't like her any more than you do, Ver. Not after the way she treated you when she was supposed to be looking out for you while I was away, not spying for your mother."

My parents had given their consent to my marrying Sidney and remaining in London at his flat on one condition. I had to take Matilda with me as my personal maid. I had disliked the idea from the outset. But I had also been desperate to remain in London, not only to assert my newfound independence as a married woman, but also to be closer to the front whenever Sidney might be given leave, not 250 miles farther north in a time when nonessential train travel was unreliable at best.

Now, as a wiser, more experienced woman, I could appreciate my parents' concerns, their desire to protect me as best they could from such a distance. But Matilda had proven to be a terrible companion, and loyal to no one except my mother. Shortly after Sidney's reported death, when I'd discovered she'd been spying for my mother all those years, sending her reports on me, I'd sacked her and sent her back to Yorkshire. I should have done so years before, when it had become increasingly difficult to fob her off with the excuse that I was going to visit a friend in the country and had no need of her, when really I was off on a field assignment.

"But that doesn't mean she was the one to search your handbag," Sidney reasoned. "There *are* fresh towels on the bureau."

I scowled at the offending white cloths. "Well, somebody has. And I can't think of anyone more likely." I turned away, dropping the bag on the vanity table with a *thunk*. "Though whether she did so on her own or at my mother's behest is up for debate."

Sidney rested his hands on my shoulders, kneading them lightly. "I agree it's the likeliest explanation," he said, speaking to my reflection in the mirror. "But confronting her will do no good. She'll only deny it, and your mother will accuse you of having a suspicious mind. Then you'll have a terrific row, and it will all just leave you feeling even worse than you do now." He leaned closer, putting his face next to mine. "So let's leave it be, and in the future we'll hide or lock up anything we don't want her to see."

I heaved a sigh. "You're right." I pressed a hand to my forehead. The entire day had left me feeling out of sorts. My normal cool confidence seemed to have deserted me, and the comfort I used to feel with my family seemed all but a distant memory. Everything felt awkward, at best. Like we were all playacting, but we weren't very good at it. Even the jests were forced.

"Give it some time," Sidney said, as ever reading my mind. "You'll find your rapport again."

I nodded, offering him a strained smile.

His eyes twinkled. "And in the meantime, perhaps the wheels can be greased by a few predinner libations."

Unfortunately, my mother did not have any predinner libations to offer—cocktails or otherwise. At least, not for me. For the men, it was an entirely different matter.

"You can't be serious, Mother," I protested with a stunned laugh. "Why, all the ladies I know, even the highest sticklers of society, on occasion enjoy a predinner drink or cordial."

"Well, I'm not sure I care for the opinion of the ladies you know. It is vulgar and inappropriate. And on this occasion you shall abstain."

She whirled away, leaving me to stare after her in shocked silence. My gaze shifted to my father, but he didn't seem willing to wage this particular battle. And why should he? It didn't affect *him*.

I stalked across the room toward where Sidney stood near the window, nursing a glass of brandy.

"Would you like a sip of mine?" he offered. "I hardly think even your mother would dare object if your husband offered you a drink."

I considered it and then shook my head. "Better not. It's not worth it." Not for brandy, in any case. I had never liked the stuff.

The lines at the corners of his eyes crinkled as if inferring my thoughts.

I started to sit in a chair near the hearth, when the appearance of Freddy and Rachel brought me back to my feet, for Freddy held his six-month-old daughter on his hip. She held her head upright steadily, gazing around her in curiosity. At the sight of my father, a tiny smile curled her perfect pink lips, and then she turned to look at me.

"Is this Ruth?" I asked in delight, my heart already softening toward the darling. Her head was covered in dark fuzz, and her cheeks were pink and chubby, and begging for kisses.

"Yes," Freddy declared with a proud grin. "We wanted her to meet her Aunt Verity before Miss Pettigrew, our nanny, puts her to bed."

I didn't reach out to touch her, not wanting to alarm her, but simply smiled brightly. "Oh, aren't you a darling. Yes, you are."

Her blue eyes searched mine before drifting toward my auburn hair, drawn to it as all babies' eyes were.

"She's absolutely perfect," I told them, lifting my gaze to my sister-in-law. "It's good to see you, Rachel," I said, leaning in to buss her cheek.

She accepted it somewhat stiltedly, though her expression was amiable. "Likewise, Verity."

The fact was, I didn't know Rachel all that well. She was the daughter of one of Freddy's superior officers with the Royal

Army Medical Corps, whom he'd stayed with during a few of his leaves from the front. Freddy had introduced her to me in London some months before their wedding took place in June 1918, but that had been shortly before I'd received word of Sidney's alleged death. Shortly before I'd lost much interest in anything but throwing myself into my work for the Secret Service and blunting all my feelings with a bottle of gin.

She was a lovely young woman about my own age of twenty-three, with dark hair and soft brown eyes. But her most distinguishing feature was the beauty mark about an inch from the left corner of her mouth. It gave her a hint of allure, and I imagined Freddy hadn't been the first gentleman to find it irresistible.

"How is your family?" I asked politely, aware she must miss them. The Yorkshire Dales must feel very rural and far away from her former home in Kent, south of London.

"They're well. My sister is now engaged to be wed, so we shall be visiting them in February."

Her expression lightened at the impending prospect of seeing them, only to be dampened by my brother Tim's following comment.

"Provided we don't receive so much snow that the trains aren't running."

We all turned to look at him where he stood in the doorway still fastening his cuff links. Though dressed in proper evening attire, my younger brother's appearance was not what my mother would deem entirely correct. His thick sandy-brown hair was too long, resisting even the copious amount of pomade he'd applied to it to keep it restrained, and there was a stain on the lapel of his black coat.

"So you've decided to finally join us," Freddy gibed.

Tim ignored this, offering me a lopsided grin as he moved forward to greet me. "Sorry, I missed you earlier," he said, though I noticed he offered no explanation. His gaze brightened when my husband sidled over to join us. "I saw Sidney drove his Pierce-Arrow."

Sidney shook his hand. "Yes. I'll show her to you later, if you like."

"Capital!"

"Just don't let him drive it," Freddy interjected.

Tim turned to glare at him while Sidney ignored them both and turned to greet Rachel. I reached up to gently grasp little Ruthie's pudgy fingers, while the pair of us pretended not to observe the silent conversation that seemed to occur between her father and uncle. The words were on the tip of my tongue to ask what all their bickering was about, when Freddy broke the standoff and turned to me.

"Would you like to hold her?"

"May I?" I asked, holding my hands out for my niece.

"Of course," he said, passing her to me.

She was not as light as I'd thought she would be, but she was certainly no burden resting against my hip. Her eyes rounded as she stared up at me, and her bottom lip began to quiver. For a moment I thought she would begin to cry, but then she settled. I would have liked to think it was because she sensed she was safe with me, but I knew it was much more likely the strand of pearls around my neck she suddenly reached for. I let her play with them, but was careful to keep them from her mouth.

"Oh, but your dress," Rachel exclaimed. "It's so beautiful, and Ruthie is drooling quite a bit right now."

I shrugged, having draped the little blanket Freddy had handed me over my shoulder. "This will catch most of it, and I doubt if anything it doesn't can't be remedied."

I found myself swaying from side to side to keep the little one soothed. Sidney leaned closer, and I turned with a smile to allow him to see her better, and she him.

"Well, hullo, there," he murmured, offering her his finger.

I felt certain she would ignore it in favor of the pearls, but I was proven wrong. She looked up at his face before reaching out to take it, and then broke into a toothless, slobbery smile. Even at six months old, the ladies were still helpless in the face of Sidney's winsome looks.

"Verity, mind your pearls," my mother chastised, appearing at my side.

"I know, Mother," I replied, fighting to restrain my annoyance. "I have a firm grip on them."

"You'll learn you can't wear such fripperies with Ruthie about," she continued as if I hadn't spoken. "Or such gowns." Her voice grew strident. "The neckline, Verity. You'll do well to wear something a bit simpler and more modest. Like Rachel."

Rachel's shoulders seemed to deflate a little, and I could see her mentally comparing my sage-green frock with draped V neck and embroidered brassiere to her pale yellow gown with its simple drop waist and three-flounced hem. Though by no means dowdy or cheap, it couldn't quite compete with Paris couture.

"Rachel looks absolutely charming," I countered.

"Of course, she does. She has no need for such brazen attire to accentuate her beauty."

I wasn't certain whether my mother had meant to insult me or not, but my cheeks stung regardless. Sensing my embarrassment, Rachel's gaze lifted to meet mine, seeming to offer her unspoken condolence. Which only made my discomfiture turn to guilt as I wondered how often Rachel had been forced to dodge my mother's barbed comments in my absence.

Mother's attention shifted to Tim, and I braced for her to flay him with her tongue next. But she merely straightened his tie before nodding her head in approval and turning away. I turned to Freddy in bewilderment, and the manner in which his eyebrows rose in emphasis seemed to say he had much more to tell me later.

"Oh, *meine Engel*," a voice exclaimed over my shoulder, and I turned to discover that Tante Ilse had joined us, looking resplendent in a gown of azure silk in a style popular a decade before. "Is this my great-great-niece?" she asked.

"Yes," I replied, turning toward her parents to continue the introductions.

"This is Ruth," Freddy told her.

"Ruth Townsend, what a darling you are," she told the little girl, distracting her briefly from her study of my pearls. "So precious." Her face had softened into an entranced smile, and I wondered if I'd yet seen her this happy since her arrival on my doorstep six days prior.

It made me breathe a little deeper, knowing I'd made the right choice to come home earlier than planned. After everything she'd endured, this was where Tante Ilse needed to be—among family. Any amount of strain or awkwardness I might experience was well worth it knowing that.

CHAPTER 10

❧

"Somehow I knew I would find you here," I proclaimed as I rounded the corner in the barn that led to the stable block.

Freddy looked up from the bale of hay he'd perched upon, a hank of brown hair falling over his forehead. "Yes, well, sometimes the horses are better company."

Tabitha, who lay on the floor at his feet, looked up at my appearance, but then subsided again when she discovered it was just me.

I leaned against the wall, studying his slumped shoulders and loosened bow tie. Its ends draped over his collar. The lantern at his feet threw his shadow up across the stall behind him. But it was the whisky bottle he dangled between his spread legs that most interested me.

"Did you bring that to share?" I asked as I approached.

One corner of his lips curled upward, and he lifted the bottle, tipping it toward me. "Don't think I didn't notice how aggravated you were with Mother about her 'no ladies tippling' policy. I figured you could use some, Pip," he remarked, using the shortened form of Pipsqueak, the childhood nickname my brothers and their friends had always called me. "No glasses, though."

"Since when have I needed one in your company?" I retorted, snatching the bottle from his hand and setting it to my mouth. The whisky was rich and peaty, and I welcomed the bite and burn as I took a deep swallow. "How does Rachel stand it?" I asked, sinking down onto the bale beside him as I passed back the bottle.

"She's never been much of a drinker, and it's best she avoid doing so while she's nursing anyway."

I looked at him in surprise. "Really?" Sometimes it was easy to forget Freddy was a doctor, a battle-hardened surgeon.

He nodded. "While expecting as well."

I sighed, sinking my head back against the stall behind me. "Lovely. Something to look forward to," I drawled sarcastically.

The horse in the stall behind us stirred, shuffling the fresh hay strewn about the floor and snorting through his nostrils. It was a comforting sound, a soft exhale in the otherwise quiet barn rife with the scents of wood, straw, and warm animals.

"You aren't, are you?"

I turned to Freddy in confusion.

"Expecting?" he clarified.

"No," I replied perhaps a trifle too emphatically. After a moment of silence, I scoffed. "Mother didn't put you up to that, did she?"

Freddy's mouth twitched around the mouth of the bottle. "No. But it would be just like her to do so, wouldn't it?"

"Like when she sent you to London a few months back to interfere."

"I didn't . . ." he began to protest, but at the sight of my challenging stare he relented. "All right, yes. It was interfering, wasn't it?"

I held my hand out to ask for the whisky. "What changed your mind about that?" I asked before taking a swig. Four months ago I felt certain he would never have admitted as much.

"Seeing Sidney with you."

I looked to him in question.

"If he's in the least upset with you for anything that happened during or since the war, he certainly doesn't show it. In fact, he seems what we might have called in our younger days 'sickeningly besotted.' " His voice wasn't derisive, as it might have been, but almost rather wistful.

"Well, I don't know about that," I replied. "But we are both dedicated to working through our differences." I stared morosely at a gouge in the opposite wall. "The war wasn't easy on any of us."

In answer, Freddy took the bottle from me and took a long drink.

Not for the first time, I pondered what his war must have been like.

When we were young, Freddy had wanted to be a veterinarian, to look after horses—thoroughbreds and racing horses, in particular. But well-born gentlemen, even untitled ones, did not become animal doctors. So he'd elected to go to medical school instead. Even that was unconventional, for as the oldest son and Father's heir, he had no need for a profession. He would eventually inherit Brock House and all its lands, and they generated more than enough income for a country gentleman and his family. But Freddy had been determined. And not simply to become a gentrified physician, but a skilled surgeon—a move that proved fortuitous once the war broke out.

He did not officially join the Royal Army Medical Corps until 1916, when he was sent to the Western Front, but while still in medical school in 1914 he'd already pledged himself, should he be needed. Of course, none of us had believed the war would last beyond Christmas when it first began, but that had swiftly changed as the number of casualties mounted higher and higher in September and October of that year. By 1916, Freddy and all of his fellow medical school graduates were desperately needed. So off he went, headlong into the bloodbath of the Battle of the Somme. A baptism in fire if ever there was one.

I could only guess at the horrifying injuries he'd encountered, at the number of wounded soldiers who had passed over his operating table, at the number who had lived and who had died. I wondered whether Freddy kept a mental tally of those he was helpless to patch up, and those he felt he should have been able to save, much like Sidney did of the men who had served under his command. It was enough to rattle me just thinking about it.

I huddled deeper into my coat, wiggling my toes in the boots I had donned after discarding my pumps. "Ruthie is an absolute darling," I told him, meaning every word, though they sounded somewhat hollow given my words immediately before. But I couldn't think of how else to segue into asking about Rachel without being too obvious. "You must be proud."

"I am," he admitted. "She's . . . wonderful."

I could read in his expression that he felt that word was inadequate to sum up precisely what his daughter was to him, and I smiled, letting him know I understood the sentiment. "And Rachel? She seems to be a happy mother?"

"Yes. She's wonderful with Ruth."

I nodded, unsurprised he'd resorted to repeating the same adjective. "And you?" I began hesitantly. "The two of you seem . . . happy."

This was a lie, but a well-intentioned one. The only thing that had become increasingly evident to me over dinner was that first impressions were fickle, and their relationship was decidedly strained.

"Don't, Verity," Freddy cautioned in a hard voice.

"I only . . ."

"No," he snapped. "We're not discussing me and Rachel. We're just fine." He turned to glare at me. "And even if we weren't, you lost the right to question me about it when you stayed away so long."

My heart ached as the truth of that statement, and the pain evident in his words, struck home.

He shifted and sank his head back so that it banged lightly against the wood behind us. "Mind your own marriage."

I swallowed, realizing I'd misstepped, or overstepped—possibly both. Either way, apologizing would only make it worse, so I allowed the silence to stretch between us. One that was at first awkward, but became more comfortable as his irritation diminished. My older brothers and I seemed to have always possessed the ability to inhabit the same space without speaking. There was a comfort and a solace in that. If only my thoughts hadn't shifted to Rob.

As if sensing the change in my demeanor, and the reason for it, Freddy remarked without looking at me, "His treehouse is still there. I'm not sure how stable it is, but it's still standing. For now."

I didn't respond. I couldn't without revealing my distress. In any case, I had no intention of visiting Rob's retreat. Not yet anyway. Perhaps never.

Regardless, Freddy seemed to realize I was fighting back tears and passed me the whisky bottle. I accepted it, taking a shallow pull—afraid that if I tried to drink any deeper I might choke on it and the knot in my throat. The burning warmth that filled my stomach helped distract me from the sting at the back of my eyes.

I turned my head toward the sound of voices coming from the front of the barn. One was Sidney's low rumble, while the other was louder and more boisterous, and undoubtedly belonged to our younger brother, Tim.

Freddy heaved a heavy sigh.

"Before they find us, tell me what all that was with Tim," I requested, having sensed earlier in the drawing room that he wished to tell me something.

He opened his mouth to answer, but then seemed to think better of it, shaking his head. "You'll see for yourself what I mean soon enough," was his cryptic reply. Before I could press him on it, they were upon us.

"See, I told you they would be out here," Tim declared before turning to me. "Sidney was looking for you." He spied the bottle cradled in Freddy's hand. "Dipping into Father's reserve?"

Freddy scowled. "It's my own."

"Then let me have a drink?"

I lifted my gaze to my husband's, who stood watching me with an inscrutable look, one hand clutching one of his specially blended Turkish cigarettes and the other tucked in his trouser pocket. I arched my eyebrows in subtle query, but his only response was an amused quirk of his lips. I supposed the situation was rather humorous. Here I was, a sophisticated married woman—and a spy, to boot—and yet I was forced to slink away to the barn like an adolescent in order to have a dram of whisky.

"Out here checking on Ruby?" Tim asked, and then continued, answering the question I must have looked. "I heard Father threaten to sell her to the knacker yard if you didn't come home for a visit." His head nodded toward a stall farther along the row where the old pony must have drowsed. "She's still alive and kicking." He rubbed his backside. "Literally."

Ruby had never been fond of Tim. He'd been an annoying child.

"You've only yourself to blame if you got too close," I quipped, refusing to feel any empathy for him.

"Yes, probably," he admitted with good grace before taking another swig from the bottle.

"Don't drink it all," Freddy groused, demanding it back. "I'll not be blamed for your having too thick a head to attend church tomorrow."

"I won't," he protested mildly, passing the bottle back to him nonetheless. "I'm well aware of Mother's intentions that we put on a great show of family unity for the other parishioners." He scrubbed a hand back through his too-long hair. "Though, we won't be in full force until Grace returns."

Freddy's mouth quirked derisively as he proffered the bottle to Sidney and then me, but we both shook our heads. "And then Bolingbroke will want to sit with us."

"Who is this Bolingbroke chap?" I asked, grateful they'd offered me the opening to do so.

"Old Fenrick's nephew," Tim replied, approaching one of the hooks where the tack hung. He fidgeted with it as if it wasn't positioned right. "He came to help convert part of Gayle Mill to provide electricity for the village."

"Then he's educated?" I surmised, trying to decipher the look that had passed between my brothers. Clearly there was something about Bolingbroke they disliked or found suspect.

"Cambridge, I believe," Freddy answered when Tim turned away, strolling down the line of stalls, his hands fiddling with every item that wasn't pinned down, and even some of those.

"Did he serve?" Sidney chimed in to query around a drag of his cigarette, leaning his shoulder against the wall.

"With the Northumberland Fusiliers." He paused, scorn lacing his next words. "Until he received his Blighty wound."

That explained it, then. Mother's hesitance to accept him and my brothers' vague contempt. The word *Blighty* had been the soldiers' rather affectionate term for Britain or home. And a Blighty wound was trench talk for an injury that was serious enough to get a man sent back to Britain—removing him from combat for a long period of time, if not forever—but that was neither mortal nor permanently debilitating. Receiving such a wound was not cause for disdain in and of itself. But if it was combined with the suspicion that the injury had been deliberately inflicted in order to escape the fighting—a suspicion evident in Freddy's curled lip—then it would explain the family's mistrust and derision. The sin of perceived cowardice was difficult for most to accept, and a taint that was all but impossible to escape when proof of one's guilt or innocence was mutable.

"Is he in your care?" I asked Freddy, curious if he'd examined the wound.

"No, he prefers to drive to Kendal."

Which was even more suspicious. For why would Bolingbroke travel all the way to Kendal when he had a competent and experienced surgeon here in Hawes? But perhaps that was my bias showing. Maybe he felt uncomfortable discussing medical matters with the man he presumably hoped to make his brother-in-law.

Whatever the case, Freddy's opinion about Bolingbroke's Blighty wound was apparently mere speculation. If he had more definitive proof, he would have shared it.

Tim returned toward us, a riding crop in his hands, which he flicked toward his feet. "When did Tante Ilse arrive in England? I didn't even know she was coming."

Freddy's gaze lifted to him in annoyance. "Mother told us over dinner earlier this week, and we've discussed it at least half a dozen times since then."

"Oh," he replied, seemingly unfazed by his brother's criticism, and also unrepentant. He tilted his head to the side as if in thought while his wrist continued to flick the crop, snapping the soles of his shoes. "I thought her maid was older. With warts."

I arched my brows. "I don't recall the warts, but yes, Schmidt was older. She died from the influenza." As so many others had. "You must have seen Bauer, her new maid." I searched his face, wary of why he'd asked about Bauer. After all, she was quite pretty.

But his gaze remained trained on his shoes as he responded almost distractedly. "No warts on her."

Detecting no inappropriate level of interest, I relaxed. "I imagine not."

"For the love of—" Freddy suddenly snarled, breaking off before he used the Lord's name in vain, an infraction that would have earned us a lashing as children. "Stop that!" he ordered Tim. "Can you not stand still for one second?"

Tim's lashing motions slowed, but never actually stopped. "I can." He grinned in a manner calculated to vex Freddy even more. "I simply choose not to."

"Well, change your mind before I rip that out of your hand and whip you with it myself."

"I'd like to see you try."

Tabitha half rose to her feet, barking.

Before Freddy could follow through on his threat, I pressed a staying hand to his chest, feeling his muscles tense beneath his tailored coat. "Stop it. Both of you. Unless you want to draw Mother out here. Or worse, Father."

My brothers might be grown men, but I knew they still dreaded receiving the raw end of our father's temper. Or worse, the heavy sigh and shake of his head that indicated his disappointment.

"Besides, your squabbling is making the horses restless," I scolded, hearing the steeds shuffling in their boxes. I turned my glare on Tim. "As is that crop."

Freddy grunted, sinking back against the wall, while Tim hung the lash with the other tack. Freddy and Tim quarreling was nothing new. They'd done so since Tim was old enough to sass his imperious oldest brother. But in the past, Rob had always been the one to keep the peace, to settle their differences. I suddenly felt the hole his death had rent in the fabric of our family keenly.

I sighed wearily. The journey might not have been arduous, as the train and Sidney's motorcar had both run smoothly, but I'd spent much of the day and the night before braced for what was to come. Even now my muscles were tense, and my nerves frayed, chary of the memories that seemed to linger in the air all around me. Memories that at one time would have brought comfort, but now only brought pain.

"I'm going to bed," I declared, pushing to my feet as I hugged my Prussian blue coat tighter around me against the chill of the air.

Sidney's eyes wavered with concern, but he didn't broach it, instead offering a casual good-night to my brothers in turn before pressing a hand to the small of my back and escorting me toward the house.

The gate leading to the inner courtyard swung easily on its hinges, and I preceded him into the enclosed space, the dirt between the tiles crunching beneath my heels. All the lamps in the servants' quarters to our right were extinguished save one that burned lowly through the kitchen window to light the way for anyone seeking late-night sustenance. Across the yard, flickering light shone through the pale curtains of one of the bedchambers in the cottage. Either Ruthie was awake, or Rachel was waiting up for Freddy to return.

My gaze lingered on the light in the cottage window, torn between empathy for my sister-in-law and irritation at her chilly treatment of Freddy over dinner. After all, I'd spent my fair share of nights sitting up, wondering if Sidney would come to bed or return to it after one of his nightmares. However, I also held a strong loyalty to my brother, who I knew was coping as best he could since the war. All the returning men were. But then I had a rather unique perspective, having spent time during the war behind enemy lines as well as at home in Britain.

Of course, my family didn't know this. They couldn't know

this, for the Official Secrets Act forbade me from enlightening them. Which made everything all the more complicated as many of them clearly believed I'd been kicking my heels about London in between my hours working in the office of an import-export business shipping supplies to the British military. What I didn't know was whether Rachel was one of them.

"You're worried about Freddy," Sidney murmured. "About his marriage."

I turned to look up at him.

"I noticed the tension between them at dinner."

"How could you miss it?"

He pulled me to a stop before we crossed the threshold of the door leading into the billiards room. "Yes, well, that doesn't mean we should presume they're always like this. After all, they must be experiencing at least some anxiety at entering into this cozy little family gathering." He lowered his voice and his head so he could see deeper into my eyes. "And being forced to live in such close proximity to your mother while the renovations on their home are completed."

The corners of my lips tugged upward in a reluctant smile.

"Perhaps they're not always at odds with each other."

"Maybe," I conceded. What couple with a spouse returning from the war wasn't facing at least some measure of strain?

Sidney lifted his hands to clasp my elbows where they were tucked against my sides, his shadowed features searching mine. "But what of you?" His voice warmed with an affection that brought a lump to my throat. "I know today hasn't been easy for you."

"I'm fine," I replied, though it came out a bit strangled. After clearing my throat, I tried again. "Just fine."

"Really?" he asked doubtfully.

"Yes." I moved to push past him, feeling the icy veneer covering my deep-seated emotions beginning to crack under his regard. I already felt like I was walking on thin ice. If I allowed him to prod too hard, I might plunge into the depths. I couldn't allow that. Not now. Not if I was to endure this visit.

I sensed Sidney's dismay and frustration that I refused to

speak of it. But really, he was the last person to chastise me for withholding my feelings. Not when much of his war and the reasons he still paced the floor to escape his nightmares some nights were still a mystery to me.

Ignoring the tightness in my chest, I walked on, not caring whether he trailed after me. Though my heart gave a traitorous flip that belied my avowed indifference when I heard him shut the door as his footsteps followed mine.

CHAPTER 11

The following day we woke to low-hanging mist, which obscured the dawn and clung to the heath-strewn slopes and shadowed woods. By the time we departed for church in a caravan of motorcars, the sun had managed to burn through some of the fog, scattering golden light over the hills and fells, but the dale bottom was another matter. Our progress slowed as we crossed the River Ure, its rippling waters still smothered by a downy blanket of mist, and did not speed up even as we reached the outskirts of the village on the other side, for the fog there was slow to dissipate.

In truth, I was grateful that my first glimpse of Hawes after so many years was through a filter of haze. It blunted the impact of revisiting the streets I had so often trod, and my memories of the faces behind every house and shop window, some of whom would no longer peer through the glass ever again. I rode in the rear seat of the Pierce-Arrow next to Tante Ilse, who was perceptive enough not to press me for conversation. Or perhaps she was equally as distracted, her eyes having taken on a faraway sheen.

Meanwhile Tim burbled away in the front seat, quizzing Sidney about every aspect of his motorcar. Under normal circumstances my brother's chatter might have exasperated me, but that morning the sound of it washing over me was almost a comfort—a bit of the mundane in an otherwise disconcerting situation. Although, from the alert glances Sidney continued to cast my way in the rearview mirror, I was aware that my silence had not gone unnoticed.

St. Margaret's Church perched on a low hill overlooking the village. To the south it was bordered by fields of grazing sheep, their coats already growing shaggy for winter, while to the east ambled the rocky stream of Gayle Beck. We entered through the simple church gate affixed in the stone wall off Market Place, the main street that ambled through the heart of the village. Shops straggled down the length of the road. Next door stood the chemist, a grocer, and the bookshop, while across the street was located the post office and a pub.

Many of the orange and yellow leaves clinging to the lime trees that lined the path leading to the church door had already dropped, rustling against the gravestones strewn throughout the yard. Whatever pattern the weathered stones had originally been laid out in was no longer discernible. The ground seemed to have buckled and twisted in places, causing some of the markers to lean toward the earth, as if they carried a burden too great for them to bear.

I paused just inside the gate, my skin prickling at the sight of the gravestones. I could only feel relieved that the newer graves were located in a neat lot to the west of the church, for I did not relish stumbling upon the sight of a familiar name engraved in sandstone, and being reminded that they'd perished from the influenza or from wounds that had festered in the hospital. Most of the war dead, of course, had not been repatriated, instead being buried in France, Belgium, Gallipoli, Palestine, and other far-flung places on the globe. But nonetheless I could feel their absence like the missing notes of a song or the lost verse of a poem.

I came to regret my hesitation, for Mother looped her arm through mine, urging me up the path. "Fifty," she declared with an aggrieved sigh. "Forty-nine men, including your brother, and one nurse. You recall that Fanny Mason joined Queen Alexandra's Nursing Service?" she asked, and then continued to speak, not requiring an answer. "That's how many young people this village, and that of Gayle and Hardraw, sacrificed to the war."

I strode stiffly beside her, unable to form a response. I had known the numbers before. Mother had made sure of it. But standing here amidst the graves of the other past residents, the tendrils of fog still curling around the stones in the distance, it struck home more sharply than before. It was an enormous toll on such a small village and its two neighboring hamlets. And though I recognized other villages throughout Britain and Europe and the world had suffered losses, to greater and lesser degrees, those deaths were largely words and numbers on a page to me, while these were all achingly personal. They burned like hot pokers thrust into my gut.

"There are plans for a war monument." She gestured toward an open space in the churchyard, presumably where they intended to place it. "Something to commemorate those who died. But the funds will have to be gathered." She leaned closer, nodding toward an older man standing beside the church doors. "It was hoped Mr. Metcalfe might agree to sponsor a large portion of it. After all, his grandson, John, was the highest-ranking member of our community to be killed." She sniffed. "But he's already commissioned a plaque to be inset in the wall inside the sanctuary for the Metcalfe boys."

That she deemed this to be selfish was obvious from her pinched expression, but it was no different from what many of the first families throughout England were doing. Replacing traditional graves with monuments and plaques—giving themselves some place to mourn, some way to ensure their loved ones' names were not forgotten. In truth, I wondered if Mother had considered doing the same for Rob, but now felt doing so would be hypocritical, especially if the rest of the village was disgruntled by Mr. Metcalfe's actions.

I lifted my gaze from the path before me, still deciding whether to remark on this, when something about the man who had rounded the west corner of the bell tower, his head low and his hands tucked in his pockets, caught my eye. He seemed familiar somehow, and yet as I sifted through my memory, trying to place his face and his shaggy, straw-colored hair, the answer eluded me. I thought I knew everyone who lived in Hawes, but of course, I had been away for five years. That was a long time, and there were bound to be a few new faces in the village or seasonal laborers here to finish bringing in the harvest.

Nonetheless, his presence for some reason struck a discordant note within me. As if the location I had seen him before did not jibe with our current surroundings. But before I could place him, he'd disappeared behind the parishioners standing near the door, and must have slipped inside.

I shook my head, dismissing him from my thoughts, for there was undoubtedly a logical explanation. He was probably a soldier I had seen sometime during the war, either on the streets of London or while volunteering in a canteen. There was nothing more to it than that.

In any case, I needed my wits about me as Mother directed our footsteps toward a pair of women standing beside the path who were waiting for us. Mother hastened us toward them, pasting a pleasant expression across her face.

"Verity, you remember Mrs. Wild," my mother declared as we drew near.

"Of course," I replied, reaching for her hand. I had always liked my mother's closest friend. Perhaps because, in many aspects, she was her exact opposite. She was round and soft where Mother was thin and rigid, and cordial and dithering when Mother was reserved and precise. They seemed a mismatched pair, but I knew they held each other in the highest esteem.

Growing up, Mrs. Wild's son had often played with my brothers and me, though being of an age with Rob, they'd always been the closest. "I was terribly sorry to hear about Henry," I told her, knowing it was the right thing to say, though I struggled to keep my voice from wobbling. His death coming so close to the end of the war, as he and his men struggled to recapture a critical railway line, had seemed all the harder to swallow, knowing he'd almost made it to the armistice. "He was a good man. The best."

Mrs. Wild nodded, her eyes unspeakably sad in her serene face. "Thank you, dear." She patted my hand. "I know he was fond of you as well." Her plump cheeks lifted in a pained smile.

"Truth be told, your mother and I long hoped that the two of you would make a match. But he told me that was all stuff and nonsense." Her gaze shifted to my left, where Sidney and Tante Ilse had come up beside us. "Even before you wed your darling husband."

I contemplated her words as Mrs. Wild and Sidney exchanged greetings. Henry and I had, of course, been aware of our mothers' machinations, but neither of us had ever had the least intention of falling in line. At least, I didn't think Henry had. It was true he'd kissed me once . . . no, twice, during the summer when I was sixteen, before I returned to Everleigh Court and he to Oxford. But I had always viewed those stolen kisses as nothing more than youthful rebellion and experimentation, and Henry had never indicated they were any more serious to him. Now, I looked back on those memories with tenderness.

Suddenly aware that I was being inspected, my gaze shifted to the left to meet the eyes of the woman standing next to Mrs. Wild. She was younger—no more than a decade older than my twenty-three years—and possessed of a fine set of crystalline blue eyes rimmed with long lashes. They were her defining feature, and without them she would have seemed rather unremarkable. Her mousy brown hair had been scraped back from her forehead in a severe style, one to match her Spartan dress, though the powder-blue shade of her garments nicely accented those arresting eyes.

"Mrs. Redmayne," Mother said, drawing me closer. "Allow me to introduce my daughter, Verity; her husband, Sidney Kent; and my husband's aunt, Frau Vischering." She turned to us. "Mrs. Redmayne is our vicar's wife."

The qualifier was unnecessary, for I had heard her speak of Mrs. Redmayne many times over the telephone. Mr. Parker, Mr. Metcalfe's cousin and the village's vicar for over forty years, had retired in late 1915 and been replaced by Mr. Redmayne from Hertfordshire.

"Such a pleasure to meet you, Mrs. Kent," Mrs. Redmayne said, clutching the books she held before her even tighter. "Your mother has spoken of you often." From the shrewd tone of her voice, I couldn't tell precisely what that meant, but I supposed it depended on whether Mother had taken her into her confidence. "And you as well, Mr. Kent." She lifted her chin, staring down her nose as she nodded to my great-aunt. "Mrs. Vischering, welcome to Hawes."

"Thank you, my dear." Tante Ilse's brow furrowed. "But haven't we met?"

My lips twitched, thinking this was her method of countering the vicar's wife's cool condescension. Especially when Mrs. Redmayne ruffled up like an affronted bird.

"Certainly not." Her gaze flicked up and down her form before she continued in a smoother voice. "I would remember you."

But Tante Ilse's eyes narrowed further in scrutiny. One that didn't seem feigned. "Are you sure? I could have sworn . . ."

"Mr. and Mrs. Redmayne only came to us here in Hawes four years ago," my mother hastened to explain. "After your last visit."

I observed her continued uncertainty with a sickening sense of misgiving.

"Oh, then, I . . . I must be mistaken," she faltered.

This was not a woman intent on bringing the vicar's wife down a peg or two. Tante Ilse was genuinely muddled. But was it because she'd forgotten who our vicar was during her last visit, or because she'd seen Mrs. Redmayne, or someone who looked very like her, somewhere else?

My gaze lifted to meet Sidney's over her head, noting that similar questions seemed to swim in his eyes.

"Well, I did not mean to offend." Tante Ilse remarked, regaining her usual poise. She smiled abashedly. "When you are my age, all the faces start to look the same."

I reached out my hand to touch her shoulder, turning my face aside as I stifled the sudden urge to laugh. Had she intended to imply the vicar's wife was unremarkable? From the choked inhalation of Mother's breath, I knew she wondered the same thing. The impish glint in Tante Ilse's eyes when she glanced at me told me yes. Yes, she had. And that puckish bit of humor did much to ease my worries.

The church bells began to peal overhead, summoning worshippers inside. But before we could do their bidding, Mrs. Redmayne seemed intent on having the last word.

"The service will be in English. I hope you will be able to follow along," she said, openly addressing the fact that Tante Ilse was German.

Not that any of us had been endeavoring to hide that fact. After all, my mother had introduced her as Frau Vischering, and any number of the other members of the congregation must remember my great-aunt from her previous visits. Though of course, that had been before the war. Before everything changed.

I turned to look at the other parishioners milling past us to enter the church, noting their curious stares. I'd become so accustomed to being observed wherever I went that, more often than not, I intentionally ignored such interest. However, I had to wonder in this instance whether the scrutiny was for me and Sidney alone, or if some of it was directed at the German in their midst.

"I suspect I shall manage," Tante Ilse answered with more grace than I would have been capable of.

Mrs. Redmayne nodded and then turned away, striding through the parishioners, who seemed to part like the Red Sea for her. I could only wonder what her husband was like, whether she ruled the roost or he possessed the same iron will that seemed to force the congregation to bend to her.

Mother's mouth was bounded by deep brackets—always an indication of her displeasure. But was it directed at Mrs. Redmayne and her condescension, or Tante Ilse for endangering her standing and influence? I had known at least a portion of the village might take umbrage with a German living in our midst, but I hadn't expected one of them to be the vicar's wife.

Father stood to the side of the doors, waiting for us, and Mother released my arm to take his, so that they could lead us down the aisle to the pews at the front all but stamped with the names of the village's first families. We shuffled into position, as I knew Mother expected us to. Freddy strode forward carrying Ruth in one arm with Rachel's arm linked in the other. Meanwhile, Sidney passed Tante Ilse off to my brother Tim before joining me in the procession behind Freddy.

A dull ache took up its place inside my chest, knowing Rob should have gone before me. Perhaps he would even have a wife on his arm, a little child burrowed into his shoulder like Ruthie did to her father, her sweet little fist clutching his lapel. My footsteps faltered, but Sidney was there to propel me forward, a look of mild query flashing across his face as he gazed down at me. I shook my head minutely, turning aside to distract myself by studying the others already seated.

My parents' servants sat at the front of the rear section of pews, as snobbish in their own way and eager to claim their rightful place as the staff to one of the first families in the area. However, I noted the gap between where Bauer sat at the far end of the pew and the others. A space that was clearly deliberate given the way the nearest maid turned her shoulder away from my great-aunt's maid. I had feared this was the type of reception she would receive. And if my parents' staff were intent on shunning her, then the rest of Hawes would follow suit and do so as well.

I had only a moment to note Bauer's drawn countenance before we whisked past, but I resolved to ask Nimble to keep an eye on her. I should have thought to ask him to do so before, and if I hadn't been so consumed with my own trepidations about returning to Hawes, I likely would have. Sidney's valet and ex-batman might not relish the task, but despite his size, he was a gentle, kindhearted fellow, and I knew he would take the duty seriously. There wasn't much he could do about the seating arrangements in church, for the unwed female servants sat separately from the unwed males, but as the guests' maid and valet they would be lumped together more often at Brock House.

The pews were filled with familiar faces, so many that I hadn't time to nod to even a tenth of them. We had barely taken our seats before the organ sprang to life, sending music soaring up to the wooden beams of the vaulted ceiling, and compelling us to our feet for the opening hymn. Though I hadn't sung this particular song in some time, the words rose from my memory, allowing my gaze to stray from the hymnal Sidney held open for us.

Beyond the brim of my hat, I could see Mr. and Mrs. Wild seated across the aisle, and next to them, Violet Capshaw. Even though Violet was two and a half years older than me, we'd always been friends. We'd had little choice but to be, living in an area where there were few girls and an overabundance of boys of our social class. Even so, I'd always liked Violet. While not quite so daring as me, at least physically, she'd never shied away from an adventure. And even when she'd matured before I did, happily leading the adolescent boys on a merry chase, she'd never placed her flirtation with them over our friendship.

Violet had always dressed herself with a seemingly effortless stylishness, and I could see from her smart indigo velvet gown and jauntily tipped hat that hadn't changed. She flashed me an arch smile, which I was hard-pressed not to return despite the fact that Mrs. Redmayne was scowling at me from the pew in front of her.

Next to Mrs. Redmayne in the front pew sat old Mr. Metcalfe, his expression as stern and surly as ever. I had not expected his surviving grandsons to be cooling their heels in Hawes of all places. I knew them too well for that. But it was disconcerting all the same to see him there all alone when not so long ago he'd had the raising of six grandchildren, his son having been killed in Africa during the Second Boer War and his daughter having returned home with her children after her husband died from malaria somewhere in the Congo. Now they were all gone, either deceased, wed, or preferring to reside elsewhere.

I felt I could hardly blame them. Mr. Metcalfe was difficult enough to get along with as a neighbor, and it had been evident from the comments made by his family, and their eagerness to escape, that he wasn't any easier to live with. Yet it was still sad to see him alone.

However, that sentiment lasted only long enough for him to cast a black look at Tante Ilse. One that made it abundantly clear where he stood in his opinion of her presence there, and Germans in general. Then I decided he'd gotten what he deserved.

The service was conducted as it had always been done, with the same litany and the same hymns, ones I had memorized long ago and found I still remembered. It was unexpectedly comforting, an anchor I discovered hadn't entirely become unmoored even though the war had shaken my faith, as it had so many others'. Though whether it was the meaning behind the words or purely the ceremony of speaking and singing them that so consoled me, I couldn't say. What I could say with certainty was that Mr. Redmayne's sermon was just as ponderous as I recalled his predecessor's being. Sidney had been forced to elbow Tim awake more than once.

When finally the service ended, Violet hastened over to thread her arm through mine as we filed out of church behind the vicar. "Verity Kent, well, aren't you a sight for sore eyes," she proclaimed before casting a glance over her shoulder at Sidney from beneath her lashes. "You *and* your dashing husband." She pressed a hand to her brow like a tragic heroine in a motion picture. "How good of you to bring some color into our spare, provincial existence."

I smiled at her overblown theatrics. "Cut line, Violet. I know you're here by choice."

"I am," she admitted with an unabashed grin. "Needed a break from all the gents in London." That this was a jest went without saying. After all, the number of young, eligible gentlemen were rather thin on the ground since the war, and I knew Violet wasn't spending all of her time in town husband hunting.

"How is your father?"

"Pottering along." She nodded in front of us. "Much like Mr. Metcalfe." She leaned closer. "They get rather crotchety as they age without their wives to look after them," she murmured out of the side of her mouth, letting me know she'd seen the scowl Mr. Metcalfe had directed at Tante Ilse.

"And I always blamed it on dyspepsia."

Violet giggled, squeezing my arm tighter as we came to a stop. "Oh, I've missed you." She glanced toward my parents, who were exchanging words with the vicar by the door. "I know you can't talk long now, but come see me tomorrow." Her amber eyes glinted with amusement. "It will be Monday, after all, and your mother will be making her social calls. And I would wager my last pair of silk stockings you'll be required to accompany her."

"No wager necessary," I muttered wryly in confirmation. Part charity, part social duty, my mother made her calls throughout the area every Monday—rain or shine—and she had already informed me that this time I was expected to join her.

"Well, come see me after." She arched her eyebrows. "I promise to serve something stronger than tea."

"Now, you're speaking my language."

"Of course." She greeted Vicar Redmayne perfunctorily before striding away with one last little wave, but not before brushing a finger playfully underneath Tim's chin where he stood broodingly to the side of the path.

Tim turned to watch her walk away, but my attention was soon claimed by Vicar Redmayne.

"You must be Mr. and Mrs. Townsend's daughter, Verity," he proclaimed as if I were a child rather than a woman of three and twenty.

"Mrs. Verity Kent," I replied as I offered him my hand, feeling the moist warmth of his palm even through the kid leather of my gloves and extracting my hand as rapidly as possible. "Allow me to introduce my husband, Mr. Sidney Kent."

"Welcome to Hawes," he declared jovially, shaking Sidney's hand. "Though, I daresay you've been here before."

"Yes, I spent a great deal of time here before the war."

The vicar nodded. "Right. You were Dr. Townsend's friend before you wed his sister." He rocked forward onto his toes, seeming pleased with himself that he'd remembered this tidbit of knowledge someone had shared with him.

"Yes. Though, I daresay Freddy will still claim me as a friend."

I studied my husband out of the corner of my eye, certain his echo of the vicar's speech pattern was intentional and that his reply had not been a joke, even though Redmayne chortled as if it was.

"Yes, yes. I'm sure he will."

Sidney pressed a hand to the small of my back, urging me forward out into the breezy sunshine, leaving the vicar to greet his other parishioners.

Tante Ilse stepped forward to clasp her arm through mine as I approached. "Was that Miss Capshaw?" she asked, watching the figure in indigo disappearing down the church path toward the village. A tiny pleat formed in her brow. "Or is she wed now?"

I felt absurdly pleased by the fact she'd remembered Violet's engagement after all these years, especially after that awkward moment with Mrs. Redmayne before the service. I really had to stop weighing and assessing her memory with every comment she made.

"Her fiancé died in '15," I said.

"Poor dear," Tante Ilse crooned. A similar tale could be told by tens of thousands, if not hundreds of thousands of women across Europe and the globe, but Violet had been determined that hers not end there.

Soon after, she'd joined the First Aid Nursing Yeomanry as an ambulance driver, where she had served until her mother's death in '17. I had happened upon her in London by pure circumstance, not long after she'd resigned and returned to England. Her train north had been delayed until the next day, and she had been rather the worse for wear—broken from the news of her mother's passing after witnessing so much carnage and death driving injured soldiers from the casualty clearing stations to the hospitals behind the front. I'd invited her to stay with me in the Berkeley Square flat, patching her up as best I could in such a short time before sending her home to her father.

Given her condition that night, some might have been surprised to find her smiling and jesting so easily two years later, but I wasn't. I had always known Violet was made of sterner stuff. She had simply needed some time and space to heal the surface wounds, even if those that ran deeper still remained raw and tender.

"Well, I am glad to see she looks so well, all in all," Tante Ilse remarked as a stream of parishioners strolled past us. Some stopped to exchange greetings, while others merely nodded politely and carried on.

Mother gestured for us to follow them, and I stepped forward to do so, to be brought up short when Tante Ilse did not budge from her spot. My gaze turned to search her face, finding it locked on something near the church door. A knot of parishioners now stood between us and the vicar, so I struggled to comprehend what had so captured her attention, but whatever it was, it was not welcomed. Her eyes widened and her face paled, and she seemed to stagger slightly.

At first I feared someone had made some cruel derogatory gesture about Germans, but Tante Ilse had ignored such insults before, and I couldn't imagine her allowing them to cause her such visible distress now. It wasn't until she spoke that I realized she was confronting something far more disconcerting.

"It's him," she gasped in German.

My gaze shifted from her shocked visage to search the crowd again. "Who?"

"The second deserter," she whispered before her knees buckled.

CHAPTER 12

❧

Fortunately, Sidney was there to catch her, and between us we were able to keep Tante Ilse from collapsing completely. We hustled her toward one of the benches positioned beneath the tall lime trees, but when we would have set her down, she instead urged us on.

"No, no. Not here."

Sidney's gaze locked with mine over her head, asking questions I didn't have the answers to. I turned back toward the cluster of parishioners, most of whom were now watching us, but I knew whoever my great-aunt had seen, they were now long gone.

I sighed and nodded, turning to continue down the path with Tante Ilse propped between us. By this time, the rest of the family had noticed our delay, and Tim hurried back to take my place. Between him and Sidney, they practically carried her from the churchyard.

"What happened?" my mother asked as I drew near.

"I don't know. She said she felt faint," I lied, unable to tell her the truth, though it pressed on my chest like a heavy weight. My gaze darted to my eldest brother. "Perhaps Freddy should take a look at her."

He nodded. "I'll fetch my medical bag as soon as we reach home. Make her comfortable in her bedchamber."

I hastened to the Pierce-Arrow, finding Sidney settling Tante

Ilse in the rear seat. I climbed in to sit beside her, clutching both her hands between my own and chafing them. She allowed this minute fussing while her eyes remained fixed on the view outside the window. Her chest seemed to rise and fall more rapidly than usual, but once we reached the outskirts of the village, it began to settle.

She tipped her head back, closing her eyes, and I couldn't help but study her with concern. She appeared wan and weary now that the near-frantic nature of her breathing had been calmed. Even though I had a dozen questions for her, I waited to ask them. Tim might be my brother, and he might have served during the war, but he had no idea that I had worked for the Secret Service, or that I'd set foot inside German-occupied Belgium, or Germany itself, during the conflict. None of my family did.

Tante Ilse must have realized this, for she did not try to explain either, instead mumbling in a raspy voice. "*Mir geht es gut, mein Liebchen. Ich bin einfach müde.*"

She could claim she was well all she wanted, that she was merely tired, but I'd seen the fear in her eyes. I'd heard what she'd said.

That didn't mean what she'd claimed she'd seen was true, but she'd certainly believed it to be, at least at the time. I couldn't help but think of the shaggy-haired man I'd seen entering the church. The one who'd seemed familiar, and yet I couldn't place him. I couldn't help but wonder if we'd seen the same person. Whether I also knew the man she'd called "the second deserter."

Though Sidney made the drive at a near-reckless speed, this time I didn't even think of chastising him. I was simply glad when he stopped before the front gate and hurried to help my great-aunt from the motorcar.

In short order, she was lying on her bed with her head propped up by two pillows. Sidney and Tim left us while I removed her shoes, promising to send her maid Bauer and Freddy up as soon as they arrived.

"I do not need Freddy to attend to me," she protested when

the door closed, not pretending to misunderstand why he would be doing so.

I set her second shoe next to the first one beside the bed, and sat down next to her hip. "Tante, you nearly collapsed. Please let him at least check your heart and your pulse."

"I require only my medicine." A martial gleam lit her eyes. "Bauer can see to that."

"Possibly. But is what you said true? Did you see the second deserter?"

She folded her hands over her abdomen. "Yes," she stated with certainty, and then contradicted herself with just as much conviction. "No." Her brow pleated. "I thought I saw him, but . . ."

"But now you're not certain?" I finished for her when she left the sentence dangling.

Her gaze lifted to meet mine, stark with confusion.

"What did he look like? Can you describe him for me?"

She lifted a hand to her head. "I . . . don't know."

"What was his hair color? Was there anything distinctive about his features?" I pressed, but she merely shook her head. "Please. You must recall something."

"He's . . ." She gestured outward with her hand, but when whatever thought she was trying to articulate did not translate into words, she allowed it to drop. "Why? Why would he be here? Why would he follow us?"

"I don't know." I frowned. "But if he did follow us, I doubt his explanation is innocent."

Tante Ilse's chest rose and fell sharply, indicating her distress was genuine.

I reached out to take her hands between my own. "Whatever the truth is, I will find it."

She blinked up at me, her hands turning over to tighten around my own. "You and Sidney?" Her mouth flattened. "I know you are brave and clever, *mein Liebchen*. But this is not the war. You need not do this alone."

I nodded, touched by her concern. "Sidney and I will find it."

Below, I heard muffled voices, and I knew it was only a matter of time before we were interrupted by my mother or Bauer. I leaned closer. "But my family cannot know. I think you realize this." I searched her face for comprehension.

"Yes, Verity, I know. Have no fear. I will not betray you."

"Thank you."

A light rap sounded on the door, and I turned to answer it.

"Although I think it is wrong that you cannot tell them."

I cut a glare at my great-aunt for this ending rebuke. Did she think I had not bemoaned the same thing countless times before? And then recanted it, for Mother would never understand. And neither would Father.

The work of intelligence agents was considered by some to be dishonorable, or at least unsporting, particularly by the older generations. The term *spy* was a dirty word, as was everything that went along with it. Mindsets were changing among those who were younger and had witnessed firsthand the good that such intelligence gathering could do. The soldiers at the front had recognized the necessity for Military Intelligence officers, though many still eyed them with some disfavor. In the case of men working behind enemy lines, like Alec, this introduced more shades of gray, but their bravery was still valued.

However, for a woman to embark on such work, and a lady at that, it was seen as both unnatural and a betrayal of her sex and class. Never mind that what I was doing was just as necessary, that the world was at war, and that my efforts saved lives. It was still unbefitting a woman of my station, and consequently, I was not to be fully trusted.

"Come in," I called, my eyes still locked with my great-aunt's, holding her to her pledge.

When we were not greeted by a flurry of words, I surmised it must be my aunt's German maid who had entered and not my mother. I turned to find Bauer eyeing her employer with both concern and misgiving. Her countenance was drawn, and I could well imagine the worries consuming her, not only for her employer, but at the possibility of finding herself alone in a strange and hostile country should the worst happen. I sought to reassure her.

"She says she needs her medicine. *Ihre Medizin.*"

She nodded and turned to fetch it from the top of the bureau, measuring and pouring, and then diluting it in a glass of water. I stood aside to allow her to help prop Tante Ilse upright as she drank the medicine, noting the dark tinge of the liquid, and the way her mouth puckered at the taste. The clear vial it had been poured from contained a thick, reddish-brown syrup, and even though it bore no label, I strongly suspected I knew what it was. Laudanum. A tincture of opium more popular in the last century than the present, though still readily available.

It wasn't the only medicine my great-aunt took. There were several bottles and vials lined up across the top of the bureau. But it was perhaps the most alarming of possibilities. Was she taking it for pain, or had she begun taking it to cope with the war and become addicted? After all, I had witnessed what a powerful hold opium could have over those who sought its numbing oblivion. I knew more than one society darling who had become addicted to morphine—laudanum's even darker cousin.

"Please, won't you let Freddy take a look at you?" I begged.

"No, no," she insisted, sinking back against her pillows. "I simply need to rest."

I scrutinized her features, wishing I knew what questions to ask. Wishing she would confide in me without my having to press her. "Well, think about what I said. It will be easier for us to find the second man, or even establish or eliminate the possibility of his being here, if we know what he looks like."

Out of the corner of my eye, I saw Bauer flinch and wondered how much of what I'd said she comprehended. She hadn't begun working for my great-aunt until later, months after the second deserter's visit. Otherwise, I might have asked *her* for a description of the fellow.

I crossed toward the door, turning to speak to Bauer in German just before I departed. "Send for my brother, Dr. Townsend, if she worsens. He can help."

I waited until Bauer nodded jerkily in understanding, and then slipped from the room. As the door latched, I slumped against the wooden trim, nearly overcome with apprehension and fear for my great-aunt. Had Tante Ilse seen the second deserter outside St. Margaret's or not? Was she ill and in pain or otherwise dependent on laudanum? And why wouldn't she let Freddy see her?

I lifted my head to see Freddy rounding the newel post at the top of the stairs, clutching his black medical bag, and hastened into the upper hall to speak with him. "She's refusing to let you examine her," I told him, unable to iron out all the distress from my voice.

His hazel eyes shifted to gaze over my shoulder at her bed-chamber door while I took a deep breath, trying to regain control of my frazzled nerves.

"Her maid gave her a tincture of medicine. One that I'm distinctly certain contains laudanum. And she claims that's all she needs."

Freddy heaved a sigh. "I can't force her to allow me to examine her." He tilted his head. "Well . . . I could. But I don't wish to do that. Not without a compelling reason to do so. And unfortunately, laudanum usage is not a justified reason."

I pressed a hand to my forehead, pacing away several steps before turning back and nodding. "I'm worried, Freddy," I confided, lowering my voice. "She's not been herself." I held up my hand to forestall any arguments. "I know she's seventy-nine, and she's just endured a horrific war and food deprivation, but I can't help but feel this goes beyond that."

Rather than dispute this less-than-scientific evidence, he surprised me instead by conceding. "I've not had long enough to interact with her to make such a judgment, but I've never known you to exaggerate matters. Not about something like this. If you think something is wrong, then there probably is." He reached out a hand to clasp my shoulder. "But we can't force her to admit it, Pip."

I knew he was right. Just as I knew I should mention the confusion and memory lapses I noticed, but I elected to keep those to myself for now. "Just, keep an eye on her, will you? You're a good doctor, Freddy. I trust you to notice something if there's cause for alarm."

"And how would you know that?" The words were spoken affably, but there was a glint in his eyes that told me the question wasn't quite as lighthearted as he wished it to seem. "You've never witnessed me in my capacity as a surgeon or country doctor."

"No, but I know *you*," I replied. "For all your incorrigible, high-spirited antics when we were young, you were always the chap with the coolest head when matters turned serious."

The corners of his mouth flickered upward in the approximation of a smile. "I seem to recall you weren't prone to panic either."

I shrugged, allowing him to drape an arm around my shoulders and turn me toward the stairs. "That was Tim and Grace. Though, to be fair, they were younger than us, and may have grown out of such behavior." I hesitated. "And Rob, on occasion."

Freddy was silent for a moment—I supposed contemplating the brother born between us—and then began to chuckle. "Do you remember when that haystack in one of Metcalfe's south fields caught on fire?"

My mouth quirked. "And Rob singed his hair in his frenzy to put it out. He was dashed lucky he didn't set his clothes on fire in the process."

Freddy laughed harder. "And then he elected to cut his own hair rather than let Mother see the damage he'd done."

I smiled more broadly. "It took months for it to grow out long enough to lay flat against his head rather than sticking up like a hedgehog's quills."

My oldest brother nearly doubled over with amusement as

we rounded the landing. When he was able to speak again, he shook his head in wonder. "To think, he was the one who joined the Royal Flying Corps. Turns out he had nerves of steel after all."

Unfortunately, courage couldn't save you. Not every time. Not when your luck ran out.

Freddy fell silent, and a brooding expression fell over his features, I suspect contemplating the same thing I was.

I didn't know the details surrounding Rob's death. I didn't want to. Not when I'd already heard the horrifying tales of other flyboys—some who had survived, albeit wounded, like Goldy, and some who had not, like Daphne's brother, Gil. It was enough to know that his aeroplane was shot down over France. To recognize that his being shot dead in the air—before the aeroplane caught fire, before it crashed—was the best I could hope for.

Although seeing Freddy's face, the starkness that had entered his eyes, the pain that seemed to tighten the skin across his bones, I had to wonder if he *did* know the particulars. If he'd asked to know them or been made to confront them. The very idea made something inside me scuttle away, cowering in some recess of my soul that pressed against my diaphragm.

I forced myself to draw breath into my lungs, to focus on each next step as it creaked beneath our feet, lest I grow weak-kneed like Tante Ilse.

"How is she?" Mother demanded, standing at the bottom of the staircase to meet us.

I looked up at her and then beyond at my father. "She . . . she says she's simply tired. That she wishes to rest." I glanced at Freddy. "She had her maid give her some medicine, but she's refusing to let Freddy look at her, even to check her heart."

"Well, we can't force her," Mother replied uncertainly as she turned to my father, clearly surprised by this.

But my father evidently wasn't. "Tante Ilse has always been stubborn and determined to have her way. I daresay she's merely affronted by the idea of letting a doctor other than her own examine her, even one who is her great-nephew."

"But her physician is back in Germany. He can hardly be called in to attend to her," Mother countered.

"Yes, and she'll come around to understand that in her own time. Meanwhile, we'll just have to be certain she doesn't exhaust herself."

With this verdict, Father turned and strode down the corridor in the direction of his study. Mother turned as if to follow him, and then changed course, murmuring something about altering the dinner menu as she crossed the hall toward the dining room.

I lifted my gaze to find Sidney watching me from the doorway to the drawing room. Though he leaned negligently against the door trim with his shoulder, there was an alertness to his features that told me he had noted my distress. Freddy slid past him into the room, where Rachel could be heard crooning to their child, but rather than follow him, I gestured for Sidney to join me across the entry hall in the billiards room.

I came to a stop next to the table covered in green baize, the red and white balls already racked and ready for their next game. "Did you hear what Tante Ilse said? Outside the church?"

"The second deserter," he replied, lowering his voice to match my tone.

"She claims she saw him in the churchyard."

Sidney's brow furrowed as he glanced toward the door. "Well, that frames the matter rather differently. Could she describe him to you?"

I moved a step closer. "That's the thing, she couldn't."

His eyebrows arched in surprise.

"She kept saying that she didn't know. Now, whether that's because she was still too agitated, or she can't remember, or she didn't see what she thought she did, I can't say." I pulled my cloche from my head and tossed it down on the baize before pressing my hands to the edge of the table and lowering my head. "But I'm hoping once she's calmer and has had some time to think about it she'll at least recall *something*."

"Are you afraid this might be another lapse of her memory?"
I turned my head to meet his gaze.

"That she might be becoming confused about what she sees
or doesn't see?"

"Maybe," I was lulled into admitting by the compassion I
saw reflected in his deep blue eyes. "But . . . I also saw someone
this morning," I confessed hesitantly. "A man who seemed intent on not drawing attention to himself as he entered St. Margaret's. He seemed familiar somehow, but I couldn't place him."
I searched Sidney's face, curious what he thought of this disclo-
sure. "I told myself I was jumping at shadows, seeing potential
villains where there were none. That he was likely new to the
village or a farm laborer, and perhaps I'd seen him or someone
like him on the streets of London during the war. Maybe I'd
even served him at the canteen outside Victoria Station where I
volunteered."

I thought of the lines of soldiers. Weary men just returned
from the trenches on leave, dirty and disillusioned, but also relieved. Naïve, grinning first-timers, eager to get out to the front
and cover themselves with glory. And war-hardened veterans,
their shoulders bowed low, lingering over one last hot meal, attempting to delay the inevitable.

"But now you're not so certain," he finished for me.

"It seems strange that we should both notice someone who
seemed out of place and seemed at least vaguely familiar."

"I agree. Did *you* at least get a good look at him?"

"He was of about medium height with shaggy hair of a straw
color." I shrugged. "I had little more than a glimpse of him, and
at a distance."

Sidney nodded, lifting his hand to smooth back a tendril of
hair that must have become tangled in my earring. "That's
something, at any rate. If nothing else, we can ask around
the village, find out if any strangers have been seen about." The
backs of his fingers slid down the length of my jaw. "If it is the
second deserter, I assume you think he followed us here, not
that he happens to live here."

"Wouldn't that be too great a coincidence?" I turned to lean back against the table, crossing my arms over my chest. "No, I think it would have to mean he followed us. Though I haven't the foggiest notion why."

"Maybe he works for German Intelligence."

"And, knowing of my aunt's connection to me, was sent to track me down?" I shook my head. "Germany's intelligence agencies entirely fell apart after the war. They're of no threat to us now."

"Maybe not to Britain. But perhaps this particular agent hopes to profit from you individually."

His words sent a chill through me.

"Blackmail?" I murmured.

"It wouldn't be difficult to deduce how much damage even the suggestion that you were in contact with German agents and passing them information, perhaps even through your aunt, might do to your reputation. Or that it could prompt an investigation into your activities."

There were already men among the intelligence services who would be only too happy to see me investigated for treason. Men like Major Davis, C's second-in-command; Sir Basil Thomson, the newly appointed Director of Intelligence; and even Lord Ardmore. For certain, there were many who would also defend me, among them C, the chief, and Captain Landau. The trouble was that for many of my forays into German-occupied Belgium, I had been answerable to no one but myself for weeks at a time. I'd been given objectives to complete, as well as any intelligence that might assist me in succeeding, but then it was up to me to figure out how to achieve them. There were simply too many variables that could not be accounted for, making it all but impossible for Landau and others to attempt to formulate the plan for me.

My ability to adjust, to plan for multiple outcomes and alter my course in a split second, relying on little but my observations and intuition to guide me, had made me a great agent. But it also made it next to impossible to explain the *why* of each decision I'd made. How could I explain why at times I would veer off my intended course, prolonging my journey and its hardship by several hours purely because my gut told me to? Or why it was better to choose the line at a border check manned by an uncouth lout rather than the reserved, doe-eyed female? Or when to risk requesting shelter from a farmhouse deep in the countryside and when to carry on through the driving rain?

And that said nothing of the little indignities a female agent was forced to endure at the hands of the occupiers, alongside the rest of the women trapped in Belgium and northeastern France. Indignities that men like Davis and Thomson would seek to use against me as proof of my collusion with the enemy. As if being groped, and pawed, and pestered merely for traveling down a road or taking up space in a shop was a thing to be desired.

Sidney was right. A German agent, present or former, who knew any information about my activities with the Secret Service could certainly be a threat.

"Perhaps somehow Ardmore even sent him."

I blinked at Sidney in surprise, not having yet made the possible connection to Ardmore's machinations. "That would imply he was and/or is still involved with German Intelligence on a deep level, and we have no evidence of that." I frowned. "Besides, if he knew about my aunt and the deserters, he would probably have already had the second man decry me."

"And miss the opportunity to beleaguer your conscience? No, Verity. Ardmore is more cunning and vicious than that. You know full well how much he likes toying with you. He would enjoy watching you squirm after he offered you the chance to save yourself as long as you dropped your investigation of him." Sidney leaned closer. "When has he ever simply outwitted someone when instead he can corrupt and demoralize them?"

He was right. For Ardmore, the enjoyment wasn't so much in winning, as in manipulating others into debasing and compromising their own morals. We'd seen that with Max's father, the late Earl of Ryde, as well as Lord Rockham—to some extent—

and Flossie Hawkins, among others. Ardmore delighted in out-maneuvering those who saw themselves as heroic, twisting and exploiting them until they were forced to accept the fact that their motives and actions were not only selfish and tainted, but heinous.

I clutched my arms tighter around myself as a fear that was different from any I had faced before gripped me. I swallowed the sticky coating of panic flooding the back of my mouth. "If that's true . . ." My words faltered—I was unable to finish the thought.

"*If* it's true," Sidney repeated, grasping my upper arms, "and it's *only* a possibility, then we'll confront it when it happens. Together. But you should be prepared, in case you receive a letter or some sort of visit from this fellow."

I took a shaky breath, feeling grateful I wasn't facing the possibility alone. Though I might be less glad if I discovered Ardmore was involved, after I learned just what he was threatening. The thought of exposing my loved ones to his machinations made my blood run cold.

Sidney's hands rubbed up and down the silk covering my arms, as if sensing the chill that had settled over me. "Now, what were . . . ?"

"And just why are you lurkin' here?" A voice interrupted before Sidney could finish.

Recognizing that the voice belonged to my mother's maid, the much-dreaded Matilda, I turned to see her standing before the open doorway leading out into the back corridor that led to the enclosed walkway between the servants' quarters and the main house. Who she was speaking to wasn't immediately apparent, until a cowering Bauer stepped into view.

Matilda loomed over her. "Spyin', were ye?"

Bauer's cheeks flushed a fiery hue. "I was not spying," she protested in her thick German accent, clearly understanding what the word meant. "I must a question ask."

Matilda made a very rude noise. "Then why did ye not knock?" But rather than wait for an answer, she stomped off toward the servants' wing with a gown draped over her arm. I knew within minutes half the staff would know about Bauer "lurking" outside the billiards room door. Perhaps I needed to have a private word with her.

"What did you wish to ask?" I queried gently.

Bauer's hands were clenched into fists at her sides, and I could see the frustration and humiliation cresting over her in the reddening of her skin above the neckline of her simple gown of blue serge. The blush slowly faded as she took a calming breath, stepping into the room. "Frau Vischering has . . . *Medizin*, and other things, she needs."

I comprehended what she meant, but elected to answer in German. "I'm sure my brother, Dr. Townsend, could replenish them for you. Or if you prefer, I'm going into the village tomorrow. Make me a list and I will pick up what she needs from the chemist." This would also give me a chance to find out exactly what medications my great-aunt was taking.

However, Bauer surprised me by lifting her chin and replying determinedly in English. "Thank you, but I must go. I must learn to do for myself."

"Of course. Then let Mrs. Grainger know. She will be able to tell you when Mr. Kidds will be running any errands in town and can give you a lift. Or you may take one of the bicycles, if you prefer."

She nodded and backed out of the room before following in Matilda's wake toward the servants' quarters.

"Brave girl," Sidney remarked.

"Yes, especially considering the welcome she's received." I frowned, wondering if I should say something to my mother or speak to the staff directly. But would that help or make matters worse?

"The other servants will come around. Surely they must see that a slip of a maid can't be blamed for all their troubles any more than an old lady can. It's not as if she was a soldier aiming a gun across No Man's Land."

That was true, but I knew from experience that a slip of a

maid could still be a remarkably effective soldier in the gathering of information. Young women were often dismissed and discounted by the enemy, hence my own success.

But this wasn't the war, and there was no intelligence to be gathered in the depths of the Yorkshire Dales.

My brow furrowed as I glanced back toward the door through which Bauer had retreated. Though perhaps I should be taking my own advice. Bauer may have been hovering outside, waiting to ask a question, but she might also have been listening to our conversation.

CHAPTER 13

❧❀❧

Some hours later, I reclined on the jonquil-print fainting couch in our bedchamber, with one arm draped over my head as I gazed up at the ceiling. I should have been dressing for dinner. My modest willow-green gown was already aired and pressed, and hanging on the outside of the wardrobe. But I was stalling, rather foolishly attempting to ignore the clock while still finding myself glancing at it every few minutes, noting each passing second more acutely than if I simply got up and got on with it.

I should have been pleasantly exhausted from the bicycle ride Sidney and I had taken earlier that afternoon, and my muscles certainly registered the day's exertions, but my mind was as sharp as ever, and as keen with dread. The trouble was that Sunday dinners had always been a family affair, even more so than the rest of the week. And so I knew Rob's presence would be more keenly missed. While I had been able to blunt my perception and overlook his absence the previous evening, I knew tonight it would be far more difficult.

The door opened, and Sidney paused on the threshold, obviously surprised to see me still lazing about in the blue serge split skirt I'd worn on our outing, which enabled me to ride a bicycle more easily. He looked at the ormolu clock on the mantel over the fireplace. "Didn't you say dinner was at a quarter after six?" he asked as he shut the door.

"Yes," I said with a sigh.

"Are you intending to feign illness?" he asked as he removed his leaf-brown Norfolk jacket.

I shook my head back and forth where it rested against the cushion. "Mother would never allow it." I arched my eyebrows cynically. "Or she would leap to a conclusion I would rather not address." Not that I had any hope of avoiding it. At some point during this visit, my mother was bound to raise the issue of us starting our family.

Sidney paused with his jacket draped over his arm, his gaze dipping to my abdomen. I wondered if he would say something, but then he turned to toss the coat over the back of a chair and reached for his tie. "Is there a particular reason for your reluctance?"

"Does there need to be?" I quipped, hoping he would leave it at that. But I was not so lucky.

"It's Rob, isn't it?"

I stared at my stocking-covered toes peeping out from the hem of my skirt, refusing to look at him. I couldn't. Not if I had any hope of keeping my emotions bottled up inside.

When I didn't respond, he moved closer, his tread soft against the Aubusson rug. "Ver, I know this isn't easy for you. What can I do to help?"

The weight that had been pressing on my chest all day suddenly felt unbearable, and I sucked in a harsh breath, feeling it rasp against my windpipe. "Didn't it seem as if nothing had changed?" I remarked with forced lightness. "The fields, the countryside . . . It looked as it ever has. As if five horrible years hadn't passed as it has elsewhere."

But I knew it had. Perhaps its marking couldn't be seen on the landscape, but the horribleness was still felt in every inhabitant's breast, in the memory of those forty-nine men and one woman who had been lost.

I shied away from this thought, for once again it veered toward reminiscences of Rob.

"Did you recognize that barn we passed?" I asked with a strained smile.

Sidney sank down beside me, and I could tell by his expression that he wasn't fooled. That he knew I was still sitting here, racked with dismay because of Rob. But I continued to grin determinedly at him anyway, begging him with the pained stretch of my lips not to press this. Not now.

He reached out to take my hand, his gaze dipping to where our fingers tangled. "Yes." One corner of his lips quirked upward roguishly. "How could I forget?"

My expression softened into one more natural. The barn in question—one of the many such stone structures that dotted the hillsides throughout the dales, providing shelter for the animals out to pasture or temporary storage for crops or equipment— had also proven to be a handy refuge for Sidney and me during a rainstorm that golden summer of 1914. We had been all but inseparable during the months following the Lucases' spring soiree when we'd shared our first dance, until war was declared and he'd rushed off to enlist, like every other young, hot-blooded Englishman it seemed. But that hour trapped by the deluge inside the stone barn along the road toward Hardraw Beck proved to be a particularly pleasant memory.

"I thought for a moment you intended to revisit it. Or Hardraw Beck."

Where we'd shared our first kiss.

My gaze slid to the side, my thoughts straying toward the past.

It was bittersweet now to think of that summer. Of each picnic and stroll over the dales. Of his teaching me to drive his Pierce-Arrow and my beating him at billiards. Of the stolen moments—kissing, caressing, longing for more.

The trouble was that so many of those memories, and the places where they'd occurred, were also tangled up with other reminiscences. Ones that contained Rob. Of splashing through the waterfall or besting him at darts. Of watching Freddy and him string a rope line from the rafters of one of the stone barns in order to glide down the rigging like the privateer in one of their favorite swashbuckling books. That adventure had ended with a dislocated shoulder.

As we'd pedaled through the sunlit autumn countryside—the

amber fields shorn of most of their crops and the trees nearly stripped of all their burnished leaves—and stood next to the stone wall separating the road from the steep crevice that cradled Hardraw Beck below, I'd struggled with that realization.

"At least, that's why I'd hoped you'd chosen that route, and not that you intended for us to ride up over Buttertub Pass, because I would have adamantly balked at such a suggestion. A little exertion is all well and good, but I've slogged through quagmires at the front that were easier going than that climb would have been on a bicycle."

While amused at his jest about the road that ascended toward Great Shunner Fell, I was more heartened by the fact he was able to make even a small jest to me about his time in the trenches. "No, I never intended to go that far. Truthfully, I'm not exactly certain why I chose to go in that direction."

"Because it holds pleasant memories without Rob," he replied without having to give the matter a moment's thought.

I lifted my gaze to his face, watching the play of light and shadow across his features from the crackling flames in the hearth.

"Because if you face those memories first, then it will be easier to confront the harder ones."

I took a ragged breath scented with wood smoke, my woolen sweater, and a hint of Sidney's bay rum cologne. "When did you become so wise?" And perceptive.

His deep blue eyes refused to release mine. "It's what I would do. It's what I've done."

I understood what he meant. There were certain places even in London that I knew he associated with the war, where he refused to go, except when compelled to by the circumstances of our investigations. Places like Victoria Station, where the trains arrived and departed carrying troops bound to and from the coast and the transport ships to France; or the Cheshire Cheese, a restaurant we'd eaten at on more than one of his leaves. He even avoided Kensington Gardens, less because we had walked there upon occasion during those same leaves, and more because of the idealized model of the trenches that had been dug and displayed there for the public during the war. The reality of the trenches had been much more ragged, foul, and grim.

The creak of the wood flooring and the familiar clump of footsteps alerted us to the fact that we would soon be interrupted before the rap fell on the door. Sidney squeezed my hand before rising to his feet and calling for his valet to enter.

Nimble poked his head through the gap in the door—to ensure he wasn't about to stumble into an embarrassing situation, I supposed—before venturing inside. "Your evenin' clothes, Cap'n."

I could see Sidney visibly suppress a sigh. He'd instructed his former batman dozens of times not to call him that anymore, and yet he persisted in doing so. Not intentionally, I suspected, but because he had done so for so long without thinking. "You can hang them there," Sidney directed. "I'll dress myself this evening."

"Very good, cap—er . . . sir," he replied, catching himself that time.

"Nimble, before you go," I called, swinging my legs over the side of the fainting couch and sitting forward.

He paused, turning to face me.

"How is Fräulein Bauer getting on?"

Nimble shifted his feet uncomfortably.

"Are the other servants being unkind?" I asked, putting into words what it seemed he was struggling to say.

He lifted his hand to rub at the scars blistering the left side of his face near his hairline, courtesy of a shell explosion. The same explosion that had taken part of his ear. I noticed he often did this when he was uneasy about something.

"They don't like her much."

"Yes, I suspected that," I admitted sadly. "Because she's German?"

He nodded.

I tilted my head, studying his hulking frame and neat appearance, wondering if I'd presumed too much from his easygoing nature. "You don't dislike her, do you?"

He shrugged. "I don't really know her. But if ye mean, do I

hold her bein' German against her." He shook his head. "Naw. She can't help where she was born. And what could a slip of a girl like her ever 've done to harm anyone?"

I could name half a dozen slip-of-a-girls that would prove that assertion wrong, but I kept that thought to myself.

"Would you keep an eye on her?"

Nimble shuffled his feet again, his gaze flicking toward Sidney and then back.

"Just . . . let me know if anyone is harassing her in particular. If they're cruel."

I'd decided that saying something to the servants would only make matters worse. They tended to resent any interference in such things, and would only take it out on Bauer, but in more subtle ways. However, I also didn't want to see the girl harmed or mistreated. If the other servants took matters too far, then I would step in.

He hesitated a moment longer before nodding. As he left, I couldn't help but wonder at his reticence. Had he worried my intrusion would harm Bauer more? Or did he fear that his intervention would not go unmarked by the other servants and turn their opinions against him? Nimble had not seemed the type to allow such considerations to sway him from doing what was right, but I supposed we all had our vulnerabilities we were afraid to expose.

My gaze met Sidney's watchful one, but before he could speak, the reverberating chime of the clock in the entry hall propelled me to my feet. "Dash it!" I exclaimed, reaching for the buttons at the side of my skirt.

Thanks to the ease of styling my bobbed hair, and Sidney's nimble fingers on the buttons of my gown, we stepped through the doorway into the drawing room seconds before the quarter hour. My mother gave me a knowing look, but the position of the minute hand prevented her from scolding me outright. In any case, we were not the last to arrive. As I crossed the room toward where Tante Ilse sat conversing with Rachel, I noted Tim's absence.

"She looks much better," I murmured to Freddy, relieved to

see our great-aunt's color had returned and her eyes were lively as she relayed a story to my sister-in-law.

"Yes, perhaps it was just fatigue," he replied evenly, though I could tell by the look in his eyes he still reserved judgment.

"Is Ruthie with Miss Pettigrew?"

He nodded. "She refused her afternoon nap, so she's already been put to bed." He glanced toward the door. "As for Tim, I couldn't say." There was a note of disapproval in his voice, but also resignation, which made me wonder how often my younger brother tended to disappear.

Abbott appeared in the doorway promptly at 6:15, and we all turned to follow Mother and Father from the room. As we crossed the hall, I caught sight of Tim pattering down the last rise of stairs, still adjusting his bow tie. He flashed me a sheepish grin, slipping into line with the rest of us as we filed into the dining room.

The chamber remained unchanged from my grandmother's days. It was papered in dark slate-blue toile wallpaper with heavy matching drapes drawn across the large window that offered an expansive view of the dales during daylight. To compensate for the darkness, a gaslit chandelier glinted overhead, and a number of candles were lit down the length of the table as well as on the fireplace mantel. A large mirror above the hearth reflected back the light, as well as giving me a view of the portraits of my great-grandparents gracing the wall behind me.

I refrained from looking down the table toward the chair where Rob had always sat to my mother's left, the place where Rachel now settled across from her husband. Tim's tardiness had spared me a few moments of anxiety, but I could feel it stealing over me again, beating a tattoo in my ears.

As if conscious of this, Father cast me an encouraging smile as he settled his napkin in his lap. Or perhaps he was merely commiserating. I knew he'd seen the look Mother had cast my way as I entered the drawing room. Across from me, I could see Tim's shoulders braced for the coming rebuke, but Mother remained silent.

That is, until after Father uttered grace and the first course of consommé was set before us. Just as Tim was starting to relax, she slipped her spoon into her bowl of soup—barely making a ripple—as cleanly as her barbed voice sliced into my brother.

"Timothy Harold Townsend, don't fool yourself into thinking I didn't notice your tardiness." Her gaze remained trained on him as she ate a spoonful of soup before continuing in the same level tone that belied its lethal edge. "Nor have I failed to note you didn't deliver the basket to Mrs. Wild I asked you to."

He flushed, and I couldn't help but wonder just what he'd gotten up to this afternoon. He had expressed an interest in joining me and Sidney on our bicycle ride, but by the time we'd changed clothes and wheeled the cycles out of the shed in the inner courtyard where they were stored, he was nowhere to be found. We'd assumed he'd been called away to assist Father or Freddy, or had simply changed his mind. But that didn't seem to be the case.

"My apologies," he mumbled. "I forgot. I must have been up too late drinking with Verity and Freddy."

One would have thought from his guileless, hangdog expression that this confession had slipped out unheeded, but the darting glances he cast down the table made me suspect differently. One look at Freddy's tight-lipped face confirmed it. Tim's heedless words had been no accident. He'd meant to betray us, no doubt to shift attention from himself.

His pronouncement was met with predictable results.

After a fleeting look at Freddy, Mother's icy stare shifted to me. "I see. And after I made it abundantly clear how I feel about imbibing in this house."

It was on the tip of my tongue to reply that we hadn't been in the house, but I was no longer seventeen, and such a sarcastic retort would only have brought my father into the argument. Instead I channeled my ire into the glare I aimed at Tim, whose attention remained absorbed with his soup.

"I raised you to be a lady, and to behave with more decorum than that," Mother huffed. "Apparently you've forgotten that while you've been in London, what with the type of establishments you've been frequenting and the low company you've been keeping."

That she was referring to Matilda's reports when she had still worked for me, and the articles in the scandal rags and newspapers—which still penetrated into the heart of Yorkshire—was obvious. I had begun to feature in them during the midst of the war when I began venturing to the swankiest nightclubs and restaurants, partly as a means to distract myself, and partly in my role with the Secret Service, gathering intelligence. Not that my mother would ever, could ever know about that.

"Mother, you must know those scandal rags exaggerate," Freddy said.

I didn't know why I was surprised by his defending me, except he'd come to London not four months earlier to scold me about the very same thing. In any case, I was grateful, particularly as his remark had earned him a glower from his wife.

Mother ignored his comment, keeping her focus on me. "What your husband's family must think, I dare not speculate."

"I found her desire to reconnect with her brothers last night quite reasonable, admirable even," Sidney remarked, lowering his spoon before dabbing his mouth with his napkin. By his carefully controlled movements, I could tell he was restraining himself, but to the others at the table he must have seemed at ease as he flashed me a gentle smile. "I know how much she's missed them. And given the amount of time they spent outdoors growing up, it seemed perfectly natural for them to converse in the stables. Not to mention polite, so as not to wake anyone.

"As for my parents, and the rest of my family, they've never paid much heed to what is in the society papers." He reached for my hand, clasping it briefly with his own. "They've always adored Verity, and still do."

How this could be true, or how he could possibly know it if it was, was doubtful. Sidney's parents were, in the best of terms, uninvolved. I had spent only a handful of days in their company over the past five years, and one of those had been to discuss my widow's settlement after we'd received the news of his supposed death, and another to welcome his return to the living. Not for a moment did I doubt they were glad he was alive, but they seemed entirely content to be tangentially aware of his existence. Though we never discussed it, I could sense that Sidney wished there were more to their relationship than the merest formalities.

However, I would never reveal any of this to my mother. Doing so would feel like a betrayal. And so I returned his smile with a grateful one of my own.

His words forestalled my mother, but I knew it wouldn't last long. As if sensing this, my father spoke, asking after Sidney's parents and his uncles. Since Father had been the one to turn the conversation to more amenable subjects, I knew Mother wouldn't attempt to return to the subject of my drinking whisky in the barn. But I was not foolish enough to believe that meant the matter was dropped entirely.

"You're fortunate your husband is so understanding about your less-than-favorable habits," she declared the following afternoon as we set off on her round of Monday social calls.

The motorcar rocked back and forth as we rolled over the rough gouges scored at the end of the drive before turning onto the road proper. I sank back against the plush seats redolent with the scent of new leather and my mother's familiar eau de cologne, and glanced at the reflection of my parents' chauffeur in the rearview mirror. I was surprised Mother had spoken thusly in front of him, though he didn't seem to be paying us any mind. A vague recollection stirred in my brain of her telling me that one of the new servants they'd hired after the war had made it through physically unscathed but for some hearing loss, and I suspected this must be the chap.

"If you're talking about my drinking, it's not a habit, Mother," I replied evenly, determined to keep my aggravation to myself. "It's simply what people in society do."

Though, not so long ago, I couldn't have claimed the same thing, for drinking had definitely become part of my ritual. Especially during the dark months I'd believed Sidney to be dead.

Then drinking had been a means of survival, of numbing and forgetting. While I still worked for the Secret Service, I'd kept it under control, aware of my limit so that I was still capable of doing my job. But after I was demobbed, there had been no reason to regulate myself. If not for Sidney's return and that fateful house party in June, who knew where I would be?

She sniffed. "None of the society I know."

I stifled a sigh, refusing to argue this point. She would undoubtedly be shocked by the substances even the most respectable members of society were willing to indulge in. Turning to gaze out the window of the Rolls-Royce, I studied the low ceiling of clouds, which cast a pall over the landscape. Rain didn't appear to be imminent, but a stiff breeze riffled the tall grasses bordering the road and rattled the branches of the trees. One more blustery storm would finish off the last of the leaves clinging to the oaks and elms.

"I'm worried about you, Verity."

I turned to find her eyeing me with concern, and the sight of that tender emotion did much to soften my irritation with her. "There's no need, Mother. I'm well. I promise."

"So you say, and yet I see all the things they write about you in the papers. These nightclubs with their drinking and dancing and that American music."

"It's called *jazz*."

"And the murders," she exclaimed before lowering her voice. "How many have you become involved in?"

"I help to solve them," I replied sharply, resentful of the way she spoke about them, as if I was partially to blame for the deaths themselves. "And I don't keep count."

This wasn't strictly true, but I wasn't about to tout the actual numbers for her. Especially when the delineation between the deaths I could speak of and the deaths that had been part of my Secret Service work that I had to keep silent about was not always clear.

"That's my point! You've become so involved with them now you actually need to keep a tally to keep track."

"There haven't been *so* many," I argued. Though many would

say one was already too much. "And besides, you and Aunt Ernestine *asked* me to investigate the last two."

"But not to the degree it seems you did." Consternation knit her brow as she clasped her handbag tighter between her hands in her lap. "You act as if all of it is nothing but a lark."

My voice hardened. "No, I don't." I had never treated what I did as a lark. Never.

"And what of your refusal to come home?" Mother demanded, once again ignoring my response. "It took a threat to make you return."

"Imagine that," I drawled sharply. "I can't comprehend why I didn't return earlier to be subjected to such an affectionate interrogation."

Her shoulders stiffened and her mouth tightened into an angry moue, but there was a fleeting glint in her eyes that told me that beneath her affronted exterior she was genuinely hurt. "Someday when you have children of your own you'll understand." She turned to stare through the windscreen at the road ahead, her composure seeming more brittle to my eyes than it had before I'd seen that flash of pain.

My hands tightened into fists, my fingernails digging into my palms at the realization that I'd been the one to cause her such heartache. I knew I should apologize for my absence, for my snippy words, but why did she have to make it so difficult? Why was it so hard to tell her that it hadn't been so much the threat or even Tante Ilse's arrival in England that had driven me home, but the realization that it was time? That I hadn't stayed away because I didn't care—about Rob, about her, about all of them—but because I cared too much.

I sat smoothing the pleats of my navy-blue botany serge skirt, trying to force the words out, when she turned to look at me sidelong.

"You aren't expecting, are you?" she asked as her gaze slid up and down my figure, inspecting it.

I straightened my already correct posture, uncertain whether I should feel affronted or not. "No."

Her eyes lifted to scrutinize my face. "You say that with such certainty."

I frowned, vexed that she should press this. "Because I am certain."

Her chin suddenly arched. "Tell me you aren't adhering to the guidance in *that woman's* book?"

"If by 'that woman' you mean Marie Stopes, then yes. At least, to some extent," I hedged, not truly wishing to discuss this topic with my mother, whose advice to me on my wedding night had been very Victorian in nature. Fortunately, Sidney had not expected me to lie still and think of England.

Stopes was the author of the controversial book *Married Love*, and a proponent of birth control and family planning, concepts that clearly shocked my mother.

"Verity, that is both sinful and immoral."

The chauffeur glanced at us in the rearview mirror, clearly having heard her outburst, though hopefully not her exact words.

I leaned toward her, lowering my voice. "Is it so wrong that Sidney and I wish to become reacquainted before we produce a child?" I demanded to know. I refrained from confessing that when he'd first returned from the dead I hadn't been certain I even *wanted* to remain married to him, but she was not so oblivious to my thinking as I'd hoped.

"You would have had at least nine months to become reacquainted," she sniped, and then her eyes widened. "Verity Alice Townsend Kent, do not tell me you are thinking of divorce."

"No. Not now," I amended for the sake of honesty.

She shook her head. "After all he's been through."

Fury shot through my veins. "All *he's* been through? What about everything he put *me* through? Letting me believe he was dead for *fifteen months*."

"But for a very good reason."

"Maybe so, but that doesn't wipe away the pain and anguish . . ." I broke off and turned away, unwilling to expose those hurts to her when I could see she felt no sympathy for what I'd endured. "It doesn't matter," I said once I'd regained my composure. "What happens in our marriage is between me and Sidney. I just wish . . . I just wish you could show me a bit of empathy once in a while."

"You want *me* to show *you* empathy?" She scoffed. "And what about mine? Where was *my* empathy when your brother died? When you refused to come home. I see how much I mean to you. Your own mother."

I turned my head to look at her, seeing that same pain I'd witnessed earlier mixed up with the anger that shimmered in her eyes. "I know I hurt you when I didn't come home. I know I should have returned sooner. But you are not the only one who lost him. And . . ." I nearly choked trying to swallow around the lump that had risen in my throat. "And there is more than one way to grieve."

I jerked my head around just as the tear I could feel quivering at the edge of my eye spilled down my cheek, unwilling to let her see it. My heart pounded in my chest and my ears, making me feel sick. I forced myself to take deep, calming breaths while internally I ruthlessly hammered down the lid on the mental container into which I'd poured all my grief over Rob.

Under the cover of adjusting my smart blue cloche hat, I swiped the wetness from my cheek and risked a glance at my mother's reflection in the window. From the hollow ache in my breast, I recognized that part of me had hoped she might reach out to me, but instead she sat stiffly, her head turned away. All our words had done nothing to close the gap between us, but instead had only widened it.

CHAPTER 14

Purgatory was an afternoon of making social calls with my mother. Somehow, somewhere I must have sinned more egregiously than I'd ever realized, and this was to be my penance. It was brutal. It was agonizing. And it was all administered at the mercy—or lack thereof—of my mother's hands.

The same conversation topics were repeated at every home, served with the same tea and tiny sandwiches. The same questions were put to me, the only variation being how strenuously I was probed. Mrs. Redmayne had seemed prepared to bring out the thumbscrews, while Mrs. Wild had delicately hinted around the more sensitive issues, such as the deaths of so many of the young men who had been my friends and neighbors. Part of me wondered whether my mother had orchestrated matters, all in an effort to break me, but my mind balked at the notion that she could be so cruel.

Truth be told, I wouldn't have minded reminiscing with Mrs. Wild about her son, Henry. Perhaps because I knew she wasn't trying to coerce a reaction, and the fact that her tone was comforting and consoling. It wasn't that I wished to avoid talking about our lost boys all together, but I resented the topic being forced upon me, and my emotions being poked and prodded as if to examine their authenticity. Did I grieve too much or too little? Was I too cold or maudlin? Their expectations were as exhausting as my own efforts to maintain my composure.

Our final visit of the afternoon was to the Hardcastles, who lived in a pretty stone cottage near the river, its walls covered in ivy. Mrs. Hardcastle was a slim, wizened widow of about fifty. She had always been a bit of a hypochondriac, and Freddy had warned me that the war had only made it worse. It was difficult to tell whether there was something to her claims of poor health or not, but she could expound on the subject for hours if you let her. Mother, thankfully, did not. But that didn't mean Mrs. Hardcastle didn't craftily try to bring the topic of conversation back around to it time and again.

"Mrs. Kent, you look the picture of health," she declared as she settled in her chair before the partially opened window, draping enough blankets around her shoulders to nearly smother herself. The table at her elbow was covered in all manner of jars and unguents, and likely responsible for the scent of camphor and mint that filled the room along with wood smoke. She shook a finger at me. "You're incredibly lucky. Don't take that for granted."

"Yes, Verity has always been vulgarly healthy," my mother replied, drawing a frown from me. "She even avoided catching the Spanish influenza, when we all know how it rampaged through London."

I barely resisted the urge to roll my eyes. Both women had been born to a generation that prized feminine delicacy. In their minds, too hearty a constitution was seen as unladylike and a decided blight against a female. Not that they wished for me to suffer and die, but I should at least have the decency to succumb to some deficiency of health. Ironically, the fact that the Spanish influenza, which had raged throughout the world through 1918 and early 1919, had disproportionately infected and killed those who were in the prime of their lives and at the peak of their health seemed to reinforce their mindset. Better to be delicate and live than alarmingly healthy and die.

"I was terrified my Isaac would catch it, you know," Mrs. Hardcastle confided. "What, with his asthma, hay fever, and all. But by the Lord's will, he came through unscathed."

I hated that phrase. *By the Lord's will.* Why was it that the people using it were usually the ones who had come out the better in the end? I'd heard it spouted far too often these past five years. It was recited to comfort the grieving—though it truly only consoled the speaker—and offered as an explanation to the unexplainable. I refused to believe the slaughter of so many lives for so little cause had been the Lord's will. No, that was all man's doing.

"Ah, here he is now," she exclaimed as her son entered the room, oblivious to my thoughts.

I was, of course, acquainted with Isaac Hardcastle, having grown up in Hawes, but not as well as with many of the other boys. Isaac had not been allowed to play with the rest of us very often, his asthma and breathing issues often becoming inflamed from time outdoors. I remembered him as a short, scrawny fellow who stood no taller than me in my stocking feet, but apparently he was a late bloomer.

My eyes widened in surprise, for some time in the last five years he had not only grown a good six or eight inches taller, but also packed on several stone of weight. Now his figure was far more round than emaciated.

His eyes crinkled with good humor. "I look a bit different than the last time you saw me, don't I?"

I gave a startled laugh at his addressing the issue so forthrightly. "Yes, you do. How are you?"

He sank into the chair his mother indicated. "Very well. I can't complain."

Yes, I remembered that about him. While his mother voiced more complaints than the entire village, he rarely ever grumbled, even when his face was red and his breath was wheezing in and out of his chest from climbing a small hill.

"Isaac is on the parish council," Mrs. Hardcastle declared proudly, as well she might be, for the councilmen were usually older gentlemen. "And he was an administrator for the local Volunteer Training Corps."

The VTCs had served as home defense militias, their ranks filled with men over military age or prevented from volunteering to the armed services for various reasons. They were usually geographically based, but not always. I remembered hearing about one unit of deaf and mute volunteers who had drilled using sign language.

"He couldn't enlist, of course, because of his health." She reached over to pat his hand where it rested on the arm of his chair. "And he was needed here."

Isaac offered her a tight smile in response, and I couldn't help but wonder if it bothered him that he hadn't been able to serve like most of the other men his age. It was true his asthma would have made it all but impossible. No one who knew him doubted that. But that didn't mean he was pleased to have escaped military service.

"Was that your husband's Pierce-Arrow I saw on the road from Garsdale Head two days ago?" he asked in an obvious attempt to change the subject.

"Yes," I replied. "He's incredibly fond of that motorcar."

"And well he should be. Quite the goer."

"Sidney was awarded the Victoria Cross, you know," Mother said, slipping that in as she had to every conversation that day, even though I suspected most of the people had already heard this bit of news.

Then they would turn to me as Mrs. Hardcastle did. "You must be very proud."

And I would smile and say, "Yes, very proud." Which was true. I was proud. But my feelings over his receiving a medal for valor were much more complicated than that. Especially knowing how Sidney himself felt about the honor. I knew he would despise the fact that my mother was bandying it about the village repeatedly.

"I heard rumors you would be returning for the holidays," Isaac stated, redirecting the conversation yet again. "But I said I would believe it when I saw it."

"Good heavens," I laughed with forced cheer. "Don't tell me the entire village has been talking about it?" I glanced at my mother, knowing that if they had, she had been the cause of it.

She ignored me, leaning forward to answer something Mrs. Hardcastle had said as an aside.

Isaac shrugged, his eyes twinkling. "There isn't much else of interest to discuss. Surely you haven't forgotten that?"

I exhaled resignedly at his teasing. "No, I haven't." Village life could be slow. More often than not an ailing cow or a letter from a relative living far afield passed as newsworthy. I'm sure that had altered slightly during the war, but less than one might expect.

"And you've brought your great-aunt with you." His expression turned wry as he muttered under his breath, "That's set the hens, and the roosters, to clucking."

"Yes, I must say I was distressed to hear of that," Mrs. Hardcastle interjected, pressing a hand to her chest. "I was barely able to rise from bed yesterday, and so I missed services, but I was absolutely aghast to hear of there being Germans in our midst." Her mouth screwed up in affront and distaste. "After all the young men we've lost to their savagery. It's shocking."

My skin flushed with anger. I had suspected that some of the people of Hawes had discussed Tante Ilse, and Germans in general, in such a manner, but I hadn't been prepared to actually hear it. I understood they were worn out by the war and that, having no definitive target on which to fix their anger and hatred, they'd directed it toward the entire German populace. But it still made me outraged on my great-aunt's behalf that she should face such rancor simply because of her nationality.

"Frau Vischering is my husband's aunt," Mother replied calmly, though her chin had lifted so that she spoke down her nose at the other woman. "She is old and frail, and she has nothing and no one left back in Germany. Besides, she is family. As a good Christian woman, I could hardly turn her away."

"No, I suppose not," Mrs. Hardcastle relented, though I wasn't certain that in my mother's shoes she would have done the same. "And a woman of her age must be harmless. So long as there are no German men showing up, taking jobs when so many of *our* men are in need of the employment." She nodded at Isaac, making me suspect this was a common topic of discussion in their household. Though I had to wonder how many

Germans had actually shown up in the depths of Yorkshire seeking jobs. My guess was none.

"I recall Mrs. Vischering from before the war," Isaac said. "I always liked the old gal."

"Isaac, really," his mother scolded. "Your language. You've been spending too much time at the Crown." The local pub.

He appeared to take her chiding in stride. "She always seemed like a kind and generous woman," he amended. "And as Mrs. Townsend said, her being an old Christian woman in need of your care, no one should begrudge them that."

I couldn't tell whether the last was directed at me or his mother. Either way, it didn't sit well with me. My mother's cool defense and appeal to people's Christian duty had been bad enough, but hearing Isaac reiterate it in such a manner rubbed me raw.

Unable to stomach another moment of the present company, I decided it was past time to make my escape. "If you'll excuse me, I promised Miss Capshaw I would pay her a call this afternoon."

Mother turned to me in disapproval, but I pretended not to see. After all, I'd paid my respects, behaving with decorum all afternoon. But I'd danced on her puppet strings long enough. Duty done, I felt no qualms about departing now.

"Lovely to see you," I told Mrs. Hardcastle. "I'll see you at home, Mother."

"But how will you . . . ?"

"Violet will give me a ride," I assured her, though I knew no such thing. However, I didn't want Mother waiting around on me. I would find another way home if Violet wasn't capable of taking me.

"I'll walk with you." Isaac surprised me by offering, rising to his feet.

Knowing I couldn't decline without sounding churlish, I thanked him and passed through the door he held open out into the gloom of late afternoon. The clouds from earlier that day had not dispersed, so even an hour before sunset, a melancholy air hung over the countryside.

The Capshaws lived a short distance from the Hardcastles, across the River Ure, but still within sight of their cottage. I directed my steps toward the road and the bridge over the pebble-strewn waterway. Now it trickled merrily over rocks and through shallow eddies, but I knew when the rains came it could turn into a gushing torrent, pouring through the valley.

I nodded to my parents' chauffeur as we passed the Rolls, but waved him back inside when he began to open the door. Leaves scattered before us as we strode up the drive, clattering over the dirt and grass, or, occasionally lofted by the wind, whirled away. One such leaf tangled in the hat of the cyclist on the road, her head bent low over the handlebars. She looked up as she passed the drive, and I realized it was Fräulein Bauer.

"Isn't that Mrs. Vischering's maid?" Isaac asked, apparently also recognizing her.

I opened my mouth to ask how he knew, but then realized the answer was obvious. After all, strangers never went unnoticed in a village like Hawes. Especially not foreigners.

"Yes, she told me yesterday that she had some things to pick up from the chemist for my great-aunt," I explained, and then felt angry at myself for doing so. As if I needed to make excuses for Bauer's use of the bicycle and visit to the village.

"Couldn't your brother have taken care of it for her?"

I had asked the very same thing because, after all, Freddy was a doctor, but resentment stirred in my breast at Isaac for doing so. "Things other than just medicine," I replied a bit too sharply.

Isaac flushed, perhaps reading more meaning into that statement than I intended, but in the end it worked to the same purpose—discouraging his questions. "I see," he said, after clearing his throat. He'd neglected to put on a hat, and his pale hair was now riffled by the wind.

We turned to silently stroll up the road, watching as Bauer's form disappeared down the hill on the opposite side of the river. As we reached the bridge ourselves, I spotted her form again in the distance, pedaling intently onward, and it prodded at something in my brain. If Isaac had noticed Bauer so quickly, then undoubtedly he would have taken note of any other outsiders who had arrived in Hawes.

"Your duties with the parish council must keep you busy," I remarked.

He shrugged. "To some extent."

"I imagine life was quite different here during the war."

"Not as much as you'd think." He glanced sideways at me. "It seemed like our young men were always coming and going. Mostly going. And we had Land Girls coming in to help at the farms that were then short of labor. They caused a minor scandal a time or two, mainly because the local women objected to the trousers that were part of their uniform. But beyond that, it was much the same."

I contemplated this and how different London was, where the faces I'd glimpsed in the street altered every day of the year.

"Any new faces in Hawes since I left?" I asked in an off-handed voice as we stepped around the muck left in the lane by a passing horse to cut across the lawn leading up toward the Capshaws' house.

"No."

"Not even holidaymakers?"

"We did see the return of some of those this summer, but now that the weather has turned colder, and the most brilliant flush of autumn color has passed, they've disappeared again." He tilted his head. "I'd say, it's been a good three weeks since last I saw an unfamiliar face. Well, save Mr. Kent's manservant and Mrs. Vischering's maid."

I nodded, feeling less reassured by his answers than I'd hoped. If there'd been a new resident, or even a stranger seen about Hawes, then perhaps I could have at least tracked them down and discovered why they had seemed so familiar to me, and whether there was any reason to believe Tante Ilse's assertion that she'd seen the second deserter was true. Now, I was faced with two alternatives. Either there *was* an unknown man skulking about whom Isaac had not heard of or seen yet, and who had chosen to lie low rather than draw attention to himself, which was worrying in and of itself, or the man I had seen at St. Margaret's had been a child when I left town and had since grown up to look like someone familiar to me.

Although the latter would be the preferred answer, instinctively I doubted it. For one, the man I'd seen had seemed older than twenty or twenty-one, which was the oldest I estimated he could be for him to have still been boyish in appearance five years prior. For another, I had sensed he was out of place in Hawes, and yet if he resembled a former or current resident, that shouldn't be the case.

The path we'd taken skirted the trees growing alongside the river. Here amid the shade of their boughs, the air was rife with the scent of the river and the earth that lined its banks. "It's good to hear the holidaymakers have returned," I said, trying to tamp down my own frustration.

I'd known the seaside had been swamped during July and August, as everyone was eager to return to some semblance of normal after four and a half terrible years. But I admitted I'd given little thought to the impact that might have had in Hawes.

"Yes, well, fortunately our town doesn't rely on tourism. Though we anticipate that changing in the coming years."

"Oh?" I replied, listening with half an ear as he expounded on his research and plans to bolster the town's economy and revenues. From the sounds of it, he took his new duties on the parish council quite seriously. His enthusiasm and creativity could be just what the town needed, but convincing the other aging councilmen would not be easy. Not when they tended to think that the way things had always been done was the way things should continue to be done. I wished him luck.

Violet must have seen us coming up the lawn, for she came out onto her portico to greet us, a thick woolen cardigan swaddling her frame. Her dark bobbed hair was tucked behind her ears and a mischievous smile lit her eyes. "Made your escape before she could bring up her piles, didn't you?"

Isaac's already-flush cheeks reddened further, and his mouth curled in a resigned smile, clearly accustomed to her teasing. "I was in no danger of that, for Mother knows full well that Mrs. Townsend would never let her burble on about her hemorrhoids." He cut a sideways glance at me. "She saves that for Dr. Townsend."

I groaned on my brother's behalf and then laughed.

"Poor Freddy," Violet agreed. "But after all, he did choose to become a country doctor, so I suppose that goes with the territory."

She was right. Freddy could have joined the staff at a number of hospitals about the country as a surgeon, and they would have welcomed him with his distinguished war service. But instead he'd chosen to return to Hawes and take over Dr. Paley's practice. I knew part of the reason was that he would wind up here eventually anyway when he inherited Brock House, but I suspected there was more to it than that.

I thanked Isaac for his escort, and then followed Violet into the house. A vase filled with seasonal flowers graced the table in the entry, just as it always had when Mrs. Capshaw was still alive. In fact, I discovered very little of the house had changed since her death two years prior, and I wondered if that was by Violet's choice or because of her father's dictates. After all, Mr. Capshaw had never been the most congenial of men, though he did seem to hold a soft spot where his only child was concerned.

"Father is at the Crown playing backgammon, as he does every Monday afternoon," she explained as we entered the drawing room, where a tray had already been prepared with glasses, gin, sparkling water, sliced limes, and a bucket of ice. "So we can enjoy a proper hobnob without him interrupting," she declared with arched brows before lifting the tray and leading me out into the solar overlooking the gardens. After all, she *had* promised me something stronger than tea.

It was a lovely room decorated in bright white and sunny yellow, and quite the cheeriest space in the house, if not all of Hawes, even on an overcast day. While Violet set the tray on the sideboard and prepared our cocktails, I settled in a wicker chair and turned to gaze out over the gardens, admiring the neat beds and late-blooming flowers. Violet had certainly inherited her mother's green thumb, and I knew her mother would be proud of the way she'd kept things up.

"Didn't you at one time have plans to offer your services to design other people's gardens?" I asked as she handed me a gin rickey.

She nodded before taking a sip of her own drink. "Mrs. Phelps wanted to hire me to arrange the gardens at her new husband's home."

"Mr. Metcalfe's daughter?" I asked, impressed by the connection.

"Yes. But then the war dragged on, and Norman was killed." She sighed. "And there just didn't seem to be any point to it anymore."

I nodded, understanding exactly what she meant. My gaze strayed to the autumn garden once again. "Well . . . some years have passed now. Maybe you feel differently?" When she didn't balk at the question, I pressed on. "You should contact her. Find out if she's still interested."

Her gaze wandered over the pretty vegetation beyond the window, as if caressing each leaf as she gave the matter some consideration. "Perhaps I will."

I smiled encouragingly at her, and she suddenly leaned forward.

"Now, tell me. What's it like having a man like that hound you?"

CHAPTER 15

❧

It took me a moment to realize she was speaking of Sidney. From her flashing eyes and eager grin, I knew she could mean no one else, even if I felt the verb to be more appropriate to the hovering specter of Lord Ardmore or the second deserter. She couldn't possibly know of either of them.

"He hardly hounds me," I finally managed to reply with a breathy laugh.

"Well, of course. If I had a husband like that, he wouldn't need to hound me for anything either. But he does seem rather . . . intense." She sat back, a puckish smile lurking at the corners of her lips. "It just made me wonder what it would be like to have so much intensity focused solely on me."

I had never been one to blush. Not about such topics. But her words made the tips of my ears redden. "Is *this* what you talked about with the other girls in your FANY unit?"

"That and other things." Her gaze dipped to her glass, and she lifted a finger to run it around the rim. "Anything that would help us forget whatever we'd seen on that night's run."

Though it was spoken lightheartedly, I could imagine the terror of those ambulance runs. Particularly in the darkness over pocked and rutted roads, desperately trying to peer just a little bit farther than your eyes were capable of, knowing one false turn could send the vehicle careening through the mud into a water-filled shell hole. And all the while hearing and smelling the pain and horror of your injured passengers—the blood, sweat, and vomit.

After all, I'd seen the roads and experienced the conditions they were forced to drive in. I'd ridden in one of those ambulances after the shelling outside Bailleul, France, had ended, when I'd been injured after Brigadier General Bishop's temporary headquarters had been blown up.

Keen not to have our discussion descend into such morbid ponderings, I decided to answer her question, albeit rather vaguely. The details of my and Sidney's physical relationship were no one's business but our own. "It's flattering, and wonderful. And truthfully at times a little overwhelming."

She grinned. "In the best sort of way."

I couldn't halt a rather self-satisfied smirk from curling my lips. "Yes. But, what of you?" I asked after taking a drink. "Any chap catch your fancy?"

"In these parts?" She scoffed. "I'm afraid the pickings are rather slim on the ground."

As they were in many parts of Britain.

A devilish glint lit her eyes. "Though your brother Tim is quite easy on the eyes."

"And four years younger."

"Well, that's not going to stop me."

I couldn't tell whether she was being serious or merely teasing, and then I decided it didn't matter. They were both adults, and entirely capable of conducting their own relationships. Whatever I thought about it was of no consequence.

I took another sip of my gin rickey, allowing my gaze to stray toward the river and the cottage in the distance. The Rolls-Royce no longer sat in the drive, so presumably Mother had gone home. "You must see a lot of Isaac."

Violet gave a shout of laughter. "Well, don't go lumping *us* together. Isaac is all well and good, but he's not the most competent of chaps. And his mother is a bitter pill to swallow."

"That's not what I meant. But, I am curious. What do you

mean he's not the most competent? Are we talking romantically?"

She recoiled.

I shook my head at her antics. "Or in general? He was elected to the parish council after all."

"Because no one ran against him."

"You mean . . ."

"They felt sorry for him." She gestured with her glass toward town, presumably indicating the older gentlemen in our community, the likes of her father and mine. "They wanted to give him something to do since he couldn't serve, on account of his health, so they got him elected to the parish council."

I sat back in slightly sickened astonishment.

"They meant well," Violet continued, her own fervor dampening. "His mother practically keeps him chained to her side because of her poor health, playing on his duty to her as well as his own ailments. You remember how rarely he was allowed to play with us all. And when he was, how he more often than not made a hash of it by repeating his mother's criticisms. He's not gotten any better about that."

I grimaced. "Which I'm sure goes over well with the council."

"Like a load of bricks." She sighed. "In truth, I feel sorry for him. He's a nice enough chap. If only he could escape his mother. The war might have helped him there . . ."

"But his body betrayed him," I finished for her.

She nodded.

Poor Isaac, I thought, and then immediately cringed. Everyone, it seemed, pitied him. Including me.

I wondered if he knew. If he was aware of the motivations behind his election to the parish council and the way we all thought of him. Recalling his kind smile and the enthusiasm he'd exhibited when talking about his plans to entice more holidaymakers, I suspected not. But then, maybe he was just good at hiding it. After all, he'd been met with the same looks and comments all his life.

Either way, I vowed to stop looking at Isaac as such a pitiful figure. He might have been dealt a bad hand, but he'd done his best with it. That was something to be admired.

Violet and I enjoyed chatting for another hour until her father returned home, then she happily gave me a lift back to Brock House in his motorcar. She lifted her hand in a jaunty wave as she drove back down the drive. Tabitha came to greet me as I entered the courtyard, and I leaned down to scratch behind her ears before prodding her toward the house. I could see through the window above the entry that a lamp was lit in our bedchamber, and I wondered how Sidney had entertained himself that afternoon. I was headed toward the stairs to find out, when my mother called out to me from the drawing room.

Stumbling to a stop, I took a calming breath before retracing my steps. "Yes, Mother?" I queried as I continued to remove my gloves, braced for another lecture.

Perched on the sofa near the hearth, she removed a pair of gold-rimmed spectacles from her eyes and lifted the letter she'd been reading. "Grace will be returning from Everleigh Court on Friday. She'll be arriving on the 4:15 train. I want you to collect her from the station."

It took me a moment longer than it should have to respond because my attention was still focused on the fact that my mother had been wearing eyeglasses after years of insisting she didn't need them. When had that changed?

It was a sharp and unexpected reminder of all that I'd missed in the last five years. Like Grace growing up. She was no longer eleven, but sixteen—a young lady traveling home from finishing school.

My mother's eyebrows arched, recalling me to the fact that she was still awaiting my response.

"All right," I finally stammered past the confusing swirl of emotions in my chest. For the first time, I found myself wondering if I'd lost more by staying away than by forcing myself to face Rob's absence and death.

"I'll write to her then to inform her you'll be there."

I nodded and turned to go, ignoring the puzzled furrow of

her brow. I knew I was acting strange, but I couldn't seem to help it. Not when I was struggling to comprehend this new and sudden aching sense of loss.

As I rounded the landing and began to climb the second flight of stairs on silent feet, I heard low voices above me in the upper foyer near the entry to the servants' stairs. I couldn't make out what they were saying, but their sharp whispers indicated it wasn't precisely a pleasant conversation. I craned my neck to see beyond the banister as my head grew level with the floor to discover Matilda standing over Bauer, pointing a finger in her face. However, contrary to what I'd expected, the girl did not cower, but glared fiercely back at the older maid, her hands clenched into fists by her side. So Tante Ilse's little maid had more spunk in her than I'd realized. Good for her.

"You mind your own matters," Bauer retorted. "You know nothing."

"Oh, I know plenty. You think . . ." Matilda broke off at the sight of me, her narrowed eyes tightening further. "Just know that I see plenty," she snapped before turning to disappear.

Bauer's gaze met my own, her features tight with residual anger. Before I could speak, she hurried away, a silver gown draped over her arm, undoubtedly for Tante Ilse. Clearly she didn't wish to be reassured again, but perhaps it was time I had a discussion with Matilda.

I opened the door to our bedchamber to find Sidney buttoning a crisp white shirt over his chest. Through the remaining gap I could see the dark whirls of his chest hair. The hair on his head was still damp, its unruly waves tamed, and I could smell the bay rum of his aftershave.

Seeing him thus, in his bare feet with his shirt untucked, I was struck again by how intolerably handsome he was. Dropping my hat, gloves, and reticule on the bed, I crossed to him, arching up on my toes to kiss his lips.

"And just what have you been up to?" I teased, trailing a finger along his freshly shaven jaw.

"Freddy and I went for a hard gallop, and then spent an hour or so playing billiards."

"Hence the bath." I tucked a stray hair back in place. "That's nice," I ruminated, and meant it. After all, he and Freddy had been close friends long before we began courting and then married. Yet they hadn't spent much time together since the war broke out.

Sidney's lips quirked upward at one corner. "Just how many gin rickeys did you have this afternoon with Miss Capshaw?" he asked, having known of my plans to pay a call on her after my mother was finished with me.

"Not enough to be considered incapacitated." After all, I could still walk a straight line and my words weren't slurred. "But probably one more than I should have," I conceded. I smoothed my hands down the fine lawn of his shirt where it stretched over his broad chest. "Why? Are my cheeks flushed?" A curse of my auburn tresses.

"A little. But you're definitely more . . . pliant."

"Hmm," I hummed in reply, studying his full lips. "Speaking of pliant, my mother asked me to collect my sister from the train station Friday afternoon."

"Then since we'll be headed in that direction anyway, shall we make plans to visit that chap in Kendal earlier that day? The one Xavier tracked down for us?" The man who might hold answers about the bomb that had killed Brigadier General Bishop and most of his staff.

"Yes, let's," I replied, my mood sobering. I sank down on the edge of the bed with a sigh. "Though I'm still not sure what, if anything, he can tell us."

"It's worth asking."

"Of course."

I tipped over sideways, resting my head on my pillow, suddenly conscious of how tired I was. I hadn't slept well since our arrival, my mind too conscious of what, or rather *who* was missing to slumber deeply. I might be sleeping in my childhood bedchamber, but everything felt different. *I* was different. And somewhere inside me I was still struggling to reconcile all of that.

I slid my hand under the pillow to grasp it, only to encounter something. I stilled and then pushed myself upright.

"What is it?" Sidney asked, noting my odd behavior.

I pulled a folded piece of paper from beneath the pillow and lifted my gaze to meet his. I could tell from his expression that he hadn't placed it there. A sinking feeling began in my stomach. Slowly opening it, I read the single line of stark text.

I know what you did.

My insides turned cold and I blinked, as if that might change the words. Sidney reached for the paper, and I allowed him to take it from my numb fingers while I turned the sentence over and over in my mind.

Given our conversation in the billiards room the previous day, my first thought was naturally of the second deserter and Ardmore. But how could he have entered the house and found his way to our bedroom without being seen? There were six people in residence in the main house, and over a dozen servants coming and going throughout the day.

Sidney lowered the paper, searching my face. "It must have been placed here while I was out riding."

"That makes sense." For then they would have faced the smallest chance of being caught. "But they still took a helluva risk sneaking into the house."

"You're thinking of the deserter?"

"How can I not?"

He nodded, looking at the paper once more. "Perhaps he had an accomplice."

I considered his words carefully. "Yes, that makes sense. A servant would have an excuse to be in and out of chambers. Particularly a maid." I frowned, my suspicions immediately shifting to Matilda. I could well imagine her taking delight in seeing me accused of some wrongdoing.

But her loyalty was to my mother first and foremost, and I struggled to see her playing the part of accomplice to such a scheme. She would be more likely to take the note directly to

Mother, along with whatever information the sender had conveyed to her.

I shook my head, feeling anger rise within me. I snatched the note back from him, staring down at the words again. "What is this supposed to mean anyway? 'I know what you did'?"

"It is rather vague."

"It's *extremely* vague. That could mean a hundred different things." I turned the white paper over. "And there's no other markings, no clue as to what they actually mean. And no direct threat." Only the implied one.

Sidney crossed his arms over his chest. "You think it's bogus?"

"I think taken alone it's fishy." I tossed the paper aside. "And why would you go to the risk of sneaking such a vague note into the house when you could get your entire message across, in a more thoroughly threatening manner, in a single letter."

"To keep you on edge."

My gaze lifted to his. "Maybe," I conceded. "But I still say it's all rather slapdash."

He sank down beside me on the bed. "Then I suppose there's nothing for it but to wait and see." Whether more notes appeared. Whether they took that risk.

I nodded, still puzzling over it, trying to understand their motivations.

"Hey!" He nudged his shoulder into mine. "Don't fret over it. If this is a ploy by Ardmore, that's exactly what he wants you to do."

"You're right. I refuse to let this trouble me," I stated firmly, though whether I could actually hold fast to that declaration remained to be seen. "What were we talking about before?"

"My bathing, and your pliancy." His midnight-blue eyes twinkled with roguish intent as he leaned toward me. All the better to distract me, I supposed.

"Right." My gaze fell to his lips again. "How long is it until dinner?"

"Long enough."

CHAPTER 16

Four days later, we arrived on the outskirts of Kendal shortly before midday. The journey had taken longer than expected due to the driving rain and gusty winds. It was a thoroughly dreich day, as the Scot who had been assigned to the desk next to mine at the Secret Service offices in Whitehall Court would say—wet, dismal, and dreary. I huddled inside my warm Donegal tweed coat and matching forest-green Torin-style side cap wondering if I might have been better off wearing my dowdy mackintosh.

As I shifted position for perhaps the fourth time in the last five minutes, Sidney's concentration darted from the road beyond the rain-splattered windscreen to me. "Nervous?" he asked, before taking another drag from his Turkish cigarette.

"Yes." I still didn't know precisely what I was going to say to this man we were meeting.

He stubbed out his fag and then reached over to touch my knee. "He must be a decent enough chap. Helped you out of that rubble, and stayed with you until after the shells stopped falling, and they could get you sent off to the hospital, didn't he?"

"He did. But remember he thought I was just a French refugee. What's he going to say when he realizes that's not the truth?"

"He'll probably be surprised, but I'll be right beside you. My war-hero status should count for something," he muttered wryly. "Is this the turn?"

Having skirted around the base of the hill on which perched

the ruins of Kendal Castle, its crumbling walls barely visible in the gloom, I could see we were now approaching the River Kent. "It should be."

We'd learned that Sergeant George Williams had worked as an auctioneer clerk before the war in a handsome whitewashed brick building east of the river. Though we were able to locate the address swiftly enough, I had misgivings we would find Williams inside, but hoped the staff might be able to tell us where we could track him down.

Sidney parked along the curb a stone's throw from the entrance, and held an umbrella over our heads as we dashed toward the door. Little good it did with the wind gusting the rain into our faces. He fumbled with the closure by the door while I attempted to brush the worst of the water from my clothes and repair my appearance. As such, I was the first to get a look at the man in a gray suit who strode through the door leading deeper into the office.

Even though I had only seen Sergeant Williams covered in sweat and grime, a helmet crammed down on his head, I recognized him immediately. And when he spoke, it removed any lingering doubt.

"Terrible weather we're having," he remarked in his mild Lancashire accent. "Not fit for . . ." He stumbled to a stop as his words dried up. His eyes scoured my features, clearly recognizing me, but unable to recall why.

It was those eyes that so identified him. Not that they were particularly distinctive, being naught but a muddy shade of brown. But because they had looked so directly into my own as he'd screamed into my face, trying to get me to move from the spot where I'd been thrown from the explosion after he and his men had dug me out of the debris. My ears had still been ringing, and I'd been unable to hear what he'd said. And later, when we'd cowered in the makeshift trench nearby, our eyes locked with each other's and his hand clutching mine, while shells continued to fall all around us.

I watched his face now, bracing for the moment he realized

who I was. It didn't come to him straightaway. I supposed I'd been beaten up pretty badly the last time he'd seen me—covered in blood and dirt, my cheek swollen from a blow. In fact, he appeared to recognize Sidney first when he approached to stand beside me, from the photographs in the newspaper. Consequently, perhaps he also recognized me in that capacity first. But I could see his mind was still searching for the other context in which he knew me as he extended his hand to my husband.

"Mr. Kent, a pleasure to meet you. How may I help you?"

"Sergeant Williams, I presume?"

If he was surprised we knew his name, he didn't show it.

"Lately with the Lancashire Fusiliers."

This made him straighten up and take more notice.

"It's my wife who needs your help, actually."

His eyes darted to me again, confusion shimmering in their depths.

"Perhaps if you imagine me a little . . . ," I began, only to break off as his eyes flared wide in shock.

"You . . . ," he gasped, stumbling back a step as his gaze flicked up and down over my appearance before homing in on my face once again. "You survived, then?"

"Yes," I replied. "In part, thanks to you."

Though my injuries had not been severe, they might have been much worse had he and his men not unearthed me from that rubble. Or had he not propelled me toward that makeshift trench. I hadn't had the presence of mind to note which pile of debris I'd been buried under, but when the shelling ended and we'd emerged from the ditch, I could see that the shells had destroyed large swathes of the surrounding area.

He blinked several times, his thoughts plainly struggling to catch up to the revelation of who I was. "But how . . . ? What . . . ? *Why* were you there?"

I looked to Sidney for guidance, waiting on him to exert that war-hero status he'd alluded to.

"Is there a place we can discuss this in private?" he asked.

Williams appeared at first as if he would like to argue, but then he glanced behind him before shutting the door through which he'd entered. He gestured toward the desk to his left. "Miss Lacey is currently out, so I'm afraid I must monitor the door and telephone. But there are no scheduled appointments, so we shouldn't be disturbed. Not on a day like this."

The auctioneer's reception area was nicely appointed, if spare, with shelves filled with brochures and a number of ficus plants. Two comfortable leather chairs sat before a broad desk, with a row of file cabinets lining the walls behind, and a smaller escritoire situated in the corner bearing a typewriter concealed by a dark dust cover.

"I know you must have a number of questions," I began as we took our seats. "But unfortunately, I can't answer most of them."

His mouth pinched.

I glanced at Sidney. "However, I hope the fact that you are aware of who my husband is, that the strength of his reputation will in some part vouch for me."

His gaze bounced back and forth between us, seeming to weigh and assess us. That he held at least some measure of respect for my husband was obvious from the glint in his eyes. I could only presume he'd read all about Sidney's dashing exploits during the end of the war, and how he'd captured and exposed a ring of traitors. The details had been splashed all over the newspapers when the story broke in June and just a month earlier when he'd received his Victoria Cross. Though Williams hadn't seemed to have connected the wife on Sidney's arm in those photographs with the woman he'd helped outside Bailleul, France, before now.

He grudgingly conceded with a heavy sigh, "I suppose I can safely assume you weren't actually a French refugee."

Though this wasn't phrased as a question, he still seemed to expect an answer, but I couldn't give him one, not so openly. After a moment he seemed to realize this. He turned his head to the side, swiping a hand over his mouth as he surveyed the deserted street outside the rain-lashed window. Nonetheless, I suspected his thoughts were really on a muddy road outside Bailleul in April 1918.

"Why are you here, then?" he asked as he turned back to face me somewhat warily.

"You were questioned after the incident?" I verified, trusting he knew what I was talking about without having to spell it out for him.

"Yes, though I never heard if the matter was ever resolved."

"It wasn't. Due to conflicting information and lack of evidence."

What there might have been had been destroyed or compromised by the shells that had fallen, and then the brief infiltration of the Germans into the area before the Allies had pushed them back for what proved to be the final time, and the prelude to the end of the war.

"But some new information has come to light that might help in determining precisely what happened," I continued, brushing a stray trickle of water from my cap off my brow.

"Then why isn't someone from the War Office speaking to me?"

It was a legitimate question, and one I didn't truly have a satisfactory answer for.

"They hopefully will be in short order." My gaze met Sidney's. "But they may need a bit more convincing that there's adequate reason to reopen the case."

He ruminated over this for a moment, his fingers tapping on the edge of the desk in obvious agitation. Sidney extracted his battered silver cigarette case—a gift from me before he set off for war—from inside his inner coat pocket and extracted a fag before offering one to Williams. He accepted, nodding his thanks, before both men went about the rituals of lighting them.

As he exhaled a stream of smoke, Williams's shoulders dropped and he seemed to decide in our favor. "What do you want to know?"

"The initial explosion. The one that sent me flying through the air. What do you remember about it?"

He frowned. "I'm not sure I understand what you mean."

I clasped my hands more tightly in my lap as I tried to find the words to explain. "I was so dazed." Both from being hurled through the air and from the fact that, immediately before the blast, the man who had escorted me from the temporary headquarters after I'd delivered C's missive to General Bishop had then pulled me behind an adjoining shed and slammed my head against the wall in his quest for information about my presence there. "My ears were ringing. I couldn't even hear you screaming at me directly in my face."

"I'd forgotten that," he admitted. "We had to pull the roof of that shed off you. And then all hell broke loose."

Sidney visibly flinched. "Go on," he urged, though his complexion was a shade paler than normal.

I stared at the potted plant on the corner of the desk as I thought back. "I remember running to that makeshift trench with you. I remember the other bodies. And I remember the shells." We'd lain in that ditch for hours, waiting for the bombardment to end, just a small taste of what these men, what all our boys, had endured for years. "But I don't remember much of anything about the explosion that destroyed the HQ." I searched Williams's face. "I thought it was caused by a shell because of what happened after, but I've since begun to doubt that. Do you know . . . ?" I couldn't seem to complete the sentence, and fortunately he didn't need me to.

"It wasn't a shell," he stated definitively, his gaze stark.

I exhaled, only just realizing I'd been holding my breath. This was proof, then. Before now I'd had to rely on my own doubts, prodded by the nightmares of the event I'd kept reliving, and the word of Major Scott—the man who had accosted me outside that temporary HQ. That Scott had accused me of planting the bomb, while I had believed he was the traitor among General Bishop's staff we'd been warning him about, only muddied the waters further. But Williams's account could be considered impartial testimony. Or at least as impartial as could be found, under the circumstances.

"What else do you remember?" I prodded again when he didn't continue.

"Not much."

"Just go back over it anyway. Tell us anything you can recall, even if it seems inconsequential."

He looked to Sidney as if for confirmation from a superior officer, which I supposed he was, even now, and my husband nodded.

"How did you come to be there?" I prompted.

Williams sank deeper in his chair, taking another drag on his cigarette. "We were being sent up the line as reinforcements. The brass expected the Germans to resume their push that night, and we'd been sent at the last to shore up a weak spot along the line. We'd been marching for hours and the captain had just ordered us to halt and given us our ease for a few minutes while he conferred with some other officers. I was leaning against a stack of crates, smoking a fag . . ." He gestured with the one currently gripped between his fingers. "When we saw a woman emerge from the hovel across the road we later learned was a temporary HQ." He nodded at me. "You."

"Did you have a clear line of sight to the door?" Sidney asked.

He shrugged one shoulder. "Clear enough, as there was a bit of a lull in the traffic marching up and down the road at that moment. In any case, despite all the refugees we'd passed fleeing the Germans' advance, the sight of a female in those surroundings did not go unnoticed. Especially when the officer she emerged with yanked her behind an adjoining shed." His gaze dipped as he tapped the ash from his cigarette into a pewter dish and then pushed it forward to the edge of the desk so that Sidney might use it. "I'm afraid some of the men started making rather crude insinuations about why you were there, and I didn't stop them. They were all keyed up for what was to come, and I figured it was better to let them blow off a bit of steam."

This last was evidently said for Sidney's benefit. I could only guess what lewd remarks had been made, but I was certain my husband was fully aware.

"Though it didn't look to me as if you'd gone willingly." There was a question in his eyes and I answered it.

"I didn't."

He nodded. "But then another man exited from the HQ."

I sat forward at this pronouncement.

"I didn't get a clear look at him because a pair of wagons came rattling past, but he was an officer. That much was clear."

His uniform would have differentiated him, and in any case, if he'd emerged from the HQ after me, he would have had to have been one of the officers on General Bishop's staff.

"Was he in a hurry?"

He shook his head. "No, he just strode out of it past the sentries, even paused for a moment to speak to our captain, who was approaching. Then he walked on. I would say it was only a matter of five seconds later that the HQ exploded. Knocked us all flat."

"Did your captain identify the officer?" For surely, he'd been questioned.

Williams's expression turned grim. "The old man was killed in the blast, along with another officer of the line and the sentries. As well as the men inside," he amended.

I sat back in shock. I had known about Bishop and his five subordinates, but none of the others. Then ten men had lost their lives in that explosion. Just moments after another officer had walked away.

I looked at Sidney, still trying to grapple with this revelation. "And you reported all this when they interviewed you after the incident?" I asked Williams.

"Aye. Not wot they seemed to do much about it." He leaned forward to tap off some more ash. "Though, as you said, I suppose with the shells having blown everything to pieces and the Jerries having overrun it all, it complicated matters."

Yes, but surely the testimonies they did have, attesting that the explosion had not been a shell, but a bomb, and Williams's and possibly others' assertions that they'd seen an officer leave the HQ just moments before the blast, would have been enough to detain the man. Had they at least interrogated him? And if so, why hadn't Alec alerted us to his existence when he'd found Williams's name in the records?

Unless he hadn't gained access to the official records, but uncovered Williams's identity another way.

Whatever the case, we needed to view those records. Who knew what other revelations they might contain, including this mystery officer's name.

"The rest I think you know," Williams said, taking one last drag before stubbing out his cigarette.

I met his gaze levelly across the expanse of the desk. "I never got to say it before, but thank you." I took a shaky breath as emotion began to stir in my breast. "Thank you for helping me that day. I'm glad you were there."

If he'd noticed the waver in my voice, he was kind enough not to mention it, responding with a simple nod.

We pushed to our feet, and Sidney stepped forward to shake his hand while I took a moment to compose myself.

"Hopefully we won't be the only ones to speak to you about this, but if you should think of anything else in the meantime, please send word." I passed him one of my calling cards. "You can reach us at this number and address, and if we're not in London, they'll know where to forward your message."

He glanced at it before sliding it into his trouser pocket. "I will."

Sidney and I were silent as we motored away from Kendal, each of us lost in our own ruminations as rain steadily drummed on the roof of the Pierce-Arrow. For my part, I was already composing what I was going to say when I telephoned the number given to me by C from the train station. The number I was to use whenever I needed to report anything urgent or schedule a meeting in my unofficial capacity as an agent for C and the Secret Service.

"I'm still grappling with the fact that an officer was witnessed leaving the temporary HQ just moments before it exploded and yet the matter was still left unsolved," I huffed in astonishment, gazing out at the gloomy landscape of fields and forest.

"Yes, but consider the facts from the investigators' standpoint," Sidney replied. "They had no physical evidence to speak of, it all being lost or destroyed by the shells and advancing Germans. What statements they did have from witnesses were conflicting." He glanced at me. "Presumably you weren't the only one to believe the HQ had been destroyed by a shell. I imagine that officer claimed the same thing to cover his tracks." He tipped his head to the side. "Add to that the fact that shells *did* begin to fall soon after, and the realization that there were much more pressing matters to contend with—namely halting and repelling the Germans' advance—and I think it's easy to understand why the inquiry was never resolved."

"I take your point," I grumbled. "Though now that I recognize that the HQ wasn't destroyed by a shell, a fact corroborated by Williams and Scott, I think the case against this unnamed officer needs to be reexamined. He might be the very traitor C had sent me there to warn Bishop about."

Sidney adjusted his grip on the driving wheel, narrowing his eyes to peer more clearly through the rain-splattered windscreen. "Yes, but what of the bomb itself? Did this mystery officer simply have it on hand, ready to be used at a moment's notice should his identity be threatened or discovered?"

I could appreciate that he was playing devil's advocate, but I stiffened in affront all the same. "Why not? He could have kept it stored with his dispatch case or his kit. Somewhere near his person. And after seeing me and surmising my reason for being there, put his plan into motion."

"So he set some sort of timed explosive, a pencil detonator or what have you—without anyone noticing—and then simply waltzed out the door?"

"Why not?" I countered again. "If Bishop and most of his staff officers were absorbed with going over the plans for the night's offensive, as they seemed to be when I barged in on them minutes before, then why couldn't it have happened that way? Perhaps he made some excuse to leave the HQ or maybe just walked out of his own accord. I don't know. What was the general's reaction likely to have been? Would he have ordered his sentries to detain him or even shoot him?"

Sidney gave the matter some consideration. "If, as you suggested, Bishop and most of his staff were distracted, then he wouldn't have noticed until the officer was already at the door or out of it. He might have called after him, or even sent one of the other staff officers after him, but it's highly doubtful he would have ordered the sentries to abandon their posts or open fire. Depending on his relationship with the officer in question, he might have even given him the benefit of the doubt and decided to call him on the mat for his behavior later."

"Even after he'd just been informed that he had a traitor among his staff?"

Sidney's resigned gaze shifted to meet my more skeptical one before returning to the road. "Even then. I had no direct experience with General Bishop, but if he was like many of the officers of his rank, then he believed his knowledge and opinions were superior to what anyone else might tell him. Especially about his own men. He may have taken the information in the letter you delivered under advisement, but given the fact that he knew he was on the cusp of battle, it's doubtful he would have taken any action."

I felt mildly stunned. For such a revelation was not just baffling to me, it was infuriating. After all, I'd risked my life to relay that intelligence to General Bishop. Did he honestly think that C would have sent an agent, a *female* agent, into the very heart of the line of retreat without being certain of the information contained in his missive?

Perhaps I spluttered, or perhaps my pale complexion betrayed my fury. Either way, Sidney seemed aware of it, for he tempered the matter-of-fact tone of his voice in an attempt to console me. "It's just the way things were."

I swallowed the scathing retort that had been building at the back of my throat, knowing Sidney was not to blame, and did not deserve the sharp edge of my tongue. Instead I focused my gaze on the rain-washed fields and undulating hills beyond the window, the tips of the fells lost in the gloom and low cloud cover.

Several moments passed before Sidney ventured his next comment. "So we've proven it's possible this mystery officer is responsible. But do we have any idea who he was? He would have to be a cool cucumber, striding out of the HQ as Williams described, and pausing to speak with that captain. He must have known precisely how much time he would have before the bomb went off." He braked as we rounded a curve to be confronted with a lumbering lorry. "You entered the HQ. Do you recall any of their faces?"

Rather than answer immediately, I continued to stare out the window, though what I saw before me was not the English countryside but rather a hovel in France lit by the yellow glow of lanterns swinging from their hooks on the wooden beams overhead. I could see General Bishop's face before me, measuring, scrutinizing. But as for the other men, they all melted together in a blurry haze. Even those who had drawn their pistols and pointed them at me as I rushed past the sentries and down the three short steps into the temporary HQ.

I waited until Sidney had maneuvered the Pierce-Arrow around the lorry at a place where the road widened before speaking. "I don't."

His gaze darted toward me before returning to the road.

"Surprising, isn't it?" I turned back to the window. "All that training. All those missions during the war where I can still recall every minor, insignificant detail. And yet, I can't recall something that might prove to be so important."

"No one is infallible, Ver," he said gently, though I could still sense the curiosity lurking at the edges of his words as he wondered why this incident was different. Why I'd failed to note all those fine particulars.

It was only a matter of seconds before he would recall that the incident had occurred a few weeks after I'd received the telegram informing me of his supposed death. By all rights, I shouldn't have been charged with such a fraught task, but I had begged C to let me keep working. I'd argued that it was what he would have demanded of the men on his staff, and so I should be no different. I'd been desperate to distract myself from the hollow, aching pit of my grief by doing something useful, and so he'd relented.

But I'd realized soon enough that it had been a mistake. I wasn't ready. I was distracted and reckless, tempting fate to end my suffering. In truth, had Major Scott not pulled me aside to question me, had that bomb not exploded and the shells begun falling, had I been escorted to the rear of the line of fleeing refugees as I was supposed to be, I'm not sure I wouldn't have just lain down in a ditch and stayed there until death claimed me.

However, Sidney didn't need to know all that. He didn't need those memories of my misery heaped on his head, not when I'd already accepted his deception as necessary and forgiven him. So I swiftly turned the subject.

"Well, fortunately the records should contain the information we seek. When we reach the train station at Garsdale, I'm going to telephone London and find out what they can dig up for us. I'm sure C will want to know." If he didn't know already.

The cynical thought lodged in my brain, for C was nothing but thorough. After everything that had happened with Major Scott a month prior and the information I'd brought to him, I couldn't imagine he hadn't already read the investigation reports. And if he'd done so, he should already be aware of the mystery officer and Sergeant Williams's claims about him. But then why hadn't he informed me of it? And why hadn't the inquiry been officially reopened?

CHAPTER 17

The train station itself was all but deserted when we arrived at half past three, even though the rail yard and accompanying buildings still bustled with activity. As such, the stationmaster said he was more than happy to allow me to use the telephone. He even accepted Sidney's offer to step out with him for a smoke, the rain having stopped falling about thirty minutes prior. I flashed my husband a smile of gratitude, grateful for the privacy. I'd been trained how to relay my coded number and letters through what seemed to be normal sentences, though nothing could prevent them from sounding stilted and at times bizarre.

Having rung up the private number set aside for just such a purpose, and requested a return call to this number, all I could do was wait. I imagined the secretary who'd transcribed the message passing it off to her superior, who then delivered it to an errand boy to be run over to Kathleen Silvernickel's desk. As C's secretary, Kathleen read all such correspondence first, often deciding what urgently required his attention and what did not.

At one time, my desk had been positioned next to hers as I'd analyzed and correlated the CX reports from the field before passing on the data to C and the other officers. At least, that was what I'd done before I'd taken on increasingly more frequent and demanding field work. Until I'd been demobbed earlier that year like most of the women who had worked for the various intelligence agencies. Kathleen was one of the few to remain.

I stood shivering in the drafty train station—the wood-burning stove in the corner not being large enough to provide much heat—and waited for the telephone to ring. I wasn't certain how long I would have to wait, though I hoped the call would come before the arrival of my sister's train. Circumstances being what they were, I didn't anticipate her being particularly pleased to see me. After all, I hadn't precisely been the most attentive and caring of sisters, and Mother had forced her to leave Everleigh Court a fortnight before the end of the term. Add to that the fact that Grace was only sixteen, and I was prepared for a very chilly if not outright antagonistic reception.

When the telephone did ring, I picked it up immediately, flashing the stationmaster a smile through the window before Sidney distracted him once again.

"Garsdale railway station," I spoke into the mouthpiece.

"What do you have for us, Lorelei?" the voice over the line asked in crisp tones, using my code name.

I wasn't shocked to hear Kathleen's warm voice. For the past few months, while recuperating from an injury, Alec had been assigned as my handler. But now that he was in Ireland, they would have to find someone else trustworthy for the clandestine job, since officially I was still decommissioned. Until then it fell to Kathleen.

"The bombing of Brigadier General Bishop's temporary HQ in April 1918. I just spoke with witness Sergeant George Williams about it, and he claims an officer departed the HQ moments before it exploded," I told her, rattling off the facts as succinctly as I could, and trusting she was already well-informed of the events that had come before. "I need access to the official investigation records. Specifically the name of that officer, and whether any of the other witnesses corroborated Williams's story. As well as a list of who else was interviewed."

"I'll see what we can do."

My breath quickened. There had been a slight hesitation in Kathleen's voice—one that most people wouldn't have noticed— but I knew her too well.

She knew something. Possibly even the answers to my questions. However, she would have to get C's permission before she shared any of it with me. It was standard procedure.

"Of course," I replied before giving her my parents' telephone extension. "You can reach me there. Unless it's something particularly sensitive," I added at the last. "Then we might want to make alternative arrangements."

If Kathleen found this suggestion surprising, she didn't say so. But perhaps she thought I was merely concerned with one of my family members eavesdropping. Instead, I was thinking of Ardmore, whom we'd suspected of tapping our telephone in London, or bribing one of the telephone operators to listen in to our conversations. It was almost certain he knew we were in Yorkshire at my parents' home, and as such, what was to stop him from having their telephone monitored as well?

We rang off just as the stationmaster and Sidney returned inside, and then we settled in to wait for the 4:15 train.

However, the 4:15 came and went, and yet Grace did not disembark. At first I thought perhaps I was simply unfamiliar with my sister's appearance and so searched the faces of the few people who had arrived at the station again. Yet, none of them were of the appropriate age or sex to be my sister. I stood on the platform, frowning as the train continued on down the line toward Carlisle.

"Maybe she missed the train," Sidney suggested.

"It's possible."

She might even have done so deliberately. Perhaps this was her way of foiling Mother's insistence she return home early.

Seeing our confused expressions, the stationmaster bustled over, fretting to himself. "Oh me, oh my. I should have thought. You were Miss Verity Townsend before you married Mr. Kent, weren't you?"

"Yes," I replied uncertainly.

He wrung his hands, the chain of his pocket watch clinking. "Oh, well, I do beg your pardon. I should have recalled that before now. And I suppose you're here to collect Miss *Grace* Townsend."

"Yes," I repeated, finding myself having to exercise great restraint not to snap at the man to get to the point.

"I'm afraid she arrived on the 1:29 train."

I stiffened. "Then where is she now? Did she use the telephone to call someone to come and get her?"

"Oh, no. There was a chap waiting here for her. Nice fellow in a pin-striped suit. Took her off in a Crossley."

I shared a speaking look with Sidney and then thanked him.

"Apologies for the confusion," he called after us as we hurried off, arm in arm.

"Do you think it was a matter of miscommunication?" my husband asked as he opened the door of the Pierce-Arrow for me.

"No, I do not." If Grace was anything like me or our brothers, it was not a mistake.

"Then . . . ?" he began as he slid into his own seat.

"She planned this all along," I stated with certainty, crossing my arms over my chest while anger simmered inside my veins.

"And the chap who picked her up?"

"Bolingbroke." Grace's beau whom Freddy and Tim had mentioned.

Sidney nodded, seeming to accept this as easily as I had. But I didn't miss the grin he was attempting to hide as he turned the electric starter.

I scowled. "You find this amusing?"

"Only because I can imagine you doing the exact same thing at her age."

My first instinct was to refute this, but after a moment's deliberation, I had to concede he was right. That is, if the man in question had been Sidney, and I had an older sister I wished to aggravate. I wondered for a moment how serious Grace was about this Bolingbroke fellow, or if she was just *that* determined to thwart Mother and hurt me, as I imagined my disinterest had hurt her.

Sidney chuckled as he pulled onto the road. "What? No argument?"

"You're right," I replied evenly, my anger having cooled somewhat with these realizations.

"What was that?" He leaned toward me, holding a hand up to his ear. "Say that again?"

I narrowed my eyes at his teasing. "You're correct. I only have to think back to that summer before the war, and all the mischief we got up to." I turned my head to stare at his handsome profile. "I'm afraid I rather lost my head where you were concerned."

His deep blue eyes met mine, softening with some tender emotion before he turned back to the road.

"Though I promised myself I wouldn't," I added in chagrin.

His hand briefly stole into mine where it rested in my lap. "I lost my head, too, Ver."

"Did you?" My brow furrowed, not in criticism, but uncertainty. "I'm not so sure."

His gaze darted between me and the road, as if trying to decipher my tone. From the manner in which his jaw hardened, it was clear he didn't like what I'd said. "You consider me to be an honorable gentleman, don't you, Ver? An upstanding fellow?"

"Yes, of course," I replied, surprised this was his response. "Sidney, I didn't mean to offend . . ."

"You could even say I prided myself somewhat on that?"

"I . . . well, yes."

"And yet there I was sleeping under your parents' roof, dining at the same table as one of my closest friends, and all the while I was coaxing his sister to sneak off with me for the afternoon, to climb out her window at night and down the trellis into my arms." His hands tightened around the driving wheel. "I had so *lost* my head that I ignored or was oblivious to the consequences of what would have happened had we been caught and I'd not been willing to do the honorable thing. Because there was no doubt or hesitation in my mind that I *would* do the honorable thing. Because it was *you*. And because I couldn't stand to imagine *not* being with you. It was all only a matter of time." He turned to meet my gaze, which hadn't moved from him since he'd begun speaking. "Do you understand what I'm saying? I never wanted anyone even a fraction of the amount I wanted you. All of you." His gaze dipped to my lips before re-turning to the road.

I swallowed, his words resounding deep inside me in a place I'd needed to hear them.

A short distance up the road sat a scenic pull-out, and Sidney jerked the Pierce-Arrow to a halt and set the brake before reach-ing for me. His mouth met mine with the same urgency I'd felt whenever he returned from the front on one of his leaves, as if he was in danger of falling and I was the only one who could steady him. An odd metaphor perhaps, for his touch always had the opposite effect on me, making me forget myself and tumble into him completely.

Whatever the case, I kissed him with the same intensity he kissed me, knocking his hat askew and digging my fingers into the dark hair at the nape of his neck. His lips trailed across my jaw, finding the spot behind my ear that always made me arch with pleasure, while his hands sought a way past my layers of coat and blouse. I had begun tipping over onto my back, pulling Sidney over me, when the sound of a passing motorcar recalled us to our surroundings.

We sat gazing at each other, our breaths coming fast, our lips swollen from kisses.

"Perhaps it's still possible for us to lose our heads," he quipped in a husky voice.

I huffed out a laugh, shifting upright and smoothing my clothing back in place.

He grinned, readjusting his hat before he released the brake.

"At least we're married now," I remarked, thinking of all the times during the summer of 1914 we'd necked in Sidney's other Pierce-Arrow—the one that had been destroyed in Belgium in July. "And I won't have to wear high-necked blouses to hide what we've been doing," I added coquettishly.

He laughed long and hard, a sound that had always made my heart clutch with joy. Particularly as over the difficult years of the war and our reconciliation those laughs had become so rare.

His eyes sparkled as we chatted the rest of the way to Brock

House, putting me in such good spirits that I only smiled and shook my head when I saw the blue Crossley parked near the end of the drive. It was conveniently out of sight of the house behind the trees, but impossible for me and Sidney to miss. The doors opened as Sidney slowed the Pierce-Arrow, drawing up beside it, giving me a strong suspicion just precisely what my sister was about.

I had last seen Grace when she was eleven years old, so the young lady who emerged from the passenger side was a bit of a surprise. She was tall and slim like our mother, and a twist of rich brown hair rested against the nape of her neck beneath the broad brim of her hat. She was beautiful, with smooth, creamy skin, and Cupid's bow lips, but I'd expected nothing less. Her green eyes when she lifted them were cool and composed, but I suspected they barely obscured a wealth of emotions snapping underneath. After all, she was young and inexperienced. She hadn't yet mastered the art of concealment. With the slightest prod, they would spring forth.

A suspicion that proved true when Cyril Bolingbroke stepped forward, his mobile face creased with anxiety. "I do beg your pardon. I had no idea you were meant to fetch Miss Townsend from the train station until just now when she told me."

Grace's mouth tightened into a moue and her eyes flashed, clearly displeased with his sacrificing her to save his own skin. I had to admit, I was none too impressed myself. I couldn't imagine Sidney ever having tattled on me like that, even if he'd been irritated by my roping him into such a deception, which was doubtful. He was more likely to have been amused by it all.

I supposed he was a handsome enough chap. He was as tall as Sidney, if not more, and possessed of a head full of thick ash-brown hair, which riffled in the wind since he'd left his hat in the car. However, he had a weak chin and a skittish nature. But perhaps that was merely because of the circumstances.

I opened my door, stepping out to speak with him rather than hollering through Sidney's lowered window. "Of course, but why are you sitting here? Why don't you motor on down the drive and join us for tea?" I queried, already knowing full well the reason why. Something Grace also anticipated I was aware of, for her flashing eyes shifted to me and then narrowed.

"Oh, well. But Miss Townsend said it would be better today if it were just family," he stammered, glancing over the hood of his Crossley at her.

"Did she?" I murmured, feeling the devilish impulse to continue taunting them both, particularly as she was roping us into her deception, and without the least amount of the grace her name would imply. "I shall have to convey your kindness to our mother."

Grace's chin came up slightly at this comment. "Mother is already aware of Cyril's incredible kindness. It is one of his many exemplary traits."

Under other circumstances my sister's prim voice might have grated on my nerves, but just then I happened to find it comical. She was skating a thin edge, and yet she couldn't rein in her resentment of me even for her own good.

"Well, then, come greet me properly, sis," I dared her.

She rounded the bonnet of the Crossley, those green eyes of hers, so like my own, glinting like hard jewels in the ebbing light of the afternoon. "Welcome home, Verity," she declared once she stood before me. "We have greatly missed you." Her tone was sarcastic and slicing, but I did not fault her that.

"You are lovely, Grace," I replied with sincerity, though I couldn't help tweaking her nose just once more. "And you've mastered Mother's cutting tone. I suspect that comes in handy at school." I turned to offer her beau my hand. "And you must be Mr. Bolingbroke."

"Yes," he replied. "Pleased to meet you." He shifted toward Sidney. "And your husband. I've seen your pictures in all the newspapers. Congratulations on your Victoria Cross."

"Thank you," Sidney said flatly, as always unhappy with the reminder. Though normally such felicitations came from civilians and not former soldiers.

But Cyril had served. Surely he understood how conflicted

many men felt about the awards they received, how undeserving they believed themselves to be.

I remembered then what my brothers had said about his Blighty wound, and my gaze dipped to his left hand covered in a glove. I wondered again at the scorn I'd heard in their voices. Had Bolingbroke injured himself purposely in order to be sent home, or was his wound legitimate, and yet he had to live with the derision and questioning of people who believed otherwise? Either might make you anxious around a man like Sidney, who had been lauded so widely as a war hero.

My regard softened toward him as he turned to extract Grace's case from his motorcar and pass it to Sidney. However, from my sister's sharp expression, she seemed to think my scrutiny of her beau meant something less complimentary. I did not attempt to disabuse her of that notion. Not then, in any case. For I couldn't do so without alerting Cyril to my thoughts. But I prompted her in a far gentler voice than I might have, "Shall we?"

She brushed past me to say her goodbyes to Cyril, arching up onto her toes to press a kiss to his cheek. He smiled down into Grace's upturned face, and her eyes softened with affection. However, his ease vanished when he lifted his head, replaced with something that looked very much like trepidation.

I turned, trying to understand what had caused such a drastic change in him, and was surprised to see Bauer pedaling by on one of the bicycles before she turned down the rutted track that led around the back way to the barns. Given his reaction to her, I couldn't help but wonder if they knew each other.

Grace whirled away, stepping forward to greet Sidney as he held the car door open for her. But Cyril still stood stiffly in place, and when his eyes shifted to meet mine, finding me watching him, spots of color rose into his cheeks. He nodded his head once to me and then slid behind the wheel of his Crossley while I retreated to the Pierce-Arrow.

But not before allowing my gaze to trail over the trees to the west of the drive as I hadn't done since our arrival. I knew the sight that sooner or later I would need to face stood too deep in the woods for me to see from this vantage, but I still feared being confronted with it until I was ready. Shaking my head at my foolishness, I climbed into the car.

An uncomfortable silence reigned as Sidney accelerated up the drive, one that I waited for Grace to break. After all, this was her ruse. But when we passed over the little stone bridge, the stream below swelled with water, and still she hadn't spoken, I broke it for her.

"I suppose you expect us to carry on with this charade and pretend we collected you from the train station as planned." I looked over my shoulder to find her glaring out the window, her arms crossed over her chest.

"Do as you wish," she retorted. "You always have."

I heaved an exasperated sigh, gazing heavenward. This was what I remembered about having a sister seven years younger. How bloody infuriating she could be. She was only repeating what Mother had said *to* me or *about* me a hundred times, but it irked me that she'd accepted it as truth when she knew no such thing.

"I never took *you* for a quitter."

Her head snapped around just as I'd known it would.

"You expended all this energy to pull off your scheme, and now at the very end, you're going to give up just to spite me?"

She opened her mouth to respond, but I wasn't finished.

"You can be angry with me all you want, Grace. I undoubtedly deserve it. But don't play the martyr." I turned away. "And be certain you know of what you speak."

Her mouth snapped shut, and she continued to glare at me even when Sidney pulled to a halt before the house. Ignoring her, I opened my door to the sound of Tabitha's cheerful barking. I rubbed her ears, fussing over her a moment before she scrambled around the motorcar to give Sidney and Grace the same exuberant welcome.

Having followed steadily behind the happy collie, Father moved forward to greet Grace, accepting her proffered kiss on his cheek, and asking about the comfort of her journey. Then he turned to me and Sidney. "Any trouble?"

My sister's gaze met mine over the roof of the motorcar, silently awaiting my pronouncement.

"No. None at all," I answered with a forced smile.

There was a watchfulness in Father's eyes that made me wonder if he knew more than he was letting on. Perhaps he'd seen Cyril's motorcar parked at the end of the drive. Or maybe he was simply attuned to the tension between his daughters. Either way, he merely nodded in acceptance.

Sidney pulled the Pierce-Arrow around to the carriage house, while Mother greeted the rest of us at the door. I couldn't help but notice how much more warmly she embraced my sister than she had me, but I had known that was the way it would be. In any case, this brief display of affection did not prevent her from unleashing her usual criticisms thinly veiled as mothering.

"Grace, your skin is looking a bit dry and flaky," she proclaimed, grasping her chin and turning her face left and then right. "Go up and have an oatmeal bath here in a moment."

"Yes, Mother," she replied dutifully.

"Was your sister prompt?"

I met Mother's gaze evenly before turning to Grace, curious to hear her response. It took everything in me not to give in to the urge to arch a single eyebrow in cynicism.

"Yes, she met me on the platform," she said, removing her hat.

"In the rain?" Mother queried.

"By then it had stopped," I replied.

Mother frowned, eyeing the water spots that marred the hat's silk ribbon, but said nothing more.

CHAPTER 18

❧

The following day dawned to bright blue skies dotted with downy clouds, but blustery winds—a typical late-autumn morning amid the Dales. Having been confined to the Pierce-Arrow and the house much of the day before, I was eager to stretch my legs, and set off for a ramble shortly after midday with Sidney and Tim, while Tabitha scampered along after us. We returned mud splattered and windblown, but in happy spirits, only to be met in the yard by Freddy.

"Have any of you seen Fräulein Bauer?"

"No," I replied. "Is Tante Ilse looking for her?"

The furrow in his brow deepened. "Apparently, she's been asking for the girl for three hours, but no one can find her."

My gaze met Sidney's as a vague stirring of alarm began inside me. "Maybe she took a bicycle to run an errand in the village," I suggested.

Freddy shook his head. "We checked. All the bicycles are accounted for."

Tim stared in puzzlement at his feet, but he didn't offer any other suggestions.

"Well, she must be somewhere." I turned to survey the courtyard, trying not to allow my fears to race ahead. But she was a German in the depths of Yorkshire, one who barely spoke English, and I had witnessed the antagonism directed at her. "Let me speak with Tante Ilse. Perhaps she's merely forgotten where she's gone."

I set off across the courtyard with a brisk stride, uncertain which outcome I hoped for. I didn't want to be confronted with more evidence that Tante Ilse's memory was not what it had once been, but I also wished for Bauer to be safe. I dashed up the stairs in my split skirt and half boots, only to be met by Matilda exiting my bedchamber.

"What are you doing?" I demanded, her posture too furtive for her presence there to be innocent.

She straightened in affront, as if she were the one who had been wronged. "I saw Bauer sneakin' out of your room this morn. She seemed nervous, so I went in to see what trouble she was up to."

"She's been helping to care for and press my clothes," I retorted. "Not that that's any of your concern."

"Yes, well, she was doing nowt with your clothes. Rather, she was leavin' a letter."

This surprised me, and Matilda could tell, for her beady black eyes glinted with satisfaction.

"I thowt it was for Mr. Kent, so I took it. Planned to give it to Mrs. Townsend."

"You thought it was?" I pressed, knowing full well that Matilda would have had no compunctions about opening it and reading it.

She scowled. "It was written in gibberish."

Which I took to mean German.

"But what with her havin' gone missing now, I thowt it might be best to return it. In case it explains that she's run off or summat like that."

"Where is it?" I snapped, struggling to restrain my temper.

She nodded toward the door to my bedchamber. "On your pillow."

I charged past her and across the room to where a crisp, white piece of paper lay on my pillow. I spared a thought for the note I'd found almost a week before under my pillow with its oblique warning—*I know what you did*—and then dismissed it to read the letter.

It was, indeed, written in German. But the contents were not what I'd expected. She was not leaving Tante Ilse's employ and attempting to make it back to Germany on her own. Rather, she asked me to meet her at the stone field barn near the river, not far from Violet's house. The one that was just visible in the fold of a hill from the road. I knew the one she spoke of, but I wondered how *she* had discovered it.

In truth, the entire letter was puzzling. If she needed to speak to me, why couldn't she do so here? This request for me to meet her somewhere so remote and so far from the house smacked of a certain level of stealth and secrecy—one I wasn't certain I was comfortable with.

My suspicions briefly turned to Tante Ilse's claims about the second deserter, but then I dismissed them. Bauer hadn't even been in her employ when the man showed up at her home near Monschau. It seemed implausible that she knew anything about the matter other than what my great-aunt might have told her.

Maybe that was it. Maybe Tante Ilse had told her something she felt I should know. Or maybe Bauer knew, or at least suspected, that the second deserter was an invention of my great-aunt's faulty memory, as I feared. She might be hesitant to voice such suspicions, particularly in front of my parents, who could be intimidating. Perhaps she'd thought that if she requested to speak with me privately here they might interfere. Or that the other servants who held such a dislike of her might overhear.

Whatever the case, I was not going to learn the answers by sitting there speculating on it. I hurried from our room, nearly colliding with Grace, to whom I apologized, before pattering down the stairs.

"Verity, what on earth . . . ?" my mother exclaimed, emerging from the drawing room.

"I'll explain later," I called over my shoulder as I rushed from the house. Bauer had requested the meeting for two o'clock, and it was already over an hour after.

"I think I know where Bauer is," I told Sidney, Tim, and Freddy as I reached the courtyard, and then lowered my voice so as not to be overheard. "She left a note saying she wished to speak to me." I glanced around me. "I suspect about something she didn't want someone here to overhear. Something about Tante Ilse's health or the servants' ill treatment of her. I don't know. But she's probably there waiting now." I looked at Freddy. "Will you go to Tante Ilse and reassure her? I'll return with Bauer as swiftly as I can."

He nodded and strode off toward the house.

"Shall I fetch the motorcar?" Sidney asked, but I shook my head.

"No, she's waiting at the field barn near the river. The one at the edge of the Capshaw property where the river folds back in on itself, and it will be faster to reach by bicycle. The lanes leading most directly to it are muddy and rutted—too rough for your Pierce-Arrow, which will only get stuck." I swiveled toward Tim, noticing for the first time how pale his face had grown. I broke off from what I had been going to say to question him. "What is it?"

He swallowed and shook his head. "Nothing. Just . . . a sore muscle."

I frowned, not entirely satisfied with his answer, but there wasn't time to ponder why. "Will you take the foot track through Metcalfe's wood? It's unlikely, but she might have learned about it from someone and realized it was a shortcut. I don't want to miss her if she's already set off back to Brock House."

He nodded, hastening off to do so. Tabitha bounded along after him and then turned back toward me and Sidney as we collected and mounted our bicycles. The border collie seemed undecided as to who needed herding most. As we pedaled off down the drive, she wheeled about to trot after Tim, evidently determining he would need her company more.

Sidney and I crossed the road, veering off onto one of the rutted tracks more often used by farm lorries or for herding the sheep. I kept to the grassy verge, attempting to avoid most of the mud and puddles, though my boots and the hem of my drab split skirt were already hopelessly splattered. An ingenious garment, the split skirt sported two long rows of large buttons down each hip that could be fastened into trousers or a skirt. I was glad I'd chosen the former that morning, no matter my mother's scowls.

I breathed deep, trying to quiet the flutter of nerves that had taken flight inside me. It was no good speculating on what Bauer wished to tell me. Not until we reached her. So I tried to concentrate on maintaining my balance over the rough ground, and on the sweetness of the country air.

Somehow I'd forgotten how crisp and clear the air was here, particularly after living so long amidst the soot and grime of London. It filled my lungs and flooded through my veins, reaching clear down into my toes. Even the occasional whiff of cow manure borne on the wind only served to emphasize the clarity of the breeze.

My grandfather had liked to say that was why the lads and lassies born among the Dales grew to be so tall and strapping, and perhaps there was something to that. I felt more invigorated, more anxious to stretch my arms and legs, even in spite of the tossing and turning I did at night, unable to rest. Maybe tonight after our hard ramble and this bicycle ride, maybe then my body would be so fatigued that my mind would have no choice but to be quiet.

We paused at the top of a rise to catch our breath. Below us in a fold at the base of a hill rested the stone barn where Bauer had asked me to meet her. Like most such field barns in the Dales, it had been positioned at a distance from the main farm buildings, in the midst of a hay meadow. During summer and autumn, the hay was cut and dried there, and then stored in the lofts above in order to feed the cattle who were herded into the barns from the surrounding fields during the cold winter nights and the harshest of days. Even now I could see sheep dotting the meadows all around, grazing on the tufts of grass.

However, unlike most field barns, there was also a small copse of trees abutting the stone fence that formed part of the structure's far wall. Most barns stood in the open, with naught but perhaps a single lone tree to break the rise of the fells and dales and the rambling stone fences cutting across them to divide the landscape into pastures. Beyond the copse lay the bend of the River Ure, separating the Capshaws' property from the Metcalfes' to the east.

Sidney opened the gate between two such meadows, closing it behind us as we pushed our bicycles through. "I don't see anyone." His cheeks were reddened from the wind and the dark hair at his temples dampened with sweat beneath his flat cap. "Do you think she's still waiting inside?"

"There's only one way to find out," I replied, pushing off to glide down the hill. The uneven lane followed the craggy, winding stone fence line to the square, stolid structure. While it seemed flat gray at a distance, as we drew closer I could see that the walls of the structure were splotched with colors undulating from gleaming white to darkest granite. Here and there amidst the variations in shade grew some sort of yellow lichen. The slate roof sagged slightly near the eastern peak line, just above the single window cut into the upper story.

We slowed as our bicycles drew near, and I expected the noise of the tires crunching over the dirt and the click of their spinning to draw Bauer out from the interior, but she did not emerge. Dismounting, I walked the cycle closer, before leaning it against the wall to the left of the arched wooden cattle doors. One side gaped open, and I stepped closer to peer inside.

"Fräulein Bauer," I called. "Are you still here?" I pushed the door wider, wishing there were more windows to illuminate the dark interior. "I only just received your note." I took a cautious step forward, with Sidney following close behind.

Almost immediately, I sensed that something was wrong, though I wasn't certain exactly why. Perhaps it was the stillness of the barn, which seemed almost unnatural even in its isolated setting. Or maybe it was my heightened instincts from the war, on which I'd learned to rely without questioning why.

But as my eyes and ears adjusted, I realized it wasn't them, or even my intuition that had alerted me, but rather my nose. Beneath the strong aroma of hay and the milder stench of damp stone and muck from some months past, another scent tickled my nostrils. One that was sharp and metallic, and carried with it the association of far grimmer memories.

Inching forward, I stumbled to a stop at the sight of the dark rivulet staining the earth. My gaze followed it to where Bauer's body was laid out across the floor, her eyes staring sightlessly up at the ceiling, the bodice of her simple brown coat saturated with blood.

Sidney swore savagely over my shoulder.

I swallowed against the urge to vomit, absolutely horrified for the poor girl. I was swamped by the feeling I'd somehow failed her. Alone and far from home in a hostile land, Bauer should have been able to rely on us for protection, and yet look at what had happened to her. But who on earth would do such a thing? And why?

I forced myself to push these thoughts aside for the moment, allowing my gaze to drift over the scene before me, scrutinizing every detail.

Meanwhile Sidney had circled around the body to get a different view. "What did this to her?" he queried, pointing at the multiple rends in the coat.

"That, I should say," I answered in a far calmer voice than I expected to emerge. I gestured toward the pitchfork that had been tossed to the side. Blood stained its tines. If we were lucky, the killer's fingerprints would be on it, but given the chill of the day, I wasn't counting on it.

I moved a step closer, careful to avoid the blood and any potential evidence. "But she's been moved." I gestured toward the post a short distance away. "See the blood staining the wood and the drag marks in the floor between here and there. I would say she slumped there after being stabbed and then was moved to this spot and laid out."

"By the killer?" Sidney posited, his gaze shifting to meet mine. "Or did someone else find her first?"

We both turned then, surveying the rest of the barn. Bales of hay were stacked high in the loft above, providing ample places for someone to hide. I felt the hairs on the back of my neck stand on end.

He moved toward the ladder on stealthy feet and began to climb while I backed toward the door, alert for any movement or shift in the shadows above. At the top, he made one final burst of movement to enter the loft before anyone could leap out at him while he was at a disadvantage. Then he began to systematically search the space, hindered by the towering piles of hay.

He was nearly finished, when something brushed past my right leg and then grabbed my left shoulder from behind. I whirled about, driving all my weight down on the arm of my assailant to throw them off balance. Releasing me, they stumbled backward. Which was all that saved them from me striking upward with my knee.

"Bloody hell, Verity," Tim snapped as he righted himself, clutching his right arm. "What did you do that for?"

I gasped in relief, pressing a hand over my heart. "For heaven's sake, Tim, don't you know better than to grab a woman from behind?"

"None of the women I know would react like that," he groused, eyeing me sullenly.

He was undoubtedly right, and not wishing to put too fine a point on that fact, I turned my attention to Tabitha, ordering her to stay. It must have been she who had brushed past my leg. Tim looked up to watch Sidney return down the ladder before querying in confusion.

"You thought she was in the hay loft?"

I grabbed hold of the collie's collar, restraining her unresisting body as I stepped to the side and allowed him to see deeper into the barn.

"Good God!" he exclaimed at the sight of Bauer's body. "What happened?" His gaze darted up to the loft and back. "Did she fall?"

"She was stabbed," I replied. "Probably by that pitchfork."

Tim had served for over a year at the Western Front. I knew he'd witnessed many of the same horrors Sidney had. But it seemed he was still capable of being shocked. His eyes blinked wide, and his face blanched, perhaps at the brutality of the crime.

I reached out to grip his shoulder, forcing him to look at me.

"I need you to take one of the bicycles and go get Freddy. Then drive to Hawes and fetch the police."

"Father won't let me take the motorcar," he replied softly.

"For this, I think he will. And if not, take the Pierce-Arrow."

"Just don't wreck it," Sidney added.

Tim's eyes darted to him in silent question.

"Yes, I know about the Sunbeam. Your brother was only too happy to tell me about it."

Apparently this had been a conversation I had not been party to, for I could only surmise what they were talking about.

Tim flushed and turned to go, but I stopped him before he set off.

"Take Tabitha with you. We don't need her getting curious," I added, perhaps unnecessarily.

Tim's face blanched, but he managed to call to the collie, who glanced back toward the interior of the barn once before dutifully following him as he climbed onto a bicycle and rode off up the lane. I watched their progress and then turned to note the copse of trees that butted up next to the field barn.

Curious, I crossed slowly toward the stone fence separating the wood from the meadow. Most of the trees were stripped of their leaves, but a handful of smaller shrubs and saplings still sported foliage in russet and red. It seemed as if it would be impossible for someone to conceal themselves there unseen, and yet I couldn't halt the sensation that we were being watched.

Sidney stopped beside me, his eyes searching the copse as mine did. "Are you thinking this is the way the killer came?"

"It would certainly afford him or her the element of surprise."

He nodded. "What's on the other side?"

"The Capshaw residence." And Violet's late mother's garden. "Though the trees straggle along the fence line nearly to the road leading to Hawes, so anyone could have walked up from there with a degree of concealment."

He nodded, turning to look toward the east. "And that direction? What lies there?"

"It's Metcalfe property as far as the eye can see. We actually crossed it to reach here." I turned to survey the meadow before us and the nodding heads of three sheep about a hundred feet away. "But this field belongs to the Kiddses. Or it used to. I don't know for certain now. But I daresay Freddy will."

I studied the woods again, but the sensation itching along my spine had stopped. Which meant either I was imagining things, or the person who had been watching us had stolen away.

CHAPTER 19

❦

When Freddy arrived sometime later, he didn't come from the direction of Brock House, but rather through the copse, setting his black medical bag down on top of the low stone wall before hopping over.

"I was called to the Hardcastles'," he replied to my unspoken query. "Tim found me there before driving on into town. Is it true?" Freddy's brow had drawn tight as he followed us around the corner of the field barn toward the door. "Tim said Fräulein Bauer was dead; that her chest was all sliced up."

"I don't know that I would categorize it precisely like that," I replied, conferring with Sidney with my eyes. "But she received multiple puncture wounds, and it seems evident it came from the bloody pitchfork lying near her body. However, you'll have to confirm." I led him to Bauer's body, making a wide circle to the other side. "We haven't touched her clothing or examined the wounds closely for fear of disturbing any evidence. We thought you should be the one to do so."

When Freddy didn't kneel beside the body, I looked up to find him examining me instead. My calm, straightforward tone had evidently surprised him. I supposed he'd expected me to be near hysterics, but what he didn't know, and I couldn't explain, was that I'd seen far worse during the war. In any case, whatever he was thinking, I could tell it wasn't complimentary. Maybe he assumed I was unfeeling.

"Are we correct? Did the pitchfork cause her wounds?" Sidney prodded, drawing my brother's attention away from me.

He set down his bag and squatted next to the corpse. "Let's see."

He opened her brown coat to reveal her once-dove-gray gown beneath, its bodice being soaked with blood. There were two distinct rents in the fabric at an angle slanting downward right to left—the first puncture being just below her rib cage, while the second was located below and to the left of her navel. A third rip in the fabric appeared near her hip, where the bodice and skirt joined, as if the third prong had gouged her skin there.

Avoiding looking at Bauer's face, I watched Freddy as he carefully inspected the wounds through the fabric, to preserve her modesty, though he did widen one of the gaps with his fingers to provide a better view. I'd never had the opportunity to observe my brother in his capacity as a medical officer or a surgeon, and doing so offered me new insight into the man he'd become. He was quick and precise, but also persistent and thorough, examining points on her body beyond her obvious punctures and lacerations.

"Yes, her wounds are consistent with those that would be caused by a pitchfork. And given the fact the prongs of said implement are bloody, it seems safe to say that pitchfork caused them," he replied to Sidney's query as he lifted each of her hands, turning them over to scrutinize them.

"Does she have any defensive wounds?" I asked.

His gaze lifted to meet mine, his attention momentarily faltering. "No. At least, none that I can see. I presume the police surgeon will do a much more thorough examination."

He finished his inspection and draped the edges of her coat closed over the torso. Pulling a cloth from his bag, he wiped the worst of the blood from his hands before reaching up to pass a hand over her vacant, staring eyes to close them.

I pivoted left and right, sweeping my gaze over the contents of the barn from this angle. The interior of the barn was dimly lit—even more so now as dusk approached, than it would have been at two o'clock, and yet I could clearly make out most of the contents. "She must have seen her attacker coming toward her," I postulated, ignoring Freddy's continued scrutiny. "Perhaps that's why she backed up against this wall. If she couldn't get around him, or her," I amended, conceding it could have been a woman. "Then she had no place else to go."

Sidney nodded, lifting aside the edges of his coat to prop his hands on his hips. "Though the use of the pitchfork as the murder weapon suggests this wasn't planned."

I agreed.

"But what was she doing here in the first place?" Freddy demanded. "Someone must have lured her here."

"I don't know how she discovered this place or why she picked it. But she was here because she'd left me a note asking me to meet her, remember." I scowled. "Unfortunately, Matilda took it from our room after Bauer left it this morning, and only returned it after she'd gone missing."

I rounded the body, striding closer to the door and the fresh air. Crossing my arms over my deep blue wool coat against the chill, I gazed out through the opening and over the meadow toward the top of the hill where Sidney and I had briefly rested. One lone oak tree stood at the crest along the fence line, its branches waving in the wind.

"Then Matilda knew where she was going," Sidney surmised, moving to stand beside me.

I couldn't deny that was where my thoughts had also gone, to Matilda's potential culpability. "Possibly. Though she says she couldn't read it because it was written in German." A language it was doubtful she knew. "But there are German-to-English dictionaries in the library, and Matilda is nothing if not resourceful."

"You can't seriously suspect Mother's maid of doing this?" Freddy protested, gesturing behind us toward the body.

"Of course I can. Matilda delights in making trouble for others, especially those she doesn't like. It would be just like her to follow Fräulein Bauer here, expecting to catch her doing something she shouldn't." And she would have had time to do so and then return to the house before Tim, Sidney, and I returned from our ramble.

"Yes, but following her here to spy on her and *killing* her are two very different things."

"They are," I conceded. "But she had the knowledge of her whereabouts, the opportunity, and the motive." I turned my sharp glare on my brother before he could protest further. "She hated Bauer because she was German. I witnessed for myself how terribly she treated her. As such, she's a logical suspect, and will need to be questioned."

Freddy removed his flat cap and scraped his forearm over his forehead in aggravation before replacing it. "Well, if you're going to include hatred of Germans as a motive, then that makes at least half the village suspects."

"I'm aware," I replied grimly. "But I daresay very few, if any, of them knew Bauer would be at this barn at two o'clock this afternoon. Someone might have seen her coming this way and followed her. But otherwise I doubt she advertised her intentions beforehand." Though I had to accede it was possible she'd confided in someone, but who? She knew no one but our family.

Sidney pulled his cigarette case from the inside pocket of his coat and extracted a cigarette before offering one to Freddy, who took it. "Regardless, until we have more evidence, this is all speculation." He arched a single eyebrow at my brother, speaking around the fag dangling from the corner of his lip as he lit it. "And we won't have more evidence until we begin asking questions."

"Don't you mean, until the police start asking questions?" Freddy replied as he lit his own cigarette.

Sidney and I both turned to him with cynical stares.

"Then your local policeman is experienced with murder investigations?" Sidney was the first to reply.

"Well, no. But he'll send for the inspector in Richmond, or perhaps they'll even call in Scotland Yard."

I scoffed. "Only if he's required to, Freddy. But the Sergeant Bibby I remember won't lift a finger to solve the murder of a

German. He's most likely to declare it the work of some passing vagrant."

The memory of Tante Ilse's claims about the second deserter following her to England rang in my ears, and I wondered if I should have tried harder to find out if there was a stranger in the surrounding area. But beyond the incident in the church-yard, I'd not heard nor seen anything to indicate there was an outsider in Hawes. Nothing but the note, that is. And I still wasn't convinced that wasn't the work of someone else.

I firmed my chin in resolve. "Fräulein Bauer was under our protection. It was our responsibility to keep her safe. And now that we've failed at that, it is our responsibility to find out who killed her, with or without the police's help."

I could feel Freddy watching me again, assessing me with new eyes, but there was nothing I could do about that. Not short of running away, and I refused to do that.

"The clerk for a shipping company, hmm?" he drawled, ru-minating on the job I publicly claimed to have performed for the war effort, working for a company that imported and exported supplies for the military, a cover for the actual work I did for the Secret Service. He exhaled a long stream of smoke. "Right." His eyes glittered angrily. "That's not the first dead body you've seen," he accused, gesturing with the fag clasped between his fingers.

"We *have* assisted with a murder investigation or two," I replied softly, reminding him of one of the reasons Sidney and I had appeared so often in the newspapers these past six months.

"Is that all?" he challenged.

My chest tightened at the hint of disgust I heard in his voice. What I didn't know was if it was directed toward what he sus-pected I'd done or at my having lied.

"Leave it be, Freddy," Sidney urged.

"Then you know . . . *whatever* it is the rest of us apparently don't?"

"Leave it be," he declared more forcefully.

That Freddy was not prepared to do so was obvious, but the sound of approaching voices cut off his diatribe. We strolled to the corner of the building, watching as Sergeant Bibby hoisted his not inconsiderable frame over the stone wall separating the meadow from the Capshaws' wood. Whatever rations those of us in London had endured during the war, Sergeant Bibby did not appear to have suffered the same hardship. Though, truth be told, all the people living in the countryside had been better off in that regard.

Tim had trailed more slowly behind him, but leapt over the fence with ease, earning him a sharp look from the sergeant.

"Mr. Kent, Mrs. Kent, Dr. Townsend," he greeted us after hitching up his pants. "Mr. Townsend tells me there's been some sort of accident."

"Not an accident," Sidney replied, offering the sergeant his hand to shake. "Come have a look."

I watched the four men disappear around the corner of the barn, knowing from past experience that most policemen did not welcome a lady's assistance, especially one who was viewed as nothing more than a society darling. But with Sidney being a war hero and the heir presumptive of a marquess, he would be heeded and accorded all due respect. It was best to leave the matter of showing the sergeant what we'd found to him.

Besides, my interest had been arrested by the person who had guided the sergeant and Tim to our location. Violet Capshaw remained on her side of the stone wall, a thick paisley shawl draped around her shoulders, which were braced against the chill of the onset of evening. I turned to see how close the sun had sunk toward the rolling horizon, bleeding the color from the sky, before strolling toward her, interested in what she had to share, if anything.

"Is it true, then? Was Frau Vischering's maid truly murdered?"

"Yes."

A dark strand of her hair caught in the corner of her mouth, and she lifted a hand to tuck it behind her ear. "What happened?"

I searched her amber eyes, wondering at her interest. Mild concern and curiosity shone in their depths, but she bore my scrutiny without complaint. If Violet was the killer, and I doubted that, then she was a cold-hearted one, indeed. But then I remembered she was also not a stranger to blood or death, having driven ambulances during the war.

"She was stabbed. With a pitchfork."

Her eyes flared wide. "Good heavens!"

I shifted my feet, which ached from the hours of walking, cycling, and standing I'd done that day. And yet we still had more walking and cycling to do to return the way we'd come. "Did you see anyone come this way earlier this afternoon? Perhaps around two o'clock."

"I didn't. But perhaps Father did. I'll ask him."

I nodded, my gaze drifting over the mostly bare branches of the trees behind her, their bark turning gray in the fading light. "Do you venture through this part of your property often?"

"We rarely venture anywhere beyond the garden. Except in the spring," she amended. "Sometimes I come this way then to check the wood for bluebells." Her demeanor stiffened. "Why?"

I glanced over my shoulder. "I just wondered how much use this field barn sees during the warmer seasons. Whether anyone uses it other than to store hay and shelter sheep."

Violet bit one corner of her bottom lip as she eyed the stone barn. "It does seem like an odd place to find the maid."

I elected not to mention Bauer's note, curious to hear what else she might suggest.

Her eyebrows arched in insinuation. "Maybe it was an assignation. Maybe they met here. She was a pretty girl, after all."

She had been more than just pretty. And I suspected her German nationality would not have discouraged some men from taking advantage. In fact, it might have encouraged them to do so.

Violet's eyes brightened. "Now that I think of it, I saw her speaking to someone in the village a few days ago. On Thursday." She frowned. "Or was it Wednesday?" She shook her head, brushing aside this detail. "They were standing in the narrow passage between the chemist and the book shop with their heads bent close together."

I straightened, my interest piqued. "Who was the man with her?"

"I don't know. He wasn't familiar to me."

"You mean he wasn't from Hawes?"

"Maybe. Though I'm certain there are villagers I wouldn't recognize. Servants and farm laborers and such. It's impossible to know everyone."

She was undoubtedly right, but I also couldn't ignore the way my scalp tingled with awareness. I had seen a man in the churchyard who seemed familiar, and yet I could not identify him. And Tante Ilse had sworn she'd seen the second deserter in the same place. Was he the same man Violet had seen speaking to Bauer? And if so, why had he followed us here? Why had he approached her? Had she slipped a note from him under my pillow five days earlier? Is that what she'd wanted to talk to me about?

There were too many questions without answers.

"What did he look like?" I asked, hoping she'd taken more than a passing interest.

"I couldn't see them well. They were in shadow. But he was about middling height and his clothing was that of a laborer."

I turned at the sound of voices, realizing the men had already emerged from the barn. "Let me know if you think of anything else," I told Violet. I took one step away before turning back. "Or if you see the man Fräulein Bauer was speaking to again."

"I will," she called after me as I strode away to rejoin the men.

"Aye, I'll have to inform the inspector," Sergeant Bibby was saying. He mopped his brow with a handkerchief. "A bloody Kraut murdered in Hawes," he grumbled. "Of all the rotten luck. What was she doing here in Hawes anyway?"

"She served as my great-aunt's maid," Freddy replied stiffly. "You recall Mrs. Vischering."

"Right, right. I heard she was here for a visit." He heaved an aggrieved sigh, turning back toward the barn. "Well, I suppose we can't just leave her there."

This earned him sharp looks from several of us.

"I guess there's nowt for it but to move her to the station for the time being. And the pitchfork, too. It'll have to be checked for fingerprints. If you gentlemen will assist me, perhaps Mr. Capshaw will have summat we can wrap her in to be carried," he declared, striding off to speak with Violet.

That my brothers and Sidney would be doing the heavy lifting, there was no doubt, but I thought I preferred it that way anyway. At least I could trust them to treat her body with some care and respect. Though I wasn't certain how much help Tim would be. He kept stealing glances toward the barn door, his pallor almost gray in the fading light.

Sidney rested a hand on my shoulder, drawing my attention. "Why don't you go on back to Brock House. It will be dark soon and there's nothing more you can do here."

I had to concede he was right, and my feet *were* aching. "What of Tante Ilse and our parents?" I asked Tim. "Did you tell anyone else what happened?"

He swallowed. "I had to in order to convince Father to let me take the Rolls. And . . . Tante Ilse overheard."

My lips pressed together tightly. I supposed I should have been glad he'd spared me the grim duty, but I wished we could have broken the news to her more gently.

"We'll return as soon as we can," Sidney told me as he walked with me toward the lone bicycle left. Before I mounted, he pulled me close to his side, pressing a kiss to my temple. "Be careful."

I set off down the lane, although as the terrain grew steeper, I elected to dismount and walk the bicycle up. My legs were simply too tired to make the effort. At the top, I looked behind me to find my husband and brothers had sunk down next to each other, leaning their backs against the wall of the barn to smoke cigarettes. Had the terrain been flatter and their clothing a drab uniform, they might have been any one of the nameless detachments of soldiers I'd witnessed at ease in France in the rear of the trenches during the war.

I realized then that it was a scene I would never be part of, for if I'd remained, they would never have allowed themselves to fall into such a relaxed stance. I might be just their wife and sister, but I was not a fellow soldier or surgeon, and so not part of the easy comradery that had become ingrained in their existence at the front. As such, I felt almost as if I was intruding on a private moment they wouldn't wish me to see, and so I turned away, mounting the bicycle again to set off down the hill toward Brock House.

The sky was painted with broad strokes of mauve and orange, and the tips of the fells in the distance were tinted a velvety purple in the twilight. The song of a linnet was the only sound save the wind rushing past me and the crunch of dirt beneath the tires. Cold air stung my cheeks, but I welcomed the clarity it brought me.

I'd felt in danger of sinking into moroseness, but I could not afford to indulge in such emotions knowing what awaited me. Nor could I afford to lose my head when there was a murderer to be unmasked. One who had either followed my great-aunt to England and knew of my work with the Secret Service, or one who would be found among my parents' neighbors. Given the choice, I wasn't sure which I would choose. Neither would be a welcome revelation.

CHAPTER 20

All was quiet when I returned to Brock House. I wasn't sure what I'd expected. Not weeping and gnashing of teeth, certainly. But not this.

Abbott, my parents' butler, appeared to have been waiting for me, for he opened the door before I reached it, and stood waiting to take my hat and dusty coat. His expression was as neutral as ever, but I thought I detected a glimmer of regret in his eyes.

"Where is everyone?" I asked.

"Mr. Townsend is in his study, and Mrs. Townsend is upstairs settling Frau Vischering. I believe Miss Townsend is in her chamber."

I turned my feet toward the stairs, only to be halted by Father. He must have heard my voice and come from his study to greet me. "It's true, then?" he asked. "I know your brother would never invent such a terrible thing, but . . ."

His voice fell away, leaving the sentence unfinished. I searched his eyes, seeing weariness there, but also something more. Uncertainty. It was an emotion I didn't think I'd ever witnessed in my father, and it left me feeling rattled.

"Yes," I replied simply.

His breath seemed to catch in his throat. "Poor girl."

My gaze dipped to his striped necktie.

"I suppose your brothers and Sidney are assisting the police."

"Yes, they'll be along as soon as they can."

"Then we'll hold dinner until they arrive," Mother declared.

We both turned to watch as she descended the last few stairs, her features as rigidly composed as ever. She nodded to Abbott, who slipped through the door leading to the servants' wing, understanding his orders.

"How is Tante Ilse?" I asked as she reached the bottom step.

"As well as can be expected." She lifted a hand to tug at the listless curl framing my face, her brow lowering. "She asked that you be sent to her as soon as you arrived."

"I'll go now."

But Mother halted me with a hand on my arm. "Just one moment."

I waited, wondering what she wished to say.

Her eyes scrutinized me, no doubt noting every splotch of dirt, every hair out of place. "I hope you're not planning to interfere in the police's investigation."

I clenched my fists, struggling to stifle my annoyance. "Not as long as they do a satisfactory job of it."

"Verity, I hardly think that is your place to decide."

Ignoring this, I turned to Father. "Is Mr. Metcalfe still the local coroner?"

"Aye."

"Then I imagine the coroner's inquest will be called on Monday. Sergeant Bibby said he would report the death to the inspector at Richmond, as required."

Father nodded. "As he should. Bibby's not investigated a murder before."

Mother shuddered, as if revolted by the word. "Verity . . ."

"Did you or did you not trust me to handle matters for Aunt Ernestine at Littlemote House just a month ago?" I contradicted, interrupting her. "And that involved *two* murders and the help of Scotland Yard."

"She has a fair point," my father said, earning a glare from my mother.

"Please trust me to do so here."

Before she could deny this request, I hurried past her and up the stairs. Pausing for a moment outside Tante Ilse's bedchamber door, I did my best to compose myself before rapping softly.

"Come in," she called.

I found her reclining in bed, staring up at the leaf-green canopy overhead. The drapes were drawn and only a single lamp was lit beside the bed, casting much of the room in shadow.

I closed the door behind me, leaning back against it until she turned to acknowledge me. "Oh, Tante, I'm so sorry," I said, moving to sit next to her where she lay. She allowed me to take hold of her hand, clasping it between mine. Her skin felt so thin, its texture worn, like a piece of paper that had been repeatedly crumped and then smoothed out.

"I'm the one who should be sorry," she replied in a raspy voice. Her eyes were clouded with regrets. "For bringing that poor girl here."

I squeezed her hand, wanting to console her, but knowing that refuting her statement would be a waste of time. Given what had happened, I was sorry I'd brought her here as well. So instead I turned to easier topics. "How did Fräulein Bauer come to be in your employ?"

"Anni came to me after Schmidt died from the influenza." She lapsed into German, perhaps because she was fatigued, or perhaps because it was easier to remember that way, but I didn't mind. "She was a little miracle, really. Appeared at my bedside to spoon hot soup into my mouth almost as if by magic." She patted my hand where it gripped hers, perhaps having felt me flinch in alarm. "I had fallen sick after Schmidt passed, and while I had not taken as ill as she had, I had still been confined to my bed for several days. Later I learned that Anni—Fräulein Bauer—had arrived in Monschau, hoping to find work. She'd lost her family to the war, you see, and so she'd taken to wandering from town to town, searching for a position."

Tante Ilse broke off, coughing, and I rounded the bed to pour a glass of water from the ewer on the bedside table. She accepted it with thanks before taking a drink and passing it back to me.

"When she heard in town about the old woman who'd lost her maid, she came to see me. She said she waited for three hours on my front step, and when I didn't come home or answer her knocks, she began to worry. She knew my maid had died from the influenza, so she decided she couldn't in good conscience leave without at least being certain I wasn't unwell." Her face softened at the memory. "She stayed to nurse me, and then I offered her the position of my maid."

I smiled in answer, thinking it spoke well of Bauer. After all, if she'd been alone and desperate for work, wandering from town to town, she might just as easily have been tempted to take what she wished from Tante Ilse while she was incapacitated and leave without anyone being the wiser. Instead, she'd stayed to help a frail, sick old woman. She might have hoped my great-aunt would hire her after that, but she must have known there was no guarantee.

"Where did she come from?" I asked, sitting beside her again.

"She never said. In truth, she seemed determined not to discuss her past. I assumed it was too painful for her. But by the accent of her voice, I could tell she wasn't from Westphalia. At least, not originally. She hailed from somewhere farther east. Saxony, maybe."

My great-aunt might be right. If she'd lost her entire family to the war and to the influenza and starvation, it might have been too painful to speak of. But I also couldn't help but note what a convenient excuse it was.

Pushing aside the uncharitable thought, I focused on the specifics. "Then there's no one we should notify?"

She shook her head sadly. "No one that I know of."

How incredibly sad that we should be the only ones to mourn her, and not as she doubtless deserved, I feared. It was a stark reminder of another consequence of the war.

"Was she religious?"

She nodded, understanding why I asked. "Lutheran. But an

Anglican burial will do. Sarah said she'll speak to Vicar Redmayne."

I was glad my mother could always be relied on for such things.

Now that those simpler matters were addressed, I knew it was time to turn to the harder questions, but still I hesitated. She seemed so fragile, and I couldn't help but wonder once again about the medicine she was taking. About her need for laudanum. I found myself examining her for any signs she'd taken it recently.

"Do you have any idea who might have hurt her?"

"No." She lifted her hands in a gesture of futility. "How could I? She did not know anyone. And they did not know her." The skin tightened across the fine bones of her face. "All they saw when they looked at her was a Boche, a Kraut." She practically spat the words that were used as slurs against Germans.

I felt a stirring of shame within me. Perhaps I hadn't been the one to utter the slurs, but I had made excuses for my fellow countrymen and neighbors who did. Did that not make me also somehow culpable? Swallowing the bitter taste of regret, I pressed on. "Was she being harassed by anyone in particular? Did she confide in you?"

"No, but I saw the way they looked at her, the way they treated her. I noticed how much she had withdrawn into herself since we arrived." She sighed, turning her head away. "I thought I was saving the girl. There was nothing left for her in Germany, and barely enough to eat. But instead, I only fed her to the wolves."

"There's no way you could have known this would happen. You did what you thought was best. That's all you could do. That's all any of us can do."

She didn't respond, but I knew she was listening. Guilt and sadness seemed to weigh her down like a blanket, but I could see her eyelashes flicker in the lamplight as she blinked from time to time.

"What of the second deserter?" I asked, and then further

prompted when she didn't react. "You said you saw him outside the church. Could it have been him?"

The expression on her face when she turned slightly toward me was vague and uncertain. "Oh, yes. I did say that, didn't I?"

"Have you changed your mind about that? Was it not the same man?"

Her brow furrowed as if she was searching for something, something she couldn't quite recall. "No. Maybe. I . . . I don't know who I saw." Her voice grew agitated. "But if I said I saw the deserter, then I did."

"But you don't remember anything more about him?" I asked hesitantly, suddenly reluctant to pursue the matter in the face of her rising distress and anger.

"I don't. . . . *Why* are you asking me these things?" she demanded. "I already told you everything I know. Go interrogate your neighbors. It must be one of them who killed Schmidt. And leave me in peace!"

The lump that had settled in my stomach seemed to grow in size as she referred to her old maid, not her new one. "You mean Bauer?"

"What?! Yes, of course, that's what I meant. I'm not a fool!" Her chest rose and fell rapidly, and I feared she'd overset herself. She lifted a hand to press it to her breastbone almost as if she was struggling to catch her breath.

I rose to my feet in alarm. "What can I do? Can I help?"

She shook her head. "No, no. Just send me . . ." She broke off, her eyes losing much of their luster as she remembered her maid was dead.

In any case, her breathing was slowing, but I was not going to leave this issue unexplored, no matter how she might protest. Someone needed to look after her health, and Bauer was no longer here to do it. Luckily, Tante Ilse broached the matter herself.

"Perhaps it is time I allowed Freddy to examine me after all."

I exhaled in relief. "I can send him up to you as soon as he returns."

"Yes, please do," she replied between controlled breaths as she closed her eyes. "But now . . . I would just like . . . to rest."

"Of course." My gaze slid to the bell Mother must have placed on the bedside table. Bless her. I moved it closer to my great-aunt, and then leaned over to press a kiss to her forehead. "Ring if you need us."

She nodded, and I closed the door gently as I departed. I stood for a moment staring at the grains of wood, trying to grapple with my thoughts. Clearly, Tante Ilse was even more ill than I'd suspected. And whatever that illness was, it had affected her mind. I knew age could account for some of it, but I feared not to this extent. Maybe it was merely the harshness and depravation of the long years of the war, but again, I was doubtful. Though, what did I really know? I was no expert. But at least she was now willing to let Freddy attend to her. I hoped he would be able to help her, and to explain what was wrong.

My heart heavy and my insides swirling with dread, I turned toward the stairs, only to be brought up short by the sight of Matilda exiting from Tim's bedchamber. Of all the emotions bottled up inside me, ire was the easiest to give sway, and I strode into the upper foyer to halt the maid before she could reach the servants' stair. "Matilda, a moment."

She stopped, her head swiveling to look at me for two long seconds before she pivoted to face my approach. "Aye?" she replied with the minimum of courtesy.

My eyes narrowed. "I need you to account for your whereabouts earlier this afternoon. From approximately one to three o'clock."

She scoffed, her gaze flicking up and down me even as she held the pile of laundry she clutched before her like a shield. "You cannot be serious?"

"Oh, but I am."

"But I told ye about her note. Without it ye wouldn't 've even known where she was."

"You only told me because I saw you sneaking out of our bedchamber."

She scowled. "I didn't even know where the Kraut was."

"So you say, but you had her letter in your possession, which could have told you."

Her face reddened with fury. "I *told* ye, I couldn't read it. Not gibberish like that."

"Maybe not, but someone else might have read it to you." I arched my eyebrows. "Or you simply followed her."

Her eyes narrowed.

"I'm well aware you're not above spying, after all." I stalked two steps closer. "Maybe you hoped to catch her at something you could use against her. Something you could use to further your vendetta. Or maybe you intended to kill her all along. After all, you made your hatred of her abundantly clear."

"Aye, 'cept half the staff saw me about, includin' your mother and Miss Townsend. They'll confirm I never left the house."

"Will they?" I replied.

She sniffed, turning to go, though I hadn't dismissed her. "And as far as the fräulein," she spat, mangling the pronunciation, "well, she was no better than she oughta be."

I didn't stop her from walking away, rolling my eyes at the unoriginality of her prejudiced insult. Because Bauer was not only a German, but a pretty one at that, that meant she must have loose morals. It was such a predictable accusation it was almost pathetic.

Shaking my head, I decided to claim the bath before the men returned. But as I turned to fetch my things from our bedchamber, I noticed Grace strolling up the stairs, a dreamy, secretive smile playing across her lips as she perused a letter. I had no trouble guessing who the missive was from.

At the sight of me watching her, her smile froze and then slipped from her lips as she quickly refolded the letter. "I heard about Tante Ilse's maid. How terrible."

I leaned on the newel post, feeling weariness in every muscle. "Yes, it was very . . . *unpleasant*," I finally settled on after struggling to find the right word.

She nodded, seeming uncertain how to reply.

I glanced toward the door to the servants' stair, recalling Matilda's words. "Grace, did you happen to see Matilda this afternoon? Say, around two o'clock?"

She frowned. "Well, I don't recall precisely when, but I did see her shortly after the post arrived. Abbott might know what time that was."

"Good, I'll speak with him, then."

Her eyes darted over my features, and I wondered if she would dare voice the suspicion forming behind her eyes.

"You . . . you really suspect Matilda?" she murmured aghast.

"She stole a note Fräulein Bauer left in my room this morning which asked me to meet her at the place where she was killed." Her eyes widened, and I held up a hand to stave off her questions. "I don't know why she wanted to meet with me. But at the moment, Matilda is the only person who may have known where Bauer was, and she hated her."

"You think she read her note?"

"She's already admitted she tried to, but it was written in German. Whether she found someone to translate it or figured it out herself, I don't know." My gaze dipped to the letter my sister still clutched in her hand. "If I were you, I would assume Matilda isn't above reading anything she finds. Or reporting its contents to Mother."

Her eyes widened.

"And I speak from past experience."

Grace seemed horrified by the prospect, but I chose not to say anything further. Whatever was written in those letters was none of my concern. Not when I'd been largely absent from her life these last five years.

In any case, we were soon interrupted by the arrival of Sidney and Tim, whose footsteps dragged up the steps much as mine had. I elected not to remark on the absence of their Norfolk jackets and ties, deciding they must have been removed at the door and whisked off to the laundry. As it was, Sidney's once-crisp white shirt sported a thin slash of red where the coat had not fully covered it.

But for all the unpleasantness of their most recent task, I

was not about to cede precedence. "I call dibs on the bath," I stated, pointing at Tim, as he was the likeliest culprit to steal it from me.

He scowled. "Why aren't you already in it?"

"I had to check on Tante Ilse and interrogate a suspect. Will you bring me my dressing gown?" I asked Sidney, backing down the hall toward my intended target before Tim could dart around me. "And Tim, will you be a dear and please tell Freddy that Tante Ilse wishes to see him. Thank you," I called over my shoulder.

I was seated on the edge of the tub, pouring in a liberal dollop of rose-scented bath oil and waiting on the water to fill the tub, when my husband rapped on the door. "Come in."

He slipped inside, the Chinese blue satin garment held before him.

"Thank you." I nodded toward the hook on the back of the door. "Hang it there."

When he finished, he turned to stand with his back resting against the door and his arms crossed over his chest, seeming to be in no hurry to depart.

"Anything to report?"

"Nothing but that the coroner's inquest will probably be Monday at the Crown, and we'll need to attend, of course," he replied on a weary exhale.

I turned off the tap and bent down to unlace my half boots. "I guessed as much. Not that the police will gather much information between now and then. The verdict will be *murder by person or persons unknown*, with a police inquest to follow."

"Yes, let's hope this inspector has more experience than Sergeant Bibby with such matters. I assume that's why you didn't mention the letter. You hoped the inspector would be less likely to jump to conclusions."

I shrugged. "It seemed . . . prudent."

He crossed one ankle over the other, settling in more comfortably. "Now, what's this about interrogating a suspect? I've never seen your brother and sister so bug-eyed as when you made that pronouncement."

I looked up at him with a grimace as I toed off my boots. "Matilda."

"And what did she have to say?"

I told him about her denial of any wrongdoing and her insistence she'd been here, as well as Grace's partial confirmation.

"So you'll need to speak with Abbott." His gaze tracked my movements as I removed my stockings and dropped them on the floor next to my shoes.

"Yes, though *loath* as I am to admit it, I already doubt she's the killer."

"Because of her loyalty to your family?"

"I simply can't imagine a scenario in which she would decide killing Bauer would be beneficial to our family, or more to the point, to my mother." I tilted my head to the side. "Unless Bauer did something terrible we're not yet aware of. But then it's more probable she would have simply shared the matter with Mother and hoped to see the girl sacked or arrested."

I paused in unbuttoning my blouse, glancing up at Sidney, who seemed partially absorbed with this task. "Are you just going to stand there watching me?"

His eyes took on a roguish glint. "You don't mind when I do so at home?"

"Yes, but . . . this is my parents' house," I finished somewhat lamely, feeling my cheeks begin to heat.

His lips curled upward at the corners in teasing. "Your point being?"

"I know we're married," I replied, lowering my voice to a whisper. "But if Mother learned of it, she would ring a peal over my head."

"Do you honestly think your mother would say anything?"

I glowered. "Well, I certainly don't want to find out."

He chuckled. "I take your point. I shall behave myself." He cast me a wolfish grin as he turned to go with a parting promise. "For now."

CHAPTER 21

Despite the day's sad events, Saturday's dinner was no more awkward and fraught than normal. Everyone acted more or less as they normally did, except for Tim, who was fidgety and absorbed in his own thoughts. I had to wonder whether it was because of the war. Whether the sight of Bauer's body had reminded him of things he had preferred to forget. As such, I watched Sidney and Freddy for the same signs, but either they were better at concealing their distress or it hadn't affected them to the same degree.

Sergeant Bibby arrived shortly after dinner to interview the servants and then the family. Though by the speed with which this was done, it all seemed to be rather cursory. I didn't hold much faith he'd uncovered anything of interest, or that he'd expected to. He was the curtest with my great-aunt, but Father's presence seemed to quell any harsher impulses. Given the questions he was asking, I was forced to tell him about the letter Bauer had left me, but he seemed to care very little for this scrap of evidence, except that it explained how we'd come to find her so swiftly.

Church the following morning was equally as mundane. I'd hoped to catch a glimpse of the stranger Tante Ilse and I had both seen the previous week—the man who might or might not be the second deserter—but he either kept well out of sight or did not make an appearance. So I spent much of our time before and after the service watching and listening, thinking I might witness a look or overhear a comment from one of my parents' neighbors that might offer some insight as to who harbored enough hatred of Germans that they might have killed Bauer. However, no one exhibited any particularly guilty behavior or spoke ill of the dead. Of course, almost no one went out of their way to express empathy or remorse either.

In fact, the only two members of the congregation who seemed affected were Mother's friend, Mrs. Wild, and Cyril Bolingbroke—Grace's beau. Cyril expressed what seemed to be heartfelt condolences to Tante Ilse. At least, heartfelt enough to earn him an invitation to Sunday dinner. I didn't object to his display of sympathy, but I was also hesitant to be won over by it. There was something in his demeanor that wasn't entirely natural, and I couldn't help but think of the look in his eyes the day Grace arrived, when Bauer rode past us on her bicycle. I hadn't thought much of it since then, but it needled me now. At the time, I'd wondered if they knew each other, and now that curiosity was sharper.

Later that evening, I was seated before the vanity in our bedchamber, adjusting the pearls draped around my neck and contemplating how I might broach the subject with Cyril, when there was a rap on the door. I glanced at Sidney's reflection in the mirror where he stood adjusting his bow tie and then called out for the person to enter. By the strength of the knock and the vibration of the floorboards from his approaching footsteps moments before, I knew it was my husband's valet, Nimble.

"Come to check on me, did you?" Sidney jested. "Don't think the old man can tie his own tie?" As the captain of his company, he'd often been referred to semi-affectionately as *the old man*, no matter that he was younger than some of his men.

"Nay, sir. Ye always do a right fine job," Nimble replied soberly. "Better 'an I can with these ham fists." He shifted his feet, hovering in the doorway, dithering over something. "Might I have a word?" he finally asked.

"Of course," Sidney replied, dropping his jovial manner. His gaze flicked toward me, and I pushed to my feet.

"I shall give you some privacy."

"Nay," he replied sharply, making me jerk to a halt. "That is, you can hear what I have to say, too."

I nodded, retreating back to the vanity bench.

Nimble closed the door and then stood rubbing the back of his neck above his starched collar. He looked distinctly uncomfortable.

"Miss Bauer spoke to me in the laundry two nights past."

Sidney and I shared a brief look, but did not interject.

"I was ironin' Cap'n Kent's shirts when she came in with a gown for Mrs. Vischering. At first she was quiet-like, but when I asked how she was doin', she just started talkin'." He spoke of this almost in wonderment, but I was not surprised. Who knew how long it had been since anyone of her own class had expressed concern for her. And for all of Nimble's size and ungainliness, there was a kindness that radiated from him she must have intuited.

"What did she say?" Sidney prompted, sliding one arm into his black coat.

"I'm afraid I couldn't make all of it out, but I gathered that people haven't been very nice to her. Here, nor anywhere. Least, not since she left home." His gaze dipped to the floor. "I tried to be comfortin' to her." He flushed. "But I think she mighta taken it the wrong way." He began to rub his neck again. "She . . . she clutched my arm and got this look in her eyes. Started tellin' me how good I was, and askin' questions about Mrs. Kent."

"Me?" I replied in some startlement.

He nodded. "I thought maybe she wondered if you'd take her on as your lady's maid."

Perhaps that explained why she wished to meet with me. But why the secrecy? She could have spoken to me about that here.

His gaze darted to Sidney and then back to me. "But then she started askin' about the war. About what ye did and where ye lived. She said she knew that Matilda had worked for ye for a time?" His voice lifted, as if he didn't quite believe this, but when I didn't answer, he pressed on. "Anyway, I thought ye should know. Especially, considering . . ."

Considering the fact she was dead.

"Yes, thank you for telling us," I told him, trying to get my head around this development.

Sidney nodded, and Nimble bowed out of the room. It was some moments later when I looked up to find my husband staring at me expectantly that I realized he'd spoken.

"Why do you think Fräulein Bauer was gathering info about you?" he repeated.

"I don't know."

I found myself reanalyzing every interaction I'd ever had with Bauer, and then wondering if I was overthinking it. Maybe she had simply been curious whether I might take her into my employ after Tante Ilse's passing. Maybe her questions about the war had mainly been to try to better understand my opinion of Germans. But the sinking feeling in the pit of my stomach also told me that might be wishful thinking.

"Perhaps your great-aunt knows," he suggested.

"Perhaps," I agreed before inhaling a bracing breath. "In any case, we're not going to find the answer here." I pushed to my feet, allowing my gaze to travel over his impressive physique swathed in evening attire, much as he perused the folds and curves of my russet-red gown. "Shall we?"

He gestured for me to precede him, and we descended the stairs to join the others gathering in the drawing room. Cyril was already present, with his thick ash-brown hair liberally coated in brilliantine to restrain it, and Grace clinging to his arm. And *clinging* was the operative word. Not that Cyril seemed averse to her attentions, but he didn't appear quite comfortable with them either.

"Isn't Cyril the sweetest?" Grace cooed, gazing up at him. "He wanted to ask me on a picnic yesterday, but he thought he shouldn't take me away from my family so soon after my arrival."

"Yes, well, I thought it best. And my uncle needed me up at Long Shaw much of the day anyway."

"His uncle owns Long Shaw now. Purchased it from Sir Rupert's niece and fixed it up smartly. You remember what a rubble it had become. Now it's ever so lovely."

Mother sidled up beside us. "We were so sad when Sir Rupert passed. And without an heir." She tsked. "But it's good to see Long Shaw is now in capable hands."

I couldn't tell whether the word "capable" was meant to express approval or an insult, but either way, per usual, Mother was being lavish with her faint praise.

She slid her arm through Cyril's on the other side. "Allow me to introduce you to Frau Vischering again," she declared, pulling him toward the chair near the hearth, where Tante Ilse sat gazing into the flames. Firelight flickered over her features, accentuating every crook and cranny.

"I can do that, Mother," Grace protested.

However, Mother turned a stern look upon her, one that compelled Grace to relinquish her hold on a bemused Cyril. "Go and greet your sister-in-law. You've barely spoken to her yet."

This was true, as Rachel had felt ill the evening before, and had missed church this morning, as well. I was relieved to see her looking better, and followed Grace over to tell her so.

"It's nothing," she demurred with a glance at her husband. "Freddy suspects it's just exhaustion. Too many late nights up with Ruthie."

"Which is why we have Miss Pettigrew," Freddy groused, referencing their nanny, who also currently had charge of Ruth.

"Yes, I know," Rachel sniped. "But I can't just ignore Ruthie's cries."

"Yes, you can. It's Pettigrew's job to answer them in the middle of the night, not you. And she tells us Ruth will never learn to rest in her own bed if you're forever rushing to pick her up."

I struggled not to react, feeling as if I'd stepped into the midst of a very heated battle that I should not have been privy to. Fortunately, Freddy seemed to at least have some sense of the line he'd overstepped.

"I'm worried about you," he said, lowering his voice. "You're running yourself ragged."

But Rachel was not ready yet to sheath her claws. "As if you get any more sleep than I do. You only know I'm awake because you're up half the night pacing or roaming the countryside."

Grace and I exchanged a speaking look, and despite the distance in our relationship, I was grateful we seemed to have the same instinct. She looped her arm through Rachel's, tugging her toward a pair of chairs set before the windows. "You haven't yet told me all about Ruthie's clever new accomplishments."

Meanwhile, I steered Freddy toward the sideboard, thinking he might want a glass of brandy, but he didn't pick up the decanter.

"I know what you're going to say," he grumbled, cutting a glance toward where his wife and our sister now had their heads bent together talking. "I should never have mentioned Miss Pettigrew."

"Actually, I wasn't."

His gaze returned to mine.

"I trusted you to be quick enough to figure that out on your own." I shifted so that I could observe everyone gathered about the room. Everyone save Tim, that was, who, as always, was last to arrive. My eyes settled on Sidney, where he stood conversing with my father. "You do realize she may be clinging to Ruth so tightly because she feels somewhat insecure when it comes to you."

A vee formed between Freddy's brows. "I don't know what you mean."

I turned my head to look him straight in the eye, unwilling to let him retreat behind a mask of confusion. "I think you do."

His entire frame tightened in frustration. "Everyone asks their questions, thinking they want the answers, but they really don't. Not when what they've imagined is so very different from reality. Not when they have no idea . . ." He broke off, apparently reading something in my eyes. It took him a moment to speak. "But you do, don't you?"

I couldn't answer that, *shouldn't* answer that. And after a moment's fraught silence, he seemed to realize this.

He exhaled a heavy breath, and some of the tension drained from his tall frame. We stood companionably that way for a minute or two before he ventured to speak again, clueing me in to what he'd been contemplating in that time. "Does Sidney talk to you?"

"Sometimes," I replied honestly. "But it's still difficult for him to do so. Even knowing that I . . ." I didn't finish that thought. "He tries, and that's all I can ask of him."

"Is it enough?"

I turned my head to gaze at his profile, wondering how deep the strain between him and Rachel ran. "Most of the time."

But not all the time. The words remained unspoken, but they rang in the air between us nonetheless.

Freddy nodded.

Tim slid through the door then, coming to a halt beside us, just as Abbott arrived to announce that dinner was ready. All I could do was shake my head at him in fond exasperation, to which he offered me a crooked smile in return.

At dinner I was seated next to Cyril, and I did my best to draw him out and engage him in conversation, but these attempts were met with mixed results. For if one thing was quite clear, it was that Cyril was not entirely comfortable with me. My sister did not help matters by shooting me glares across the table. Glares that I could not comprehend, as I was doing my best to be charming and civil, despite my growing suspicion that Cyril was hiding something.

Twice more he mentioned the fact that he'd spent the previous day with his uncle at Long Shaw—a point he had already emphasized. The very fact that he seemed so anxious that we accept this as truth had the exact opposite effect, making me wonder if he was lying. I added it to my already-growing list of queries to be answered during or following the inquest the following day.

When Tante Ilse confessed her desire to retire early, I volunteered to be the one to help her upstairs, as eager to escape Grace's barbed glares as I was to assist my great-aunt. Why my offer to do so should irritate my mother, I couldn't fathom, but she reminded me and my brothers that it was to be a particularly cold night and so we would be best served to remain indoors—a thinly veiled warning for us not to drink in the stables. No matter. I was headed to bed.

I sat with Tante Ilse on her fainting couch until the upstairs maid assigned to her since Bauer's passing arrived. She clutched my hand between hers as she reminisced about a dinner party she'd attended some years earlier. Weary and uneasy at heart, I allowed her words to wash over me, not quite grasping the exact timing or context of her story, but appreciating it nonetheless. She had always had a knack for storytelling, and neither age nor the slips of her memory had dulled that. Not yet anyway.

I firmly shut the door on that thought, and then looked up in surprise as a door closed across the corridor just as resolutely. I realized it must have been Grace, and the motorcar we'd heard outside the window a moment before must have belonged to Cyril.

Tante Ilse's hand squeezed mine, recalling my attention. "Sisters should not be at odds."

I smiled tightly. "Yes, well, Grace is very angry at me." My voice dipped. "And I can't say she doesn't have a right to be."

"Yes, *mein Liebchen*, but that anger is only masking hurt." Her gaze took on a faraway cast. "When my older sister, Lina, your grandmother, married your grandfather and left for England, I was . . . sad. Upset. And, yes, angry. I felt like she had abandoned me. And I refused to visit her here for many years. But later, when I was older, I better understood. She had not left me. She had merely gone on to live her life. As we all do, in time." She tapped the top of my hand as she looked up. "Your sister will realize this in time, too. If you keep trying."

I considered what she'd said, and how I'd just encouraged Freddy to keep trying with Rachel. How Sidney and I had made a commitment to do so. Did Grace not deserve the same effort?

There was a rap on the door preceding the entry of the maid, and I leaned in to press a kiss to Tante Ilse's papery cheek before pushing to my feet. "Sleep well."

She nodded to me in encouragement, perhaps already knowing what I was about to do.

Then before I could reconsider, I crossed the hall to Grace's door and knocked.

A moment later, I heard her footsteps stomping across the room before the door was flung open. I didn't think she could have expected it to be me, but her expression was sour anyway. "What do you want?"

"May I talk to you?"

Her green eyes searched mine mistrustfully before finally relenting. She backed into the room, allowing me a glimpse of the tidy space in which she lived. At least, it was far tidier than I had ever kept my bedchamber. Painted in a soft shade of primrose, with pale oak furnishings and white bedding and curtains, it was bright and airy, and well-lit even at this hour by the two lamps placed on opposite sides of the room. Porcelain bird statues lined several shelves hanging above her bureau, something I hadn't known she collected. That realization caused a pang in my heart.

Given the overall orderliness, I couldn't help but note the letter peeking out from beneath a pillow on her bed. Recognizing I had seen this, Grace hurried over to shove it farther underneath and plopped down on the bed in front of it. I supposed she had been rereading Cyril's correspondence to her, just as I had done when Sidney was away from Brock House the summer of our courtship.

"Well, you're here," she burst forth as I sank down on the edge of the bed several feet from her. "So, talk."

"Grace," I began tentatively. "I don't blame you for being mad. If I were in your shoes, I would be, too."

She turned her head to the side, as if unable to look at me.

"All I can do is say I'm sorry. And I am." I hesitated, uncertain how to go on. Uncertain whether making excuses would help or make it worse.

"Is that all?" she snapped when I didn't say more. When I continued to vacillate, her gaze swung back to me, narrowing. "Why did you stay away?"

My gaze dipped toward where my hand rested against the

downy counterpane. "Well, it was partly the war. I had my bit to do. No matter how much others might belittle it," I added, hearing her draw breath to repeat one of Mother's disparaging remarks, thinking I'd been a shipping clerk. I lifted my chin. "I had agreed to my duty, and I was as determined as anyone to do it to the fullest." I swallowed. "And it was partly apprehension of missing Sidney when he was home on one of his leaves or, God forbid, missing a telegram informing me he'd been injured. He often had little notice when his leaves would be, and obviously, no notice of the latter." I pressed a hand to my quavering abdomen, forcing myself to go on haltingly. "And partly the fact that I couldn't face Rob's death. Being here . . . knowing . . ." I shook my head. "I couldn't do it, coward though I might have been."

Grace didn't reply immediately, but when she did, her voice was not so brittle. "And after the war ended?"

"I was still reeling from Sidney's reported death. And then his return."

She nodded, perhaps not having considered this before.

So I pressed on before she spoke. "War isn't easy on anyone. We all make mistakes. And in times like that, all anyone can ever ask is that we each do the best we can with the hand we've been dealt."

Grace reached out to pass her finger over a bit of stitching along the counterpane. "Cyril said something similar to me once," she murmured, and I could only wonder at the context.

"When did the two of you meet?"

"The summer before last, at a garden-party fundraiser thrown by Mrs. Wild." She shook her head. "Otherwise Mother would never have let me go." She smiled at the memory. "He looked so dashing. He was one of the lone young gentlemen there, and all the girls were vying for his attention."

If Cyril was like most of the other veterans I'd met, I imagined he hadn't been precisely comfortable being at the center of all that attention, especially not knowing how many of his fellow soldiers had been buried over in France and would never have the chance to receive such adulation.

"Of course, I was too young at the time for him to take more than a passing notice of me, but when I was home for winter break just before I turned sixteen, well, it was a different story."

"You're in love with him, aren't you?" I asked, merely intending to clarify matters, but her guard instantly went up.

"Yes," she replied, crossing her arms over her chest. "And he loves me. He's told me so."

"Calm yourself, Grace. I'm not questioning your affection. Has he asked you to marry him?"

Her brow lowered. "No. But I'm certain it's just a matter of time."

But her body language said she was less certain than she claimed.

As if recognizing this, her scowl returned. "You didn't have to badger him at dinner."

I frowned. "I was hardly badgering him. I was conversing with him on the most mundane of topics, trying to set him at ease."

Her expression turned skeptical.

"It's true." I lifted my hands in defense. "I don't know why he was so discomfited."

She opened her mouth as if to protest this description and then allowed it to fall shut.

Deciding any further discussion of Cyril's odd behavior would rile her further, I switched subjects. "Does Mother approve of the match?"

She retreated a bit. "I don't know. She keeps insisting I'm too young."

Which she was, though not by much. After all, I had been just a little over a year older when I wed Sidney.

Her eyes suddenly flashed and her mouth tightened. "But otherwise Cyril's prospects seem to wax and wane according to her opinion of you. One moment she's talking about taking me to York or London to introduce me to some more people my age, and the next she's perfectly happy to see Cyril court me."

That she blamed me for this, as well, was obvious, but I wasn't about to apologize for Mother's behavior. Particularly when my staying away had seemed to serve Grace's purposes just fine.

"Well, as the youngest you were always her favorite," I replied. "I'm sure you can convince her to come around to your way of thinking."

She shook her head. "Not anymore."

"What do you mean?"

She unclasped a bracelet from her wrist and dropped it onto the bed beside her. "That honor now belongs to Tim. Haven't you noticed?"

"I did notice he seems to be rather restless and forgetful," I admitted.

"It's more than that. Father is forever exasperated with him for not following through on the few small tasks assigned to him. He just wanders about, meandering aimlessly through his days, expending the bare minimum of effort."

That she was repeating some of what she'd overheard from others was obvious, but I was still curious to hear her impressions.

"Father thinks he needs some sort of occupation, but Mother coddles him and tells Father to leave him alone. That is, until Tim fails to do something Mother asks of him. But then he makes certain to let slip something one of the rest of us has done wrong, so her ire will turn on us."

"Yes, I noticed that," I admitted, recalling how he'd revealed the fact that Freddy and I had shared a bottle of whisky in the barn.

"Tim has turned into a little sneak," she brooded, crossing her arms over her chest.

With Tim being the closest to her in age, the two of them had always had a contentious relationship, squabbling one minute and best mates the next. I was more interested in learning what insights she held about others in the household. "What about Freddy? What have you observed there?"

Her gaze snapped to mine and she sneered. "Do you really care?"

I arched my eyebrows at this display of contempt. "Careful, sis. I'm the one who's a rotter, remember?" I mocked. "Don't say something now to change that."

Her brow remained furrowed, but I could tell by the wavering of her features that she was fighting to hold on to her indignation.

"Of course, I care," I retorted, growing annoyed with her determination to dislike me. "Now, tell me."

She lowered her arms. "He's different, too. Sharper. More serious." Her fingers toyed with the links of her bracelet. "He hardly ever cracks jokes anymore. And sometimes he wanders at night."

I nodded, for none of this was surprising to me. I'd witnessed much of the same in Sidney, as well as in other men returning from the war. But her next comment came as somewhat of a shock.

She peered through her eyelashes at me. "Mother thinks he might be having an affair."

I stiffened, for the very idea of her suspecting such a thing angered me. I knew men who were philanderers and I knew men who were haunted by the war, and I had witnessed the differences in their demeanor. Freddy was definitely the latter.

"But I don't think that's it," Grace said, perhaps sensing my anger and misinterpreting it.

"It's the war," I stated with certainty. "The number of men he watched die under his knife and in his care disturbs him."

She seemed shocked speechless by this, and her face paled at the thought. Perhaps I should have been less blunt, but she was nearly seventeen and she wished to marry a veteran. She needed to understand at least some of what these men had experienced, some of the demons they'd brought home with them.

"I take it Cyril hasn't spoken to you about any of this."

She shook her head. "But I know what Freddy and Tim and some of the others say about him." Her voice hardened. "And it's not true."

"You've asked him about it?"

"No, but I know what kind of man he is. He would never do something so dishonorable."

"You would be surprised what otherwise honorable men might be convinced to do when faced with the hell they fought in," I cautioned. Sticking their hand above the parapet to be shot by a sniper or firing a bullet into their own foot was sometimes preferable to enduring the trenches for a single day more.

"He didn't do it," she practically growled.

Given her stalwart defense, it seemed fruitless to continue pressing her on the matter, but that didn't mean I was satisfied. Grace might be blinded by infatuation, but I was not. His intentions toward my sister were reason enough to look into the matter, and his fretful behavior and reaction to Bauer only cemented it. It was time for Sidney to call in a favor of his own.

CHAPTER 22

The coroner's inquest progressed much as expected the following morning when it adjourned in the parlor of the Crown, with a few exceptions. For one, the inspector from Richmond had been needed elsewhere, and so he had left the matter in Sergeant Bibby's dubious hands. Given the fact that the death was obviously manslaughter, and that no immediate suspect had been uncovered to bring forth on charges, the inspector's presence wasn't truly required anyway. Once the expected verdict of *willful murder by a person or persons unknown* had been pronounced, the police would be asked to conduct a more thorough investigation into the matter.

It was hoped that this would lead to the inspector's greater involvement, but given the lack of evidence, the victim's foreignness, and the little hope there was of retrieving fingerprints from the pitchfork handle—save those belonging to the Kiddses' farmhands who had used it to bale hay—I didn't hold much hope of that happening. Not when the inspector was in charge of such a large area. He might call in Scotland Yard, but I also thought that to be doubtful. No, the inquiry would be left in Sergeant Bibby's hands, with predictable results.

Or so I believed. Though I hadn't counted on Mr. Metcalfe, the coroner, stepping forward to voice an accusation of his own.

"Aye, well, I can't say that the chit wasn't asking for trouble walking where she shouldn't have been," he pronounced with the same utter lack of compassion he'd shown through the entire proceedings. He glanced toward where Bauer's body lay covered by a sheet on a table to his right in the slanting rays of the sun shining through the pub windows. Earlier the jurors had gathered around her as Freddy had explained her cause of death. His testimony as a surgeon and former RAMC officer had been deemed enough, and so no official police surgeon had been called in to examine the body. "But I believe I've seen the culprit."

This caused a minor stir among the people seated at the scarred trestle tables scattered about the room, most of whom were men puffing on cigarettes or pipes.

It was evident from the keen expression on his craggy face that he'd expected this reaction. He'd always possessed the grandiosity of a born showman. "My foreman caught a German sleeping in one of my field barns some nights past."

Sidney and I shared a look of astonishment. The second deserter?

"The Kraut ran off before he could summon assistance, but he'd been there all right. I saw with my own eyes the nest in the hay he'd created for himself." He sat back, clasping his hands over his abdomen and watching in satisfaction as the jurors and audience murmured among themselves. "Perhaps he was conspiring with the maid and they had a tiff, or maybe he was working alone. But it's clear he's up to no good."

"How did your foreman know he was a German?" my father asked from his seat on my other side, speaking in his usual measured voice but somehow still being heard above the din.

"I trust my foreman to know the difference," was Metcalfe's oblique response. He glowered at my father. "Perhaps you don't appreciate the connection being pointed out, but I think it strains credulity that three Germans should appear in our small community at the same time and not somehow be connected."

"Aye," Father conceded, the only evidence of his agitation being the furrow between his eyes. "But it seems unnecessary to make spurious accusations about the girl when we've no proof that she did anything more sinister than enter the field barn of one of our neighbors without permission."

I felt a surge of affection toward him for defending Tante Ilse's maid. In truth, I'd given little thought to how Tante Ilse's arrival and Bauer's murder had affected him. He'd always been fond of his aunt, but accepting her into his household so soon after the war was not without its difficulties, and yet he'd done so, without hesitation. And here he sat, defending her maid, despite all the questions and unknowns of her brief time with us and her unfortunate death, simply because it was the right thing to do.

Metcalfe dipped his head in acknowledgment of this. The old man might be pompous and controlling, but he also recognized how well-respected my father was. When he spoke, people listened. It was a trait he and Sidney shared. One among many.

"Did your foreman give a description of the man?" Isaac Hardcastle suddenly stood up to ask from the audience. "For I think I may have seen him myself." He glanced about the room, as if to gauge the effect of his words on others. "I saw the maid in question speaking with a straw-haired fellow outside the chemist some days past, and they were speaking German."

I stiffened, unable to suppress my reaction to this bit of news, and Sidney and Father both turned to look at me, but I shook my head minutely. I would not discuss it here. Not while the rest of the audience speculated aloud about straw-haired strangers.

Sergeant Bibby pushed to his feet, asking for quiet from the audience before he addressed the jury. "Well, it seems clear to me we have a likely suspect."

"Aye," Metcalfe agreed. "But as we don't yet know his name, I ask the jury to return a verdict of *willful murder by a person or persons unknown.*"

As this was all but a formality at this point, Sidney, Father, and I left the pub to stand under the eaves of the rough-hewn stone building overlooking Market Place. The structure blocked much of the wind, but its chill still cut to the bone, and the weak sunlight filtering through the clouds did nothing to counter it. Winter was upon us.

"Why did you react when Hardcastle mentioned he'd seen

Fräulein Bauer speaking with a man?" Sidney mumbled around his cigarette as he cupped his hands around the tip to light it.

"Because Violet Capshaw said she'd also seen Bauer speaking with a strange man near the chemist's shop, though she couldn't describe him because they were in shadow."

I elected not to mention the fact that I'd also seen a straw-haired man, this time in the churchyard. Just as I withheld the fact that Tante Ilse may have glimpsed the same man and accused him of being the second deserter. I could read in Sidney's eyes that he was thinking of these things as well, but he obeyed my unspoken wishes and didn't speak of them in front of my father.

"Of course, that still doesn't mean the fellow was German, or that he killed Bauer," I added. But based on the sheer number of reported sightings, it seemed obvious there was some sort of stranger hereabouts, and that he was somehow familiar to Tante Ilse and Bauer.

Sidney exhaled a stream of smoke into the breeze. "But that won't stop people from believing he did."

Father's grim gaze remained fastened on something across the street. "Sidney's right. And if the fellow does happen to be German, I'm afraid that may see him convicted without any further evidence."

Sidney seemed to hear something behind his words that I hadn't, for he stilled with the fag pressed to his lips, but didn't inhale. "Would your neighbors take justice into their own hands?"

My heart rose into my throat as I turned to Father, curious to hear his answer.

He spoked measuredly. "If their anger was great enough."

And it was, considering all the lingering, pent-up resentment aimed at Germany, and the fact that their armies and allies had killed forty-nine of the villagers' sons and one daughter.

"If they could justify it to themselves as stopping a man from murdering again or fleeing from his crimes, then yes." He looked at Sidney with a mournful glint in his eyes. "Yes, I think some of them are capable of it."

I'd witnessed how cruel and unforgiving people could be to one another. I'd watched a German soldier break an old man's arm because he didn't obey his order fast enough. I'd seen a young woman pulled out of line and led away by an officer, knowing full well what he intended to do to her. I'd watched as a pair of French citizens who had been stripped of nearly all their possessions, and reduced to near skeletons by the food restrictions, had then been shot mercilessly in the street when they were discovered concealing one small loaf of brown bread beyond their allotted restrictions. And I'd endured such things without being able to say or do anything, not only out of fear that they would turn on me, but that I would draw their attention and unwittingly reveal my true identity and endanger my mission, as well as the lives of those intelligence-gathering agents within Belgium and France who had helped me.

But I had never expected I might witness such behavior at home, among the peaceful neighbors of the Dales. I wanted to argue that it wasn't possible. That the people of Hawes might be grieving, but they would never let such hatred or their desire for vengeance sway them. But Father knew them far better than I did, and he was not prone to speak without careful consideration. For him to admit to such a fear, there must be a great deal of truth behind it.

When his gaze dipped to meet mine, I could see concern deeply etched in the lines of his face. "Which is why you had better uncover the truth first."

I blinked in surprise. "Are you actually *asking* us to investigate?"

"It's what you did for your Aunt Ernestine, and she had high praise for you."

I arched a single eyebrow sardonically. "Don't you mean Sidney?"

"Aye, well, we all knew who was the brains behind that operation," he jested, outright shocking me, and making Sidney's lips quirk upward at the corners. "Whether or not they wish to admit it."

Father looked behind him as the door opened, nodding at a

neighbor as they ambled away. When he turned back, he moved a step closer, lowering his voice. "That girl deserves justice for what was done to her, and I don't wish to see the wrong man punished simply for the crime of being German." His gaze shifted to the side, his brow darkening. "I'd also like to know if one of my neighbors is capable of killing a woman in cold blood for the same reason."

I couldn't say no. Not when I wanted the same answers. Not when I already intended to continue investigating. But there was one last hurdle to overcome that he might be able to help us with. "Mother won't like it."

"I'll handle your mother."

I looked at Sidney, who had observed this exchange without speaking, but who I knew was already aware of my intentions. Then I nodded. "But we'll need your help," I told my father. "We need you to keep your ears open and speak with any neighbors you can. People may tell you something they won't tell us."

We all looked up as the door opened again, but this time it was Freddy, who emerged without his coat and hat. He hunched his shoulders, huddling against the wind.

"Metcalfe has agreed to release the body," he told us. "Shall I handle the arrangements? I'm headed in that direction anyway to make a call on Mrs. Askew."

Father accepted his offer, and the two of them conferred briefly over what was to be done while Sidney and I moved off toward Father's Rolls-Royce. On the drive home, I was largely silent, staring out the window and contemplating Bauer's death while Father and Sidney conversed in the front seat. The last of the autumn leaves scattered in our passing, pinwheeling down the side of the road, a bright blot in the gloomy landscape.

My thoughts slipped to the coming holidays at the end of the month, and whether my parents still chopped down an evergreen to be decorated for Christmas, a tradition my grandmother had brought with her to Yorkshire over sixty years ago. A German tradition.

During the war, there had been high anti-German sentiment, and a push to abandon all things German. I wondered if in that fervor my parents had abandoned the use of a Christmas tree. And if they had, would they revive it now that the war was over, now that Tante Ilse was here with us?

As we slowed to turn onto the drive that led up through the copse of trees to Brock House, I contemplated whether I should be the one to request we still do so.

That was when I spotted him. The man watching us from behind a tree about fifty feet away.

"Stop the car," I ordered, sitting forward.

"What?" One of the men broke off to ask.

"Stop the car!"

Father lurched to a halt at the edge of the drive, and I threw open the door to leap out. I set off at a run through the trees, hurdling the shallow ditch at the side of the road. Sidney shouted my name, but I didn't have time to turn and address him. Not if I was to catch the man. Where had he gone? There! Between the pair of twisted rowan trees. The distance separating us was growing.

"Stop!" I called after him, pressing onward, grateful I'd chosen to wear half boots instead of pumps for the inquest. Dirt and decaying leaves churned up beneath my feet as they pounded over the earth. The man swerved out of my sight behind a cluster of gorse bushes. When I reached the other side, I could no longer see him, though I ran several more steps in the direction I thought he'd gone before blundering to a stop. I swiveled left and then right, gasping for breath as I scoured the woods.

"What are you doing?" Sidney demanded as he caught up with me.

"I saw him . . . in the trees," I panted. There was no need to explain who "he" was. "He ran . . . I think that way." I pointed. "But I lost sight of him." I began to move forward again, but Sidney grabbed hold of my arm.

"Verity, stop. Think. What exactly were you going to do if you caught up with this man? He could have a gun."

I could see now that he was angry. The muscles in his jaw ticked and his eyes snapped. His hat had been abandoned somewhere behind us, either in the motorcar or on the ground, and his dark hair had fallen over his brow, curling as it was wont to do when not kept ruthlessly restrained.

"He doesn't," I protested. "I could tell." I pulled against him. "Come on. We're losing him."

He yanked me back. "There's no way you could tell that. Not from the brief glimpse you must have gotten of him. Verity, please."

It was the pleading note in his voice that made me stop struggling and turn to face him. He was right. I couldn't have known. Not for certain. Perhaps it *had* been foolish of me to run after him, but if I hadn't reacted immediately, I'd feared he would be long gone before we could return to search for him.

However, these woods didn't stretch on forever. They were merely a small copse bordered by open meadows in three directions, and the road to the south.

I turned in that direction, realizing he almost certainly had doubled back, and perhaps had already slipped across the road and south toward the forests bordering the river. But what I saw before me made me stiffen.

"I understand your desire to catch the fellow, to find out who he is, but not at risk to yourself," Sidney scolded, only to break off at the look on my face. He turned to follow my gaze. "What? What is it?"

In my pursuit of the man, I hadn't taken note of my surroundings or which way we were running, and so I suddenly found myself facing the sight I'd most wished to avoid since our arrival.

The crude treehouse was anchored in a large pocket formed between two thick branches and the trunk of an old oak tree. Its boards had aged and were riddled with divots and speckled with moss, but otherwise it appeared as stable as it had always been. I wondered when the last time it had been used. Freddy had said it was still standing, but had he, or Tim, or Grace even, climbed up into it? Or had it lain empty since Rob had left home for the last time to join his squadron in early 1915?

I flinched away from the thought, just as I flinched away

from the structure. My heart now beat more wildly in my chest than it had moments before. Blood roared in my ears, and I feared I might be sick if I didn't leave this place. Now.

I pulled from Sidney's grasp and began to stumble away, slowly at first, and then faster. Back the way we'd come. I didn't know if Father would still be waiting for us at the end of the drive, but it didn't matter. I simply had to get away.

Sidney soon caught up with me, taking a firm grip on my elbow lest I trip in my blind flight. He didn't speak, but I knew he must have questions. Despite my father's jest outside the Crown, we were all well aware of Sidney's intelligence. He must have realized the treehouse held some significance for me, and given my adverse reaction, it didn't require a genius to realize it must have something to do with Rob.

By the time we spied the Rolls-Royce still waiting on the drive beyond the trees, with my father standing beside it, I had mostly managed to compose myself, shoving the grief that had threatened to overwhelm me back down into the hole inside me where it belonged and stamping on it with my proverbial foot, for good measure.

"There was a man lurking in the woods," I explained in answer to my father's unspoken question. "I thought it must be the man Isaac Hardcastle and Violet Capshaw were speaking of."

Father's troubled gaze lifted to scan the trees beyond us before he nodded. "Good. Then maybe he already realizes we can help him if he knows something."

That was one possibility. But there was also a far more nefarious reason why he might have been lurking there. One that made my decision to recklessly run after him even stupider. My gaze lifted to Sidney's stern one, realizing he was thinking the same thing.

Father swiveled to stare down the drive. "I'll alert the staff and tell them to inform us if they notice anyone watching the house."

We were silent as the motorcar continued its journey up the drive to the house. A curtain twitched in the window of the cottage as we rolled past, so I was not surprised when we entered the inner courtyard from the carriage yard that Rachel was waiting for us.

"Is Freddy with you?" she asked, her arms crossed before her against the cold.

"Sorry, lass," Father told her. "He said he had to make a call on Mrs. Askew, and so I asked if he'd transport Fräulein Bauer's body to Faber's"—the local undertaker—"on the way."

She nodded stiffly, and then turned to retreat to the cottage, but I called out for her to wait. When I told Sidney to go on, I could tell from his arched eyebrows that he suspected I was stalling, not wishing to have the conversation he clearly intended to. But I had other reasons for wishing to speak to Rachel alone.

When the men had departed, Rachel stood in the doorway, the sharp glint in her eyes not precisely inviting conversation. "Is everything all right?" I began tentatively, worried she may have sought out Freddy for an urgent reason. "Can I help?"

She scrutinized me, and I realized I wasn't entirely certain what her opinion of me was. "No," she finally replied. "Miss Pettigrew has Ruth, and I'm . . ." She exhaled, releasing some of her palpable aggravation. "I just wanted to speak to Freddy."

I nodded, still uncertain how to broach the subject I wished to, or how she would react to my interference. I didn't know Rachel well enough to read her, and I wasn't certain she wanted me to. But for my brother's sake, I decided to forge ahead.

"You said that Freddy paces at night. That he sometimes roams the countryside."

Her gaze dropped to the ground, and I could tell she regretted disclosing those things before dinner the previous evening.

"Sidney does the same thing," I rushed to say before she withdrew.

Her eyes lifted, glittering softly in the veiled light.

"They all do. The men who returned. It's . . ." I swallowed. "It's the war, you see." I shook my head. "Not you or me. They . . . don't know how to leave it behind. Not after everything they've seen. So they try to outpace it, to drive it from their minds with exhaustion. They're simply trying to find a way to live with it, with the memories, the best they can."

For a moment I thought I was helping, that perhaps Rachel might have feared the same thing Grace had said our mother did—that Freddy was having an affair. But then the skin across her angular features tightened and her shoulders stiffened. "Well, he's home now. And he has a family counting on him. He needs to get over it."

With that she slammed the door of the cottage, leaving me standing on the doorstep feeling as if I'd been chastened as much as Freddy.

CHAPTER 23

⌖

Abbott greeted me at my parents' door, and I was so absorbed in my thoughts over what had just happened with Rachel that I almost missed what he was saying.

"You received a telephone call while you were out, ma'am."

I turned toward the butler abruptly. "Did they leave a message?"

He traded me a piece of paper for my coat and hat, which I opened immediately.

Plan on it. Rosalind

Hurrying to the telephone on the bureau, I dialed the number I used to contact the Secret Service, leaving nothing but my code name as the message before ringing off.

"I'm expecting another telephone call from Rosalind," I told Abbott. "And I'll be somewhere in the house until it comes through."

"Very good, ma'am," he replied as I turned away.

I spied Sidney through the door to the drawing room, but hurried on past and up the stairs, trusting he would follow. As expected, I'd done little more than remove my necklace and bracelet before he came striding through our bedchamber door. Before he could speak, I lifted the note to him for his inspection.

"I trust that Rosalind is actually Miss Silvernickel," he murmured, leaning against the bedpost as I traded my teardrop earrings for some more understated pearl studs.

"Presumably," I replied, for C's secretary had never actually been assigned a code name before. At least, not any that I knew of. But since Rosalind was one of Shakespeare's heroines in disguise, it seemed an appropriate sobriquet for the situation. " 'Plan on it' means she has information for me. Had she messaged something like 'can't make it,' that would mean the opposite."

"Then she's found something."

"About the bomb that killed General Bishop and his staff," I reminded him, swiveling to face him. "I can't imagine it has anything to do with Bauer's death." I frowned at my reflection in the mirror. Though I'd said such things about seemingly disparate intelligence before and been proven wrong.

He crossed to the fainting couch and dropped down on the edge of the cushions, scraping a hand back through his hair. "I suppose there's no use speculating on what."

"No," I agreed with a sigh. "But . . . I am wondering . . ." I nibbled my bottom lip, trying to find the words to voice what I was trying to say. Sidney waited patiently as I sorted through my impressions. "Well, frankly, I don't know what to make of the suggestion that the man I saw in the woods, the man so many people have seen lingering about, speaking with Bauer, is the second deserter."

"Maybe he isn't."

I nodded, my troubled gaze lifting to meet his. "There's been no further notes. No attempts at blackmail. And if he's truly meant to intimidate me, he'd doing a rather shoddy job of it. Tante Ilse's memory isn't what it once was," I regretfully admitted. "And I'm starting to think she might have been mistaken."

"You said Landau swore that second deserter hadn't been sent by him, or anyone else in the service. Do you believe him?"

"I do. And yet I still don't understand how the second deserter knew to go to Tante Ilse's home. Despite her recent memory problems, I doubt she mistook the matter. Her former maid,

Schmidt, would have still been alive then, and she would have been canny enough to see through most fibs. So whoever the man was, he must have been convincing." I reached out to trail my finger over a shallow gouge in the wood at the edge of the vanity table. "I know we speculated he might have been a suspicious villager intent on entrapping her, but . . ." I tilted my head uncertainly. "That still doesn't make sense to me."

"Maybe he learned about her from the first deserter."

I looked up at Sidney as he sank deeper into the couch, much struck by this idea.

He shrugged. "Maybe he wanted to help another friend or family member escape from the fighting."

"That actually makes a great deal of sense. Becker was obviously a man who cared significantly for his loved ones. It would be logical that he might attempt to help another soldier in that way." I sat taller in my eagerness. "He could have described the route we'd taken, assured them Tante Ilse's was a safe place to transform themselves before escaping farther into Germany. They wouldn't have had the forged papers and documents Becker had been given by us, but they would still have had a chance of passing unchallenged if they feigned an injury or some such thing."

I breathed easier having this possible explanation. At least, for a moment. I frowned. "But then why would the second deserter then follow Tante Ilse and her maid to England?"

"Perhaps it's just as you said a moment ago. Maybe he didn't, and your great-aunt is mistaken." His brow knitted. "Or he followed her hoping she would help him. After all, she'd assisted him in the past under difficult circumstances. Maybe he hoped she'd do the same now."

I tilted my head, considering this. "So he approached Bauer, hoping she might intercede on his behalf since Tante Ilse rarely, if ever, ventures out on her own. Her health is too frail for that now." I felt a pinch in my chest just stating those words. "It makes sense. It even explains why she might have been asking Nimble questions about me, and why she asked me to meet her

in that field barn. Maybe she intended to introduce me to him."
I grimaced in skepticism. "And then he killed her?"

Sidney cradled his jaw in one hand, running his index finger
back and forth over his lips as he contemplated the matter. "It's
possible he became angry when you didn't appear, and they
fought and he stabbed her." He shook his head. "But I doubt it.
A man capable of making his way from Germany all the way to
the North Riding of Yorkshire, through what I would term hostile territory, given his nationality, would be both patient and
cool under pressure. I can't imagine he suddenly snapped and
skewered the girl out of disappointment. Not when he must
have known she was his best hope."

I nodded, agreeing with his assessment. "But he might have
arrived at the barn before we did. After all, someone laid out
Bauer's body, perhaps even tried to help her." My gaze dipped
to the floor as I imagined the barn. "If he was hiding in the hay
loft, maybe he even witnessed her murder."

If so, he must have known that if he tried to come forward
with what he knew, *he* would be the one arrested. After all, he
was a German in hostile territory, and if he admitted to being in
that barn when Bauer was killed, then he would all but sign his
death warrant.

I sat forward, pounding my leg with my fist in emphasis. "We
have to find him."

"Yes, before someone else does," Sidney agreed, but then his
gaze sharpened. "But that doesn't mean you can go charging off
after him into the woods."

I pressed a hand to my brow guiltily. "I know."

"All of *this* is mere speculation. He might *be* the murderer.
He might intend to harm you." His voice turned slicing. "I can't
imagine racing off half-cocked after a suspect was part of your
training."

I narrowed my eyes, knowing this must have been the voice
he'd used in the trenches whenever his men had required repri-
manding, and not appreciating his turning it on me. "Yes, well,
I didn't often have the pleasure of pursuing a suspect. Normally

I was the one being hunted," I snapped, anticipating the manner in which his features then blanched.

Shame infused me as I recognized I'd said that with the precise intent of hurting him. The very fact that I'd expected such a response, expected it to silence him, told me I'd known perfectly well what an effective weapon it was.

I knew how much Sidney hated the thought of me being in danger. He still struggled with the reality that I'd so often chosen to place myself at peril during my assignments with the Secret Service during the war while he'd believed I was safe at home in London. To his credit, he had never doubted my capability, nor had he tried to obstruct me from doing what needed to be done in our investigations since. No matter the risks. And my actions today *had* been foolhardy. I'd already admitted as much to myself. I'd deserved a scolding. Wouldn't I have done the same to Sidney if our situations were reversed? And yet I'd lashed out cruelly, aiming for his weak spot—his fear for me.

I moved over to the fainting couch, sinking down beside him as I pressed a hand to his arm. "Sidney, I'm sorry. That was uncalled for. And you're right. I wasn't thinking clearly, I wasn't thinking *at all*, when I ran off after that man in the woods." I squeezed his arm, hoping he could sense my remorse. "It won't happen again."

His deep blue eyes searched mine, perhaps trying to tell how earnest I was, and I let him, not withholding anything. "If something happened to you . . ." he murmured, lifting his hand to grasp my jaw between his thumb and forefinger. The callused pads gently abraded my skin.

"I know," I said, not needing him to complete the sentence, for I felt the same.

His gaze dipped to my lips, and I thought he meant to kiss me, but apparently his thoughts had not gone in the same direction mine had. "That treehouse in the woods."

I stilled, my heart thudding against my ribs.

"I know Rob built it."

I pulled away, turning so that he couldn't see my face, though he grabbed my arm, trying to stop me. "I'm not discussing that."

"Verity, look at me."

I shook my head and broke free of his grip to rise to my feet. "No."

"Verity, you can't keep refusing to confront this. I know you're not sleeping. I watch how you pick at your food at most meals."

I remained resolutely turned away, unfastening the buttons at the shoulder seam of my sapphire-blue dress.

"We came here so you could finally grieve, but you'll barely even speak Rob's name."

My chest was so tight I thought I might never draw a proper breath again, but I kept my fingers moving, taking off my sash belt and throwing it on the bed.

"And this investigation is yet another distraction to keep you from facing it," he continued relentlessly. "Verity, talk to me!" he pleaded.

"I can't." I shook my head again, pulling the tunic over my head before dropping the skirt, racing now to change clothes as if my life depended on it.

"Verity," he chided.

"I can't!" I finally shouted at him. My body shook with repressed emotion, and the pained look in his eyes made me want to bury my head in my hands. Instead, I snatched up my slate-blue voile blouse and thrust my arms into the sleeves. "I just can't."

"Why?" he asked tightly as I stepped into my charcoal-gray skirt and pulled it up over my hips.

Because if I started, if I let loose the torrent of emotions I'd buried deep inside me, I feared I would never be able to stop. I had hoped that being here I could confront small pieces of that pain one at a time. I still hoped it. But to speak of what I was feeling—and with Sidney, who I'd believed was dead for fifteen long months—the very idea choked me. For I knew that some of my grief over him was mixed up with my grief over Rob, and there was no way to separate them. To speak of one was to speak of the other. And though I'd shared some of the pain Sidney's alleged passing had caused me, I had never let him witness the full impact of it. The thought of doing so now shook me, for it was a hole so dark and so deep, I wasn't certain I would ever reach the bottom of it.

I moved toward the door, intent on escaping, but I couldn't leave without saying something. "Just . . . give me time," I said over my shoulder, and then hastened from the room before he could object.

I hurried down the hall, intent on finding Tante Ilse, but when I rapped on her bedchamber door, no one answered. Whirling away, I intended to retrace my steps to the staircase, only to be brought up short by Matilda's scowling visage. Given my unsettled emotions, she was about the last person I wanted to see, but when I moved to stride past her with a curt nod, her words halted me in my tracks.

"I caught Miss Bauer in your bedchamber the day you arrived. She was searchin' through yer things," she continued as I turned to face her.

I thought back to our arrival, how I'd noticed my handbag had been rifled through. Because of our contentious history, I'd blamed Matilda. But perhaps I'd been wrong.

As if reading my thoughts, her eyes narrowed. "Given wot ye seem so intent on blamin' the Kraut's murder on *me*, I thought ye should know." She scoffed. "Though, no doubt you'll decide I'm lyin' about that, too."

"It's your own fault I don't trust you, and you know it," I replied crisply. "You made it abundantly clear who your loyalty lies with, and it isn't me."

She clasped her hands beneath her substantial bosom and arched her chin. "Aye," she admitted. "But that don't mean I didn't have your best interests at heart." The hard black chips of her eyes softened the tiniest fraction. "I know ye grieved Mr. Kent when ye believed he'd died. Just as I know ye grieved yer brother Rob."

Why this acknowledgment should leave me feeling like I'd been punched in the gut, I didn't know, but Matilda *had* been my maid for three years during the war. She had been my most constant companion, even as little as we liked each other. She had been there when Father telephoned to tell me about Rob, and she had been there when the telegram arrived to inform me of Sidney. That she had seen me at my most vulnerable and still betrayed me was undoubtedly wrapped up in my extreme dislike of her. And yet, something in her eyes told me she hadn't meant to hurt me.

"But grief can make ye do things ye never would otherwise. It can tear ye up and turn ye around, till ye don't know which way's up and which way's down, and what's right and what's wrong. Only what stops it." Her mouth firmed. "I'll not apologize for doin' what I could to keep ye from harmin' yourself. Even tellin' yer mother."

The matter was hardly so black-and-white, and I still believed she could have handled matters better, but when phrased in that light, I felt less out of charity with her. Though I wasn't about to tell her that.

In any case, she didn't expect a response as she turned to go, but she did pause to deliver one last pronouncement. And per usual, it was the most enticing one. "Oh, and your bedchamber isn't the only place I saw Miss Bauer where she shouldn't 've been." She arched her chin. "She crept out of yer brother's room a few nights past. And by the rumpled sight of her, she wasn't changin' the linens."

I frowned at her retreating back, wondering if what she'd said was true. I wanted to dismiss the possibility, but while Matilda was prone to framing things in the worst possible light, I had never known her to lie outright. And it was difficult to see how Bauer leaving Tim's room at night in a rumpled state could be entirely innocent.

If my feckless younger brother had been intimate with the girl, it might explain his strong reaction to her death. I'd thought it odd at the time, given the fact he'd served in the trenches for more than a year, but his having known the maid—in more than one sense—could account for it. He'd also been remarkably jittery and distracted, even more so than before.

My insides twisted at the possibility that there might be a

more disturbing reason behind his behavior, but just as quickly I dismissed it. Tim was not a killer. But he might know something important.

I pattered down the staircase to the entry, glad to find Abbott was still hovering about, completing his duties. "Do you know where I might find Tim?"

"I believe the young Mr. Townsend went for a walk."

Taking Tabitha with him, no doubt. That's why she hadn't greeted us upon our return.

"What of my great-aunt?"

"Frau Vischering is in the conservatory."

I thanked him and hurried down the corridor to the farthest chamber on the right. Though it wasn't grand by any measure, my mother was still justifiably proud of the space. Various plants and hothouse blooms were placed near the large windows spanning the two outer walls, while species that required less sunlight were set closer to the door. A cabinet and worktable stood to the left, while the wall to the right was painted with a large mural of the Garden of Eden, complete with a strategically shrouded Adam and Eve nestled in the background.

I found Tante Ilse perched on one of the wooden benches, her gaze turned toward the wind-whipped landscape outside the window and the lowering clouds. The scenery was a stark contrast to the humid air and floral scents in the room. It was obvious she was lost in thought, and unhappy thought at that. When she failed to acknowledge my presence, I was forced to speak, lest I startle her.

"May I sit with you?"

She looked up at me then, though it seemed to take her a moment longer to recollect where she was. "Yes, of course. This is a pretty blouse," she remarked, fingering the fabric at my sleeve as I sat.

"Thank you."

Her gaze trailed over my features, searching for something. "Sarah said you returned. That they are still looking for Bauer's killer, but we can bury her."

"Yes. Freddy transported her to the undertaker, and I believe Mother is arranging everything with the church."

She nodded, turning away. "Yes, yes. She said as much." She sighed wearily, her shoulders seeming to bow beneath the weight of her grief and guilt. "Poor girl. I wish I had never let her convince me to bring her here."

The hairs on the back of my neck stood up in interest. "You didn't want to bring her?"

"I did not intend to even come myself," she admitted sadly. "I knew how it would be. I did not wish to make trouble."

"But the threats you received?"

She nodded. "Yes, they upset me. But I hoped that in time they would stop. Bauer saw it differently. And she knew . . . she knew how much I longed to be reconciled with all of you. After all, you are the sole family I have left."

"But surely there was nothing to reconcile," I contradicted. "I certainly don't harbor any ill will toward you. We were simply trapped on different sides." I paused, pondering something I should have long ago. "Do you harbor any ill will toward me?"

She reached over to clasp my hand. "*Nein, Liebchen*. I know you have only done your duty, just like your dear husband and your brothers. Just like your cousins did fighting for the kaiser. But I could not know for sure that you would see things the way I did. Just like I could not know how your parents really felt." Her head dipped. "After all, they lost Robert. They have the right to feel angry."

I swallowed hard, choking down the lump that had gathered at the back of my throat upon hearing Rob's name. "But not at you."

She shrugged one shoulder. "Maybe. Maybe not." She gestured almost listlessly. "Anyway, I did not know. And I thought merely to continue to write letters, hoping some of them would make it to you and to Yorkshire. But Bauer convinced me that it would be better to go to England and speak to you myself before it was too late."

My heart stilled upon hearing these last words, but she continued on as if they were of no consequence.

"She also knew well that I no longer had family there to look after me, and I think the sentimental girl wished to change that. Especially since her own family was gone."

"Tante, are you sick?" I asked, forcing the words past my lips.

She turned to look at me, her eyes registering less surprise at the question than I expected.

"You said, 'before it was too late.' "

Her lips softened in a consoling smile. "I am old, *mein Liebchen*."

Which wasn't actually an answer.

"Sick or well, I am not much longer for this earth. But do not fret. We still have time."

But rather than reassure me, her words left me feeling even more conscious of the passage of time, and the fear that it was running out.

I found myself thinking of Bauer, and wondering whether she'd had any inkling that day when she went to the field barn that death would find her. She must have had hopes and plans, thoughts beyond serving as Tante Ilse's maid. Had she hoped that coming to England would offer her a fresh start? Had her reasons for encouraging Tante Ilse to come here truly been so selfless and pragmatic? Or had she harbored ulterior motives?

"Did Bauer mention meeting anyone in Hawes? In particular, meeting another German?" I asked, wondering if Tante Ilse had remembered anything. The last time we'd spoken of the matter, she'd claimed her maid didn't know anyone, but she'd been grieving deeply, and her words had grown confused. I thought that with more time, she might have recalled something.

"Another German?" her voice creaked in surprise. "Here in Hawes? No, no, she did not tell me anything about that." She frowned. "Is there?"

"I don't know. But Bauer was seen speaking with a strange man in the village by several people, and one of those witnesses claimed he was a German." I elected not to bring up the incident in the churchyard when she had claimed to see the second deserter, as that had only seemed to fluster her the last time I'd mentioned it.

Her face flushed with fury. "And let me guess, evidence or no, they've decided that he must be the killer." Her eyes snapped to me. "Have you?"

"I don't know who did it," I replied honestly. "But whoever that man is, whether he's German or not, it's important we find him and speak with him before the others do. He might know something that can help us." I reached up to help drape the side of her floral shawl that had slipped behind her back around her shoulder. "You're certain she said nothing about him?"

Some of the color faded from her face, and the rigid line of her jaw softened. "No."

"If she had met another German, if he'd needed help, do you think she would have tried to do what she could for him?"

"Yes, that would be very like her. In Monschau she always tried to help others, even when . . ." She gasped and her eyes widened. "Oh, wait. There *was* a man."

I straightened eagerly.

"Not here, but back in Germany. She told me she had given him something to eat once, but then he had started following her. That she didn't like it. He unsettled her."

"But she didn't say he'd followed her here?"

"No, and I hope she would have."

I drummed my fingers against the edge of the bench beneath me, wondering how likely it was that the man had actually followed her all the way to England. And what Bauer's reaction would have been if he had. The probability seemed slim, but if he had, that might cast an altogether different light on the fellow. A far grimmer light.

My ruminations were interrupted by the appearance of Abbott. "Mrs. Kent, you have a telephone call."

I pushed to my feet, belatedly turning to ask Tante Ilse to excuse me before striding toward the entry hall.

"Rosalind?" I asked, speaking into the mouthpiece.

"I see you correctly construed my message," Kathleen's dry voice quipped over the connection, which crackled slightly at the edges.

"You've got something for me?"

"I do, but it's not what you're hoping."

"Oh?"

"The report has been sealed. The War Office is denying access to it."

My shock at this pronouncement must have been more obvious than I realized, for Abbott turned to look at me in query. I responded with a strained smile, lowering my voice even further so as not to be overheard. "But I thought the inquiry had been shut down for lack of and conflicting evidence?"

"It was."

"Then why would the report be sealed?"

"I don't have the answer to that now. But we agree it's suspicious."

And by "we," I knew she meant she and C.

"We're looking into it," she added in a suppressed tone, which let me know that someone was in the room with her, and she was not at liberty to speak freely.

"Do you know when the file was sealed? I was under the impression that a mutual friend had gained access to it recently."

She would understand I was referring to Alec, as he had been my handler, but I wasn't certain how much he had shared with C, and by consequence, her.

"I don't know that either. Although, our friend sometimes uses his own sources."

I'd figured as much. And with Alec out of reach, on assignment in Ireland, there was no way to gain access to those sources ourselves.

"I'll telephone if I have more information."

I didn't miss that tiny "if," which was a very different conjunction than "when," but it wasn't as if I could object. If C couldn't gain access to that file, then I wouldn't be able to do so on my own. And without examining its contents, I wasn't certain how we would ever uncover the identity of the officer Williams claimed he saw leave General Bishop's temporary HQ moments before it exploded.

CHAPTER 24

I thanked Kathleen and rung off, staring broodingly up at the Francis Nicholson landscape hanging on the wall over the bureau.

"Was that Rosalind?"

I turned toward Sidney as he reached the bottom of the stairs, knowing that my taut features must have made the answer to this question obvious. But rather than speak openly, where any of the staff might hear, I ushered him into the billiards room, closing both doors behind us.

He leaned against the billiards table, listening intently as I explained in a low voice what Kathleen had informed me.

When I'd finished, his expression was as forbidding as mine. "You know not just anyone has the power to restrict access to a file in the War Office. I hate to say it, because until now we've had little reason to suspect him, but this has the whiff of Ardmore about it."

"Yes, and I'm no more pleased about it than you are," I retorted, lest he think otherwise. I paced away several steps before whirling back around to demand, "How is it possible that the man has his fingers in so many pies, and yet no one beyond us suspects he has underhanded intentions?"

"Because he's cultivated the right friends, all of whom are greedy, ambitious men, and he never tries to take the credit or the limelight. In fact, he never attaches his name to anything, if he can avoid it. He's not even the chess player moving the pieces about the board, but the man seated in the shadows behind the players, coaxing them to move a rook here and a bishop there, and allowing them to believe it's all their own idea."

I was much struck by this analogy, for if our suspicions about his endgame were correct, then the chess players were Britain and Ireland, and Ardmore was attempting to influence them both to some unknown conclusion.

I planted my hands on my hips, turning to glare out the window at the gloomy courtyard. "If it's true, if Ardmore is responsible, then he probably didn't realize I was involved in the matter until Major Scott started pursuing his vendetta against me." I narrowed my eyes. "And yet he pretended not to know why."

"Yes, well, we already knew not to trust him. We should have realized he was much better informed than he let on."

Out of the corner of my eye, I could see that Sidney still leaned against the table with his arms crossed over his chest, projecting the bearing of a man perfectly at his ease. But I could sense the roiling of his emotions and the watchfulness of his gaze as it traced my profile.

"Should we ask Ryde to try to use his connections to have the file unsealed?"

I turned to look at him, recognizing now the reason behind his sudden intensity. It wasn't about Ardmore, or my failure to confide in him about Rob. Or rather it was. But it was also wrapped up in the lingering insecurities in our marriage, in the trust we both seemed hesitant to give each other entirely.

"I'm not sure that would be wise," I replied, feeling somehow that I was being tested. I just didn't know precisely how. "Especially since we don't know for certain what we're dealing with." I turned to face him more fully. "Let's wait to hear if C can bring his influence to bear. There's nothing we can do about the matter until we return to London anyway."

The murmur of voices passing outside the door drew my attention away from his dark stare. One of them was merely Matilda, but it jostled a memory in my brain.

How many days ago was it that Matilda had accused Bauer

of eavesdropping on my and Sidney's conversation in this very room? I had dismissed Matilda's accusations as malicious at the time, but now I couldn't help but wonder if I had been too hasty to defend Bauer. Maybe she *had* been intentionally listening to us.

Hadn't our conversation been about the second deserter, and the potential that they'd followed us in order to blackmail me? And not a day later that note had been left under my pillow. *I know what you did.* Could it have been left there by Bauer, either of her own accord or at someone's direction? We'd observed at the time how a servant was likely involved.

"What are you thinking?" Sidney asked, breaking into my thoughts.

"Just that I'm beginning to think Fräulein Bauer wasn't exactly who she seemed."

Tim's voice rang out in the entry hall, greeting Abbott with some sort of anecdote about Tabitha's behavior on their walk.

My lips twisted. "Case in point." Striding to the west-facing door, I yanked it open.

Tim's words stopped, and the smile brightening his face withered at the sight of my glaring visage.

"Tim, may we have a word with you?"

He looked at Abbott, as if the butler could rescue him from this situation, before replying in a choked voice. "Of course." He passed off the rest of his things and then slumped into the room. His brown hair stuck up around his head in cowlicks, making him appear more boyish than his twenty-one years.

Intent on being included, Tabitha slipped through the door before I could close it, her muddy paw prints mussing the floor. Her paws should have been cleaned off before she'd ever entered the house, but as it had fallen to Tim to do so, of course, it hadn't been done. I opened the door, asking Abbott for a towel, and then hurled it at Tim, not about to do the task for him.

He knelt, whistling for Tabitha, who obediently lifted each paw for him to rub. "How was the inquest?" he asked in a taut voice.

"About as expected," I replied, waiting until he rose to his feet to put the question to him I most wanted to know.

He nodded. "Then they don't know who . . ."

"Fräulein Bauer was seen leaving your chamber several nights past."

He stilled at this pronouncement, and color rose in his cheeks.

I sidled a step closer, scrutinizing his features. "Were you sleeping with her?"

His expression underwent a paroxysm of tiny movements as he fired back with multiple denials. "What? Of course not. Why would I do such a thing? How can you think that of me?"

Unfortunately for him, I had always been able to tell when he was lying. For one, he wasn't very good at it, usually overdoing it with protestations of his innocence, as he was now. For another, his left eyebrow twitched, a spasm he had obviously still not been able to gain control of.

I had elected to wait out his display of offense, but apparently Sidney was of a different mind.

"Cut line, Tim. You're a rotten liar." He had straightened from his slouch and now turned to face my brother as he growled, "You *did* sleep with her."

Tim lifted his hands as if to ward him off. "She came to me."

"In your room?" I quizzed doubtfully. I would not have expected such boldness from the maid.

"Well, no. In the courtyard. I . . . I was smoking, and she came out of the servants' quarters. But I don't think she saw me, not at first, because she started crying." He spread his hands, pleading with us. "I couldn't see her like that and just walk away."

"And so you . . . *comforted* her?"

He scowled at the scornful tone of my voice. "Not like that. Not at first. But she looked so sad, so alone, and . . . and she is"—he seemed to choke on the word—"*was* . . . a dashed pretty girl."

"And so . . . what? One thing led to another?"

"More or less."

I glowered at my brother in disapproval, though my ferocity

couldn't match Sidney's. For a moment I wondered if he was going to box my brother's ears.

"You took advantage, Timothy," I snapped. "She *was* sad and alone, and surrounded by people hostile to her because of her nationality. She deserved our protection, not your dubious attentions."

The fight abruptly went out of him, and his shoulders slumped in defeat. "I know," he groaned. "I *knew* it when I first let myself kiss her. I should have stopped myself then. I nearly did. But she seemed to *want* me to. I certainly didn't force her up to my room or . . . or into my bed."

"That doesn't excuse it," I retorted, though I was relieved to hear that at least it sounded as if Bauer had participated willingly.

"I know. You're right." He rubbed the back of his neck. "Afterward, I felt so guilty I lay there for hours just letting her talk. It seemed the least I could do."

I exchanged a glance with Sidney, my interest heightened. "She talked to you for hours?"

"Well, I don't know precisely how long, but it seemed like hours."

I sneered at this typical male complaint. "What did she say? What did she talk about?"

Tim eyed me warily, seeming alarmed by my interest. "Her . . . her family mostly. What they had been like. How she missed them."

"Did she tell you where she was from?"

"Berlin."

"Talk, Tim," I ordered, tired of these drips of information. "Tell us everything you remember. It could be important."

"Well, I think I understood most of what she said," he stammered. "But my German isn't as good as yours."

The way he fidgeted and the manner in which his gaze kept darting between me and Sidney as if we might pounce made me realize we were unnerving him. Perhaps even overwhelming him. Recognizing this as a sign of shell shock, I pressed a hand to Sidney's arm, urging him to take a step back with me so that we were no longer crowding Tim. Then I spoke again in a calmer voice. "Just tell us what you could comprehend."

He nodded, and his Adam's apple bobbed up and down as he swallowed. "She said she'd had a brother and a sister, both younger. They and their mother died from the influenza late last year. She said they had been weak to begin with, from . . . from lack of food. That she'd been surprised she'd survived." Tim's expression was bleak, and I understood why. I felt the same yawning sense of dismay in the pit of my stomach knowing how terrible conditions had been in many parts of war-torn Europe. How terrible they still were.

"Her father had served in the German Army, but she didn't know what had become of him. She said that they'd had no word of him since his last leave. When the war ended, and he still hadn't come home, she said she'd realized he must be dead. And so she set out to look for work."

"But she was from Berlin. She couldn't find any work there?" I asked in confusion.

"I don't know. I guess I didn't listen carefully to what she said about that. All I know is that she eventually found herself in Monschau." Over four hundred miles away. "And was grateful Tante Ilse took her on."

I nodded. "Go on. She didn't have any other family, then?"

He tilted his head. "She mentioned a cousin—Kurt—but I gathered he'd also been in the army and she didn't know what had become of him." His face scrunched up, trying to recall. "Or she did know, and then she lost him. I'm sorry. I think she must have used some words I didn't translate properly."

I struggled to stifle my frustration, realizing most of this wasn't in the least helpful to our current predicament. She sounded like a lonely orphan, far from everything and everyone familiar, just as she'd seemed. And yet, something was nagging at me. Something I couldn't quite place.

"Was there anything she said that you found either surprising or interesting?" Sidney asked, perhaps sensing my growing agitation. "Anything out of place?"

Tim sank down on the edge of a leather armchair, staring at

the rug before him. Either sensing his distress or simply eager to be petted, Tabitha followed, butting her head against his hands where they dangled between his legs. Almost unconsciously, he began to scratch her ears as he shook his head. "No, I don't think so. Although . . ." His eyes lifted to me in query. "She did seem to have a lot of questions about Verity."

I met his searching gaze levelly.

"What kind of questions?" Sidney prodded with a glance at me.

"About what kind of person she was, and what she did during the war."

Tim's expression turned thoughtful, as if he was just now giving these topics due consideration. It made me wonder how he'd answered them when she asked them. Or whether he wasn't being entirely truthful and instead was trying to pass the blame and focus to me, as he'd done to me and Freddy at dinner a week ago.

Sidney's tone was wry, making me suspect he harbored the same suspicion. "Did you ask why she was so interested in your sister?"

He shrugged. "I figured she hoped Ver would hire her."

I narrowed my eyes. "Yes, because hiring a lady's maid who's slept with one's brother is ideal."

He flinched.

"Then you slept with her just the once?"

A fiery blush of red crested his cheekbones. "Well . . . just the one night."

I closed my eyes against this excessive bit of information, before opening them to glare at him. "Tim, you are a cad."

"I suppose I am," he admitted. "But for heaven's sake, I wasn't going to marry the girl. The situation wasn't that dire. And clearly the girl was searching for some fairy-tale prince. Which I am not. The way she carried on about her parents' marriage, how her father was such a gallant soldier. How he called her mother his snow fairy. Honestly, it was enough to make one sick."

I had begun to turn away, disgusted by my own brother's callousness, but these last few statements made my head whip around again. "Wait! What did you say?"

Tim stared at me dumbstruck for a moment. "What did I say? About . . . ?"

"What did her father call her mother?"

His gaze slid to my husband, plainly asking him if I'd lost my mind. "His snow fairy?"

I pressed my hand to my forehead as a horrifying realization washed over me. "Good heavens! I think I know who she is."

Whirling around, I charged from the room, only to collide with Freddy.

"Oh, I beg your pardon," I gasped, turning to hurry away.

But Freddy grabbed hold of my arm, hindering me. "Verity, I need to speak with you," he bit out.

"Yes, of course. But first, I must . . ."

"Now!" he barked.

It was then that I realized what a towering fury he was in. My oldest brother had always had a temper, but rarely had I seen him as worked up as this. His face was bright red, his eyes nearly protruding from their sockets, and the veins stood out from his forehead.

Rather than wait for my reply, he turned on his heel and marched into the drawing room, expecting me to follow. When I moved forward to do so, Sidney—who had followed me from the billiards room—walked in step with me, seeming hesitant to leave me alone with his friend when he was in such a state. But I shook my head, deterring him. I wasn't afraid of my brother. In any case, the last thing this moment needed was Sidney and Freddy breaking into fisticuffs over me. Especially when I suspected I already knew what Freddy was so furious about.

Having witnessed my and Sidney's brief unspoken exchange, Freddy nodded at his friend, seeming to promise he would not resort to violence, and then shut the door firmly. "What did you say to Rachel?" he demanded.

I clasped my hands before me and forced myself to meet his gaze without wavering. "I wanted her to know that your pacing and rambling about the countryside at odd hours was because of the war, not anything she or Ruth had done."

He whirled away, striding toward the hearth and back, his hand clutching the back of his neck.

"I was merely trying to help."

"Well, no one asked you to," he roared as he turned to face me, making me jump. "My marriage is not yours to meddle in, Verity. Do you know what you've done?" He turned away as if he couldn't look at me.

"I'm sorry."

"Rachel thinks I've been talking about her now. Complaining about her to my long-lost sister, who only now remembered that her family exists."

I felt as if he'd just slapped me across the face. "That's not fair, Freddy."

"No." He turned back to me, laughing humorlessly. "No, it's not, Pip."

Tears rushed into my eyes.

"Sure, you telephone, you write letters, but you can't be bothered to come see us. Why is that, Ver? Why?"

"I . . . I . . ." I couldn't speak beyond the lump gathering in my throat, the bubble of pain pressing on my chest.

"Too important?" he sneered derisively.

I shook my head, horrified that he should think that, and stumbled forward a step. "That's not it."

"Then what?"

My face felt hot, my insides quavered, and I feared I might be sick all over the rug.

"What?!"

I quailed at the fury in his voice, but the word finally popped from my mouth. "Rob."

He stared down at me for a moment as if he couldn't believe what I'd said. "Rob's been dead for over four years now."

I pressed my hands to my ears and closed my eyes, unable to face his words, his disdain. But I could still hear him.

"For God's sake, Ver, you haven't fallen off your rocker. You know that."

There was too much sorrow inside me, too much pain—for a moment I thought I might burst. "Yes, I know that. But I don't *want* to know that," I screamed back at him, hating him for making me say it.

He stared at me as if I *had* gone a bit rocky upstairs, and I flinched away, wishing I hadn't spoken, furious that he'd forced me.

"Pip, have you honestly been pretending all these years that Rob is still here?" He asked in a slightly calmer voice. "That if you didn't come here to see with your own two eyes that he's gone, that you could go on believing so?"

When he phrased it like that, it sounded incredibly foolish, but the alternative . . . the alternative had been too much to bear. It still seemed like it might be.

"What is going on in here?" my mother suddenly demanded to know, striding into the room.

I sniffed, swiping at my tear-stained cheeks before I dared turn to face her.

"All this shouting and carrying on like a couple of fish-wives." She turned to glare over her shoulder. "And half the household standing outside the door listening."

At this, the audience in the entry hall scattered. All except Sidney, who watched me with worried eyes.

"I will not have my children behaving like this. We will be receiving callers soon, and I will not have them arrive to the sound of your caterwauling. Whatever your squabble, you will discuss it like civilized adults." Mother's stern gaze shifted from Freddy to me, scrutinizing my features. "Verity, go wash your face. Freddy, I need to speak with you about Fräulein Bauer's funeral."

"Yes, Mother," he replied dutifully as she turned to leave.

I kept my gaze lowered, too ashamed to look at him as I passed by. But he surprised me by reaching out to touch my elbow, momentarily halting me. I glanced at him sideways, finding his expression far more forgiving than I'd expected. His brow was still lowered, holding on to his anger, but his hazel eyes were soft with a compassion I was certain I didn't deserve.

I allowed Sidney to pull my arm through his, but rather than turning my steps toward the stairs as he intended, I towed him in the direction of the servants' quarters. I swiped my fingers under my eyes, dashing away any lingering wetness as I firmed my resolve. "We need to search Bauer's affects."

Nothing was going to make me feel better about Rob. Nothing was going to ease this ache. But Bauer's murder was different. That was a problem I could tackle, a wrong I could do something to right. And if I was lucky, it would distract me from the rest.

CHAPTER 25

Mrs. Grainger, the housekeeper, was able to direct us to the tiny room Bauer had been given to use. Barely larger than a closet, it contained a bed and a small bureau, and enjoyed only the dim light that could filter through one tiny window. Three hooks hung on one wall, and a cross on the other. Tucked up under the eaves as it was, she would have had to be careful not to hit her head on the ceiling when she sat up in bed. But she would have had privacy—a choice commodity among servants. Though, sadly, in this instance, I suspected it was also a reminder that none of the English staff had wished to share a room with her.

I wasn't certain why we hadn't searched Bauer's effects yet. It seemed obvious now, but truthfully it had never even occurred to me. I had seen how small her valise was, how little she owned. But that didn't mean there wasn't something among those things that couldn't yield some sort of clue. Of course, thanks to her ramblings to Tim, I now also had a much better idea what to look for.

Once Mrs. Grainger's footsteps had receded down the hall, leaving us alone in the small room, I slid open the top bureau drawer to rummage through the contents. I was met with the clean scent of soap and crushed lavender, and I soon discovered she'd stored several stalks with her garments.

"In the billiards room, you said you'd figured out who Fräulein Bauer was," Sidney reminded me.

"It was pressing on my memory almost from the moment Tim started telling us what she'd told him about her family. But it wasn't until he mentioned that her father called her mother 'his snow fairy' that I made the connection." I turned to look at him. "That's what Becker called his wife."

He frowned. "Becker? Wait. You mean the deserter you helped over the border into Germany?"

"Yes. Heinrich Becker was from Berlin." I began ticking the items off on my fingers. "He had two daughters and a son. And his term of endearment for his wife was 'his snow fairy.' I cannot believe it's a coincidence that Bauer's family was the same. Not when she supposedly had to travel four hundred miles away from home to find a position, and it just happened to be with Tante Ilse."

"She was looking for her father," Sidney deduced.

"That's what I think, too. After all, Captain Landau told me Becker had succeeded at his first mission. Landau didn't know whether he'd visited his family while he was in Germany, but I'm willing to wager he did. If you were in his situation, wouldn't you?"

I didn't wait for Sidney's reply, instead turning back to my search of the top drawer, which seemed to be filled with nothing but a few undergarments. I closed it and opened the second drawer.

"We have no way of knowing what exactly Becker told his family, but it's not inconceivable that he revealed some of what he was doing. Perhaps he even told them about my great-aunt in Monschau." My hands stilled for a moment as I contemplated the precariousness of his having done so, and how little I liked the idea that he had put Tante Ilse at such risk when she'd helped him. "Whatever the case, he then returned to Holland to report to Landau. But when he was sent back into Germany on a second mission, he disappeared. I privately hoped that meant he'd simply returned to his family with the money given to him. At least, that was better than the alternative—that he was captured and killed. But if Bauer is, in fact, his daughter, and he didn't return to them, then that must mean something unfortunate happened."

I glanced over my shoulder. "Search the garments on those hooks," I ordered as my hands stumbled upon something more solid in the drawer filled with serviceable skirts. Pulling it from beneath the fabric, I discovered it was a worn leather journal of some kind, penned in German. The first page proclaimed it belonged to someone with the initials *ALB*, but that was of no help since Bauer had been clever enough to choose a surname that began with the same initial.

Skimming through the pages, I found the usual ramblings of an adolescent girl's private thoughts interspersed with lists, some of which were self-explanatory, while others were not. The first entries were dated before the war, and then as the war progressed, the span between writings seemed to increase. Thirty or so pages into the journal, for whatever reason a large hunk of pages had been ripped out, leaving nothing but their worn edges where they'd clung to the binding.

After that, the content changed. Here were various notes, likely gleaned from her father. Words like *Frau Vischering/ Vissering(?) in house at edge of woods to northwest of Monschau—German or British person pretending? Helene—British, spy, young, auburn hair.* As well as my code name and description, she'd listed Landau's and the *passeur* who had helped me and Becker over the border between Holland and Belgium. And then her questions began. *Last seen? Who betrayed? Why?*

I was frankly surprised by the depth of information she possessed. Her father must have shared nearly every identifying feature he'd collected, though I was uncertain to what avail. Plainly he hadn't trusted us. Not completely. In his shoes, I wouldn't have either. But what had he expected his daughter to be able to do about it?

Whatever his reasons, this seemed to be confirmation of my suspicions. Fräulein Bauer was, indeed, Becker's daughter. And Sidney turned to pass me another piece of evidence that corroborated it.

He had fallen silent as I scrutinized the journal, but now his deep voice broke into my thoughts. "Look at this."

A label had been sewn inside the sleeve of the maid's dark

woolen coat that read "Becker." It was likely the best coat she or her mother had owned, and she had been loath to part with it.

"Then it is her," I stated with finality, handing the garment back to him.

"It certainly appears so," Sidney agreed, hanging the coat beside the other clothing. "But then, why didn't she simply tell your great-aunt who she was? If she was searching for her father, wouldn't that be the easiest way to gain information. Why this charade?"

"I think I can answer that." I passed him the journal, opened to the page with my great-aunt's name.

His gaze flitted over it, taking it all in.

"If she'd believed her father was betrayed, then she would be wary of trusting Tante Ilse," I said.

He flipped through several more pages of the journal, filled with additional notes. Notes that made clear her suspicions about me. She'd evidently deduced that Helene was a member of Tante Ilse's family long before they'd come to England. And her growing suspicions about me were evident in the flowing script.

"Clearly, she was an amateur," he stated, brandishing the journal.

"Yes," I agreed. Sidney well knew my aversion to putting any intelligence in writing. No experienced agent would have dared keep such an incriminating piece of evidence. It was far safer to store such facts in your brain unless or until it became absolutely necessary to transpose them to paper.

"She even went so far as to blab it all to Tim."

A move that many of my male colleagues would have classified as typical of female spies, and evidence of why we couldn't be trusted as intelligence agents. However, the women in the service I knew were far from fools, and I was quite certain they were no guiltier than men of falling prey to the illusion of safety that intimacy inspired. Perhaps less so, as we were often confronted with such prejudice, and so were on our guard against it.

But even though Bauer had not been in the service, as a woman I felt the urge to defend her.

"She hardly gave herself up," I countered. "After all, she didn't offer any real identifying figures. She almost certainly didn't know her father had shared the story with me about how he came to call his wife his snow fairy." I took the journal back from him, gazing down at her fluid handwriting. "Besides, she could safely assume Tim didn't know her father, had never even heard of him. And I imagine it got rather lonely never being able to speak of her family, to actively remember them." I stifled a pang of empathy for her. "Even the best of agents are caught out by such miscalculations and assumptions, believing a small piece of information is untraceable or the man you're speaking to isn't really listening but purely pretending to as he dozes off." I couldn't resist turning a pointed glare on Sidney as I uttered this last statement.

He arched his eyebrows. "Is that supposed to be an indictment of all men or just me?"

"Merely an observation," I replied crisply as I closed the journal with a snap. "But now that we know Fräulein Bauer was Fräulein Becker, the question is, What was she intending to do? Was she planning to confront me? Blackmail me even? Is that why she asked me to meet her at that field barn?"

"If that's the case, then do we still think the straw-haired German fellow she's been seen speaking to is someone seeking help?"

"Honestly, I don't know what to think," I admitted in exasperation. Was he the second deserter? Was he the man from Monschau that Bauer had told Tante Ilse was following her? Or was he simply a German searching for work? Perhaps even a prisoner of war who had been released, but never made his way back to Germany.

I shook my head, still not understanding how all the pieces of the puzzle fit together. "Whoever he is, we still need to find him. That's our best bet for getting answers."

"Then let's hope he hasn't gone far."

But that wasn't to be the end of our concern for the mystery man that day. The family had all gathered in the drawing room following dinner, when there was a knock at the front door.

It had been a long day and a tedious afternoon. Mother had

elected not to make her usual round of Monday afternoon calls, correctly deducing that instead people would come to her. Or at least, the women of Hawes and the neighboring villages. As a female member of the family, I had been obliged to sit through these calls with Mother and Grace, as well as Rachel and Tante Ilse, who were present for at least part of the afternoon.

I'd expected to glean some sort of useful information from these visits, but people had come to gossip and ask questions, not to answer them. So I spent most of the time discussing my life in London and my dashing husband, while hopelessly trying to turn the discussion back to Bauer and dodging Rachel's icy glares.

Exhausted from the effort, I'd considered retiring early, but Tante Ilse had expressed an eagerness to play bridge, and I had agreed to be their fourth. Tim was just dealing out the cards when the knock on the door came. I turned from my seat at the table, curious if anyone had been expecting a late caller, but everyone seemed to sport varying looks of perplexity. All but Freddy and Rachel, that is, who seemed resigned to the fact it must be for him. I supposed life as a country doctor meant he was called from home at all hours of the day.

However, when the door to the drawing room opened and Violet Capshaw came bustling inside, still bundled from the cold, it became clear this was not the case. For if either of the Capshaws had required a doctor, they would have telephoned or sent a servant to fetch Freddy.

"Violet," I exclaimed, rising to my feet.

"So sorry to barge in on you like this," she gasped, seeming slightly out of breath.

"My dear, please sit down," Mother coaxed, guiding her toward the sofa nearest the door. "Whatever is the matter? Is it your father?"

"No, it's not that." Violet perched on the edge of the cushion. "Though I did scold him soundly for tramping about in the cold with his rheumatism. And he's likely to be a perfect beast because of it tomorrow."

"Then, what has you so flustered?" Mother pressed, offering her the sherry cordial Father had poured.

"No, thank you." She pressed a hand to her chest, as if to still her heart. "I'm terribly sorry. I'm not explaining myself well." Her gaze lifted to seek mine out. "I understand you were at the inquest earlier today, but I take it you left early?"

"Yes," I replied, glancing at Sidney, Father, and Freddy in turn. "We all did."

Her mouth twisted grimly. "Well, it might have been better had you stayed. Apparently, the men got themselves worked up over the possibility there's a murdering German prowling our streets. The things Father was spouting when he returned home . . ." Her cheeks flushed and she shook her head. "They're not worth repeating. But at any rate, they weren't just muttering threats. They actually set out to comb the countryside, looking for the fellow, determined to find him and . . . do who knows what to him."

I looked toward Tante Ilse, whose face had turned ghastly pale. I was not the only one to notice. Freddy sat forward in his seat, almost as if he meant to go to her, and I found myself wondering if it was merely the shock or something else he knew about her health that concerned him.

Violet gave a little gasp, seeming to have forgotten she would be present. "Oh, Mrs. Vischering, I am so sorry. I didn't mean . . ."

But Mother cut her off kindly, patting her knee. "It's all right, dear. This isn't your doing." Then she pushed to her feet. "But I don't think we all need to be present for this. Grace, come with me and Tante Ilse to the parlor," she urged as she coaxed Tante Ilse to her feet. "You can play that minuet for her I heard you practicing earlier."

Grace appeared as if she wanted to object, but she rose to her feet to dutifully follow.

Mother's gaze cut to mine, her lips tightening, but she didn't attempt to remove me. And then she was too preoccupied with supporting Tante Ilse's shuffling steps. I darted another look at Freddy before focusing on Violet's next words.

"I'm sorry," Violet tried again to apologize as soon as the door shut behind them. "I should have thought."

I sat in the space vacated by my mother, clasping Violet's hands between my own. "No more of that. Mother is right. This isn't your doing. Now, go on."

She swallowed and nodded, trying to regather her thoughts.

"I take it your father joined them in their search," I prompted. "That's why you're so cross with him."

"Yes, he was gone all day, making me fret something awful. I was on the verge of telephoning the police when he returned home exhausted about an hour ago. After hearing all his talk, I settled him as quickly as I could and came to tell you." Her eyes passed over the faces in the room as the notes of Grace's minuet penetrated dimly through the wall from the next room. "I doubted any of the Townsend men or Mr. Kent would have taken part in such a farce."

"Do you know if they called the search off for the night or are they still at it?" Father asked.

"I . . . I believe they halted for the night, but plan to resume tomorrow." Her eyes darted to my face. "But you should know, from what I could gather, Isaac Hardcastle was one of the ring-leaders."

"Isaac?" I queried in shock.

She nodded. "He's been rather vocal in his feelings about Germans in the past few years. He put forth a few measures with the parish council, statutes that would make it illegal for villagers to hire Germans or recent immigrants of German origin and whatnot, but the rest of the council felt such measures weren't necessary. After all, it's not as if Hawes was expected to receive an influx of foreigners."

"But now, here's his proof that the Germans are coming for us, after all," Freddy bit out.

"I can't say I'm surprised." Father stared into the flames of the hearth as if it held answers. "I knew about some of Hard-castle's ideas. Metcalfe even asked me to speak with him."

"Did you?" Tim asked.

"Yes, and it seemed obvious to me that those statutes were his way of staving off the guilt he felt for not being allowed to fight because of his health. He knew perfectly well that his seat on the parish council had been given to him out of pity. I warned everyone he would. That no matter their good intentions, it would make his feelings of ineptitude worse." He scratched his chin. "I suppose, in a way, he saw passing those statutes as his fight. His way of defeating the Germans. And now that a German maid has been killed after she was seen speaking with an unknown German man, he sees it as vindication that he was right."

There was a rap on the drawing room door, followed by the entrance of Abbott.

"Pardon me. This just arrived for Dr. Townsend."

We all waited tensely for Freddy to read it, his face creasing into a deep frown. Seated beside him, Rachel remained turned away, her eyes trained on the same spot across the room where they had been focused before the message's arrival.

"Speak of the devil," he remarked as the door closed behind the butler. His gaze lifted to Violet. "Did Hardcastle take part in the search?"

"I presume so," she replied.

"Well, his mother claims he's nearly at death's door."

Which could mean anything, given Mrs. Hardcastle's hypochondria and excessive use of hyperbole.

He folded the missive in sharp movements. "I'm not surprised his asthma is acting up if he's been tramping through meadows and in and out of field barns. I wasn't pleased to see him at the inquest this morning either, given the fact that smoke exacerbates his condition, but what do I know," he practically growled. "I'd best collect my medical bag and be off." He turned to drop a kiss on Rachel's temple. "Don't wait up for me."

I sat forward in my seat. "May I come with you? To speak with Isaac," I clarified as everyone turned to me in astonished silence. "We need to know if he knows anything more about Fräulein Beck—" I corrected myself. "Bauer's death that he hasn't already told us, or if he's merely taking advantage of the situation." I turned to Violet. "For instance, did you tell him that you'd seen Bauer speaking with a strange man outside the chemist?"

"No, but . . ." She inhaled as if regretting she must continue. "You aren't the only person I mentioned it to."

This didn't entirely surprise me. After all, I hadn't insisted Violet keep the matter to herself. But it wasn't reassuring either. Regardless, I elected not to dwell on it when I had a point to make. "I couldn't help but find it odd when he mentioned it this morning. Just as I found it odd that he was so certain the man was German. But when you described their meeting, Violet, it was furtive and done in shadow. You couldn't hear their voices."

"That's true." She shrugged one shoulder. "But maybe they met there more than once."

"Yes, that's possible. But it will be easier to judge once I've questioned Isaac about it."

"I don't think that's a good idea," Freddy said in a stern voice. "If Isaac is having one of his asthma attacks, he won't be able to answer you anyway. And Mrs. Hardcastle is likely to object to your presence in his bedchamber."

"She won't if you tell her you require my assistance."

He scowled blackly. "I'm not going to lie. No, Pip, it simply won't do."

I clenched my hands in frustration.

"But . . . I'll see what I can find out myself."

Rachel opened her mouth as if she wanted to object to this, but then snapped it shut again. Her already-furrowed brow lowered farther.

Recognizing I was not going to win this dispute, and that perhaps doing so would compromise my brother's professional integrity, I acceded. "Thank you."

He strode from the room with a sharp nod.

Father rose to his feet, tugging downward on his coat. "Meanwhile, the rest of us will begin our own search of the Townsend property and the surrounding hills at first light. With any luck, we'll find this fellow before the others do and prevent them from doing anything rash." He bid us all a good-night, and followed after Freddy.

"I should be going as well," Violet murmured with a regretful smile.

"I'll walk you to the door," I said, looping my arm through hers. "I do hope your father won't suffer too much for today's activities."

"Well, if he does, it will serve him right. Of all the nonsense. He knows better."

Abbott tactfully withdrew, allowing us some privacy in the vestibule as Violet adjusted her driving gloves. One glance at the window showed me that a gentle snow had begun to fall.

"You're all right to drive?"

"Oh, yes, of course," she replied with a light laugh. "I drove in much worse conditions than *this* in France."

I smiled, not having really doubted her, but it had been the polite thing to ask. With her garments settled, I expected her to buss my cheek and go, but instead she stood for a moment, her amber eyes searching mine.

"Is this what it's like, then? Investigating murders."

I tilted my head quizzically, uncertain exactly what she meant.

"Questioning everyone around you. Wondering if they're lying, if they're telling the truth. Wondering if they're capable of taking another person's life."

"At times," I hedged, not really knowing how to answer.

The corners of her mouth curled upward in an empathetic smile. "It must be weary on the soul."

"No more so than the war," I answered before I could think.

But she nodded, seeming to accept my meaning as a general statement on the entire conflict rather than the slipup I momentarily feared it to be.

We said our farewells, and I watched through the window as she crossed the courtyard toward where her motorcar waited on the other side of the gate, leaving footprints through the dusting of snow. I spared a moment's worry for the German man, hoping he'd found somewhere safe to weather the night. If the snow continued to fall, then it could hinder the morning's search. Or help us, if the German left footprints. But of course, anything that helped us would also help the other villagers.

I turned as Rachel stepped into the entry, crossing toward the billiards room and the door that opened out onto the covered walkway that led to the cottage. If she was aware of my and Freddy's very vocal argument earlier that afternoon over my interference in their marriage, she hadn't shown it. Though she must have noted the tension between us. What *was* clear was that she hadn't forgiven me for my remarks to her in the courtyard, despite my good intentions.

Perhaps I should have offered her another apology, but after everything that had occurred that day, I decided that was something I was not equal to. Not when Rachel looked at me with such frosty eyes.

"Goodnight," she said in clipped tones, and I bid her the same.

Civil I could be, but until I understood what my sister-in-law wanted from me, I would offer no more. Such a bridge had to be built in both directions, and I was tired of trying to judge the angle of hers only to have it shift.

CHAPTER 26

❧

I returned to the drawing room expecting to find that everyone except Sidney had wandered off, but Tim stood by the window, parting the drapes to peer out. At my appearance, he dropped them and whirled about.

"Miss Capshaw is off?"

"Yes," I replied, stumbling to a stop at the anxious energy that appeared to radiate from him. I looked at Sidney, seated a short distance away, noting that one corner of his mouth was crooked wryly.

Tim cleared his throat, rocking back on his heels, his hands clasped behind his back. "I wondered . . . if I might have a word. Will you shut the door?"

"Yes, of course," I replied, doing so.

I expected I knew what was coming. After all, our last conversation had not been the most amenable, and Tim had certainly ended it looking like a great heel. Accordingly, my brother's opening line didn't disappoint.

"I wondered, that is, I mean, you won't *say* anything to Father and Mother about Fräulein Bauer, will you?" He moved closer to where I'd perched next to Sidney on one of the oatmeal damask sofas. "It's just, I don't want them to . . . They needn't *know* about it. Right?"

I appreciated the reasons he didn't wish our parents to know, but the fact that he'd led with that, proving it his chief concern rather than his regret over what he'd done, did not endear him to me. Perhaps that was obvious from my expression, for Tim sank down on the sofa opposite, leaning forward in appeal.

"I mean, I'm *dashed* sorry about what happened to her. As you can imagine, it was quite a shock seeing her lying there like that, especially after"—he fumbled for his words—"what happened between us. And I know I *should* have exercised restraint. I treated her shoddily, I did." His gaze dipped to the rug beneath his feet. "But it's different since the war. Everything seems so . . . dull. Flat." His entire face scrunched, almost in pain, at not being able to find the right words to convey what he wanted to say. "When something comes along that jars you out of that reality, something that doesn't make everything seem so pointless, it's difficult to turn away from it." He lifted his somber eyes to study what effect this confession had on us. "You think that makes little sense, I'm sure . . ."

"Actually it makes perfect sense," I replied, and then reached for Sidney's hand. "Why do you think we launched ourselves into the London social season and all those murder inquiries with such fervor?"

His chin lifted, and he seemed to study us with new eyes.

"Your feelings are not unique," I told him. "But out here on the Dales you have no way to divert yourself. Freddy has his patients, as well as helping Father to manage the estate, and a wife and child to care for. But you have no claims on your time, no responsibilities. Not really." I crossed one leg over the other, warming to the topic. "What you need is an occupation. Something to not only occupy your time, but also your thoughts." I knew this had also been Father's council, but I wondered if mentioning that might actually hurt my argument rather than help it. "Why didn't you enroll at Oxford this autumn?"

He rubbed a hand over the back of his neck. "I wasn't ready and . . ."

I arched my eyebrows. "Mother didn't want you to go?"

His grimace was answer enough.

"Then, have you thought about enrolling somewhere in January?"

He shook his head.

"Then what about a hobby? Or a trade that doesn't require a university degree? It doesn't have to be elaborate. It could be anything from training horses to writing poetry to building bird-houses. It doesn't matter what it is, as long as it interests *you*."

His mouth clamped shut as he turned to stare into the crackling fireplace.

"Tim, I don't care what it is you choose," I added gently. "But you can't just continue to wander aimlessly through life. That won't help you."

"But what if what you want to do is forbidden to you? What if it's simply not possible?"

My heart stilled at the frustration and desolation in his voice, knowing he wasn't speaking hypothetically. I wondered what he could possibly be referring to. One look at Sidney told me he had a suspicion, but I was completely in the dark. "Like what?"

When his jaw hardened, I thought he would refuse to answer. But then Sidney stepped in. "It's aeroplanes, isn't it?"

Tim's gaze flew to his. "How did you . . . ?"

"The interest you took in my Pierce-Arrow's engine," he replied in answer to his unfinished question. "The way you watched that Sopwith that flew overhead on our walk and all the specifications you were able to rattle off about it. It's clear you're mechanically minded, and what else could possibly be forbidden to you but aeroplanes. Because of Rob."

Because he'd been shot down over France in an aeroplane.

I stared at my younger brother, waiting for him to speak and trying to pretend my stomach hadn't hollowed with dread.

Tim's hands clenched into fists, as if he was struggling to control some equally strong emotion. "I wanted to join the RAF when I came of age. But after Rob, well, Mother forbade it. I could have disobeyed. I could have joined anyway." He shook his head. "But I couldn't do that to her. So to the army I went. And into the trenches." His lips peeled back from his teeth as if flinching at the bitter taste of those memories. "She hates them, you know. Aeroplanes. Calls them 'infernal contraptions.' If I told her I wanted to fly them, if I admitted that, I know what it would do to her."

I did know, for I felt a sharp swell of panic just at the thought of him going up in one, and I was only his sister. How much more so must it terrify our mother?

But I had also seen the look in Tim's eye when he had watched that aeroplane on our ramble. I had seen the sparkle of wonderment, of longing, and I had not been unaffected. I should have realized sooner, as Sidney had, where Tim's interests lay. If flying aeroplanes was what he wanted, if it was what would help him heal, then it would be wrong to stand in his way.

Not that Mother would see it that way. After all, she had a determined penchant for trying to bend her children's will to match her own. This was one reason why she and I had so often clashed. I was not content to do what I was told, to stay firmly in my appointed place. I had always kicked against her traces. So seeing one of my siblings stifled and constrained by them made me want to slice the ribbons myself.

I inhaled deeply. Perhaps in this instance there was no need to be so drastic.

"Must you fly them?"

Tim looked up at this query.

"Would you be content studying and designing them? At least, at first. Surely Mother wouldn't object so much to that. To your efforts to make the 'infernal contraptions' safer and more efficient for other flyboys. Then, in time, perhaps you could work Mother around to the idea of your going up."

Tim seemed to be much struck by this idea. His eyes brightened and his rigid posture softened, while his mind seemed to turn over the suggestion.

"I'm sure Goldy could offer him some advice, don't you think?" I said to Sidney.

"Goldy is Captain Fitzwilliam Goldwater, lately of the RAF. His family owns an aviation company . . ."

"I know who you mean," Tim interrupted excitedly. His gaze darted between us. "Do you really think he'd speak with me?"

"I'm sure he'd be glad to. He could tell you what steps you need to take. What qualifications they're looking for." A smile hovered at the edges of Sidney's lips as he witnessed Tim's sudden enthusiasm. For my part, I was fighting to withhold a far more watery emotion. "Shall I give him a ring?" he offered.

"Yes, please do!"

Sidney nodded, glancing at the ormolu clock on the mantel. "Tomorrow, then. I imagine he's at Grafton Galleries with Etta at the moment."

"Of course. Thank you." Tim leapt to his feet to leave, and then swung back around. "And about our earlier conversation, you won't . . ."

"I won't say anything to Father and Mother," I assured him. Not when it would do nothing but cause further pain and disappointment.

"Thanks, Pip."

I shrugged one shoulder, brushing this expression of gratitude aside.

Sidney waited until Tim had disappeared through the doorway to speak. "You're still meddling."

My instinct was to take umbrage at this remark, especially considering the row between me and Freddy earlier that day over the very same subject. But I caught the teasing glint in his eyes in time to stifle my rebuke.

"Yes, well, can you honestly say I was wrong to do so this time?"

"No. Every brother should have a sister so concerned for his happiness." A tiny furrow formed between his eyes, which told me he was thinking of his own largely absent and self-absorbed sister. Not that I could claim I'd been much more than that to my own siblings in the past five years. But then it was smoothed away as he draped his arm around my shoulders and pulled me closer to his side.

I allowed my head to rest against him for a moment, enjoying the warmth and comfort of his presence. As always, he smelled of the bay rum in his aftershave, the pomade in his hair, and the spicy smoke of his Turkish cigarettes. The weight of all the day's revelations already seemed heavy, and yet I felt certain there was more to come. That is, if Freddy could calm Isaac's breathing enough to convince him to speak. I considered closing my eyes just for a short while, but first there was one more thing to be done.

"I should look in on Tante Ilse," I murmured, though I made no effort to actually do so.

"Stay," Sidney urged, tightening his arm around me. "I heard your Father assisting her up the stairs some time ago. She's probably already in bed."

I realized then that the piano had been silent for some time. Sighing wearily, I allowed my eyes to drift shut as I lifted my hand to his chest to feel the reassuring beat of his heart. After Sidney's brush with near death, I'd found myself doing so whenever I was apprehensive or overwhelmed. I supposed because that steady beat muffled by skin and bone and muscle had proven to be so vital to my own well-being and happiness.

He brushed aside the hair at my temple, pressing his lips to my skin. "Why don't you go on up to bed and let me wait up for Freddy?"

I shook my head against his shoulder. "No, I'll be fine. I want to hear what he says."

He exhaled a frustrated breath, but relented, perhaps correctly apprehending he would never convince me.

I don't know how long I dozed that way, but when I stirred I became aware of the sound of voices. One was felt as much as heard, rumbling from Sidney's chest beneath my ear. I blinked open my eyes to discover Freddy had not only returned, but that he was seated on the sofa opposite with a glass of whisky cradled between his palms. Both men fell silent, watching me as I rubbed the bleariness from my eyes.

"You've returned."

Freddy tossed back a drink, clenching his teeth at the bite. "Aye, and contrary to his mother's claims, Hardcastle was not at death's door. Oh, he was having trouble breathing all right, but I've seen him in much worse shape. Just a few days ago, in fact." He scowled into his drink. "But fortunate for you, he was in the mood to talk."

Resisting the impulse to immediately demand he tell us everything, I instead addressed the anger vibrating from him and the fatigue evident in the dark shadows beneath his eyes. "I'm sorry, Freddy. It must be difficult dealing with such patients."

He lowered his glass, having drained it, and then set it aside. "Aye, well, it was my choice to take over Paley's practice rather than taking a position at a hospital in one of the cities, so I suppose it's foolish to complain. But no matter," he declared, brushing this all aside as he came to the point of why we'd been waiting for him. "Hardcastle is dead certain he saw Fräulein Bauer speaking to a straw-haired chap outside the chemist. *And* that he heard the chap speaking German like a native."

Which was no guarantee he was German, but I had to allow it was indicative of it.

"But he didn't hear what they said?"

"He claims he didn't comprehend it, since he doesn't speak German."

I frowned. "Really? I could have sworn he did."

Freddy shrugged. "That's what he claimed."

"But wasn't he the one who was showing off his command of the language at that church fete some years back. The one commemorating St. Margaret's sixtieth anniversary. Remember? It was Halloween and the vicar had pulled out some old Reformation hymns written in German in honor of Martin Luther."

"I would have been up at Oxford. But I thought it was Eddie Metcalfe who had the ear for languages and liked to show them off."

I pressed a hand to my brow, trying to recall the event more clearly from my sleep-addled brain.

"Whatever the case, he claims he doesn't know what they said. But that the fellow was furious. That he looked 'perfectly capable of murder.'" Freddy held up his hands to ward off any objections. "His words, not mine."

"Of course, that's what he would say," I muttered. "It supports his objective."

"Yes, but Hardcastle's suppositions aside, it does tell us that whoever the man was who was seen speaking with Fräulein Bauer, he wasn't happy," Sidney pointed out.

"True. But that's also not proof he killed her. A lot of people were unpleasant to Bauer."

"Interesting you should mention that," Freddy said. "Because I told Hardcastle the same thing, and he had something unexpected to tell me." He leaned back, draping his arm over the back of the sofa, drawing out the moment for dramatic effect. An action that was so like the Freddy of old—the young man he'd been before the war and all that had come after—that I found I couldn't be annoyed with him for it. "The German chap wasn't the only person he saw speaking to Bauer."

"Who?" I burst forth to demand.

He nodded in the direction of the door, his nose wrinkling as if he smelled something foul. "Bolingbroke. He claims he saw Bolingbroke speaking to the maid the morning of the day she was killed. Says he was driving to Askrigg when he saw them conversing on the side of the road—Bolingbroke in his motorcar and Bauer with a bicycle."

Before I could voice my reaction to this, the door suddenly flew open.

"That's a lie," Grace shouted, her face twisted into an ugly sneer. "That's a filthy lie!" She pointed a finger at Freddy. "You've never liked Cyril, and so you're happy to use any excuse to smear his good name."

"He took the coward's way out," Freddy stated flatly.

"He did not! Stop spreading *lies*, Freddy."

"Now, hold on," I intervened, leaping to my feet. "Let's all just take a deep breath." I turned to Grace, whose chest rose and fell rapidly with anger. "First of all, Freddy was only repeating what Isaac Hardcastle told him this evening."

"Yes, but it's obvious he believes it." She gestured toward our brother. "You can see it plainly written on his face."

I could not argue that, not when Freddy's mug was viciously smug. "Well, I'm not prepared to take anything for fact based solely on one person's word. But we do need to ask Cyril about it."

Grace rounded on me. "You think he's a killer?!"

"Now, I never said that," I replied, trying to remain reasonable. "Just because he spoke with her that morning does not mean he then killed her some hours later. But maybe he's aware of something about Fräulein Bauer the rest of us are not. Maybe he saw something."

Her eyes narrowed, telling me all I needed to know about her trust in my motives. "Not before I speak with him first," she snapped before turning to storm out of the room.

I stared after her, wondering if I should go after her or if doing so would make matters worse. Turning my head, I arched a single eyebrow at Freddy in impatience. "Do you know for a fact that Cyril's injury is suspicious?"

He shot me a black look. "I saw enough of them to know the difference."

Which while seemingly a logical conclusion, was not actually based in fact. Just because most of the injuries he had seen of that type had been caused by men trying to be sent home, it did not by necessity mean that *all* such injuries were sustained in that craven effort.

"Have you heard from your friend?" I asked Sidney, not caring if Freddy knew we'd asked someone in London to look into the matter for us.

A tendril of dark hair had tumbled forward over his forehead, escaping the efforts of his pomade to restrain it. "Not yet, but I'll telephone him again tomorrow to see what he's uncovered so far."

My gaze swept over the shadowy corners of the room. "It's late. There's nothing more to be gained by continuing this discussion tonight. And I'm sure Rachel is waiting for you," I told Freddy.

Contrary to his instructions, she had doubtless been listening for his motorcar to return, and even now lay in bed waiting to hear the cottage door open and his footsteps climb the stairs. I knew I would be.

"Aye." He pulled the collar of his coat up around his neck as he rose. "There will probably be a couple of inches of snow on the ground by morning."

"Ruthie's first?"

He glanced over his shoulder, his mouth softening as if he'd just thought of this. "Aye." His gaze shifted to Sidney. "Tell Father not to hold the search for me. I'll join in later to help."

I smiled at his retreating back, contented to hear him thinking of Ruth, of Rachel.

Late the following afternoon, I returned to our bedchamber after a leisurely soak in the bath to find Sidney sprawled across our bed. We'd spent a long, tiring, cold day on horseback, searching one swathe of the hills and dales that constituted Father's property. There had been little shelter from the slicing wind, except for the handful of field barns we'd flushed, looking for signs of human disturbance.

My cheeks felt raw, and my muscles and joints had only just loosened from the cramped positions they'd been braced in all day to stave off the chill. I'd been reminded of muscles I'd forgotten I possessed. Apparently I'd grown soft in the year that had passed since the end of the war, unaccustomed to such harsh conditions and strenuous activity.

For Sidney's part, he hadn't complained. Likely because he'd suffered much worse during the winters in the trenches. After all, what was one afternoon spent on horseback, knowing there would be a soft bed, hot bath, and warm food at the end of it compared to weeks in the muddy, confined trenches and dugouts, with little but their own clothing to shield them from the cold, their meals from a tin can, and a bit of watery lukewarm tea if one was lucky.

All the same, I could see the fatigue written in the lines bracketing his eyes and mouth, and the dead weight of his muscles as he lay splayed across the counterpane.

His eyes opened to thin slits to look up at me as I moved closer to stand over him, gazing down at him fondly. I lifted my hand to play with the dark curl that had fallen over his brow. "If you hurry, you might be able to beat Tim to the bath."

But even as I said the words, the sound of sturdy footsteps could be heard striding past our door and down the corridor in that direction. I offered him a sympathetic smile.

"No matter," he replied drowsily. "It just gives me an excuse to lie here longer."

Hugging my Chinese blue dressing gown tighter around me, I sat down on the end of the bed next to his hip. Not only had it been an exhausting day, but also a thoroughly fruitless one. We had uncovered no sign of the German mystery man, and I could only hope the other villagers had no better luck.

I frowned, for it puzzled me that several people had reported seeing the man, but no one knew where he was staying. It was almost as if he appeared and disappeared at will, but I knew that wasn't possible. He must be taking shelter somewhere.

"I spoke to Babbage."

My gaze dipped to Sidney in interest. Somehow in the weariness of the day I'd forgotten he was going to telephone his friend about Cyril, but apparently he had not.

Sidney lifted his arms, cradling his hands behind his head. "He hasn't yet been able to view Bolingbroke's army medical records or learn any details about the precise nature of his injury, but he did confirm he was honorably discharged, and he was able to locate the incident report. It involved a motorcar."

I reared back slightly in astonishment. "That doesn't sound like a typical Blighty wound."

"No, it doesn't."

And yet it appeared Cyril had done little to defend himself or discourage the belief of men like Freddy that he'd injured his hand purposely. I wondered if that had something to do with the nature of the crash. Though, I knew how serious vehicle smashups could be. The chief's son had died in a motorcar collision in France at the start of the war—the same crash that had cost C part of his leg.

"There's more," Sidney declared in solemn tones, breaking into my thoughts. The grim look in his eyes told me I was not going to like what he had to say next. "He worked for Military Intelligence."

I lurched forward. "What? Babbage was certain?"

Sidney nodded.

My hand crushed the silk at the collar of my dressing gown

where I clutched it. "Army, not Naval Intelligence?" I wanted to verify.

"Yes. Though given what we know about Ardmore, I'm not certain the distinction matters."

He was right. I pushed to my feet, pacing back and forth before the bed as my mind wrangled with all the possible implications of this information. When exactly had Cyril been injured? Where had he been stationed? Did he have anything to do with the bomb that had killed Brigadier General Bishop and his staff? Was his presence in Hawes merely a coincidence or something more? After all, he had been unknown in these parts until he'd arrived to assist his uncle in converting part of the mill to provide electricity for the village. Or so he claimed. Was Fenrick truly his uncle?

Sidney pushed himself upright. "It doesn't necessarily mean he's up to no good, but . . ."

"It is suspect," I finished for him. I came to a stop, inhaling and exhaling a deep breath so that I could think calmly, rationally, rather than putting the cart before the horse. "All right, what do we know for certain? Freddy said he served with the Northumberland Fusiliers, is that true?"

"Yes, so he must have been an intelligence officer attached to their regiment."

"Grace told me she met Cyril at Mrs. Wild's garden party during the summer of 1918, which usually takes place in June when her roses bloom. So presumably he was injured some months before that." Which meant that feasibly he could have still been in France in April 1918 when Bishop's temporary HQ exploded, but it wasn't certain.

"Except the date of his honorable discharge was the thirtieth of April. Which means he must have suffered his injury some months earlier."

The wheels of the military never moved swiftly in such matters.

I felt my shoulders lower in relief. "Then he couldn't have placed that bomb."

I thought back to that crude partially submerged shelter, trying to envision the men gathered around General Bishop, but their faces wouldn't come into focus. I wanted to believe I would have recognized Cyril had he been there, but the truth was, I wasn't sure.

In any case, just because he couldn't have had anything to do with that bombing didn't mean he was entirely innocent of Ardmore's influence, or that his presence here—and his courtship of Grace—wasn't suspect.

My heart surged in my chest at the thought of Grace. She had been seated in the drawing room when we returned from the day's searching, so if she'd gone to Cyril to speak with him about Freddy's accusations, then she'd returned unharmed. Part of me wanted to caution her not to be alone with Cyril again until we'd had time to uncover the truth, but the other part of me realized that would only drive her into his arms quicker. No, it was best to remain quiet about our suspicions. At least, until we knew more.

"Cyril will likely be at Fräulein Bauer's funeral tomorrow." Which was to be just a simple graveside service. "We should question him after."

Sidney's expression was dubious. "You'll have to find a way of separating Grace from him."

I glanced toward the door. "Leave that to me."

CHAPTER 27

At least the sun decided to shine. That was about all I could say in praise of Fräulein Bauer's graveside service. Vicar Redmayne, it appeared, had been determined to make a point, and had not even bothered to speak with Tante Ilse to learn more about the young maid. Instead the service was all about reckoning and righteousness, relying much too heavily on Revelation.

Only Mrs. Redmayne and Isaac Hardcastle seemed to show any appreciation for the vicar's message, while the rest of us stood silently, allowing his words to drone over us. Even Mr. Metcalfe, who had surprised me by attending, seemed to grow vexed at the vicar's chosen texts, harrumphing loudly with each new quoted verse, rattling the man. When at last he lost all patience with the clergyman, snarling, "Oh, let the poor girl lie in peace already," I wanted to cheer, grateful for his interference. After that, Redmayne wrapped up the service rather rapidly.

Metcalfe was also the first person outside the family to approach Tante Ilse to offer his condolences. Though I couldn't hear what was said, I could gauge by its effect on my great-aunt that it had been compassionate and heartfelt. I supposed that while most of us in attendance were well-versed in the language of loss, he was the most fluent. I was struck by the sadness that seemed etched into the very lines of his face when he turned to depart. His eyes trailed over the gravestones as he walked away, perhaps thinking of all the loved ones buried there, or perhaps thinking of the three grandsons that were not. Who were instead buried somewhere in France—where they had fought—along with Rob.

This reminder that Rob was not here, resting where he ought to be, struck me sharply, and was all the more agonizing for its unexpectedness. I stood stunned, struggling to breathe evenly as the pain washed over me. Though I had turned away and I thought had not uttered a sound, Sidney still somehow knew something was wrong, for I felt his arm settle around me, offering me what support I would accept. He tried to pass me his handkerchief, but I shook my head, sniffing back the tears and then dabbing lightly at the corner of my eyes to wipe away any that threatened.

While settling myself, I took the opportunity to allow my gaze to travel over the surrounding fields. The newer section of the church's graveyard was set a slight distance from the church, and was bordered by nothing but sheep pastures and dry stone walls. As such, there wasn't much more than a few lone trees to conceal anyone's approach or shield them from prying eyes. Given this fact, it would have been the height of folly for the mystery man to come here today, but I had still thought he might risk it. It appeared I was wrong.

It was while I was studying a figure that had emerged from the rear of one of the shops on Market Place, which backed up to the graveyard, that Isaac Hardcastle approached us. Gone was his easygoing manner from that day Mother and I had paid him and Mrs. Hardcastle a call, to be replaced with something harder, something much more self-important. If this was the type of man he became when given any sort of power, then it was not a good look on him.

"I heard your family had no more luck than we did locating the German yesterday." He narrowed his eyes. "Or is that just a ruse?"

"Why would you suggest that?" I countered. "We have more reason than anyone to want to speak with him."

"Then you're not trying to prevent justice? Or pass the blame onto someone else?" He edged a step closer, but halted when

Sidney crowded even closer to my side. "Isn't that what your brother's questions were really about the other night?"

"His questions were in aid of us trying to get to the truth. Yes, Fräulein Bauer was seen speaking to a strange man by more than one person." I tilted my head, scrutinizing him. "A man that thus far only *you* have claimed to hear spoke German, and as such he must be a person of interest. But that's far from proof that he had anything to do with her murder."

"He's a Kraut," he spat. "What more proof do you need?"

I shook my head. "That is not a legally sound argument, and you know that as well we do."

"Then you *are* defending him!"

My hands clenched together inside the muff I held before me as I struggled to retain control of my temper. "No, I simply refuse to *accuse* anyone until the facts prove otherwise."

His eyes flicked up and down over me as if examining me like an insect. "Maybe you should be the one being questioned. After all, you conveniently found a note telling you where to find her."

I arched a single eyebrow at this absurd accusation. "Except I was with my husband and my brother Tim during the hours in which the murder happened."

His gaze darted to Sidney's face and back. "Maybe they're lying for you. Or maybe they're part of it."

Rather than take the same umbrage at this suggestion as I did, Sidney seemed coolly amused. "And what earthly motive would we have had to do so?"

Isaac's face reddened with anger. "Maybe she was spying on you. Maybe she knew something about you that you didn't want others to find out."

I continued to glare at him in silent disdain despite the fact that this insight was not far off the mark. We hadn't killed Bauer, of course, but I did wonder what she knew about me. And whether she realized I had worked for the British Secret Service.

But how had Isaac come up with such an idea? He had never

been particularly insightful, and I doubted that had changed in the past five years. So what had inspired his notion that there might be something Bauer knew that I wished to hide?

"Really? A German spy in our midst. How terribly cliché," I drawled. "And what, pray tell, could she possibly have been sent to the wilds of Yorkshire to learn? The secret to making Wensleydale cheese perhaps? Or worse, maybe she meant to lay siege to Bolton Castle." I knew I was outright mocking him now, but he had made me so irate that it was all I could do not to slug him as I'd done when we were children and he'd derided Tim for not knowing the proper order of his kings and queens.

Isaac was practically shaking with fury, and finding I had no desire to hear what else he had to say, I turned and strolled away.

Tante Ilse stood huddled inside a fur-lined greatcoat that was now much too large for her shriveled frame, gazing down into the hole where Bauer's coffin rested. Her expression was so haggard, so forlorn, I worried she might tumble over the edge. So I hastened toward her across the snow-trampled ground, wrapping a supporting arm around her waist, and threading my other arm through my muff so that I could clasp one of her hands. She looked up at me with watery eyes and then resumed her contemplation of the earth.

"Come away from here, Tante," I urged gently. "It is cold, and Fräulein Bauer would not wish you to catch a chill on her behalf."

Mother stepped away from the vicar and moved to her other side. Her gaze was hard as it cut to me. "Yes, let us return to the house. Frederick?" she called over her shoulder, asking for my father's assistance.

"I can help, Mother. You and Father have already done so much." And it was true. Mother had remained by Tante Ilse's side more than any of us, caring for her in her grief as best she could.

"That's quite all right, Verity. Let Tante Ilse take your father's strong arm."

I frowned at her icy tone, not certain what I'd done to upset her.

Father patted my shoulder, his consoling gaze telling me he knew. Not that he would explain it to me. I passed my great-aunt off to him, watching their slow progress across the uneven ground. It had just occurred to me to wonder if Father had forgotten our discussion the previous evening, when he called out to my sister in his measured voice. "Come, Grace."

She turned from where she stood with Cyril in surprise. "But I thought to ride with . . ."

"You'll see him at the house. I have need of you now."

This was a statement Grace couldn't argue with, not without sounding insolent and childish. But it didn't stop her from casting a mistrustful glance my way. My sister was far from stupid.

Aware of our intentions, Freddy did his part by taking Tim's arm and directing him toward his motorcar, leaving me and Sidney to manage Cyril alone.

"There's no reason for you to drive out to Brock House on your own. We can give you a lift," Sidney declared, draping his arm around Cyril's shoulders in a bonhomie fashion.

"Oh, but how will I return to Hawes?" he balked, staggering along as Sidney propelled him forward.

"I'm sure someone will be coming back in this direction. Besides, this will give us a chance to get to know one another better."

I might have told Sidney that these words and the amount of teeth he flashed at Cyril when he smiled were not doing anything to soothe his anxieties, but then I realized that was precisely Sidney's intention.

Cyril swallowed. "Oh, well, yes. But this is *really* not necessary."

"Oh, but it is." Sidney opened the rear door of his Pierce-Arrow, staring at him until he relented and slid inside. Meanwhile I settled into the passenger seat, turning to gaze over my shoulder at him.

I made pleasant small talk until we reached the outskirts of the village, while all the while Cyril tugged fretfully at his collar.

But as the motorcar's speed increased, my banter grew more serious.

"We understand you spoke to Fräulein Bauer on the morning of the day she was killed?"

Cyril rolled his shoulders, undoubtedly having anticipated this question. "Yes, Grace told me that Mr. Hardcastle told you he'd seen us talking, but I don't know why he did so."

"Are you saying he lied? That you didn't pull your motorcar to the side of the road by our drive to say something to her?"

"Well, I might have greeted her on my way to Long Shaw."

"Might have?" I asked incredulously, sharing a look with Sidney.

"All right, yes, I greeted her. But it was merely a passing comment."

"And yet, you stopped and pulled to the side of the road to do so. You didn't simply wave."

"I . . . I believe I asked after your great-aunt," he added in a choked voice.

I searched his face, trying to understand why he was lying. He must have realized he wasn't very good at it, and yet he persisted in doing so. Either he was playacting, or the most ill-suited Military Intelligence officer I'd ever met. But which was it?

I decided to try a different tack. "You told us *multiple* times that you spent most of the day at Long Shaw with your uncle. And yet every minute of your time there can't be accounted for. Not to mention the fact that Long Shaw is but a short distance from the field barn where Bauer was murdered. You could have slipped out, killed her, and then returned, hoping everyone would be none the wiser."

Cyril's eyes widened with panic. "But I didn't! I didn't kill her! Do you think I'm mad? Why would I do such a thing?"

"It seemed to me you already knew each other," I countered. "Your reaction to her presence, pedaling past on her bicycle when you dropped Grace off at the end of the drive the day of her arrival, seemed unduly strong. In fact, it looked very much like fear."

"It wasn't fear!"

"Then what was it?"

"Surprise maybe," he hedged.

"Surprise?"

But then he tried to backpedal. "I don't know. How would you feel if someone suddenly appeared where you hadn't expected them to?"

"So, you'd met before?"

"No! I didn't say that. I only meant . . ." He broke off, turning away in exasperation.

I gripped the back of the seat to steady myself as the Pierce-Arrow swung through a turn. "You were surprised to see her *here*," I finished for him. "But where else would you have expected to see her?"

"I don't know. In the village, maybe."

"In the village?"

He stilled as if he'd just realized he'd admitted something he shouldn't have.

"Then you *had* seen her before."

He eyed me with acrimonious dislike. "Yes."

"Did you speak with her?"

"No more than a cordial greeting," he sniped.

Now this I could tell was the truth, though it was counter to what I'd wanted to hear. I tilted my head, studying him closely. "And yet somehow I don't think you left the encounter with a good impression of her. Why is that?"

He didn't answer, but he also didn't refute what I'd said.

"Was it because she was German?"

"No. Besides, I didn't know that then."

"Not pretty enough?" I baited, catching Sidney's eye as he listened intently, though he was focused on the road before him.

His jaw tightened with anger. "No."

"Not taken in by your charms?"

He glared at me in response, the veins standing out on either side of his forehead.

"Perhaps she all but ignored you."

"It was because of the way she looked at me!"

I stared at him in disbelief, not understanding. "The way she looked at you?"

"Yes." He made a sound of disgust, whether at himself or us. "Do you think I don't see it? Do you think I'm not accustomed to it by now? The way people see or hear of my damaged hand and instantly assume I'm a coward." He flexed the fingers of his left hand and then cradled it in his lap. "I don't know how she knew about it. Maybe the servants were gossiping or she saw the scars. People assume it's a bullet hole, but it's not." He laughed bitterly. "I wasn't even in the trenches when it happened."

"What did happen?" I asked evenly.

"A motorcar accident. I was driving a couple of brass to a forward command post when a shell hit the road just before us. I swerved, but the left front tire clipped it and rolled us. Broke my collarbone and a leg, but those knit neatly. The large shard of glass that got embedded in my hand was not so forgiving."

By then we'd reached the house, but Sidney halted the motorcar at the edge of the drive.

"And yet everyone assumes the worst?" I pressed, not without sympathy.

Cyril had turned to stare forlornly out at the barren trees still dusted with snow. "Though I'm not certain the truth is any better." His pale skin flushed with shame. "No one wants to hear of a junior staff officer wrecking a motorcar. Not when there are genuine war heroes like Sidney Kent and the Townsend boys about." His face twisted with acrimony. "Ironic, isn't it? I had the easy war. Suffered a minor injury and returned home, for the most part, in one piece. I should be thanking my lucky stars. But instead I find myself envious of those poor bastards lying in the hospital, missing a limb."

Cyril's confession was so raw it had to be genuine. For he was not only ashamed of his injury, but also ashamed of his desire for glory and his inability to cope with other people's assumptions about him. Was that why he allowed Grace to cling to him? For the sake of his own vanity? It would explain the embarrassed reluctance he sometimes exhibited. He craved her adulation, but was also chagrinned by his need for it.

Grace had said the other girls had flocked about him at Mrs. Wild's garden party, but I wondered if that was still the case. If the gossip surrounding his injuries had soured their interest.

"Fräulein Bauer looked at you as if she thought you were a coward?" I prompted him, trying to bring him around to the original reason we'd corralled him into the Pierce-Arrow.

"Yes," he mumbled sullenly. "I didn't know at the time she worked for Mrs. Vischering. That's why I was surprised to see her."

"And when you stopped to speak with her on the road."

He didn't answer at first, and I thought he might continue to deny it, but then he heaved a sigh. "I was trying to explain how I'd gotten the injury, but she didn't want to hear it. She rode off before I could finish." He turned his head so that he could meet my gaze. "I know it's foolish. Why should I care what a maid thought? But the judgment in her eyes, it had been so . . . cutting. When I happened upon her on my way to Long Shaw, I found I couldn't not try to make her understand."

He was right. It made little sense. But that was what also made it so believable.

I nodded to Sidney, telling him to drive on.

"Did you follow her later and try to *make* her understand?" I posited, scouring the trees in the direction I'd last seen the straw-haired stranger for any sign of him before turning to gauge Cyril's reaction.

His shoulders had slumped and his expression turned bleak—all of the fight having gone out of him. "Did I follow her to the field barn, do you mean?" He shook his head. "No. As God is my witness, I did not."

I found I wanted to believe him, but simply wanting to did not make it true. After all, he'd just provided us with a possible motive for his murdering Bauer, even as mad as it sounded.

Grace was waiting at the gate to the courtyard as we rounded the drive, her arms crossed over her chest in evident fury. Much as I regretted the necessity, I could not regret the tactic we'd employed to get Cyril alone. We never would have gotten the answers we needed from him with Grace present. She not only would have hindered our efforts, but he would have also balked at confessing them in her presence.

I offered Grace an apologetic smile as I passed by her on my way up to the house, but the cold glare she continued to aim at me told me I would not be easily forgiven.

Once inside, I hurried up to Tante Ilse's bedchamber, where Abbott had told me she'd been taken to lie down. My chest tightened with worry. I knew Bauer's death had been hard on her, and funerals were never easy, but she seemed weaker with each day that passed. More than ever, I was certain something else was wrong.

I opened the door to find her reclining in bed. Her face was pale, and the lines scoring it more pronounced, as if she was in physical pain. I glanced at Mother where she stood next to the bureau, surmising she'd just dosed her with her medicines, including laudanum.

"Tante," I said, sinking down on the side of the bed to take her hand.

"Verity," she said, patting my hand as she offered me a faint smile. "You are a good girl."

Guilt lanced through me at receiving this praise. "I'm sorry I haven't been here to sit with you more."

"Nonsense. I know you are out searching for Bauer's killer."

I glanced at mother again as Tante Ilse continued to speak, finding her mouth clamped in a tight line. Her anger had evidently not abated.

"That is where you are needed. You were always a clever girl, a woman of action. Just like during the war."

I stiffened at these words, worrying Tante Ilse would say something more about the war in front of Mother, but she was cannier than that.

"I know it cost you much," she murmured in a softer voice. "More than some realize. But most wounds can be mended with a bit of time and patience."

That she was speaking of my relationship with Mother, with my family, was obvious. And yet she did not really understand the full extent of our estrangement.

I could see that the laudanum was taking effect then, softening her features, and shrinking her pupils. In contrast, Mother
seemed to be growing more irate, slamming drawers and muttering under her breath. Considering the number of times she
had scolded me and my siblings for such behavior, calling it un-
genteel, I knew she had worked herself up into a righteous fury.
Past experience had taught me there was no use discussing matters with her when she was in such a state, so I remained by my
great-aunt's side, hoping Mother would take herself away to
blow out the storm brewing inside her elsewhere.

But Tante Ilse did not seem to understand this.

"Sarah, what has worked you into such a bother?" she asked.
"You seem to hold some apple of discord."

I cringed, knowing full well what her bone of contention
was. Me.

Mother finished folding the shawl in her hand and thumped
it down on the vanity table near the window. "You want to
know why I'm so bothered?" She gestured to me sharply. "This
'good girl' of mine, who has so much empathy to spare for you
after your maid's death, could not even be bothered to offer me
a *smidgen* of compassion when my own son was shot down
over France."

"That's not true," I protested, albeit with no heat. "I empathized as best as I could."

"Yes, when I *telephoned*. But you couldn't be bothered to
travel home and hold *my* hand."

My voice quavered with emotion, but I kept my calm by
staring fixedly at the bed. "You know why I couldn't. I've explained it to you many times. But I am sorry I didn't come
sooner. I truly am."

"Yes, your critical war work and the sporadic nature of the
train schedules." She scoffed, ignoring my apology. "Those excuses barely held up to scrutiny then, and they certainly don't
now." She arched her chin. "You simply didn't want to halt
your drinking and carousing."

"That's not true, Mother. You weren't there, and you don't
know." I scowled, struggling to keep the resentment from my

tone. "No matter what Matilda may have reported to you. My presence was needed in London for my war work."

"She's right, Sarah," Tante Ilse chimed in to say.

"What do you know of the matter?" Mother snapped.

"More than you do," she answered, unruffled by her niece-in-law's outrage. "Your trouble, Sarah, dear, is that you've always seen things how you wish them to be rather than what they are."

"What is that supposed to mean?"

"Precisely what I said. You were hurt and angered by Rob's death, and so rather than direct that anger at God, or your government, or at Rob himself for joining up to fight, you turned it on the person who was not here to defend herself."

"Stuff and nonsense!" Mother proclaimed with a splutter. "You're merely taking her portion. As you've always done."

"Not when it wasn't warranted. But she's apologized for not coming home sooner, and I know her reasons are justified." Tante Ilse raised her hand, halting Mother's answering tirade with a shaky flick of her wrist. "You must stop telling her who she should be, and accept her for who she is. Verity has always danced out of line. And you have more reason to be grateful for that than you will ever realize." Her gaze shifted to me, wavering, and then boring into mine with her iron will. "And you must also learn to value your mother for her strengths. There is a reason she inspires such fierce, undemanding loyalty in others, just as there is a reason you do. In times gone by, she is the type of woman on which the bedrock of many a village, tribe, and clan would have pivoted through fair times and foul, contrary to what male historians would say." Her eyes flashed at this last utterance before she subsided back into the bedding, her vitality all but draining from her.

I clutched her hand tighter.

"Mend these differences." She opened her eyes to order us. "For I won't be here much longer to bridge the gap."

My breath tightened, knowing she was not speaking about returning to Germany.

The brackets at the corners of her mouth softened with compassion. "I have cancer."

"No," I gasped, though I didn't know precisely what I was denying. That she had it, that she was telling the truth, or that she was going to die, as seemed to be the implication.

She patted my hand. "Yes."

I blinked rapidly, trying to see through the wash of tears filling my eyes.

Mother turned away, perhaps unable to watch this scene play out. Her cool acceptance told me she already knew.

"Now, I don't want you to fuss," Tante Ilse continued as I dashed away a tear. "There's nothing to be done. I've had a long, and mostly wonderful life. I've no complaints. And my mind . . . well, it is beginning to go." She lifted her hand as if to touch my face, but then let it fall. "I know you noticed it, *mein Liebchen*. And I believe it is better this way—to go before it is all gone." Her voice brightened. "But I'm not done quite yet. I may linger for a few more months. And I intend to make the most of those. Perhaps I'll learn to play the violin." She smiled at the idea. "I always wanted to."

"There's no treatments . . ." I began, but she cut me off.

"*Nein*. I've already been over and over that with your parents and your brother. We must accept what is."

I nodded woodenly, wondering how long they'd known, and why no one had told me sooner.

"The important thing is that we move forward. But first, you have a murderer to catch." She shook her head lightly. "Do not let me down."

"The guests are arriving," Mother murmured, moving away from the window.

It wasn't custom to hold a funerary meal for a member of the staff, but with Bauer being a foreigner with no family to take on the responsibility, and only Tante Ilse to truly mourn her, Mother had decided our family would assume those traditions, albeit in a limited way.

She paused to pat Tante Ilse's shoulder before leaving the room with the door cracked behind her.

I sniffed and forced myself to my feet, fighting the maelstrom of emotions churning inside me. A task, a goal, an action was just what I needed. And that's exactly what Tante Ilse had given me. On purpose. The gleam in her eyes told me so. I leaned over to press a kiss to her cheek. Then setting my shoulders, I turned and strode from the room to face what must be done.

CHAPTER 28

❧❀❧

Unfortunately, there was only so much pain and emotion a body could repress without the cracks beginning to show. The first of which splintered when I managed to corner Freddy in the drawing room while Mother and Father were ushering in the few neighbors they'd invited to the small funerary meal.

"Why didn't you tell me Tante Ilse has cancer?" I hissed.

"She finally told you?"

"Yes!"

He held up his hands. "I'm sorry, Pip. She forbade me to do so. Not until she'd had a chance to talk to you herself."

"I don't care. You should have told me anyway," I snapped, being forced to stifle my anger, as Mrs. Redmayne came over to greet us.

When I managed to extricate myself from the spiteful woman, another crack appeared when I bumped into Grace emerging from the cloak room. It was clear from her red-rimmed eyes that she'd been crying, but her miserable countenance immediately transformed to one of antagonism at the sight of me.

"What did you say to Cyril?" she demanded.

"He admitted he spoke to Bauer on the morning of the day she was killed," I replied with little sympathy. "So Isaac Hardcastle was telling Freddy the truth."

Her eyes shimmered briefly with uncertainty before being overshadowed once again by anger. "But that doesn't mean he *killed* her."

"No, it doesn't," I conceded, but was unwilling to say more. She frantically searched my face. "But you think he did!"

"I never said that."

"Oh, no wonder he left. He thinks you believe he's a murderer."

"He left?" I turned to gaze toward the sounds issuing from the drawing room, wondering how suspicious that was.

"Yes, he . . . he told me he wasn't worthy of me." Her eyes filled with tears. "Of all the foolish, ridiculous *nonsense*! Of course he is."

I didn't respond, I couldn't, for I wasn't certain he was either. Not because of his injury. I could care less about that. And not because of his resentment and frustration at people for their assumptions that he'd contrived to be sent home with a Blighty wound. I could understand that, though he was in danger of letting those emotions overtake his life. But because I didn't believe his affections toward Grace were fully engaged. It seemed to me that he cared for her simply because Grace adored him, and my sister deserved better. She deserved to be loved and adored in return.

"Now no one will want me," she bemoaned into her handkerchief.

"Don't be stupid, Grace," I replied bluntly. "Of course someone will."

She narrowed her eyes in affront. "Not like Cyril."

"Better than Cyril. Quit being a sap." I stalked away as she glared daggers at my back. I knew I could have handled that better, but truly, could she be more of a muttonhead? There were far more consequential things to be concerned with at the moment.

At dinner, Mrs. Wild was seated between me and Sidney. A seat that swiftly proved to be a trifle inhospitable when Sidney pressed a topic he knew I was not eager to pursue. Though it began innocently enough.

"Oh, Verity," Mrs. Wild exclaimed with a light laugh. "You'll never guess what one of our farmhands found the other day. Do you remember that contraption Rob and Henry built one summer? The one they tried to fly off the barn roof?"

I smiled at the memory, even as a twinge of pain stabbed my heart. "Yes." They'd modeled it on a picture of one of the Wright brothers' flyers they'd seen in a book. "But I thought it got busted into a dozen pieces."

"It was, but apparently we never got rid of them." She shook her head. "It's a miracle those boys didn't break their necks."

"Rob was always interested in flying, then? And Henry, too?" Sidney turned to ask, his gaze briefly catching mine before sliding away.

"Henry? No. But Rob, oh, yes, he was enthralled with flying machines for as long as anyone can remember." She looked to Mother, on Sidney's other side.

"Yes, he was." She agreed, setting down her glass. "Though I wish I'd realized then that allowing such an interest would lead to more heartache than merely a sprained ankle . . ."

I looked at Tim, seated across the table. His gaze remained trained on his plate, but I could tell by the flush in his cheeks that he'd heard what Mother had said.

"Rob might just as easily have died if he'd served in the infantry or the artillery, or the navy, even," Sidney pointed out not unkindly.

"Yes," she replied. "But at least, he would have had a better chance."

No one could argue with that. Our flyboys had died in alarming numbers, especially at the start of the war.

"I remember that Rob was always building things," Sidney prodded again.

"He was. When he was young, he would spend hours building with his blocks. I think he first picked up a hammer when he was about four or five." Mother's face softened in remembrance. "The first thing he made was a rickety little birdhouse." She chuckled. "The roof was rather crooked, and I was certain it would fall down during the first stiff wind, but it lasted for a good four or five years before he replaced it with a much sturdier version."

My gaze shifted to Father, finding him politely listening to whatever Mrs. Redmayne was telling him on his left, though his eyes strayed toward Mother from time to time, making me think he wasn't entirely unaware of the topic being discussed at the opposite end of the table. What Mother didn't know, and Rob had never suspected, was that Father periodically shored up the rickety walls of that little birdhouse. I'd caught him at it one summer morning, and he'd sworn me to secrecy.

"He built a number of things over the years. Shelves and stools. A dollhouse for Verity." Mother arched her eyebrows at me. "Not that it saw much use until Grace came along."

I didn't rise to her bait, knowing that if I spoke, my voice would squeak and wobble. I was already struggling as it was not to become swamped in the specter of memories their words had raised. Afraid I would choke if I tried to swallow, I pushed around the roast beef and peas on my plate with my fork.

"I seem to recall his building skills coming in remarkably handy during the mischief he, Freddy, and the others used to make," Sidney declared with a grin while purposely avoiding my quelling gaze. I was certain of that now.

But there was little I could do about it except clench my hands into fists in my lap and endure. Besides, I would be lying if I didn't admit a part of me was also hungry to hear these reminiscences about Rob. As much as they stung, they also comforted. As such, I was torn between strangling my husband and wishing I could reach for his hand under the cover of the table. But Mrs. Wild, who was laughing softly, sat between us.

"Good heavens, the things the boys and Verity used to get up to," she remarked. "And I'm sure there's many more capers we were never made aware of, probably for our own good."

I shrugged when they all turned to me, knowing better than to admit to anything.

Mrs. Wild giggled and shook her head.

"He built that treehouse out in the woods, too, didn't he?" Sidney asked.

The bite of beef I'd decided to risk eating settled in my stomach like a hard lump.

"Why, yes," Mother gasped. From the corner of my eye, I saw her reach out to touch his hand. "Fancy you remembering all this. How kind."

I couldn't recall the last time Mother had touched me with such affection or looked at me with anything approaching that level of approval. Pain and anger and guilt and grief washed over me in successive waves, making me hot and then cold, and it was all I could do not to react—to continue to sit there and breathe, even as my muscles urged me to run, to fight, to do *something* to alleviate the torment.

Somehow I made it through dinner and the exchange of small talk that followed, but as soon as the door closed behind our guests, I was out of the drawing room and up the stairs. Sidney caught up with me as I was donning my warmest hat and coat trimmed in beaver fur with epaulette and button trim.

His gaze dipped to the kid-leather walking boots encasing my feet. "Where are you going?"

I wanted to ignore him, but I knew he would only persist in asking until I answered, so I bit out a simple retort. "For a walk."

"Alone?"

I glared at him in challenge, and then turned to yank open the drawer of the bedside table to extract his Luger pistol. After brandishing it before him, I tucked it into my pocket. "Yes."

He watched as I pulled open a drawer in the bureau and removed a pair of gloves. "Is this about dinner?"

"If you have to ask . . ." I began to retort before he interrupted me, grabbing my arm to prevent me from leaving.

"I'm only trying to help. I thought if I raised the subject of Rob in a less direct way, you might find it easier."

"Easier to discuss him in front of a dozen people when I can't even talk about him when we're alone?" I snapped incredulously. "I *told* you to leave it be. I'll discuss it when I'm ready to discuss it."

"It seemed to help your mother and Mrs. Wild," he stated defensively, his jaw hardening as if *he* was the injured party.

I rounded on him. "Then would you like me to raise the subject of your war service and exactly what you experienced in the trenches the next time my family hosts a dinner party? It might help my brothers." My voice was skirting the edge of mockery, but I was too angry to care.

"That is not the same thing," he bit out.

"Oh, but it is." I squared off before him. "*You* were out of line. And you know it."

"You've given me no choice, Ver. How else am I supposed to help you?"

"Maybe you aren't."

His hard, glittering gaze flinched, and I narrowed my eyes, contemplating why that, of all things, had made him falter.

"Is that what this is all about, then? *You* helping me." I stepped back. "You've made this all about yourself."

"That's not true."

"Isn't it? After all, you said it. *You're* supposed to help me."

I could see the moment he began to question whether I might be right, and pressed my point. "*I'm* the one grieving, Sidney. So give me the space to do so." With that, I twisted away, and pounded down the stairs toward the entry.

I didn't stop to speak, or to even acknowledge anyone. I needed room to breathe, to move, to scream to the heavens if I so wished.

Everyone, everywhere, throughout the entire war and after, had always been watching, scrutinizing, assessing. Judging whether you were grieving right. Too little and you either hadn't cared enough or weren't acknowledging the loss. Too much and you were maudlin and overemotional, and damaging the war effort by not keeping enough of a stiff upper lip. You weren't supposed to cry too much or talk too much about your pain, but drinking or taking morphine, or any of the other things you might do to excess to numb the ache were also frowned upon. You were compelled by society to conform to an impossible set of strictures, one that no one could hope to maintain for long without cracking.

In addition to the strain of those untenable strictures, I had also needed to be able to perform my job with the Secret Service. And that was a place where there was absolutely no room for error, no space for emotion, and no time for weakness. I became so good at denying those feelings either by will or the use of gin and dancing, that even when the war had ended and I had been demobbed, and finally there had been an opportunity to actually grieve, I found I no longer knew how. The pain had become planted so deeply inside me that I was no longer certain I could uproot it without also uprooting a large part of myself.

My angry strides took me down the drive to the old stone bridge that spanned the brook separating the house from the larger part of the woods. Here I paused, pressing my hands against the rough, craggy rocks to gaze over the side at the water trickling past. It burbled musically as it cascaded over the rocky bed, the only sound save the soughing of the wind through the trees and my own breaths. The caw of a rook pierced the air, shattering the peacefulness of the setting, and I lifted my gaze to watch it glide to a stop on the roof of the cottage.

The cold wind stung my cheeks, and sent the heavy clouds racing across the sky. I shoved my hands deeper into the pockets of my coat, huddling against the breeze and contemplating how far into the wintery landscape I wanted to tread. The trees in the copse would serve as a type of windbreak, but that meant confronting Rob's treehouse. There was also the matter of the implied promise I'd made to Sidney not to venture there alone, lest the German mystery man be lurking in the woods again, though I felt less than inclined to uphold that oath after what he'd done. My fingers traced the barrel of the gun in my right pocket. And in my defense, I would not be unarmed.

I was still standing there deciding what to do when Tabitha came running toward me, barking to alert me to her presence. She stopped beside me to spin circles in greeting, and I reached down to rub her ears while I waited for the man striding down the drive in his usual unhurried way to reach me. Given the fact it was my father, I knew there would be no shouting or histrionics, but that didn't mean I wasn't about to be scolded.

I straightened as he reached the bridge. He nodded to me in greeting, his stoic face telling me nothing about what he was thinking, before turning to gaze over the stone railing down the winding course of the brook as it trailed into the woods. Tucking my hands back in my pockets, I turned to stand by his side. He didn't say anything at first, as content in his silence as I remembered. And soon enough, I became content in it as well, as my anxiety over what he might say began to fade.

I'd always admired my father, and though he was no more demonstrative than my mother with his affection, he had a way of making me feel loved nonetheless. It was in the way he looked at and spoke to me. The way he never questioned I knew my own mind, which hadn't meant he'd always agreed with me or let me have my say. But since I'd wed Sidney, he'd always respected my choices, regardless of what his opinion might have been of them.

"There'll be more snow by morning," he finally remarked as he surveyed the skies and breathed deep of the cool air. "Enough to coat the fells."

I made a noise of assent, trusting he knew what he was talking about.

"But Mr. Kidds will make sure all the ewes make it into the field barns for the night," he said, speaking of his foreman.

As would be the priority of all the other farmers in the area. Which meant if that straw-haired German stranger was staying in one of them somewhere, he was at greater risk of being discovered.

"Well, Verity." He inhaled and exhaled, finally coming to the reason he'd followed me. "Your arrival has certainly caused no small amount of turmoil."

It wasn't said with rancor—far from it—but his words smarted all the same.

"I don't try to cause problems," I replied in a small voice.

"Oh, I know that. Just as I know the reasons you didn't come home after Rob's death must have been good ones." He turned to look down at me, a kindness reflected in his eyes that I had not expected. "Just as I know that you've been grieving as much as the rest of us, whether you show it or not."

A lump formed in my throat, grateful he, at least, had recognized that.

"But your mother is hurting, Verity. She thinks you don't care about her, about Rob, about any of us. And nothing anyone else says will convince her otherwise." He adjusted the flat cap on his head, narrowing his eyes to see into the distance. "I know she's always been particularly hard on you, but it's simply her way." He chuffed. "To hear tell, she thinks she's been too soft on you, considering how strict her own mother was. But all the same, it's only because she wants to see you safe and settled. Unfortunately, it's her lot in life to have a daughter who thrives in the chaos she most hates."

I could tell the last was said mostly in teasing, but it was also the harsh truth. Mother had always craved order and constancy, while I had sought—not so much chaos, but adventure and excitement, and the thrill of trying new things. Even at a young age. When exasperated with me, Mother liked to tell the story of how at the age of two I'd toddled off from the churchyard while she was helping to decorate for Easter Sunday. Our nanny had been ill, and so she'd taken me with her. Once she'd realized I was gone, she'd spent half an hour frantically searching for me, only to find me happily climbing up and down the barstools in the Crown.

"Talk to her, aye?" he urged.

I nodded.

"And, Ver, I know it's painful. I know you don't want to do it. But I also know one of the reasons you came here was to finally face what you've been afraid to." He tipped his head, fixing me with a gently reproving look. "So get on with it. Stop dragging your feet, lass. Waiting any longer will not make it better. But it will certainly make you crosser, and everyone else in the family as well."

I choked down the lump that had settled at the back of my throat, unable to argue with that even though I wanted to.

His gaze flicked toward the house and back. "Tante Ilse told you about her cancer."

"Yes," I whispered in a broken voice.

His stalwart frame seemed to sag with weariness. "Then you have that to confront as well." He nodded toward the woods. "So go on." His eyes dipped to the dog, sitting at my side. "Take Tabitha with you, if you wish." He reached up to press the back of his hand against my cheek. "But go make what peace you can."

With that order, I turned my steps toward the woods, trudging forward on feet of lead. I didn't turn to look back, but I knew Father was standing there watching me, perhaps knowing I would turn chickenhearted if he did not.

As my footsteps broke through the unblemished snow, trailing off into the trees, they became lighter. As if the momentum alone was enough to carry me onward. Rather than gamboling ahead like normal, Tabitha remained faithfully by my side, as if she sensed my turmoil. We wound our way through the oaks, rowan, and downy birch to the treehouse deep in the copse.

At its base, I paused to look up, trying to remember the last time I'd been inside, but I'd not marked the occasion. It must have been during that final summer before the war, but I hadn't spent as much time up there as usual that year, being too wrapped up in Sidney and his courtship.

What had Rob thought of all that? After all, he hadn't only been my brother, but my oldest and dearest friend? It was true that Tim and I were closer in age by a few months, but Rob had been the brother I'd most related to and relied on. He'd been the peacemaker between me and Freddy, between all of us, really. Had he felt abandoned by my absorption in Sidney? He hadn't seemed upset, but then I'd been too blinded by my own giddiness to notice.

The wood appeared warped and faded, overgrown with moss and riddled with gouges, but it still looked stable. I reached up to tug on the boards hammered into the trunk of the tree, and finding them sturdy enough, hitched up my skirts, and began to climb. It wasn't high off the ground. Even if I fell, I would only twist an ankle or bruise my backside. But still I tested each rung before pulling myself upward.

Tabitha sat obediently at the base of the tree. When I reached the top and gave a mighty shove to open the door fashioned into the floor, she barked at the thwack of it hitting the boards on the other side. The hinges had creaked with age and disuse, but they'd held.

Cautiously peering inside, I noted that a corner of the roof had been damaged by a falling branch, letting even more light filter inside than the two small windows allowed. Spiderwebs draped the darkened corners, but I trusted the cold had either killed or driven the leggy weavers to warmer locales. Rotting piles of leaves had drifted to the edges of the space, giving the treehouse a damp, moldy odor.

Climbing the two remaining rungs, I sat on the edge of the floor with my legs dangling through the door, tentatively testing the wood. It seemed solid, but I decided it would be best not to press my luck, sliding backward a few feet along where the sturdy junction of the two tree limbs rested, bracing the floor beneath me. Pulling my knees up to my chest, I cradled my chin in the well formed between them. Then I closed my eyes and exhaled a long breath, releasing the shaky grip I held on my emotions.

When nothing happened, I sat dumbfounded. I'm not sure precisely what I'd expected to happen, but it was more akin to a dam breaking and torrents of water coming rushing out than this numbing sense of disbelief. It was like believing an angry mob was battering at your door, fighting to get in, only to open it and find there was no one there except a squirrel.

I lifted my chin to look around me, worried that this was all there was. This hollow emptiness forever and ever. Then my gaze caught on something poking out of the leaves to my right, and I leaned over to pull it toward me.

I wasn't certain what it was at first. It was definitely wood, and it had been carved and smoothed by human hands, most likely Rob's. But it seemed unfamiliar, until I recognized the distinctive long, thin shape and the wave-like design with the hole at the center for what it was. An aeroplane propeller. Likely from a model Rob had built.

My hand tightened around the wood, feeling a surge of emotion at the knowledge that my brother had touched this, had sanded it, had taken such care with it. It felt almost as if it was an invisible tether somehow connecting him to me. And I knew, I suddenly *knew* to the core of me that Rob was never coming back. He was never striding through my parents' door, or climbing the rungs to this treehouse, or wrapping me in the arms that it seemed had always been there to hold me. He was gone.

The pain inside me first escaped with a whimper and then with a sob, and then I could only clutch my knees as I wept. I cried so hard that I felt my ribs would crack and my heart would break. They were the tears I would not let fall when I'd learned Rob had died. And Henry, and Daphne's brother Gil, and cousin Thomas, and every friend and family member since. Including Sidney.

Oh, Sidney. That he'd miraculously come back to me mattered, but it didn't vanquish all the pain I'd suppressed at learning of his supposed death. It didn't erase it like the flip of a switch. The fear and darkness was still mixed up in all the other grief I'd repressed.

Then, as if conjured by my thoughts, he was there beside me, pulling me into his arms, holding me as I completely came apart. He didn't speak. He seemed to know better than to try. He simply held me close.

There was no going back. There was no returning to the way things were, the life and innocence that we'd had before. There was no returning to the people we were before. The only choice left to us was to shrivel up and die or to move bravely forward. To abandon hope or continue to clutch it to our hearts with all the might we possessed.

It was a long time before my sobs began to subside. By then the woolen front of Sidney's coat was soaked through, as well as his handkerchief. My face felt puffy, my eyes stung, my head pounded, and my ribs felt as if they'd been cracked. It was worse than the morning I'd lain battered and bruised, trying to rest in a Belgian farmer's attic after taking a tumble into an unseen rocky ditch in the middle of the night and then having had to hike three more miles to reach the next safe house. Then I'd ached in body, but now I also ached in spirit.

Barely able to lift my arm, I fished around in the pocket of my coat to locate my own handkerchief, blowing and wiping my already-raw nose. Truth be told, all of me felt raw, like the outermost layer of my skin had been scraped off. Or perhaps it had been sloughed off, like a snake shedding its skin. Maybe I'd emerged a new person.

Either way, I felt too weak to sit upright, let alone stand, so I sat slumped against Sidney, staring down at the toy propeller I still clutched.

"Was that Rob's?" Sidney asked, the first words he'd spoken other than crooning comforts since his arrival.

I passed it to him. "I found it."

He turned it over in his fingers, clearly recognizing its purpose. "I wonder where the rest of it is?"

"Maybe buried in that pile of four years' worth of decaying leaves, but I'm not about to dig for it."

Tabitha barked below, apparently having heard us talking.

"Stay, girl," Sidney called down through the door in the floor, and the collie settled back down, resuming her patient vigil.

"How did you find me?" I said into his chest.

"Your father sent me. He thought you might have need of me. And if that were true, I knew there was only one place you would have gone."

I trailed my fingers over one of the buttons fastening his coat. "I miss him," I admitted simply. "I miss them all."

"I know," he replied, needing no further explanation. "I miss them all, too."

All. All those we'd loved and cared for who were now lost to us. At least on this earth.

We both sat silently, remembering them. Grieving them. Wishing they were still with us. But there were some acts that could not be undone, some planes that could not be crossed. Not until our time had also come. But not yet. Lord, not yet. And so we pressed on. Without them.

Sidney's hand lifted to my chin, gently tipping my head back so that he could look into my eyes. I wavered a moment before meeting his gaze, feeling exposed and vulnerable. All the walls I placed between myself and others were down, some of them crumbled to dust. There was nothing to shield my thoughts from him.

As if aware of this, his fingers played over my skin with the lightest of caresses. "Verity, I'm sorry I pushed you. You were right. I did make this about me." The emotions swimming in the depths of his deep blue eyes were as clear and unfettered as I'd ever seen them. "The truth is, I feel guilty for having left you alone to deal with all of this for so long. Yes, I was at war and then pursuing traitors," he admitted, voicing the argument I was about to make. "But I still hate that I couldn't be there when you needed me most. And that I only added to your pain with my own deception." The rough callus of his thumb rubbed across my bottom lip. "I knew how upset you were with yourself for avoiding your family for so long, and how deeply you were grieving Rob, and I . . . I wanted to be there for you like I couldn't be during the war, yes." His face scrunched in pain. "But I also somehow got it into my head that if I could help you heal, then maybe that meant that eventually I would be able to heal, too."

"Sidney," I murmured, understanding now why he'd placed so much stock in helping me grieve for Rob. "I hope you realize now that one doesn't necessarily follow the other. That grief isn't something that ever truly ends. We grow and we heal in stages, but that doesn't mean we're ever completely whole again."

He nodded. "I should have let you lead, not tried to force you to grieve how *I* wanted you to, and at the pace I set. I simply should have supported you."

"And I should have *let* you support me. I should have let my family," I admitted in a voice grown hoarse from all my crying. "I'm no better, you know. I suppose I got so used to having to be strong and do everything on my own, that I forgot what it means to have others to lean on for emotional support." My gaze dipped to Sidney's square jaw as I swallowed, feeling tears threatening again. "I've always been the resilient one. The one others turn to."

He lowered his chin, forcing me to look him in the eye. "But Verity, everyone has their breaking points. That's not a weakness. It's just evidence of your humanity."

I blinked as tears burned my eyes again. "I'm just so angry at myself for not handling Rob's death, and your death, and everyone's death better. For causing everyone more pain."

"You need to let that go. You did the best you could. I know deep inside you know that. And that's all you can ask of yourself." He swiped away a tear as it fell from my eye. "War is hell. No one comes out unscathed. No matter how hard we try." His eyes shimmered with intensity. "Give yourself the same grace you give all of us."

His words hit me squarely in the chest, and I felt myself exhale for what seemed like the first time in years. I pressed my hand to his cheek, feeling the bristles along his jaw abrading my palm, and nodded in acceptance. His mouth found mine, and I reveled in the reassurance and love he offered me in that kiss.

We sat wrapped in each other's arms for a short time longer. Long enough for me to steady myself and to regain some of my strength from him. But the cold and discomfort of the hard floor soon recalled us to our senses.

Sidney insisted on descending the ladder first, to catch me lest I lose my grip. It wasn't until I was about halfway down in my descent that I realized Tabitha was no longer barking or circling below us. Confused, I turned my head to the left and then right, searching for her, wondering if she'd run off after a hare or a fox. That's when I saw them. The footprints in the snow. Coming from a different direction than the house.

CHAPTER 29

❧

"Sidney, the footprints," I murmured, moments before a man emerged from behind the wide tree trunk.

He appeared to be unarmed, but there was a wildness in his eyes, a stark detachment that made me nervous and uncertain what he would do. An impression that was only emphasized by the fact that his clothes were worn and dirty, likely from sleeping it rough.

I felt Sidney reach up to grasp my waist, steadying me. Then his hand slid into the pocket of my coat where the weight of his Luger pistol still rested.

"What did you do to Tabitha?" I asked the man, anxious to keep his gaze on me and not on what Sidney was doing. "The dog? *Der Hund*?"

"I gave dog food. From house. Dog is safe," he replied in a thick German accent, struggling to translate.

"What do you want? Why are you here?" I asked in German as I continued down the ladder. The man's intent would be clearer conveyed in his own language, and while Sidney was not as fluent in German as I was, he was certainly better versed than this fellow seemed to be in English.

"I apologize for sneaking up on you, particularly under these circumstances." His pale eyes glittered with sympathy as they flitted over my strained features, making it obvious he'd been here long enough to understand I'd been sobbing. "I mean you no harm. So you have no need of that pistol." He nodded to my hip, where Sidney's hand gripped the gun inside my pocket. "I simply want to talk."

I could see Sidney weighing his options, trying to decide whether to trust this man's word. As I reached the ground, I felt his hand release its grip on the pistol, leaving its heft behind.

Meanwhile, I had been scrutinizing the German fellow's face. He had the shaggy straw-colored hair I'd expected, but there was also something else about him that seemed familiar. The sun had sunk low in the sky behind him, so that his face was cast in shadow, but I could still see well enough to note that there was something in the tilt of the tip of his nose, in the shape of his eyes, and the heaviness of his brow that pricked my memory. I was also startled to realize I'd seen him before. At the church in Hawes, yes, but also before that. In London on the street outside our building. Bauer had been talking to him, and I had thought him to be an importuning bloke.

But there was more. I had seen those features before on another face. I had seen the same solemn frown. And just like that, some of the pieces to the puzzle began to slide into place.

"You're Anni Bauer, or should I say, Anni Becker's cousin."

Sidney's gaze darted to me sideways in surprise, but the man before me did not seem astonished.

"Yes."

"You're Heinrich Becker's nephew."

He nodded once in assent. "Right again. I am Kurt Becker."

I narrowed my eyes. "And you are the second deserter who appeared at my great-aunt's home."

He looked to the side. "Yes, well, it seemed a necessary ruse at the time."

But not because he was himself deserting. No, it was far more personal. "You were searching for Herr Becker."

He shrugged. "It was the logical place to start."

"Wait a moment," Sidney interrupted. "I'm struggling to follow. Heinrich Becker, as in the first deserter? The man you led to your great-aunt's in Monschau?"

"Yes. Do you remember me telling you that I'd learned that Herr Becker had been successful in his first mission? That he reported to the British in Holland and then was given another task, but was then never heard from again?" I turned to Kurt. "Well, I presume he made a visit to his home at some point during that first mission." We'd surmised as much after reading Anni Becker's journal and seeing all the information she'd possessed.

"He did, and explained to his wife what he was doing. Anni overheard their conversation, and was very angry at him for deserting the army and taking the British's money. She'd had it drilled into her brain at school every day how important the German ideal was, how Germany's honor must be upheld." He sighed, shaking his head. "She had no idea of the real toll the war was taking on her countrymen other than the increasingly meager amount of food they had to eat. But even that was something to be endured for the good of the country."

That sounded remarkably like many of *my* fellow countrymen, minus the near-starvation conditions.

"So you will understand she was not the most gracious of daughters when Uncle Heinrich departed. And when he never returned, she carried the guilt of that with her. Particularly as conditions worsened and she realized that her father had not been as selfish and dishonorable in his actions as she'd assumed."

"So she decided to try to find him," I concluded.

Kurt shifted his feet in the snow, making it crunch, and clasped one fist in the palm of the other hand before him as he thought back. "When I was next home for leave, she convinced me to go to Frau Vischering, posing as another deserter to learn all I could. I told her the idea was faulty. That I was unlikely to learn anything. But she would not be swayed. It was the only link we had, you see. The only tangible information we had to go on. And so I went, hoping to prevent Anni from doing something even more reckless."

"Did you learn anything?"

"Other than the fact that Frau Vischering was not a cold-hearted traitor, but merely a woman who chooses to view the worth of each person on their merits alone and not that of their nationality, no." He heaved a sigh. "But Anni, she would not accept that. When I returned to Berlin after the war, I discovered she had gone to Monschau to search for answers herself. And that she had contrived to get herself hired as her maid." He shook his head, his face forlorn. "I begged her to let it go. To return to Berlin with me and move on with her life. But she would not listen. She began leaving threats."

"*She* left the threats?" I repeated.

He grimaced. "Childish things. Anonymous letters and messages scrawled on walls. But they frightened Frau Vischering, and it was cruel to do so, especially when the old woman had only ever been kind to Anni. When that didn't work, she became determined to come to England, to search for the truth here, though I didn't understand how." He straightened his shoulders. "That was when I threatened to go to Frau Vischering and tell her everything if she did not abandon her plans, but she outwitted me. She told her that I was a scorned suitor who badgered her, and soon after they departed for England."

"But you followed them?"

"Yes, though it was not easy." He cleared his throat. "I am not here legally."

I had already guessed as much.

Tabitha came trotting out of the woods then, licking her chops, and I shook my head at her, for what a poor guard dog she'd turned out to be. But I also wanted to howl at the uselessness of Anni's charade. "I wish she'd come forward and told us who she was. For the truth is, we don't know what became of Herr Becker. As I said, he was sent back to Germany on another mission, one that was admittedly more dangerous than the first, but he agreed to it and he was handsomely compensated. I'd hoped he'd simply returned to his family, taking the money given to him with him. After all, he'd made it clear his loyalty lay with his family above all else. But sadly, it appears that's not where he went. Or, at least, he never arrived."

I turned to gaze out over the quiet woods as the shadows lengthened, casting strange elongated patterns across the snow. "You were seen by several people speaking to Anni in the village."

"I figured as much. That's why they've been hunting for me, isn't it?" Kurt's jaw hardened. "I'm a stranger, and a German at that. They think I killed her."

"Did you?" I asked evenly.

His brow furrowed, as if he wished to take offense, but then he abandoned it, perhaps recognizing it was a legitimate question. "No." He tilted his head in candor. "Honestly, I thought at first that you might have done it. That you'd realized who she was and tried to silence her. But then I realized that made no sense. What had *you* to fear from her? And also I watched you and listened to the villagers when I could, trying to learn more of you. I realized then that you were not content to accept the police's conclusion." His gaze flicked to Sidney, who despite his deceptively relaxed stance was still on guard. "That you and your husband were searching for the truth yourselves."

"How did you learn such things without drawing people's attention?" Sidney questioned. "Where did you conceal yourself?"

His gaze darted between us, as if hesitant at first to share. "The church. The bell tower."

Of course. I wanted to kick myself, for I should have realized sooner that the church would be the perfect place to hide. It was always open, but also often deserted. Particularly at night.

"People do not often guard their tongues in a church. They think they are not overheard. Except by God. But then, you English tend to believe he's always on your side."

I couldn't fault him for this assertion. It was true. But I turned my queries back to the matter of Bauer's murder.

"What happened in the barn?"

Kurt's eyes dimmed. "I don't know. Not for certain. That is the truth. She planned to leave you a letter, asking you to meet her there so that we could both confront you. I was to arrive later than her, after the two of you had begun to talk. But when I reached the barn . . ." His shoulders sagged and pain etched his brow. "She was already dead."

"You were the one who laid her out on the floor," Sidney guessed.

"I thought I might be able to save her, but . . . she was already gone."

I was not insensitive to the grief I heard in his voice. Not after just battling my own. But what we needed most right now were answers. And I hoped Kurt could help us to find those.

"You were also in the woods." It was a statement more than a question. "Watching us."

"I needed to be sure she would be found, to know who would find her."

"In case they were the killer returning?"

"Yes."

I did not fault him for this thinking. I would have pondered the same thing. After all, it was unlikely someone would have just happened upon such an isolated spot except a field hand come to bale the hay.

"So you didn't see or hear anything or anyone that might tell us who killed her?" I pressed.

"No, but . . ." He frowned, wrestling with himself. "A few days before, she told me that she'd been confronted by a man as she was leaving the village. She said he all but accused her of being a spy, and that he would be watching her."

I shared a look with Sidney. "What man?"

"I can't recall his name. Hard-something. She called him a soft egg, a slacker." He began to speak faster, perhaps in reaction to my jolt of realization, which he seemed to interpret wrong. "I heard the man she was speaking of talk several times, heard the way he struggled for breath. I thought he had been gassed and told her she was cruel to label him so. But she said he'd not been gassed. That he'd not fought at all. I realized then that his health must have been poor."

I turned away, pacing a tiny circle as I considered the ramifications of what he'd just revealed.

"You know who this is?" Kurt asked.

"Yes, and I think . . ." I broke off, unwilling to say more until I was certain. "I need to speak with Freddy." I turned to stride off, but then paused to turn back. "Where are you staying? The church still? Is it safe?"

He shrugged. "As safe as anywhere."

I glanced at Sidney, who was watching me, and then made a decision. "Will you wait? I'm going to send someone to you. Someone who will bring you some food and lead you to a place to shelter on my father's property. I give you my word that as long as you have been honest with me, you will not be harmed."

He studied me and then Sidney in turn, and for a moment I felt certain he would refuse. But then his shoulders dipped, as if bowed beneath the weight of a heavy burden. "Yes, I will wait."

I nodded once and then turned to stride off toward the house, whistling for Tabitha to follow.

Sidney caught up with me in half a dozen steps. "Isaac Hardcastle."

"Yes." I pressed my lips together grimly. "What Kurt told us isn't proof of anything, of course, but . . . I think Freddy might be able to tell us more."

Whether Sidney understood what this oblique statement meant, I couldn't tell, but he didn't question it. Instead, he gripped my elbow to help me over a fallen tree limb. "Then let's go see him."

After a quick word with Father, who agreed to have one of his staff provide shelter for Kurt in one of the outbuildings, and to keep the matter hush-hush from everyone else, we knocked on the door of the cottage. Freddy answered, and the looks on our faces must have conveyed our urgency.

"What is it? What's happened? Tante Ilse?" he asked in rapid fire, giving me some idea of what his manner had been in the operating theater at the front after battles. When one broken soldier's body after another was placed on the table before him to repair, or at least stave off the prospect of imminent death, before being whisked away to be replaced by another.

"No, I'm sorry. It's not Tante," I told him. "It's about Fräulein Bauer's murder."

"You've thought of something."

It wasn't truly a question, but I answered it as one nonetheless. "Yes."

He glanced behind him before stepping back to allow us

entry. "Rachel's upstairs with Ruth and Miss Pettigrew," he explained as we moved toward the wooden table with four spindle-backed chairs that stood closest to the door. A bowl of pine cones and evergreen boughs sat at the center, lending their aroma to the room. A small stove stood near the wall along with a cupboard, while the other half of the room was arranged as a cozy sitting area with chintz sofas. Pale green paint covered the walls, and a coordinating shade of chintz adorned the windows. Beyond the sitting area lay the stairs and then the bath and a workroom.

"You have questions for me," he deduced, not forcing me to have to explain myself.

"When Tim came to collect you and the motorcar after we'd found Bauer, you weren't here," I began.

"That's correct. I'd been summoned to the Hardcastles'. Isaac had one of his asthmatic episodes . . ." His voice broke off almost midword, as if realizing the same thing I had.

I leaned across the table toward him. "Did they tell you what brought it on? Did he or Mrs. Hardcastle explain?"

He began to shake his head, but then stopped. "No. They didn't. But hay is one of the chief culprits, and I found some on my coat when I departed." His gaze shifted to Sidney and then back to me again. "Mrs. Hardcastle had hung it over Isaac's on the hook." He sat back, plainly staggered, and swore. "Isaac Hardcastle. Do you really think so?"

"In your medical opinion, would he be physically capable of it?" Sidney asked. "Could he wield a pitchfork like that?"

"Of course," Freddy replied without question. "Even in the midst of a minor attack, I suspect he would be able to do so. Only while suffering a more severe incident would he be truly incapacitated, and he suffers from those far less than Mrs. Hardcastle would have everyone believe. Because he listens to medical advice and normally avoids strenuous physical exertion and known triggers, like hay."

"Was his attack the day Bauer was killed severe?" I queried. "Severe enough it may have been brought on by both strenuous physical exertion and exposure to hay?"

His voice was solemn. "Aye."

I pressed my hand to my mouth and turned to gaze out the window toward the inner courtyard. The sun had set, leaving naught but a dusky light in the sky. "Good heavens, he did it," I finally said. "It has to be him."

Freddy stood to turn on a lamp, as if just recognizing it was needed. "Not the missing German?"

"He's not missing anymore." I glanced at Sidney. "We just spoke with him. He was Bauer's cousin, and I'm certain he didn't kill her."

Freddy turned to Sidney, and I felt a twinge of annoyance that he should expect my husband's opinion on this to be more valid than mine.

"Verity's right. He didn't do it," he concurred. "It makes no sense for him to have done so. Not when everything he'd done before then had been to try to keep her safe."

I pressed my finger to the table, further laying out my case. "He also told us that Isaac had approached Bauer one day when she was leaving the village and essentially threatened her. He told her that he knew she was a spy, and he would be watching her."

"So he followed her to the field barn . . ." Freddy surmised.

"Or overheard Bauer and her cousin planning to meet there," Sidney chimed in to suggest. "He might have denied knowing German." He nodded to me. "But I would wager Verity's memory is correct, and he does know it."

Though we would have to ask Kurt if he knew precisely what Isaac had overheard them discussing.

Freddy nodded, conceding this possibility. "And expecting she was up to no good, he decided to confront her. Matters turned heated . . ."

I arched my eyebrows. "Maybe she called him a coward and a slacker, as she'd already told her cousin she believed him to be."

He cringed. "Aye, that would certainly get under Hardcastle's skin. So, he picked up the pitchfork, whether intending to use it or just threaten her, and then ended up skewering her."

I grimaced. "That's the gist of it."

Sidney shifted in his chair to face me. "Is that what a 'soft egg' means? A coward?"

I realized he was referring to what Kurt had said in the woods. "Yes, some Germans would call a coward a *weichei*, a *weich ei*, which literally translates to a 'soft egg.'"

He tilted his head in consideration. "So is a 'hard egg' someone brave?"

I scowled at him, for now was not the time for such a discussion. "The trouble is, we don't have any proof. Isaac's fingerprints might be on the handle of that pitchfork—and he would undoubtedly have a difficult time explaining them if they were—but he might just as easily have worn gloves. It was cold enough."

Freddy nodded. "And very like Isaac to do so in order to avoid touching anything that might trigger a fit. Have the police tested the pitchfork for fingerprints yet?"

"I don't know, but I'm going to ask Father to speak to Sergeant Bibby about it tomorrow, and pressure them to do so if they haven't. Threatening to go over his head if he must."

"Aye, Bibby will want to keep on Father's good side. He'll see it's done." He sighed, sitting back in his chair and crossing his arms in front of his chest. "But if there aren't any fingerprints, I'm afraid there isn't much of a case against him. Any barrister worth his salt would argue that the asthmatic attack could be attributed to any number of sources. It's certainly not proof he was in the barn, though it is indicative."

"Not that he would even be arrested on the evidence we do have," Sidney stated matter-of-factly. "After all, who other than us is going to believe the word of a German who snuck into this country illegally over a parish councilman?"

He was right. It was more likely that Sergeant Bibby would arrest Kurt on Isaac's flimsy evidence, no matter what we said. And I couldn't reveal my connection to Heinrich Becker, or why Bauer and Kurt had come to England, or explain any of their odd behavior without compromising myself and breaking the oath I'd sworn to uphold the Official Secrets Act.

"So what do we do?" Freddy asked.

My jaw firmed. "We need a confession."

My brother studied me, clearly weighing and assessing me with new eyes given the things he'd learned about me in the past few days. "Do you think you can get one from him?"

"For him, it all comes down to pride," I replied. "He'll want to brag to someone. After all, what good is saving England from German spies if no one ever knows about it? He needs someone to know that he did his bit. Not just in serving on the parish council, but actually in a warlike capacity."

Freddy's eyes glimmered with sympathy. "Aye, I'm certain it eats at him, his not having been able to serve."

Just as I was certain he was aware everyone pitied him for it. Freddy might feel compassion for him, but he didn't want it. What he wanted was respect. That was something I could appreciate. But not if it meant he'd killed an innocent German maid in his quest to get it.

CHAPTER 30

❦

Having agreed it would be best to wait until Father returned from speaking with Sergeant Bibby on the progress of the inquest and whether the handle of the pitchfork had been tested for fingerprints, I spent much of the next morning pacing the floors. I was still undecided on what was the best way to confront Isaac, realizing I would only get one chance to elicit a confession from him. His words to us in the churchyard while Bauer was being laid to rest suggested he might already be on guard, but I was hopeful I could still play on his insecurities.

Sometime shortly after midmorning, Abbott appeared in the doorway of the drawing room. "A message for you, Mrs. Kent, delivered by the Capshaws' manservant."

Surprised by this news, I hastened over to take the missive. Turning toward the sunlight spilling through the window, I opened it.

> *I must speak with you. Come to St. Margaret's at half past eleven. Father has use of the motorcar, and I can't risk the staff overhearing. —Violet*

It was hastily scrawled, and the ink had smudged from being folded too quickly. A glance at the clock told me I must hurry if I hoped to arrive at the time requested. Passing it to Sidney, I hastened up the stairs to fetch my Prussian blue velvet coat with roll collar and matching hat. I met him coming up as I was on my way back down.

"Shall I come with you?"

"I'd rather you stay here to wait for Father," I told him while buttoning the coat up over my gown. "That way you can come straight there to fetch me should there be any immediate news. But I will need to take your Pierce-Arrow."

He glanced down at the note, clearly harboring some sort of wariness I didn't feel.

"I can't imagine there being any trouble," I assured him. "The vicar will be there, as well as any number of other parishioners going in and out about various tasks." I arched a single eyebrow in teasing. "Or is your hesitation more about my getting behind the wheel of your prized Pierce-Arrow?"

"No, I trust you to take care. After all, you drove my other one for over four years without her suffering a scratch."

I wouldn't have gone so far as to say that, but I wasn't about to contradict him. Not when I was getting my way.

"Just . . . be careful."

I arched up on my toes at the base of the stairs to press a kiss to his cheek. "Always."

Father had been correct. Another several inches of snow had fallen overnight. But the sun was now shining, and the temperature had risen over the morning, causing some of the snow to melt, and leaving behind a slushy mess on the roadways. I drove with extra caution, aware it had been some time since I'd navigated roads in such a condition, and anxious not to damage the motorcar in any way. Few people were out and about, and as I pulled into the lane next to the church and parked, I encountered almost no one. Only a terrier loping down the pavement, who stopped to sniff my boots as I climbed from the Pierce-Arrow before carrying on.

I hurried up the path leading to the church beneath the overarching lime trees, their branches limned with snow. My gaze lifted to the rough-hewn stone of the church as I approached, the slate of its steeply pitched roof a patchwork of white and gray. Under such conditions, with the sunlight breaking through the clouds to glint off the stained glass windows, the building lost some of its usual solemnity.

The heavy wooden door groaned as I opened it to step inside. A hush seemed to fill the soaring space as it shut behind me. I turned to look about me, searching for Violet. Wondering if I had arrived before she had, or if she'd entered through one of the other doors, I began to stroll up the aisle toward the chancel, my heels clicking across the stone floor to ricochet up to the wooden beams above. The air inside was cool and lightly scented with lemon polish and the lingering stench of extinguished candles.

I slowed my steps as I reached the rail separating the chancel from the nave, and turned to look behind me, suddenly a little awed and unnerved by the realization that I was alone in this echoing space.

That's when I caught a fleeting movement out of the corner of my eye. Turning back toward the altar, I stepped up into the chancel. "Violet, is that . . . ?"

My words died as Isaac Hardcastle stepped out from where he'd been hiding beyond the choir stalls. He held a Webley pistol in his hand, aimed at my chest.

"Hullo, Verity," he declared, his mouth twisting with satisfaction. "Weren't expecting me, were you?"

I forced myself to take a calming breath even though my heart pounded in my ears. "Isaac, what on earth are you doing? Put that thing down."

"I think you know what I'm doing. Don't play games with me."

I frowned. "I take it Violet won't be joining us. That this was all just a ruse to get me here."

"Her father knew she'd raced over to Brock House the other night to tell you all about our search for the German." He scoffed. "As if it was something to be horrified about and not merely the pursuit of justice. So it was no trouble to convince him to have one of his servants deliver a message to you."

"Yes, but why the need for such a charade? You could have

come to Brock House to ask your questions. I would have answered them." My gaze dipped to the Webley. "Without the need for a gun."

"These aren't the kind of questions you'll wish to answer in front of your family or your war-hero husband. But go ahead, make your denials." His eyes hardened to chips. "Though I tell you, things will go much better for you if you cooperate."

His words and the voice in which he'd said them sent a chill down my spine. It appeared I had sadly underestimated what Isaac was capable of. Sadly, indeed.

He gestured with the pistol. "Now, step into the lady chapel, if you please."

Swiftly weighing my alternatives, I decided it was best to obey him for now. But that didn't stop me from raising my voice as I passed the large Victorian font and walked through the wooden tracery-worked screen into the side chapel. "I'm not sure what it is you think I know, but I presume this is something to do with Fräulein Bauer and the man you saw her speaking with."

"If you're hoping Vicar Redmayne will come to your rescue, then you're mistaken. He spends his Thursdays over in Askrigg at St. Oswald's."

My heart stilled, for I had not known this, though I refused to give him the pleasure of seeing that.

"You've been away from home too long, Verity," he mocked. "You're no longer familiar with our ways."

"Do those ways include threatening an unarmed woman in a church at gunpoint?" I retorted angrily.

"When that woman is a *traitor*, aye, they do."

I swiveled to look at him, realizing just how deeply in trouble I was. "You can't be serious?" I shook my head in shock as well as denial. "I'm not a traitor."

"Then why did Miss Bauer and her German fellow want to meet with you in secret?" he challenged.

"I don't know why they wanted to meet with me. My best guess is that it's because she knew my great-aunt is ill and not long for this earth, and she wanted me to hire her and this German man."

"Lies!" he snapped, moving several steps closer and jabbing his gun toward me.

I shrank back a step in reaction, my breath catching in my throat for fear he would fire the pistol in his anger. But then I planted my feet as my training took over, refusing to cower, and apprehending that my best bet of escaping unharmed was to disarm him. And I couldn't do that unless he came close enough for me to strike out and grab his arm to force the barrel away from me before it discharged.

"Don't lie to me," he snarled. "I heard them talking about a turncoat and a spy."

I inwardly flinched. Could Isaac have overheard two worse words, and then misunderstood them? I was certain Bauer or Kurt had used the word *Überläufer*, which could mean "deserter" or "turncoat." Of course, Isaac had grasped on to the latter.

"But I didn't connect it to you until I learned about that letter she left you, asking you to meet them."

"I thought you told Freddy you didn't understand German," I replied, gauging the distance between us. Just two more steps, and I might be able to attempt it.

Unfortunately, he came to a stop, his mouth twisting into a spiteful grin. "Aye, well, you aren't the only one with hidden talents."

"Then you overheard their plan to meet in the field barn." I shifted on the balls of my feet, wondering if I could slowly close the gap between us. "You knew they would be there."

He scowled.

"Were you there waiting for Bauer when she arrived?"

"I . . ." He shook his head, his face flushing with anger.

"Did you confront her with what you'd overheard?" I pressed, shifting another quarter step closer with every sentence. "Did she call you some nasty names in return?"

"She was a spy," he spat, spittle flying from his mouth and nearly striking my cheek. "And an insolent, foul-mouthed girl."

"So you killed her."

He opened his mouth and then snapped it shut, his eyes narrowing in suspicion. As his gaze dipped to my feet, I recognized I was about to lose my chance to disarm him, and I might not get another chance. So I made the split-second decision to lunge for him and strike out from where I was.

My hand connected with his wrist just as the pistol fired. The bullet tore into my shoulder, knocking me backward, and I fell to the ground. I gritted my teeth against the sharp pain that lanced through me. Pressing my right hand over the wound, I stared up at the vaulted ceiling.

This was what Sidney had felt when he'd been shot during the chaos of the retreat from St. Quentin. The thought briefly flickered through my mind. Blood soaked the coat underneath my fingers, but I knew I had to keep pressure on the wound.

Then a figure moved to stand over me with wide, wild eyes, the gun now dangling from his hand at his side. "Now, see what you made me do," he taunted in a shaky voice. "All you needed to do was confess. That's all I wanted from that German maid. But neither of you understood what's good for you." Air rasped from his lungs, growing more labored with each breath.

Lying there at his feet, reeling from a bullet wound, in an empty church save for the two of us, I realized I was entirely at his mercy. All he needed to do was lift the Webley and fire it into my head or my heart, and my life would be over. And sooner or later he would realize that. He would emerge from his stupor and silence me, blaming it on the German, on Kurt. It was the only choice he had if he was to save his own skin. After all, I was a Townsend, not merely some German maid.

The sickening irony of it all was that until five minutes ago, I hadn't been worried about what Isaac Hardcastle might do to me. Lord Ardmore and the unknown bomber of General Bishop's HQ had been the biggest threats to my life and future. I had never anticipated that a childhood acquaintance—if not friend—and neighbor would be the one to kill me.

I hardened my resolve. But not without a fight. I hadn't survived four bloody years of war, of sneaking in and out of the

German-occupied territories, and losing my brother and colleagues and so many others, only to die on the floor of the church in my quiet English village, executed like a mangy dog.

Tightening my abdomen muscles, I shifted to the side and struck out with a sweeping kick. Isaac tumbled to the ground, landing partially on my legs. I yelped in pain, but then forced myself to roll, to keep moving. My shoulder throbbed as if it were on fire, but I heaved myself upright, searching for the gun. It had clattered across the floor to my left, out of our reach. But rather than dive for it and risk him tackling me, I rammed my knee into his side—once, twice.

"That's for shooting me," I growled. "And this is for ruining my favorite coat." I pulled back my fist to punch him in the nose. It landed with a satisfying crunch, and he howled in pain.

Staggering to my feet, I stumbled across the floor to grab the pistol. I sank down on my knees, lifting it to aim it at Isaac. But when he made no effort to rise or come toward me, but just lay there groaning and cursing between labored breaths, I lowered it, my muscles shuddering in agony.

I looked up as I heard footsteps pounding over the stones in the chancel, and voices shouting my name. "In here," I called.

Sidney hurtled through the door first, followed by Freddy and then Tim.

"Tim said he heard a gunshot," my husband gasped, looking first at Isaac and then me.

I shifted so that he could more clearly see the front of my coat. "I'm afraid he's right."

The gun fell from my hand and my muscles seemed to give way, as if now that the danger was past they were no longer able to support me.

Sidney caught me, sinking down on his knees behind me and gently lowering me to the floor as he called urgently to Freddy. I blinked several times, trying to keep them in focus, but everything had become rather fuzzy. The last thing I recalled was seeing them hovering over me, their eyes filled with fear, and then everything went black.

CHAPTER 31

❧

Morning sunlight streamed through the curtains, casting a long shaft of light across the bed. If I shifted slightly to the right, it would shine directly into my eyes, but I was content enough where I was. After all, I'd woken that morning to only a mild twinge of pain rather than the dull throbbing ache I'd feared would never go away, and so I was determined to be grateful for what was.

My shoulder was healing, thanks to Freddy and the staff at the hospital where I'd recuperated for a week. I couldn't have been in better hands, though I was certain my brother had never anticipated patching his *sister* up from a gunshot wound. In time, I was expected to make a full recovery, though I would always bear a scar. Which severely limited my choices when it came to my evening wardrobe. But my modiste and I would simply have to come up with a clever solution for that.

I turned my head on the pillow to gaze at Sidney's sleeping face. His dark curling hair always fell in disarray as he slept, and I found him to be all the handsomer for it. It softened the rugged cast to his features and made him look as if he'd been up to something decidedly naughty. Though that definitely had not been the case last night.

He awakened to the sight of me tracing his features with my eyes, something I refused to feel embarrassed about. After all, one should be allowed to enjoy the sight of one's husband, especially when he was as attractive as Sidney.

"Good morning," he said in a sleep-roughened voice that always seemed to register low in my belly.

"Good morning."

He pushed up onto his elbow with a yawn, causing the covers to fall to his waist and revealing his well-defined torso, as well as the scar he sported from his own bullet wound. "Do you need some more pain medicine?"

"Not yet."

He gazed down at me, perhaps trying to gauge whether to believe me—something I couldn't fault him for doing, as after my release from the hospital I'd initially tried to wait too long between doses and wound up regretting it. He leaned closer, and then reared back as the sunlight struck him full in the face. "Shall I fix the curtain?"

"If you like." I watched intently as he rose up onto his knees and reached over me to draw the curtain closed tighter, causing a ripple of movement in the muscles of his abdomen and arms.

Looking down at me, he caught me avidly scrutinizing him, and his lips twitched in amusement. "So that's your game."

"Just appreciating beauty where I see it," I explained as he settled on his side next to me, his elbow bent and his head propped in his hand. "And glad we're both alive."

His gaze dipped to my shoulder, the thick dressing evident beneath the loose sleep shirt I'd borrowed from him. "I've been scared many times in my life, Ver. Especially during the war. I'm not too proud to admit that." His deep blue eyes shimmered with emotion as they lifted to mine. "But I've never been more scared than when I saw you kneeling on that church floor with your coat covered in blood."

I lifted my left hand as much as my injury would allow, and he reached out to twine his fingers with mine. "I'm sorry I frightened you."

"I know. I just . . . wanted you to know." He pressed a kiss to my lips, but pulled back before things could get interesting. "Your brother should be here shortly to check your dressing." His eyes scoured my features with concern. "Maybe you *should* take your medicine."

"Yes, you're probably right."

Not that Freddy wasn't gentle, but manipulating my shoulder about, exerting the muscles that had been damaged, always caused me pain.

He fluffed up the pillows behind me and helped me to sit upright before measuring out the medicine and waiting for me to drink it.

"I forgot to mention, we received a telegram from Becker yesterday evening," Sidney remarked as he whisked the glass away. "He made it to Berlin safely."

I exhaled in relief. "That's good to hear." Though my father had offered him a position here at Brock House, Kurt Becker had told us he wished to return to Germany despite the hardships there. So Sidney had made arrangements for him to do so, without suffering any ill consequences. His cousin, Anni Becker, would, of course, remain buried here in Hawes, but I hoped now she would at least be able to rest in peace.

Tante Ilse had looked tremendously sad and weary when we'd explained who Bauer was and why she'd come to Monschau and then England. I'd expected her to be a trifle angry as well, for no matter her reasons, the girl had deceived her and betrayed her trust. But she merely shook her head and lamented the fact that she hadn't simply told her who she was.

I grieved knowing what had become of Heinrich Becker's family, wishing it could have been different. Wishing I could have shared my admiration for him with his daughter, and told her how very much he'd loved her. How everything he'd done, every choice he'd made had been for them, even if it hadn't made sense to her. I wished she could have known it. But such were the choices one made in life, whether during war or peace. Even those decisions made with the best of intentions could turn out horribly wrong.

"And Miss Capshaw," Sidney added. "She called after you'd retired to bring you some bulbs from her mother's garden."

"Oh, she didn't need to do that," I protested. Violet had been horrified when she'd learned what her father had done. She and Mr. Capshaw had visited on my return from the hospital some days past so that he could apologize for being taken in by Isaac and sending me that note. Given the fact that Mr. Capshaw had appeared appropriately contrite and was notoriously stingy with his apologies, I'd accepted it with grace. I only hoped he wasn't the only villager who'd realized the error of his ways. But Violet clearly still felt guilty.

"Your mother and I told her so, and we reiterated that you placed no blame on her and that you had already forgiven her father. Though I'm not sure I have," he muttered under his breath as an aside. "But she insisted."

I shook my head against the pillow propping me up. "It's as much my fault as anyone's. I should have been more suspicious of that note. I should have wondered why Violet hadn't simply telephoned. I should have recognized the missive wasn't written in her hand. But I saw the scrawl as merely an indication of her haste. And I sorely underestimated Isaac." I tilted my head to the side. "Of course, I'd not realized he'd pegged me for a German spy, but I still should have been more wary. I knew full well that when one of my fellow agents was caught it was usually because of a small slipup on their part. Those thoughtless little mistakes more often than not were what led to their apprehension. And yet still I blundered in without thinking."

Sidney sank down on the bed and reached for my good hand. "Don't beat yourself up. None of us suspected Hardcastle was capable of such a thing. And we never would have thought to be concerned had it not been for your mother. When we told her where you'd gone, she was the one who expressed doubts, telling us Violet always spent Thursdays in Richmond volunteering at the orphan home, and that the vicar went to Askrigg. That's when we began to worry that perhaps everything was not as it seemed."

"Well, I still blame myself for not stopping to think. Perhaps that will keep me from making the same mistake in the future."

His hand squeezed mine, and I looked up in time to see doubt flash in his eyes.

"Don't tell me you're about to turn into an ogre, and try to lock me in a tall tower. Because I won't stand for it."

"No," he conceded, though he didn't sound certain. "But I do want you to be more careful."

I tightened my grip on his hand. "Isn't that what I just promised to do?"

"You can't fault me for worrying about you, Ver?"

"No, but I will if it makes you a wet blanket," I jested. "There's no need for you to turn into a Mrs. Hardcastle." I frowned. "I suspect she's taken all of this rather hard."

"I believe she's still in denial, even though once pressure was brought to bear, her son essentially confessed to everything. I think she's most furious you broke his nose."

"She's lucky I didn't break anything else," I grumbled.

There was a knock on the door.

"That'll be Freddy, no doubt." He pushed to his feet to pull on his dressing gown, knotting it at the waist before calling out for Freddy to enter.

"Good morning," my older brother declared, already dressed and freshly pressed, the hair at his temples still damp.

Behind him another person poked his head around the door like an eager puppy. "May I come in as well?"

"Yes, Tim," I replied, struggling to repress a smile. "As long as you don't make me laugh while Freddy is changing my dressing." I'd witnessed a remarkable change in my younger brother since my return from the hospital. He was lighter, happier, and much more inclined to resort to the comedic antics he'd indulged in before the war.

He held up his hand as if taking an oath.

"Well, then, Pip, how is my patient this morning?" Freddy queried, rounding the bed to stand over me.

"The pain was less when I awoke."

"Good," he declared, and then like a typical big brother dampened my hopes. "Though once the wound has finished knitting back together, it's going to hurt like the dickens again when you begin moving it about to rebuild the muscle."

The talk shifted to my injury while Freddy carefully prodded and examined it and then changed the dressing. Then as I pulled the nightshirt back over my shoulder to button it up, I turned to

Tim, who was clearly anxious to share some sort of news. "All right, out with it. Before you burst."

He grinned, unabashed. "First of all, I shared with Freddy what we discussed." That he was speaking of his desire to work with aeroplanes was evident, and I was pleased to see the approval in Freddy's eyes.

"I'm glad," I replied, for Tim would need someone to talk to about it, someone who understood once Sidney and I returned to London.

"And Sidney put me in contact with Goldy. He's invited me to come down to view his family's aviation company, and what they're doing there. Even offered to hire me on as an assistant, show me the ropes, so to speak, until I decide what to do."

"That's wonderful," I said in delight, though I knew I should have expected nothing less from our friend.

He nodded, rocking forward onto his toes. "I'm going down sometime in January."

"Then you'll stay with us," I ordered. "At least until you know what's what."

"Thanks, Ver." A curious glint lit his eyes before he dropped them, toeing the base of the bedpost with his foot. "It felt all wrong, you know. Getting to come home when Rob . . . when so many others didn't. I just"—he turned to the side—"I just kept thinking, why should I get the chance to live when they don't?"

All three men fell silent, each plainly contemplating their own losses, their own feelings on this matter.

"I know it's hard, but if the situation was reversed," I murmured softly, knowing I spoke to them all, "if you were the one dead, and they were still living, wouldn't you want them to embrace it?"

He nodded, meeting my gaze again. "That's what I realized. That there's no shame in feeling excited about the future. That what I'm wishing for is that *they* were *here* with me, not that *I* was *there* with them. But what's the use of my living if I'm not really doing so."

I smiled at him even as tears burned the back of my eyes. "You're wiser than I remember, Tim."

A snort of laughter escaped from Freddy's chest.

"Hey, now, I've always been the sharpest of us lot," Tim protested and then flashed an impish grin. "I just chose to keep it a secret so as not to trample your delicate pride."

It was my turn to snort.

"Speaking of which." His eyes narrowed at me. "I know you weren't just some shipping clerk during the war."

A taut silence filled the room as I fretted over just how much Isaac Hardcastle had uncovered, and how much I might have revealed unwittingly in my unconscious state.

Tim's nose wrinkled grudgingly. "But I suppose you can't talk about that. At least, that's what Freddy thinks. Secrets Act and all that stuff."

I turned to look at Freddy, but his steady regard never wavered. That, more than anything, told me he suspected the truth, and had accepted it. Perhaps even approved.

"So I suppose we'll have to leave it at that," Tim added, though the quirk of his mouth suggested he hoped I would say otherwise.

My dressing having been changed, Sidney shooed them out so that I could dress. Something he saw to himself, unwilling to pass the duty off to a maid. However, I balked at allowing him to style my hair.

"Send Grace to me," I requested. At Everleigh Court, she was more often than not forced to groom herself without the assistance of a maid, so I knew she would have some semblance of an idea what to do. Besides, I wanted to talk to her alone, and we'd not yet had the opportunity.

Sidney left me perched on the bench before the vanity table, gazing into the mirror at myself. My skin had lost much of its luster over the past ten days. Dark circles ringed my eyes, and my collarbone protruded slightly more from the weight I'd lost. At this rate, I might achieve the slim, boyish figure that was now so desirable. But in time I would recover. At least, externally. My healthy flush would return and my curves regain their lushness, but I knew it would be some time before I trusted my judgment so readily again.

A trifle more caution was a good thing. After all, if I'd exercised it when I'd received that note that was supposedly from Violet, I wouldn't be in this predicament. But I also feared it would make me hesitate when I could not afford to. When my confidence in my instincts and intuition was needed to extract me or others from a grave situation.

I breathed past the tightness in my lungs. I supposed only time would tell.

The door opened, and in the reflection of the mirror I saw Grace tentatively peer inside.

"You need my help?" she asked uncertainly.

"Yes. Please, come in."

She slowly edged up behind me, her eyes dipping to my shoulder and the sling fashioned to cradle my arm against my torso.

"It's my hair. I can't do anything with it," I confessed. "And I absolutely refuse to let Sidney make a hash of it."

Her gaze shifted to my bobbed auburn tresses, perhaps wondering why I didn't simply summon a maid. "I can try."

I passed her my hairbrush, watching as she cautiously pulled it through my tresses, gaining confidence with each stroke.

"Why don't you have a lady's maid?" Her gaze darted to my reflection in the mirror and then back to my hair, as if expecting me to be angry with her for asking.

"Well, as you know, I had Matilda for a time. But she was really there to spy for Mother."

Her eyes widened as if she'd not known this.

"So I sent her back here. And then . . . well, the war was still on, and I'd just found out Sidney was allegedly dead, and . . . honestly, I wanted privacy more than anything. So I hired another war widow who lived out to come during the day to take care of my clothes and the flat, and I suppose I just got used to doing the rest for myself." A corner of my mouth quirked upward in chagrin. "Though, I admit now I rather wish I'd hired someone."

Grace listened to this with interest, but I couldn't tell what she was thinking.

"Have you considered bobbing your hair?" I asked.

She reached up to touch her brown tresses. "Some of the other girls at Everleigh have, but Mother would have a fit if I did it." Her gaze darted to me guiltily.

"Yes, I know she hates mine," I said with a smile. "It's brash and boyish and unbecoming."

She smiled timidly.

I shrugged my good shoulder. "But I like it." I grinned wider. "And so does Sidney."

My smile faded as my sister's eyes turned downcast. I knew what, or rather who, she was thinking of.

"Grace, I'm sorry about Cyril. If I could have spared questioning him I would have."

"I know," she replied automatically, though I didn't think she truly understood.

I braced myself, knowing I was about to risk her enmity, but my next words needed to be said. "Grace, Cyril has a number of issues he must confront before he will ever be ready to be with someone on good terms."

She stiffened. "He is *not* a coward."

"I know."

The stark certainty of my pronouncement startled her, and I couldn't help but wonder whether a small piece of her had feared that he was despite her protestations to the contrary.

"He was injured in a motorcar crash while the enemy was shelling our boys. His injury and discharge were entirely honorable. But *he* still feels ashamed of it."

"Why?" she asked in bewilderment. "Because of the way some people make him feel, thinking he injured himself on purpose." Her eyes flashed, clearly thinking of Freddy.

"I'm sure that plays a part of it, but it has more to do with the fact he was injured behind the lines driving a motorcar rather than serving in the trenches. He feels conflicted."

"But that's ridiculous!"

"To you and me maybe. But not to him. And I imagine many of the men who served would understand."

She stared at me in utter bewilderment, and I swiveled on the bench to face her directly.

"Grace, until Cyril confronts the shame he feels, until he is able to stand up to your family's scrutiny and feel worthy of you . . ." I shook my head. "A relationship between you will never work. It will be wretched and painful. And whatever love you feel for him will eventually be snuffed out or twisted into something much less noble."

Her jaw hardened stubbornly. "No, it won't."

"Yes, it will," I insisted sadly. "I've seen it happen before."

The mutinous set of her lips told me she refused to believe me.

I reached out to take her hand. "Grace, I just want to see you happy, and unless you wed someone who wants you as much as you want them, then it will only be a misery." I gripped her hand tighter when she would have pulled away. "But if your heart is set on Cyril, then at least wait until he's ready. At least wait until after you've visited me in London over the summer holiday."

Her eyes widened at this pronouncement.

"Please, say you'll come. Just for a few weeks. I should have asked you before. I should have done a lot of things. But we've already established I've been a dreadful sister. Positively beastly."

Her lips quirked.

"But let me make it up to you. Please, say you'll come."

"Well, I suppose I can hardly refuse when you put it like that."

I beamed. "Good. We'll have the most fabulous time."

It was a risk bringing her to the city, into Ardmore's sphere, but I was certain he already knew of her existence. With any luck, by the time she visited he would already be locked away for his crimes. And if not, we would simply have to brave it, keeping a sharp eye out for trouble while she was with us. Because I refused to sacrifice my relationship with my family any more than I'd already done. Five missing years was long enough.

CHAPTER 32

Later that evening, it was my mother who assisted me up to my bedchamber and helped me to prepare for bed. As she settled the loose nightshirt around me and brushed my hair before folding back the covers for me, I wondered when it was that she'd last done such a thing for me. Our nanny had normally seen to such tasks, but from time to time Mother had performed them. Particularly when we were ill. I remembered a week when I was nine when she'd sat by my bedside, reading Beatrix Potter books to me while I lay sick with a fever.

I had been amazed by how quickly she'd adjusted to the fact that her daughter had been shot, but then I realized I shouldn't have been. Rob's death aside, Mother had always been steady and calm in the face of calamity and difficulty. And I would never dare criticize her for her reaction to Rob's death. He was her son, after all. And in the end, her manner of grieving had been far healthier than mine.

She tucked the covers in around me and turned to go, but I stayed her with a hand to her arm. My words faltered as she looked back at me in surprise, but there was no disdain in her eyes, only concern. "Will you sit with me for a moment?"

"Of course," she replied after another brief pause. She perched on the side of the bed at my hip, smoothing out the nonexistent wrinkles in her skirt.

I faltered in the face of her scrutiny, even uncritical as it was, and the words I wished to say all seemed to jumble together and lodge at the base of my throat. Brushing my right hand over the stitching on the counterpane, I swallowed and forced myself to speak. "I want to say something, and I'm probably going to say it badly, but . . . please let me try."

She gazed back at me evenly, the lamplight glinting in the silver hairs now threaded through her brown. "Go on."

"I'm sorry that it took me so long to come home. And I'm sorry that I wasn't here to support you as you wanted me to. I never meant to hurt you." My voice wavered with emotion as I spoke my next words. "But just because I wasn't here doesn't mean I wasn't grieving Rob. I grieved him deeply. I still do. But people grieve differently, and I just couldn't face being here, surrounded by all my memories of him. I had . . . *people* relying on me, and I simply couldn't afford to break down." I searched her face for some crack in her reserve, some sign that she understood what I was saying. "I care about you, about everyone in our family, *very much*. That hasn't changed. Even if I have."

She didn't speak at first, and I couldn't read her expression, though I was desperately trying to. When her gaze dropped and she smoothed her hands over her lap once again, I thought for a moment she was simply going to nod her head and leave. It made a hollow open up behind my breastbone, that familiar aching place where I felt all of my mother's slights and criticisms.

"Thank you for telling me that, Verity," she said in a tentative voice that gained strength with each word. "For all that you seem to imagine me to be, I'm not a mind reader. When you don't visit and barely telephone, I can only assume you don't care. Unless you tell me otherwise." Despite her poise, I could hear the pain fraying the edges of her voice and see it buried deep in her eyes. "Don't assume I understand."

That was reasonable, and I told her so, but she wasn't finished.

"I know I've often made my disapprovals of your choices clear, but that is only because I worry about you. Worry about the life you've chosen to lead." She drew herself up taller. "It's not easy to watch your children behave in ways that you know can harm them. To want to shield them, and not be able to. When you and I have not seen eye to eye, it is because of that."

"You're right. *Sometimes* I do things you consider reckless or imprudent," I conceded. "But other times, you know very well that's not the case." She opened her mouth to argue, but I cut her off. "Bobbing my hair, Mother, was not detrimental to my person in any way. Or do you think I'll catch my death of cold from a chill across my neck?" I arched my eyebrows, awaiting her answer.

Her mouth tightened in aggravation before she huffed in acceptance. "Very well. Sometimes I'm a trifle too critical. But you had such lovely, long hair. The kind many women were envious of. I hated to see it all gone."

"You never told me before that my hair was lovely."

"Oh, you knew very well you had beautiful hair. Don't go fishing for compliments."

I might have become cross at this retort, but instead I chose to view it with amusement. Mother had never been the type to offer unsolicited praise. It was foolish to expect that to change now.

"I will never be exactly the daughter you want me to be. It is as simple as that," I stated baldly. "And my life may never be as safe, and settled, and proper as you wish it, but it is *my* life. And I'm happy in it. I know approval is too much to ask, so all I ask is that you accept it."

Her sharp gaze shifted to my injured shoulder. "Even when it means seeing you shot."

"Even then."

She turned away, and I didn't know if that indicated her agreement or not. "Someday when you have children of your own"—her gaze snapped back to me—"*if* you have children of your own, you'll understand."

"Maybe. Probably. But I hope I'll also still choose to meet them where they are."

She huffed again, but then nodded. I chose to view that as her promise to do her best. And I supposed that was all I could ask.

"Cheer up, Mother," I bantered. "After all, I didn't say we would *never* have children. Isn't that an encouraging sign?"

"Aye, well, you may be following *that woman's* advice," she said, referring to Marie Stopes's book again. "But I'll put my stock in the good Lord and the Whitlock blood you inherited from me flowing through your veins. No Whitlock woman has failed to bear less than five children in the past four generations." Her eyes glinted with almost triumph as she rose to her feet. "If you don't find yourself in the family way within the next six months, then I'll buy *myself* a copy of that God-forsaken book."

I stared after her, wondering if I wanted to contradict this statement. Shaking my head in bemusement, I decided there was little point. Maybe it would be true, or maybe it wouldn't. There was no point arguing the fact now, and I wasn't certain I even wanted to.

Though, the expansion of our family would undoubtedly be less fraught if Ardmore were no longer a threat—an event that didn't seem like it would be happening anytime soon. Not unless we could find the proof we'd been seeking. And that meant locating those phosgene gas canisters.

However, a break in our other point of inquiry came unexpectedly a few days later.

The men had been hard at work earlier that day, gathering evergreens, holly, and even a few balls of mistletoe to decorate the house, as well as the Christmas tree. We had all gathered in the drawing room with the doors to the family parlor thrown open to allow us more space, each diligently at work on our assigned tasks. Sidney and my brothers were busy hanging the greens, while Father supervised, puffing on his pipe. Mother tied elegant ribbons and bows, while I arranged flowers in their vases. I was proud at how adept I'd become at working with one hand.

Meanwhile, Tante Ilse directed Rachel and Grace as they adorned the tree, her eyes sparkling with merriment. From time to time I would catch myself watching her—trying to absorb every nuance of her face, to memorize what made her laugh—all the while wondering if this would be her last Christmas. I'd not thought to store up such memories of Rob, for none of us had known what was coming, but I wasn't going to miss the opportunity to do so with Tante.

When the telephone rang in the entry hall, none of us truly marked it, too busy teasing each other and focusing on our charge. Even when Abbott informed me the call was for me, I went out into the hall laughing at something Tim had said. It was only when the voice spoke on the other end of the line that I grasped the significance.

"Lorelei, sorry to intrude at such a late hour, but we've uncovered something you should know."

"Of course," I stammered, shifting modes as C's secretary, Kathleen, continued.

"We've gained access to some of the sealed investigative files concerning the incident in Bailleul." When Brigadier General Bishop's temporary headquarters had been blown up by a bomb, killing him and nine other men. "It appears the officer who left the building before the incident in question was a Lieutenant James Smith." She kept speaking, but I barely marked it as shock reverberated through me. "He was one of the witnesses who claimed the cause was an enemy projectile."

My hand tightened on the earpiece, the wooden ridges digging into my palm. Of course, he'd blamed it on a German shell. He'd been the one to set the bloody bomb.

"Does that name mean anything to you?"

I had to lean downward a bit to speak, unable to pick up both the earpiece and mouthpiece. "Yes," I ground out. "He was involved in the Littlemote Park incident and all that followed."

It also explained why Alec hadn't taken note of it. If, in fact, he'd viewed the same report. After all, Smith was an incredibly common name, and I wasn't certain he'd ever been privy to the given name of the Lieutenant Smith I was speaking of. But I was.

Kathleen had fallen silent, and I realized I'd momentarily astounded her. "Then he's connected with the Fowler?" This was code for Lord Ardmore, and unhappily I had to answer in the affirmative.

How many times were my and Ardmore's paths to cross? How many pies could he possibly have had his hand in?

Sidney had stepped out of the drawing room, and I could tell by the way he was looking at me that my voice and expression had conveyed the fact that the news I was receiving was not welcomed.

"I'll inform C," Kathleen told me before ringing off.

I set the earpiece back on the hook and turned to face Sidney resignedly.

"London?" he murmured in query.

I nodded, swiftly explaining what I'd just learned.

He exhaled a long breath, rubbing the back of his neck, before addressing the matter. "Well, at least now you know what most likely happened. Now, the question becomes proving it."

"And proving whether Ardmore was involved."

His brow quirked in irritation. "You know he was."

"Yes, my gut tells me so. But without proof . . ." I shrugged my right shoulder.

"Without proof we have nothing. Again."

It was less satisfying than I'd expected to hear Sidney so frustrated with Ardmore's Machiavellian moves and the lack of evidence he left behind. Normally I was the one bemoaning our being perpetually two, if not ten, steps behind him.

"But this time at least we have a good idea where to look," I said, determined to cheer him. "And a face in the crowd to watch for."

"True." He lifted his hands to clasp my waist, dipping his head closer in concern. "But it can wait until your shoulder is healed."

"Yes," I agreed, looking beyond him toward the sounds of laughter floating through the doorway from the drawing room. "After the holidays at the very least. I've been away from my family long enough." I looked up into his somber eyes, offering him a hopeful smile. "Besides, C would let me know if there were any indication that Ardmore were about to make any moves to cause further mayhem. He does have him being watched."

"Yes, but will they truly be able to tell?"

My brow furrowed, and I reached up to fidget with the folds of his tie. "With Ardmore? Unlikely. But we can't put our lives on hold indefinitely for him, can we?"

"You're right." He pressed his lips to my forehead. "We've sacrificed enough of our lives to the whims of others already."

"C will let us know if there's anything anomalous happening, and that will simply have to do for now." I leaned my head against his chest as we turned to stroll back toward the drawing room with our arms draped behind each other's backs. "Besides, I have a feeling Ardmore has no intention of making any significant moves without me around to witness it. It's part of his game."

"Let's hope you're correct," he replied, not sounding as confident of that as I wished him to be. "In the meantime . . ." He paused in the doorway, glancing upward significantly.

I spied the sprig of mistletoe strung above us and eyed him with mock suspicion. "You did that on purpose."

He pulled me close. "Of course, I did, dear wife. And I warn you, I intend on inventing any number of excuses to catch you beneath them, repeatedly, everywhere they're hung."

I smiled coyly. "Well, I noticed Tim hanging one above the billiards table earlier, so I look forward to seeing how you're going to contrive that one given my current debilitated state."

His eyes flashed roguishly. "Challenge accepted."

Don't miss any of Anna Lee Huber's bestselling Verity Kent
mysteries, beginning with:

THIS SIDE OF MURDER

**The Great War is over, but in this captivating mystery from
award-winning author Anna Lee Huber, one young widow discovers the real intrigue has only just begun . . .**

England, 1919. Verity Kent's grief over the loss of her
husband pierces anew when she receives a cryptic letter, suggesting
her beloved Sidney may have committed treason before his
untimely death. Determined to dull her pain with revelry, Verity's
first impulse is to dismiss the derogatory claim. But the mystery
sender knows too much—including the fact that during the war,
Verity worked for the Secret Service, something not even
Sidney knew.

Lured to Umbersea Island to attend the engagement
party of one of Sidney's fellow officers, Verity mingles among the
men her husband once fought beside, and discovers dark secrets—
along with a murder clearly meant to conceal them. Relying on little
more than a coded letter, the help of a dashing stranger, and her own
sharp instincts, Verity is forced down a path she never imagined—
and comes face to face with the shattering possibility that her husband may not have been the man she thought he was. It's a truth that
could set her free—or draw her ever deeper into his deception . . .

Available wherever books are sold from
Kensington Publishing Corp.

CHAPTER 1

❧

You might question whether this is all a ruse, whether I truly have anything to reveal. But I know what kind of work you really did during the war. I know the secrets you hide. Why shouldn't I also know your husband's?

June 1919
England

They say when you believe you're about to die your entire life passes before your eyes in a flurry of poignant images, but all I could think of, rather absurdly, was that I should have worn the blue hat. Well, that and that my sister would never forgive me for proving our mother right.

Mother had never approved of Sidney teaching me how to drive his motorcar that last glorious summer before the war. Or of my gadding about London and the English countryside in his prized Pierce-Arrow while he was fighting in France. Or of my decision to keep the sleek little Runabout instead of selling it after a German bullet so callously snatched him from me. In my mother's world of rules and privilege, women—even wealthy widows—did not own motorcars, and they certainly didn't drive them. She'd declared it would be the death of me. And so it might have been, had it not been for the other driver's bizarre bonnet ornament.

Once my motorcar had squealed to a stop, a bare two inches from the fender of the other vehicle, and I'd peeled open my eyes, I could see that the ornament was some sort of pompon. Tassels of bright orange streamers affixed to the Rolls-Royce's more traditional silver lady. When racing down the country roads, I supposed they trailed out behind her like ribbons of flame, but at a standstill they drooped across the grille rather like limp seagrass.

I heard the other driver open his door, and decided it was time to stop ogling his peculiar taste in adornment and apologize. For there was no denying our near collision was my fault. I had been driving much too fast for the winding, shrubbery-lined roads. I was tempted to blame Pinky, but I was the dolt who'd chosen to follow his directions even though I'd known they would be rubbish.

When my childhood friend Beatrice had invited me to visit her and her husband, Pinky, at their home in Winchester, I'd thought it a godsend, sparing me the long drive from London to Poole in one shot. I hadn't seen either of them since before the war, other than a swift bussing of Pinky's cheek as I passed him at the train station one morning, headed back to the front. All in all, it had been a lovely visit despite the evident awkwardness we all felt at Sidney's absence.

In any case, although Pinky was a capital fellow, he'd always been a bit of a dodo. I couldn't help but wonder if he'd survived the war simply by walking in circles—as he'd had me driving—never actually making it to the front.

I adjusted my rather uninspired cream short-brimmed hat over my auburn castle-bobbed tresses and stepped down into the dirt and gravel lane, hoping the mud wouldn't damage my blue kid leather pumps. My gaze traveled over the beautiful pale yellow body of the Rolls-Royce and came to rest on the equally attractive man rounding her bonnet. Dark blond hair curled against the brim of his hat, and when his eyes lifted from the spot where our motorcars nearly touched, I could see they were a soft gray. I was relieved to see they weren't bright with anger.

Charming a man out of a high dudgeon had never been my favorite pastime.

One corner of his mouth curled upward in a wry grin. "Well, that was a near thing."

"Only if you're not accustomed to driving in London." I offered him my most disarming smile as I leaned forward to see just how close it had been. "But I do apologize. Clearly, I shouldn't have been in such a rush."

"Oh, I'd say these hedgerows hold some of the blame." He lifted aside his gray tweed coat to slide his hands into his trouser pockets as he nodded toward the offending shrubbery. "It's almost impossible to see around them. Otherwise, I would have seen you coming. It's hard to miss a Pierce-Arrow," he declared, studying the currant-red paint and brass fittings of my motorcar.

"Yes, well, that's very good of you to say so."

"Nonsense. And in any case, there's no harm done."

"Thanks to your colorful bonnet ornament."

He followed my pointed stare to the pompon attached to his silver lady, his wry grin widening in furtive amusement.

"There must be a story behind it."

"It just seemed like it should be there."

"And that's all there is to it?"

He shrugged. "Does there need to be more?"

I tilted my head, trying to read his expression. "I suppose not. Though, I'll own I'm curious where you purchased such a bold piece of frippery."

"Oh, I didn't." His eyes sparkled with mischief. "My niece kindly let me borrow it. Just for this occasion."

I couldn't help but laugh. Had he been one of my London friends I would have accused him of having a jest, but with this man I wasn't certain, and told him so. "I'm not sure if you're quite serious or simply having a pull at me."

"Good." He rocked back on his heels, clearly having enjoyed our exchange.

I shook my head at this teasing remark. He truly was a rather appealing fellow, though there was something in his features—

perhaps the knife-blade sharpness of his nose—that kept him from being far too handsome for any woman's good. Which was a blessing, for combined with his artless charm and arresting smile he might have had quite a devastating effect. He still might, given a more susceptible female. Unfortunately, I had far too much experience with charming, attractive men to ever fold so quickly.

I pegged him at being just shy of thirty, and from his manner of speech and cut of clothes, undoubtedly a gentleman. From old money, if I wagered a guess. A well-bred lady can always tell these things. After all, we're taught to sniff out the imposters from the cradle, though it had begun to matter less and less, no matter what my mother and her like said about the nouveau riche.

He pulled a cigarette case from his pocket and offered me one, which I declined, before lighting one for himself. "If I may be so bold . . ." he remarked after taking a drag. "Where precisely were you rushing to?"

"Poole Harbor. There's a boat I'm supposed to meet." I sighed. "And I very much fear I've missed it."

"To Umbersea Island?"

I blinked in surprise. "Why, yes." I paused, considering him. "Are you also . . ."

"On my way to Walter Ponsonby's house party?" He finished for me. "I am. But don't worry. They won't leave without us." He lifted his arm to glance at his wristwatch. "And if they do, we'll make our own way over."

"Well, that's a relief," I replied, feeling anything but. Some of the sparkle from our encounter had dimmed at this discovery. Still, I couldn't let him know that. "Then I suppose if we're going to be spending the weekend together we should introduce ourselves." I extended my hand across the small gap separating our motorcars. "Mrs. Verity Kent."

His grip was warm, even through my cream leather glove, as he clasped my hand for a moment longer than was necessary. "Max Westfield, Earl of Ryde. But, please, call me Ryde. Or

Max, even. None of that Lord business." Something flickered in his eyes, and I could tell he was debating whether to say something else. "You wouldn't by chance be Sidney Kent's widow?"

I'm not sure why I was startled. There was no reason to be. After all, I'd just discovered we were both making our way to the same house party. A party thrown by one of Sidney's old war chums. There were bound to be one or two of Sidney's fellow officers attending. Why shouldn't Lord Ryde be one of them?

My eyes dipped briefly to the glow at the end of the fag clasped between Ryde's fingers, before returning to his face. "You knew him?" I remarked as casually as I could manage, determined not to show he'd unsettled me.

"I was his commanding officer." He exhaled a long stream of smoke. "For a short time, anyway." His eyes tightened at the corners. "I'm sorry for your loss. He was a good man," he added gently.

I tried to respond, but found alarmingly that I had to clear my throat before I could get the words out. "Thank you."

It was the standard litany. The standard offer of condolences and expression of gratitude that had been repeated dozens of times since Sidney's death. I'd developed a sort of callus from hearing the words over and over. It prevented them from overly affecting me, from making me remember.

Except, this time was different.

"Did you know Sidney before the war?" I managed to say with what I thought was an admirable amount of aplomb. They were of an age with each other, and both being gentlemen it seemed a safe assumption.

"Yes, Kent was a year behind me at Eton and Oxford. Same as your brother, if I recall. They were chums."

I nodded. "Yes, that's how we met. Sidney came home with Freddy to Yorkshire one school holiday."

"Love at first sight?"

"Goodness, no. At least, not for him. I was all of eleven to his sixteen. And a rather coltish eleven, at that. All elbows and knees."

He grinned. "Well, that didn't last."

I dimpled cheekily. "Why, thank you for noticing. No, Sidney didn't return to Upper Wensleydale for six more years. But by then, of course, things had changed."

My chest tightened at the bittersweet memories, and I turned to stare at the bonnet of my motorcar—Sidney's motorcar—gleaming in the sunshine. I'd known this weekend was going to be difficult. I'd been preparing myself for it as best I could. Truth be told, that's why I'd nearly collided with Lord Ryde. I'd been distracted by my recollections. The ones I'd been ducking since the telegram arrived to inform me of Sidney's death.

I'd gotten rather good at avoiding them. At calculating just how many rags I needed to dance, and how much gin I needed to drink so I could forget, and yet not be too incapacitated to perform my job the following morning. And when I was released from my position after the war, well, then it didn't matter anymore, did it?

But this weekend I couldn't afford the luxury of forgetfulness.

As if sensing the maudlin turn of my thoughts, Ryde reached out to touch my motorcar's rather plain bonnet ornament, at least compared to his. "Kent used to talk about his Pierce-Arrow. Claimed it was the fastest thing on four wheels."

"Yes, he was rather proud of it." I recognized the turn in subject for the kindness it was. He'd sensed my discomfort and was trying to find a gracious way to extricate ourselves from this awkwardness. I should have felt grateful, but I only felt troubled.

I lifted my gaze to meet his, trying to read something in his eyes. "I suppose there wasn't much to talk about in the trenches."

His expression turned guarded. "No, not that we wanted to. Motorcars were just about the safest topic we could find."

I nodded, understanding far more than he was saying. Though, I also couldn't help but wonder if that was a dodge.

Almost reflexively, I found myself searching Ryde for any visible signs of injury. I'd learned swiftly that those soldiers fortunate enough to survive the war still returned wounded in some way, whether it be in body or mind. The unluckiest suffered both.

As if he knew what I was doing, he rolled his left shoulder self-consciously before flicking his fag into the dirt. He ground it out before glancing down the road toward Poole. "I suppose we should be on our way then, lest our fellow guests truly leave us behind to shrift for ourselves."

"It does seem rude to keep them waiting longer than necessary," I admitted, suddenly wishing very much to be away, but not wanting to appear overeager. "Is it much farther?"

"Just over the next rise or two, you should be able to see the town laid out before you."

"That close?"

"Yes, and as I said, I suspect Ponsonby will have told them to wait for us all before departing. He was always considerate about such things."

"You know him well then?" I asked in genuine curiosity.

He shrugged, narrowing his eyes against the glare of the midday sun. "As well as one can know another man serving beside him during war." It was rather an obscure answer. And yet Ponsonby had thought them friendly enough to invite him to his house party to celebrate his recent engagement to be married. Of course, the man had also invited me, a woman he hardly knew, though I assumed that was because of Sidney.

As if sensing my interest and wishing to deflect it from himself, he added, "I know he and Kent were great friends."

"Yes, since Eton. I met Walter once or twice before the war. And, of course, he attended our wedding." One of the numerous hasty ceremonies performed throughout Britain during the months at the start of the war, between Sidney's training and his orders to report to France as a fresh-faced lieutenant. I'd only just turned eighteen and hadn't the slightest idea what was to come. None of us had.

I looked up to find Ryde watching me steadily, as if he knew what I was thinking, for it was what he was thinking, too. It was an odd moment of solidarity under the brilliant June sky, and I would remember it many times in the days to come.

Because who of us ever really knows what's coming? Or what secrets will come back to haunt us in the end? The war might be over, but it still echoed through our lives like an endless roll of thunder.